THE VERY BEST OF TRUE STORY ROMANCE SPECIAL
VOLUME 5

TRUE STORY
and
TRUE CONFESSIONS
Magazines

True Story and *True Confessions* are the world's largest and best-selling women's romance magazines. They offer true-to-life stories to which women can relate.

Since 1919, the iconic *True Story* has been an extraordinary publication. The magazine gets its inspiration from the hearts and minds of women, and touches on those things in life that a woman holds close to her heart, like love, loss, family and friendship.

True Confessions, a cherished classic first published in 1922, looks into women's souls and reveals their deepest secrets.

Published by True Renditions, LLC

True Renditions, LLC
105 E. 34th Street, Suite 141
New York, NY 10016

Copyright @ 2020 by True Renditions, LLC

All rights reserved. No part of this book may be reproduced or transmitted in any form or by any electronic means, without the written permission of the publisher, except where permitted by law.

THE VERY BEST OF BEST OF TRUE STORY ROMANCE SPECIAL

VOLUME 5

From the Editors
Of *True Story* And
True Confessions

BOOKS FROM THE EDITORS OF TRUE STORY AND TRUE CONFESSIONS

A Soldier's Family	More Miracles
A Turkey Day Gathering	One Winter Night
All The Scandalous Secrets	Our True Furry Friends
Always A Mystery	Painful Love
Becoming Cinderella	Parting Ways
Coming Home for Christmas	Real Heroes
Delivered Into Danger	Valentine Delights
Enchanting Easter	Second Chances
Faith, Hope, Love and Luck	Seriously Cheating
Young And Desperate	Shameful Secrets Revealed
Giving Thanks	Shattered Vows
Grandma Knows Best	Signs Of Angels
Hope For The Heart	Untrue
Jealous Obsessions	True Memories
Killer in the Shadow	Surviving The Unthinkable
Life Is a Lottery	Tales of Inspiration
Life-Changing	Tales of Inspiration: Volume 2
Little Baby Lost	Talk About Murder
Living Through Tragedy	Ten Greatest Love Stories
Married to the Military	The Day of the Jack-O-Lantern
Miracles: Volume 2	The Most Remarkable Mom

25 Agonizing Heartbreaking Ordeals
The Very Best of the Best of Secrets Volume 1, 2, 3 & 4
The Very Best of the Best of True Confessions Volume 1, 2, 3 & 4
The Very Best of True Experience Volume 1, 2, 3 & 4
The Very Best of True Story Romance Special Volume 1, 2, 3 & 4
Thirteen Sizzling Confessions and Crimes of the Heart
Troubled Thoughts Of A Teenager
True Confessions Classic Novella Volume 1
True Ghosts—Stories from the Trues
Love After Loss—A Widow's Story
True Sisters Volume 1 & 2
True Story Romance Special 2017, 2019 & 2020
Twelve Tender Tearjerkers
Stroke of Midnight: A New Year's Eve Story Collection
Steadfast Love—Stories of Love and Devotion
Scandals, Secrets and Sensual Confessions
Finding The Way Out—Stories Of Addiction
Brides: From Blushing To Bawling
Editors' Favorites Volume 1 & 2
37 Stories Of Confession

Contents

I Married 3 Brothers!..1

The Art of Deception!...17

Sex On the Love Boat!..31

I'll Stand By My Man!...46

Four Missing Children!..62

He Married Me for My Money!...76

I Tamed the Neighborhood Bully!.....................................89

My Love Rival Gave Me the Greatest Happiness of My Life.......105

My Holy Affair...120

The Softer Side of My Macho Man...................................134

The Little Tramp Who Ran Our Home!..............................150

"Come Away with Me!"...167

"Don't Lock Up Grandpa!"...180

32—and I Can't Have Sex!...192

My Husband's Underworld Life!.......................................207

Why Would a 17-Year-Old Girl Do It?...............................224

I Hitched a Ride With a Madman!....................................240

Flirting With Disaster...Schoolgirl Crush!............................255

Love 'Em and Leave 'Em!...270

The Government Stole My Kids!......................................283

My Second Marriage Will Be My First................................298

I Hired a Woman for Daddy!..314

I Drove My Lover Insane!...329

Enchanted By a Kind Stranger..342

I MARRIED 3 BROTHERS!

Zack and I wouldn't have eloped if there had been any other way for us to be together. I know I'd have liked to have had a nice wedding in our little church, with my family and friends there. As for Zack—well, I guess things like that are never so important to a boy. He just wanted to get married.

Zack had finished high school that June, and his father wanted him to work in the family wholesale nursery business. Zack's oldest brother, Steve, was already a partner. But Zack had other ideas. He was itching to go to the West Coast and try his luck. If he told me once, he told me a hundred times that he was sick of living in a little town like ours.

"Now that we want to get married, it's different, though," Zack told me as we sat in his car. We had a special place out on a little-traveled road where we always went to park. "We'll stay here in Sunnyside. I'll even be willing to give the nursery business a try. Steve seems to like it okay. And I know that when my brother, Gary, comes home from the Navy, he's going to work for my father. One thing, my brothers and I get along fine, so I guess that's something. How does it sound to you, honey?"

"Oh Zack, it's wonderful!" I said, breathless with excitement. "I'm going to tell my folks about us. They'll be upset because I won't be going back to school in September, but thank heavens they like you. I know they're going to be so pleased that we want to get married."

Zack took me in his arms and gave me one of those long kisses that set my heart thundering in my ears. "Love me?" he said against my lips.

"Oh, yes!" I breathed, and he held me close. I got a little scared then. Not because I didn't trust Zack, but because I had such crazy feelings tumbling through me that I didn't trust myself. So I pulled away from him.

"What's the matter?" he said, reaching for me again.

"I love you," I told him, "and I think you'd better take me home."

A smile crept across Zack's handsome face. "I know what you mean, honey," he said. "We can't get enough of each other. But give me one more quick kiss, and I promise we'll get right home."

Well, it wasn't a quick kiss. None of our kisses could possibly be. It was another one that sent little shivers of excitement through me. I didn't want it to end any more than Zack did, but we did end it because we knew what could happen to us if we let ourselves give in to our feelings.

When Zack dropped me off at my house, I told him I'd talk to my parents that night as soon as supper was over.

And I did. I was full of joy and happiness as I told my mother and father I wanted to marry Zack.

My mother gave me a stunned look. "Gee, married at your age!" she exploded, making it sound as if no girl seventeen even thought of such a thing before. "I should say not! Zack's a nice boy, but that's all he is—a boy! He's not ready for marriage any more than you are. Why, a year from now, when he's nineteen, he'll probably think he's madly in love with some other girl. He doesn't know what he wants now, and neither do you!"

She turned suddenly to my father, who, up to then, had been silent, and said, "Dad, you talk to her!"

My father was sitting in his favorite chair, puffing on his pipe. His newspaper had slid from his lap to the floor and lay in an untidy mess at his feet. He looked at me and seemed so upset, I could have cried. "Cheryl," he said, his voice gently admonishing, "you must know that we couldn't agree to anything so foolish."

"Foolish!" I burst out. "How can you and Mom think it's foolish? I'm in love with Zack, I tell you! And whether you like it or not, we're going to get married."

My mother burst into tears, and my father got up and went over to her, putting his arm around her. "She doesn't mean it, dear," he told her gently. "Please, please, don't be so upset. You go upstairs and lie down, and let me talk to Cheryl. We'll get this whole thing straightened out."

I felt terrible, making my mother cry like that. I loved both my parents and never wanted to do anything to hurt them. But I loved Zack, too, and right then, Zack was the most important thing to me.

Well, my father talked to me. He reasoned and he warned, and I listened. But he didn't change my mind about wanting to marry Zack. He just thought he did, because I didn't put up any arguments.

It was the following week, over July Fourth weekend that Zack and I eloped. We pooled our savings, took one suitcase apiece, and went to California, but we were married in Nevada. We found a tiny furnished apartment on the outskirts of San Francisco, and it was there that our marriage really began.

Those first few nights of our honeymoon—it wasn't really a honeymoon, but I called it that—were all the magic a girl dreams of. Kisses, whispered words of love, and the giving of love. And the more Zack made love to me, the closer to him I felt. I was miserable if he had to be away from me for even one minute. He was the only thing in the whole world that meant anything to me. It was joy and it was pain and it was the beginning of my learning what it meant to be a woman.

If I thought I loved Zack when we were just going together back home, I was sure of it since I had become his wife. I'd find myself thinking of all the wonderful years that lay before us, the two of us together, our love growing and growing and growing. We'd never get tired of each other. Zack would get a job and become a big success. Eventually we'd buy a little house, maybe a house like my mother and father had.

I wondered about my mother and father. I could imagine what went on when they'd found the note I'd left them. My mother was a small woman, somewhat frail, really, with the softest eyes I'd ever seen. She had soft hair, too, and it didn't have a trace of gray in it. And although Dad was forty-two, no one would ever guess it. But I had seen them both when they were worried deeply about something, and the change that came over them had shocked me. My leaving home the way I did would be the worst blow of all to them. My mother would be beside herself, maybe even blaming herself for not having been able to stop me, and my father would grieve silently and at the same time try to give comfort to my mother.

I didn't feel good about any of that. I felt a kind of aching remorse. And it never got any better. Zack felt bad about his father, too. Finding Zack's note would be a shock to him. He'd worry just like my parents.

"But what else could we do?" Zack said. "We wanted to get married. We had to run away."

"We couldn't do anything else," I told him. But it was a long time before the painful lump in my throat went away.

That first week in San Francisco was like living in a dream world. We'd go swimming at one of the public beaches almost every day, and since both Zack and I got good tans, we'd sun ourselves until we got hungry and wanted to go to our apartment to eat. At night, after we finished the dishes, we'd walk hand in hand along Denton Avenue, looking in at all the beautiful big hotels.

But by the end of the week, our money was getting low and we decided to look for jobs. I was lucky. I got a job as a cashier in a restaurant. I didn't make an awful lot of money, but it helped. Zack, though, wasn't so lucky. There just didn't seem be anything for him. He was feeling pretty down in the dumps about it, too. He'd come home hot and tired—often long after I got home from work—and he wouldn't even want to eat the supper I'd cooked.

We went through about three weeks of that, with Zack not finding anything and me praying he would, and then one night he came home walking on a cloud. He grabbed me in his arms and said, "Get dressed, honey. I'm taking you out tonight."

"Oh, Zack! You've found a job!" I cried, so happy to see him his old self.

3

"I have, indeed," Zack said. "Starting this weekend, I'm a bellhop at the Oceanside Hotel."

It didn't matter that Oceanside was one of the smaller hotels, and old. Right then, it seemed like the most wonderful place in all of California, and after Zack walked me past it later that night, I had a kind of feeling of possession. I called it Zack's hotel, because that was what it had become. My husband was a part of it.

Soon after Zack got that job, though, we began to quarrel. It was over the girls I'd see him talking to whenever I'd stop in at the hotel. I was jealous, and I couldn't help showing it. Once I even made a sarcastic remark to one of the girls, and it got Zack into a fury. We had real blowup over that when he got home. He said he was getting sick and tired of me and a lot of other things that made me cry, and he made no effort to take me in his arms when we went to bed—or even say he was sorry. And the next morning he left for work without saying good-bye.

I was miserable all that day. After work I stopped at the hotel, hoping to wait for Zack until he was through and to walk home with him. Well, I saw Zack all right, and he was talking to the same girl who'd made me so mad the day before. Zack didn't even say hello when he saw me, and the girl gave me a kind of smirking smile and went right on talking to Zack. I just walked away, but was boiling inside. Just wait till you get home, Zack, I thought. And I got some small comfort in knowing he was my husband, no matter how many girls didn't think I mattered to him.

Zack didn't come home for supper that night. It was almost as though he was playing a game with me, not doing any of the things I thought he was going do. The little apartment seemed to close in on me, and all I could think was how terrible it would be if I never saw him again. We hadn't even been married two months, but he was so much a part of my life that I didn't see how I could live without him.

But that's exactly what I was going to have to do—live without him—and he told me so that night when he finally came home. I had run to him, put my arm around him, begging him to forgive me, and he just looked at me like a stranger.

"Don't, please, Cheryl," he said. "I want to talk to you. I've been wanting to talk you for days about this, and I couldn't make myself."

A feeling of panic took hold of me, because I knew what he was going to say and I didn't want to hear it. And a terrible roaring sound began in my head. I sat down. I didn't want Zack to see the trembling that I felt beginning in my legs.

"You love me, don't you, Zack?" I said, praying that he'd say yes.

"I can't lie to you, Cheryl," Zack said. "I guess I'm not in love with you. I feel all boxed in being married."

"Oh, Zack!" I cried. "Give us a chance. We were happy when we first came down here. We'll be even happier after we get over being mad at each other. I'm sorry I've been jealous, but I promise I won't be ever again."

He turned away from me, went to the closet, and pulled out his suitcase. "It wouldn't work, Cheryl. I'm sorry."

I stared at him, not knowing what I could do to stop him. I watched as he folded his things and packed them in the bag. I watched as he got his toothbrush and gathered up his shaving things. And then he put some money on the table and started for the door.

"Zack, wait," I choked, getting up and running after him. I put my arms around him and pleaded with him not to leave me. But Zack just moved me away from me and walked out the door.

I called my parents that night and sobbingly told them what had happened. "Come home," they said. "Take the first plane. We love you. We want you back." And I started to pack the minute I hung up.

For weeks after I got home, I expected to hear from Zack. I couldn't make myself believe he didn't love me. I'd think of the first night after we were married and how we couldn't stand to be away from each other. I'd remember all the nights we'd spent in each other's arms loving and whispering our love, and I didn't see how he could forget.

Even after my annulment came through, I was thinking like that about Zack. But he never got in touch with me. I didn't even have the excuse that he didn't know where to find me, because I'd left my father's address with the landlord, just in case Zack did come back looking for me. So it was over, really over, and after the shock and grief wore away, there was a deep bitterness that took their place. I had loved him, he had taken my love, and then he had thrown it in my face. I just couldn't seem to forget it.

My mother and father were very patient with me through it all. They were kind to me, but they didn't let their kindness weaken me. They waited and they watched, and when they thought the time was right, they talked to me about getting a job.

"It will do you good to get out among people," they said.

At least I could try. I got a clerical job in a real-estate office, and I'd been there about three months when I got the call from Zack's brother Steve. He apologized for calling me at the office, and told me that my mother had said it would be all right. I had never met Steve, so I was a little startled. I was sure he was going to tell me some bad news about Zack. But that wasn't it at all.

"I'm sorry things didn't work out for you and my brother," Steve said, his voice deep and sincere sounding. "We haven't heard from him since he left home, and I was wondering if perhaps you could tell us where we could reach him. My father's pretty worried about him."

I told him I hadn't heard from Zack either, that I didn't even know if he was still in San Francisco. I mentioned the Oceanside Hotel, but I was pretty sure that Zack would have moved on from that job.

Steve thanked me, and that was that. A week later, though, I heard from him again. "I have something I'd like to talk to you about, but it would be a little difficult over the phone," he said. "Could you possibly have lunch with me today?"

"Well—" I began, not too eager to accept.

"Please," he broke in.

I'd heard Zack talk about Steve and somehow I pictured him as being much older, and the kind of man who could be counted on. I was sure he wouldn't look anything like Zack. But I was wrong. When he picked me up at my office that noon, I couldn't believe my eyes. In every way, there was a resemblance to Zack that was startling, but Steve was even better looking and taller. He was a man—with a man's self-confidence and maturity.

I felt very much at home with Steve, and our lunch together was so pleasant that the hour was almost gone before I knew it. Then I suddenly realized that Steve hadn't talked to me about whatever it was that had been on his mind, so I mentioned it to him.

"I'm afraid I'm going to make you angry," he said. "I wanted to see you so I could tell my father what you were like. He feels very bad over what happened, and he thought that maybe he could do something to help out."

"If you mean giving me money," I said, "no, thank you. I have my family and a job now. There's nothing like that that I need."

"Maybe, then, I could give you a better impression of the Quinn family," Steve said with a smile. "I'd like to see you again soon, take you out some evening. Would that be all right?"

I could just hear what my family would say if I told them I was going to go out with Zack's brother. I couldn't help smiling as I thought about it.

"You haven't answered me," Steve said. "I know what you must be thinking, but don't. Will you have dinner with me this Friday?"

He was so nice and so persuasive that I couldn't say no. And for the first time in months, I found myself looking ahead to something.

When I told my mother I had seen Steve for lunch, she said, "I didn't mention it to you before because there was no reason to. But I met Steve Quinn and his father shortly after you and Zack went away. They both came over here to ask if your father and I knew where you had gone." She put her arm around me. "If you want to know what I think about your going with Steve, I say 'Fine.' Your father and I were very impressed with him. Certainly Steve can't be held accountable for what his brother did."

6

"Of course he can't," I agreed. "In fact, Steve thinks it was terrible, Zack walking out on me the way he did. So does Mr. Quinn." And it gave me a strange little feeling of satisfaction to know that Zack's family was on my side.

I started to get the dining-room table ready for dinner, spreading the floral cloth over the top and carefully smoothing it so the creases lay flat. My mother watched, eyeing me thoughtfully.

"You're still bitter, aren't you?" she asked. "Well, that's too bad. I just wish you could remember that Zack was too young to get married. He shouldn't be judged the same way you'd judge a grown man. But regardless, the sooner you close the chapter on him, the happier you're going to be."

In my heart I knew she was right, and yet I was filled with so many tormenting, mixed-up emotions that I frequently had to fight back tears. I'd no sooner tell myself that I hated Zack, that he was weak and selfish and unfeeling, than I'd be overwhelmed with the desire to be in his arms again, have him kiss me, tell me he loved me. It was seven months since I'd seen him, our marriage had been annulled, and I was free to start a new life. And yet, I went on feeling that I was still his wife. That's how strong the tie had been for me.

Steve called for me the following Friday. The weather was getting very summer-like, so I wore my new pink dress. I'd had my hair done that noon on my lunch hour, and it framed my face with flattering softness. Zack had always loved my hair, and he'd run his fingers through it. But I had to stop thinking of Zack. I had to stop thinking and remembering. . . .

I checked my lipstick, smoothing just a little more on my lower lip, then I touched my earlobes with perfume and ran downstairs. When I went into the living room, my father was telling Steve about a trip his company was sending him on. He stopped right in the middle of a sentence as soon as he saw me. Steve stood up, gave me a smiling hello, helped me into my sweater, and we left.

We went to a cute little place to eat about ten miles out of town. I felt good with Steve, and talking to him was as easy as talking to an old friend. We found that we both knew the same people in town and we both felt the same way about most of them. I even knew the girl Steve had been engaged to.

"What happened?" I asked. "Did you change your mind about her?"

"No," Steve said slowly. "It was the other way around. She's a nurse, you know, and she fell in love with one of the interns at the hospital. She's very happily married to him now. At the time, I took it hard. But I got over it."

"Then you know what it's like," I said, looking down at my hands, feeling the old, aching sadness coming over me.

"Hey, I'm sorry," he said, his voice husky. "I didn't mean to stir up any gloom. I've forgotten all about her, so how about you thinking just about us—and tonight."

I took a deep breath and looked up at him. "Okay," I said, and all at once, I was smiling again.

I saw Steve off and on for almost a year, and I had other dates as well. I began to feel myself relaxing a little, and the more that happened, the less I thought about Zack. I don't think Steve even suspected it, but I knew I was falling in love with him. He had never so much as taken me in his arms or kissed me, but I kept wishing he would.

And then one night, it just happened. Steve had driven me home, and we were sitting in his car outside my father's house. I was reaching for the radio when he suddenly took hold of my hand. I glanced up at him, wondering if he knew how wildly my heart was beating, and without knowing exactly how I got there, I was in his arms.

"Oh, darling, darling, darling!" he whispered, tilting my chin up to look at me. And then his lips slowly met mine, and I knew that love had come to me to stay.

"Is it too soon to tell you that I love you and want to marry you?" Steve said softly, his breath warm against my cheek.

He knew, of course, that it wasn't. The ice around my heart had been melting for months, and once again, it was warm with love.

We had a small engagement party, with my parents and Mr. Quinn, and it was one of the happiest times in my life, because everyone was so happy for Steve and me. Mr. Quinn hugged me and wished me well, and there were tears in his eyes.

"I'm proud to have you as a daughter, Cheryl," he said. "And you're pretty, just the way my wife was. You remind me of her in other ways, too. I know you're going to make my son a good wife."

"Oh, I will!" I promised. I had no doubts about that.

I was nineteen when I became Steve's bride. I'll always remember the fluttery feeling I had in my stomach when Steve held my hand and slipped the delicate platinum wedding band on my finger. I was his, as of that moment, and I prayed that we would always love each other as much as we did right then. I know my own heart was fairly bursting with love, and I thanked God for having given me such a wonderful man.

We had a two-week honeymoon in the Caribbean Islands, and every minute of it was exciting and happy and tender. We were the kind of married lovers who found every moment of being together, whether it was on a walk or going into each other's arms for a final good-night kiss, a joyous, thrilling experience. The more we knew each other, the more in love we were, and a tremendous contentment was born of that love. I might have thought of Zack once or twice, but only fleetingly, because my love for Steve was my key to forgetting.

Steve had put a down payment on a cute little ranch house we'd picked out and furnished, and we settled in it when we returned from our trip. Before a month had gone by, I felt as though I'd been married to Steve for years, because he was so easy to live with and so vitally a part of me.

Once in a while on Sunday, we'd visit my family or Mr. Quinn, and we loved having them come to our house for dinner. My mother and father could never find enough good things to say about Steve. He was just like a son to them. He'd help my father cut grass, put up screens, paint—anything at all, and then he'd turn right around and do the same things for his own father. All of this after he'd done what had to be done around our own home. And the harder he worked, the more energy he seemed to have. He took me out—for drives or for dinner—and there was no such thing as a rut for our marriage to fall into.

I became pregnant that August, and our baby son was born the following May. I had a very easy time of it all the way, and what a thrill it was to hold my baby in my arms. But I'll never forget Steve. He was so proud, it was really funny. He'd come back from the hospital nursery, smiling to himself, and acting as though fatherhood was something that had happened only to him. He was so boastful of his son, and full of elaborate plans. And all of it warmed my heart and made me love him even more.

On almost every Saturday that summer after Justin's birth—we'd named the baby after Steve's father—we would pack up our things and go for a picnic. And often while the baby slept in the car, Steve and I would stretch out on a blanket under the trees. My head would be on his shoulder and his arm would be around me, and we'd just lie there, making plans for the future and talking about the big family we hoped to have.

In September of that year, Gary was discharged from the Navy, and his father took him into the business. Steve was relieved to have him helping out, because his father had had a mild heart attack a year before we were married. With Gary around, Mr. Quinn could take it a little easier.

I had never met Gary. "What's he like, Steve?" I asked one night.

"Well, there's no denying we're brothers. We look alike. He's twenty-three, a year younger than me, and he's had so many girls, my father and I thought he'd have been married long ago. Maybe now that he's home, he'll settle down. I don't want to give you the wrong impression, though. Underneath it all, Gary is a pretty serious sensible guy. Not at all like Zack."

The sudden mention of Zack's name shocked me for a moment. Steve and I never discussed him. He had become sort of like a half-forgotten dream.

"Has your father ever heard anything from Zack?" I asked. I

couldn't help being curious about him, but I knew the Quinns would be too discreet to say anything about him unless I asked.

"No, nothing," Steve said, stretching his long legs out in front of him as he leaned back in his chair. "Pop tried to locate him a couple of times—I know he often worries about him—but he never could turn up anything. It's my guess Zack's too ashamed to come home."

"That's not surprising," I said, and I could feel a trace of the old bitterness. "He'd have a hard time explaining the way he treated me to your father."

Steve looked over at me, an expression of sadness on his face. "Let's forget about him," he said. "I don't want you getting all upset."

So, once again, Zack was put away in a tiny corner of my memory and covered with resentment. Steve knows what he's like, I told myself as I dismissed him. He could never fool his brother Steve.

Before I went to bed that night, I checked on the baby. He needed to be changed, but he didn't cry when I woke him. He was such a dear, sweet baby, really, and he just lay there, cooing, as I made him comfortable and dry. Even at four months, he was beginning to show signs of his father's loving disposition, and I told that to Steve when I slipped into bed beside him.

Steve gathered me close to him. He kissed me, gently at first, and then urgently. "You're the one with the loving disposition," he said huskily. "And when I hold you like this, honey, all I know is that I want you."

It was that way for me, too. It always was. That's what made us so right for each other. We never had to pretend. We were even more in love than on the day we were married.

Gary was home almost a month working with his father before I met him. He had a date, and Steve said he could borrow our car. I don't know what I expected him to be like. Perhaps I thought he'd have a strong resemblance to Steve, since Steve had given me the impression that was the case. But to me, at least, there was none—or very little. Oh, his eyes were the same, with Steve's warm friendly look, and he had the same big, muscular build. But he was dark, and very handsome in more of a Latin sort of way.

"Well," I said, smiling up at him after Steve had introduced us, "which side of the family do you take after? In spite of what Steve says, I'd never know you were brothers."

Gary clapped Steve on the shoulder. "She wouldn't say that if she saw how stubborn we can be, would she, Steve?" he said, laughing. Then he turned to me. "I'm just kidding, Cheryl," he said. "Actually, they say I take after my mother's side."

Steve went out of the room and came back with Justin in his arms. "And who do you think he looks like?" he asked proudly.

10

"I'll tell you when he gets a little more hair," Gary kidded. Then he held up his finger so Justin could grab hold of it. "Say, he's smart," he said. "I think he knows I'm his uncle."

Steve laughed and handed the baby to me. Then he tossed the car keys to Gary. "Have a ball, sailor," he told him. "And just leave the car in the driveway when you bring it back."

The only times I saw Gary after that was when he'd borrow our car. And then he got his own car, and I scarcely saw him at all. But Steve talked about him so much, telling me how hard he was pitching in on the job, that I felt I knew him. Little things would come out about him how he did this for his father or that for Steve, and I liked him instinctively. I know that Gary was aware that I'd been married to Zack, too. Steve had told him about it. But Gary was like the rest of the Quinns; he never mentioned Zack's name to me.

We had a wonderful Christmas that year. It was the baby's first, and although he was too little to understand any of what was going on, he was fascinated by the Christmas tree, the lights, and the bright ornaments. Steve had given him a big cuddly cat, all soft and white, and Justin would chew on it, pull on it, and shove it out of his crib. Then he'd squeal for it, and I'd have to go running to him and give it back. Steve's father and my family had Christmas dinner with us—Gary couldn't make it—and when the day was over, I was left with a warm feeling. I wished that everyone could be as happy as I was. Because I had so much.

Several times during the winter months, Steve went hunting on weekends with his friends. I'd stay home, taking care of the baby and house. When Steve got home, he would tell me all about his trip while we ate. He really enjoyed those times with the men.

There were times, too, when I felt the need to be with women. Quite a few of our neighbors were young mothers with babies Justin's age or a little older, and we'd get together a couple of times a week at each other's houses. There was nothing formal about it. We'd have coffee and home-baked cake or cookies and talk about our children and our homes. The nice part about it was, none of the girls I knew seemed to have problems with their husbands. They were in love the way I was, and nobody tried to poke her nose in anybody else's business. Lots of times we'd baby-sit for each other, and, oh, how grateful I was for that when there was some special shopping I wanted to do.

The baby was getting to look more and more like Steve every day. He was really a very handsome little boy, and as soon as he learned to walk, he'd toddle around after his father. Steve was very good with him, too. He'd play with him, give him a bath, and spend hours teaching him to talk. But the first word Justin learned to say wasn't "Daddy." It was "Mommy." I was very touched by it, because I knew it was Steve's doing.

We had a terribly hot, dry summer that year, and on one of the hottest days, Steve's father had another heart attack. We were all worried about him. But the doctor said that with rest, there was no reason in the world why he wouldn't recover. He would just have to take it easier, though, and let Steve and Gary do most of the work at the nursery. Of course this was a terrible blow to Mr. Quinn. He was like his sons, a very active man, and he wanted to go on as he always had. So in a way it was a problem to Steve to make his father understand that he had to slow down. But somehow Steve did it.

Then, right after we began to relax over Steve's father, things began to happen to my family. Steve and I went to see them on Sunday, and I could tell my mother was excited about something all through dinner.

"What is it, Mom?" I asked when we were doing the dishes together. I was really kind of scared. I thought maybe something bad had happened or was going to happen.

Mom was evasive. "You'll have to wait till later," she said. "Your father will tell you all about it."

My heart really sank then. "Oh, Mom!" I cried. "Is Dad's job shaky or something?"

"No, no, no," she said reassuringly. "It's nothing like that. It's good news, but I want your father to tell you about it."

Well, it was good news—for them. My father's company was transferring ring him to the largest branch office and giving him a big promotion. He couldn't hide his excitement and eagerness as he told us about it, and my mother was glowing with pride. But they were going to be so far away; I might see them only once or twice a year. The house would have to be sold. In fact, a Realtor already had someone who was interested in it.

I was happy for them, of course, but I felt sad for myself. I could only imagine what it would be like with them gone. And in a couple of weeks when it actually happened, it was far worse. I'd go to the phone to call my mother about some little thing I had on my mind, and I'd suddenly realize that she didn't live near me anymore. We could call each other long distance, of course, but it wouldn't be too often.

Late in October, Steve was away on his first hunting trip of the season, and I spent most of the Saturday afternoon with the baby in the recreation area of the park. Justin loved the sandbox there, and it was easy for me to watch him.

When I got back to the house, I hadn't been inside more than ten minutes before Gary showed up. I was surprised to see him, because he never came over unless he wanted to see Steve about something, and he knew Steve was away. Then, as I really looked at him, I knew something was wrong. His face was tense and grim, and for the first time, I believed that he could be as serious as Steve said.

"Come in, Gary," I said. "Something's happened to your father, hasn't it?"

He took a deep, shuddering breath, looked away from me for a moment and then back. His eyes were filled with tears.

"Steve's dead, Cheryl," he said, his voice ragged. "I'd give anything if I didn't have to tell you."

I stared at him, so shocked I couldn't speak. I could hear the baby talking to himself in his crib. I saw Steve's work jacket hanging near the front door. Everything was the same, except for Gary standing there in the hallway, the stricken look on his face.

Suddenly he reached for me and took me in his arms. "Don't, Cheryl!" he begged. "Please don't look at me like that!"

I didn't cry when I finally realized the truth. I wept. I couldn't escape my awful agony or my grief.

Haltingly, Gary told me Steve had tried to rescue his hunting dog when it got trapped on a rocky ledge. He lost his footing and went crashing down from a height of at least sixty feet. When the other men got to him, he was dead.

Just like that! I thought, my heart a thudding mass of pain. Just like that—and my husband is gone!

My mother and father flew east to be with me, and with Gary's help I was able to do what had to be done. I faced people who came to offer their sympathy when I wanted to cry out my grief alone in a room. I lived through that awful time to that final day of the funeral.

I sat with Steve's father and Gary for the services. All of a sudden, Mr. Quinn let out a deep sigh. I felt so numb, it's a wonder I even heard it. I glanced at him just in time to see him sliding from his seat to the floor, and I let out a startled cry. People rushed over to help. But it was too late to do anything for my father-in-law. He was dead. The doctor said it was another heart attack.

The double tragedy shocked everyone in town. Gary became hollow eyed and drawn from lack of sleep and grief, and I lost so much weight my clothes just hung on me. Then, at last, Mr. Quinn's funeral was over.

My mother and father had to get back home, and they tried to persuade me to live with them for a while with the baby. I told them I didn't want to leave Sunnyside, so they asked Gary to try to get me to change my mind.

When he spoke to me about it, I said, "No, Gary. This is where I belong. I can't run away."

He nodded in understanding. "Steve always told me you had guts. Now I can see what he meant." He patted my hand. "Maybe you're doing the right thing at that."

It wasn't easy staying on in the little house. Everywhere I looked

I'd see something that reminded me of Steve: shelves he'd put up, a book he'd been reading, a picture he'd taken of the baby—oh, there were so many things. And then I'd remember that he'd never be coming home to me again, and I couldn't bear it. I'd cry, no matter how hard I tried not to.

If it hadn't been for the baby, I might never have found the strength to go on. But he needed me so, was so confused over not seeing his daddy, that I had to spend more time with him than ever. It was impossible for me to dwell on my grief with an active little boy on my hands.

At least I didn't have any financial worries. Mr. Quinn had provided for his sons to share in the business, and since I wouldn't be taking a cash settlement for Steve's interest, Gary assured me I'd have a comfortable weekly income. I had other problems, though, of course. There were so many things to be taken care of that I didn't understand, I don't know what I would have done without Gary. He spent hours going over Steve's papers with me, and seeing so much of him, I discovered a strength in him that I couldn't help but admire.

Then, during the summer, I noticed a change come over Gary. A tenderness would creep into his voice when he talked to me, and he was always reaching out to take hold of my hand. Maybe I was being awfully stupid, but I never dreamed that Gary was falling in love with me. Yet, that's what was happening. I remember the strange feeling I got the night he told me.

"I don't see any reason to fight it," he said. "I'm not dishonoring my brother or anything. I've got to live, Cheryl, and I want to be happy. I know I will be if you'll marry me."

I couldn't answer him. I won't deny that I felt a very deep affection for him, but I'd loved Steve so much I didn't think another man could take his place. Not even Gary.

I underestimated Gary, though. I found I couldn't go on with him the way I had before. Once the awareness was between us, once I knew he wanted me, my heart opened up to him. I felt alive again, a complete woman. When Gary kissed me, my lips warmed to his. But there was a greater need that he stirred up in me—the need to belong to him. And when I could no longer deny to myself that it was really love, I told Gary.

He swept me up in his arms and held me so tight I could scarcely breathe. Then he kissed me. My heart was pounding when he finally let me go. "I'm going to make you the happiest woman in the world," he said. He didn't know it, of course, but he already had.

One night about a month after we became engaged, Gary was a little late coming to see me.

"You're not going to believe it, darling," he said, his eyes shining with excitement, "but Zack's back!"

"Zack's back?" I repeated, and as I said it, I could feel a crawling kind of sensation in the pit of my stomach. All the blood in my body seemed to be rushing to my head. "What does he want?"

"Hey—you're not still mad at him, are you? You two were just dumb kids when you ran off. You couldn't have been in love with him."

"Oh, I was in love with him," I insisted, "but he walked out on me. Maybe you've forgotten that."

Gary laughed. "Say, you're really serious, aren't you?" he said, sounding completely amazed. "Look, let's not talk about it anymore tonight. We've got better things to do."

But I wasn't ready to drop the subject. "What did Zack say when he heard about Steve and your father?"

The smile left Gary's face. "He was rocked back by it, believe me. Darling, if you'd seen the way it hit him, it would have made you cry."

I didn't say anything. I didn't want Gary to know how bitter I really felt about Zack. "How long is he going to be around here?" I said finally.

"I'm trying to talk him into staying and working with me," Gary said.

I don't remember much else about that night, what Gary and I did or said. I was too preoccupied with the news about Zack. And later, after I'd looked in on Justin, I went to bed and lay sleepless for hours. Memories of Zack flooded my mind. I could see him as he'd been in San Francisco—tanned and handsome, his hair lightened by the hot sun. I remember him stretched out in bed beside me in our little apartment. The way he'd reach for me and take me in his arms, the thrill of his kisses. And now he was back.

I wondered what Zack looked like. What would I feel if I saw him again? Would it be the way it had been once? In spite of everything, would I find I still loved him? The thought frightened me.

I compared Zack with Steve. The way I loved Steve, I knew I was safe from Zack. I adored Steve with my whole heart. I was married to Steve, who understood about Zack and me. But Steve was gone.

I was very restless and uneasy the next day. When I took Justin to the park, I sat watching him play with the other children, but I kept wishing the afternoon would go quickly so we could go home. I was angry with Gary for being so tolerant of Zack. I was convinced that Gary didn't love me as much as he said, because if he did, he wouldn't want Zack around, he'd tell him off.

When I saw Gary that night, I couldn't make him understand why I felt as I did. He thought I was being unreasonable.

"Oh, no I'm not," I told him, my voice shaking with anger. "And if Zack stays with you, it's all off with us!"

I was sorry the moment I said it, because the look on Gary's face was the same as it had been that time he came to tell me Steve was dead. He looked terribly, terribly shaken and unhappy. But I didn't take back what I said.

Of course I felt worse about it later, and in the days that followed, I was torn apart with loneliness for him. But I kept insisting that if he wouldn't take my side when it came to Zack, then I was better off without him.

Gary couldn't stay away from me, though. I knew it the night I heard his step coming up the walk. A wave of happiness rushed over me as I ran to meet him, but instead I came face to face with Zack.

I could feel the smile freeze on my lip, and I just looked at him in stony silence. But my heart was hammering.

"Hello, Cheryl," Zack said, and the next thing I knew I was leading him into the living room that Steve and I had furnished. I'll never forget the strange feeling I had as I watched him go over and sit in Steve's chair. I could see his hand shaking as he sat.

He's like me, I thought suddenly. He's scared, too. Certainly, he didn't know how I'd react when I saw him again. He was probably even dreading it. But the odd thing was, I didn't feel any of the things I thought I would feel. I didn't want to throw myself in his arms. I didn't want to lash out at him in anger. I felt peculiarly calm, the way I should feel with Gary's brother.

Then, all at once Zack was pleading with me not to break off with Gary. "I'm not worth causing you both any trouble," he said. He was so distressed, his voice cracked and trailed off. I watched as he kept gripping his hands together.

I felt sorry for him and ashamed of myself. I'd let myself be carried away by so much resentment, I thought I wanted revenge through Gary. But suddenly it seemed foolish and childish.

I found the courage to tell that to Zack, too. And then I told him I hoped he'd stay around, that I knew Gary wanted him and needed him.

"No," Zack said, standing up. "I don't really think I want to stay. I've changed enough since you saw me last to know what I should do, and I'm going to be on my way. But you'll call Gary, won't you? And the next time I'm in town, you'll both be seeing me."

I walked to the door with him and watched him go down the walk. Then I went to the phone and called Gary. The past was gone, and the lonely time was over. Because Gary still wanted me.

The End

THE ART OF DECEPTION!
I taught her to lie

That Saturday morning, as Janie and I came out of the doctor's office, I felt a cold knot of anger inside me. It's unfair, I thought savagely, as we went out into the dingy Bronx street. I felt the blast of cold air and looked down at the child. She was shivering in her coat, which the doctor had told me, was much too thin for January.

The doctor's words were buzzing in my head, making me feel guilty, as if Jack and I weren't doing enough for Janie, or for that matter, for six-year-old Michael and baby Shelley at home. Janie's chronic colds had come because she wasn't dressed warmly enough, the doctor had told me. I'd told the doctor we could just about live on the six hundred dollars a week Jack made as a clerk. But the doctor said we'd have to do more for the kids—dress them warmly, feed them better, give them vitamins.

I wouldn't have been so furious if the kids had had to do without things. But when it was just Jack's stubbornness that kept the five of us jammed into the three-room apartment over the shoe store, just Jack's stubbornness that kept us all without the things we needed.

As we turned the corner, I felt raw wind slide up my arms and again I looked at Janie. Her lips were blue. The coat was a hand-me-down from a neighbor's child, and although I'd mended it, the worn spots had stayed thin. "Cold, honey?" I asked.

"Not really, Mom," she said.

It was her eagerness to please me that did it—plus the fact that I was boiling mad at what the doctor had said. I piloted her across the street to the best children's shop in town. There was a blue coat in the window. Even from outside the store we could see the thickness of the lining, how the sleeves were pinched in to keep out wind. I saw Janie's eyes open wide.

"Do you like that coat?" I asked her.

Her eyes got shimmery, the way they had when she was six and Jack had spent his whole Christmas bonus on a doll for her. She didn't answer. She didn't have to.

I marched her into the store, and before I could talk myself out of it, I asked the salesgirl if we could see the coat.

When the girl brought the coat, Janie touched it shyly, as if she didn't want to build herself up for a letdown. "Put it on," I commanded. I wanted to see it on her before I looked at the price tag. And then it looked so beautiful, I didn't care how much it cost. "We'll take it," I said.

"One hundred dollars," the salesgirl said.

I gulped. I thought about Jack's insurance premium. I thought about the medical bills we'd just finished with on the baby, and the bills we were still paying for Jack's ulcer treatments. I thought about the rent. I told myself it was crazy to spend so much on a coat for a twelve-year-old. But then I saw Janie's eyes, and I knew from the light in them that she'd remember this moment if she lived to be twelve times twelve.

"I'd like to open a charge account," I told the girl.

She looked suspicious.

"I'm Mrs. Dowling," I said. "I live a block away. You can check on me with Mr. Nelson, the butcher next door. I've had an account with him ever since I've been married."

She called the butcher, and then she said I could charge the coat.

When we were out on the street again, Janie had color in her checks that I knew had nothing to do with the cold. She was pink with pride.

"Warmer now?" I said.

She dimpled. "Lots." Then she added, "But, Mom, what will Daddy say?"

"Leave your daddy to me," I said, but I felt scared. I didn't know what Jack would say when he found out.

Jack was working. He'd been working Saturdays for the extra money when he could, but with his ulcers, he'd had to take it easy on all strenuous work. I collected Michael and the baby from Mrs. Kootz, who'd been minding them, did my housework, and cooked dinner before he got home.

When I heard his key in the lock, I felt tense over the coat, although usually his homecoming was the high point of my day. Janie and Michael ran to him and kissed him.

As I came out of the kitchen and saw his eyes light up at the sight of me, I felt guilty. We were still very much in love, and a quarrel with him always made me sick.

Janie didn't mention the coat, but Michael had to announce it right away. "Mommy bought Janie a coat," he said.

Jack's face was tired as he turned to me. "Who donated one this time?"

I had to say it then. "No one. I did buy her a coat. I had her to the doctor's about those chronic colds. He said she needed warmer clothes."

He looked at me, his face pale. "Peg, if you think I like to see our kids in outgrown things, you're nuts. But you know the expenses we've had—you know the money troubles we'll go on having until I can get a good-paying job."

"Jack," I broke in wearily, "we started off wrong, getting married

18

on nothing. But I don't see why the kids should suffer when there's something you could do so easily." His face stiffened. He knew what was coming. "Jack, you've got to ask your father for some money."

"I'd rather dress you and the kids in burlap bags and make you live in a tent."

"Jack," I pleaded, "I never nag you about things I need. But I won't have the kids suffering when your father has money—when he said at our wedding that he wanted to help us."

"No!" he shouted, his face red and angry. "If you knew how he makes his money, you wouldn't ask him for any."

"Oh, for pity sakes," I said. "He must make it within the law; he's never been in jail."

Jack turned to Janie. "Honey," he said, softening his voice, "I want you to take the coat right back to the store. You can wear another sweater under the old coat. You're old enough to understand we can't afford a new coat for you this winter. Next year will be better." Janie's eyes filled with tears. She turned to me. It was the first time Mom had given—and now Daddy was taking away.

I couldn't let it happen. "The coat is not going back, Jack," I said.

"You heard me, Janie," he went on as if I hadn't spoken. "Get the coat and take it back."

Janie didn't move. But Michael trotted to the closet and came back dragging the coat. "Here it is, Daddy," he announced.

Jack reached for the coat, but I was quicker. I had it first. It was the first time I'd openly defied my husband, and deep down there was an ache from hurting him. But the pain wasn't as sharp as if I'd hurt Janie.

I knew I couldn't keep the coat by force; Jack was stronger than me. So I made my voice light. "Jack, this is a fuss over nothing," I said. "The coat was reduced to ten dollars. If I cut down on what I spend for food, I'll be able to pay for it with what you give me for the house." I hid the tag with my fingers.

It was the first time I'd lied to Jack, so of course he believed me. The red faded from his face. But then I noticed Janie's eyes. Under her relief over keeping the coat was surprise, surprise that I'd lied for it.

Well, I thought uncomfortably, she'll have to learn that sometimes you tell a white lie to get what you want.

"Well," Jack said, looking at the coat. "It's a good value."

So the crisis was over. The lie had fixed everything. As I began to serve dinner, I knew what I was going to do. I was going to see Jack's father.

I'd never been able to understand about Jack and his father. Maybe because of what my grandmother had done for me.

Mother had come from a town in New Jersey. She'd fallen in love with my father and eloped with him. He was the vocalist with a small-time band, and he took Mother to New York, to an apartment near Tenth Avenue.

They'd had some rough years, with him drunk more than sober, out of work more often than working. When I was born, his drinking got worse, and Mother, who'd never been strong, began to fail.

When I was five, Dad got killed in a bar brawl. Mother hadn't had much strength left, but she packed our things and took me back to New Jersey. Gran was standing in the doorway of her house when we got there, and her first words were, "Everything I have belongs to both of you now."

She meant it. She bought me all my clothes, sent me to school, cooked and cleaned for Mother and me. But despite all she did, Mother died a year later.

I went on living with Gran, and then when I was sixteen, I met Jack at a high-school dance. He told me his mother was a dressmaker, but his face darkened and he changed the subject when I asked him about his father. As we started to go steady, he told me his hopes, his plans, his dreams. But he always clammed up when I mentioned his father.

When we got out of high school, Jack went into the Army and I waited through the three years he served. I couldn't get a job because Gran was old and sick and needed me at home, and so we lived on her pension. Jack had to send most of his money to his mother; her fingers were crippled from arthritis by then and she had to stop sewing. The time Jack came home, we'd spent the last of Gran's pension. Then when she died, I had to bury her with the few hundred dollars I had left after the sale of her heavily mortgaged house.

So Jack and I were married with no money saved. His mother made me a lovely dress, though, in spite of her hands. During the fittings, I heard her and Jack whispering about whether or not they should invite his father to the wedding. Finally they decided it was his right to come.

I met him for the first time at the coffee-and-cake reception in Jack's mother's apartment. He was a big, handsome man, and seemed very pleasant. Before we left, he kissed me and said, "If you need anything, you know where to turn. I'm a rich man. I'd give you a big check now, to start you off right, but that husband of yours would return it."

I couldn't understand Jack's attitude. It had puzzled me during our brief honeymoon in a hotel in the Catskills; it puzzled me even more when we moved into our tiny apartment. I'd got pregnant with Janie right away, and the morning sickness was so bad I couldn't take the job I'd arranged to get. Then Jack's ulcers acted up and he had to take a lower-paying, less hectic job than the one he'd expected to get.

A few years later, when we were still paying medical bills for Michael's birth, Jack's mother became completely crippled with her arthritis, and we had to foot more bills for medicine. Then she died, leaving no insurance.

That was when I begged Jack to ask his father to pay the funeral expenses; he'd been her husband, and we were in debt. But Jack silenced me with a furious look and took a loan on his GI insurance.

Later, I often thought of Jack's father, but I never had the nerve to mention him to Jack. Not until the business about the coat. That was when I decided I'd see him on my own.

The following Monday, when Jack had left for work and the older kids were in school, I took the baby to Mrs. Kootz. Then I looked up Jack's father in the telephone directory. My heart was hammering as I headed for the downtown subway.

When I got to his office, I asked the receptionist if I could see him. I explained that I was his daughter-in-law. She took me into a simple inner office, and there sat the man who'd come to our wedding.

The years hadn't changed him much. The white streak in his hair was wider and the lines around his eyes had deepened into grooves. "Peg," he said, standing up and brushing his lips against my cheek. "So good to see you. What can I do for you?"

What could he do for me? Just like that! "You can lend me a hundred dollars," I blurted out. Then, before I knew it, I was telling him about Janie's colds, about Jack's ulcers, and all the other troubles that would have been so much easier to bear with just a little money.

"Good heavens, Peg," he cut in, "if you need money, you only have to ask for it. And don't even talk about paying me back. I'll make out a check for two hundred. Sure you don't need more?"

I began to cry. I cried because I thought of the bills on the kitchen table. I thought about how the extra money could chip a little off so many of them. And then I had to stop crying because two young men came in. They were ordinary-looking men with slicked-down hair, and they carried briefcases.

While I mopped my eyes and tried to smile, my father-in-law said, "Peg, I'd like you to meet Brent Reynolds and Tad Brown, two of my salesmen."

Beneath the excitement of getting so much money was the old puzzled feeling about Jack and his father. Jack had said so grimly, "If only you knew how he makes his money." Now was my chance to get one thing cleared up.

"Mr. Dowling," I said, "could you—would you tell me what you sell?"

Jack's father smiled. The salesmen smiled, too, as if I'd asked a perfectly natural question. Then Jack's father said, "Pencils, of course." He added, to Tad Brown, "Give my daughter-in-law a few samples. She can use them to jot down shopping lists."

Mr. Brown opened his case and handed me a half-dozen pencils in bright colors—red, green, yellow, purple. I took them, feeling dazed. They were sturdy pencils, and anger at Jack washed over me. But maybe Mr. Dowling had changed his business. "Have you always been in the pencil business?" I asked.

"Thirty years," he said. Then his face hardened. "I'm shifting Tad to your Greenbriar territory, Brent," he said. "You haven't done too well with it. And Tad could sell our products anywhere."

Brent's face tensed, and I got up hastily to go. My father-in-law saw me to the elevator. His last words were, "Peg, please feel free to call on me any time."

As I walked through the watery winter sunlight, I couldn't believe we were in the clear on the coat and that I had an extra hundred to play with. It had happened, though. I had the check in my handbag, and beside the check were the shiny pencils to prove it all hadn't been a dream.

That night, after we'd undressed, Jack said to me, "Honey, I just put some socks in the hamper and found it filled with clothes."

"So?" I made my voice casual.

"I can't remember when you didn't wash on Monday. Was something wrong today?"

"Do you have to check on everything I do?" I snapped. "I didn't wash. Do you have to make a production out of it?" When I saw his face, though, I knew I'd made a mistake in taking his words the wrong way.

"I only wondered if you weren't feeling well," he said, giving me a strange look.

"I'm—I'm sorry, Jack," I stammered. "I went to a movie by myself."

The words sounded false. Jack gave me a sharp look and said, "Sure you went by yourself?"

I stiffened. Never in our marriage had one of us had the slightest reason to make a remark like that to the other. "Jack," I said, "you apologize for that!"

"All right," he said, "maybe it was uncalled for. But you're acting so darn strange."

When we got into bed, he lay rigidly beside me. He didn't reach for me. I felt sick with guilt over what I was hiding. I wanted to tell him everything, but I knew what would happen if I did. The check would go back, Janie's coat would go back. And Jack had be furious with me for months.

The next day I paid for the coat, and as I settled some of our other bills with the rest of the money, I was thankful that Jack had always left the paying of bills to me.

As the weeks passed, the yellow of daffodils brightened the streets. The kids were well, and life would have been good if it hadn't been for the strain my feeling of guilt was causing between Jack and me. A thin wall had come up between us, and I thought that the only way to knock the wall down would be if I never had anything to do with Jack's father again.

Then, on a warm March morning, I got the letter. I saw my father-in-law's name on the envelope, and my heart pounded fearfully. I slipped the letter into my apron pocket while I handed Jack the rest of the mail—all bills. Uneasily, I wondered what Mr. Dowling wanted.

When Jack left I tore open the envelope. I found that Mr. Dowling didn't want anything. A check dropped out. A check for another hundred. "Forgive a meddlesome old man," the enclosed note said. "But with spring here, I wondered if the little girl who got the coat would like an Easter suit."

A new suit for Janie. A hundred dollars for it. Mr. Dowling evidently thought little girls' suits were made of gold. Why, this money would be enough for extra blouses, for a hat, for shoes, as well as a suit. Meddlesome old man indeed! Dear old man.

But what about Jack? I'd have to deceive him again. I'd have to tell Mr. Dowling I couldn't keep the check.

I worried about it all day—dreaming of Janie in the suit, and then thinking of how hard it was getting to even talk to Jack. But when Janie ran in at three, wearing the winter coat even though the weather was now too warm for it, I had to tell her.

I told her everything—how her daddy didn't care for his daddy for some reason, how I'd gone to see her grandfather and found out he was a very nice old man. And then I told her how he'd sent her money for a suit.

Her eyes were shining so I couldn't finish. "A suit!" she breathed. "Oh, Mom, I thought the coat was too wonderful to be real. But now a suit!"

"Janie!" I said, "since your daddy feels this way, do you suppose we could say Leah Kootz bought the suit and that it was too small and so she gave it to you?"

"Leave it to me, Mom," she said promptly. Too promptly, I thought, with a tug at my heart. "I'll make it sound good."

On Saturday Janie and I went shopping. We found a blue-gray suit and some pastel blouses and a hat with tiny roses in the brim. Janie was a picture in the outfit, and my heart almost burst with pride over her.

That night, at dinner, Janie said to Jack, "Dad, Leah finally gave me something she didn't outgrow. The most gorgeous suit you ever saw and a hat to go with it. She got them on sale and they were too small. The store wouldn't take them back. So she gave them to me without even charging me for them."

"That's nice," Jack said, looking at her trustingly.

My heart turned over. She was looking at me, as if for my approval. I couldn't eat my dinner.

Later, as I did the dishes, Jack came into the kitchen. "You didn't eat a thing tonight," he said, his voice warmer than it had been in a long time.

"I wasn't hungry," I told him.

"I know something's bothering you," he insisted. "Janie's big enough to be left with the kids now. Why don't you and I splurge and go to a movie? Then we can have a beer at the bar on the corner and you can tell me what's eating you."

Our wall thickened. How could I tell him I'd just made our daughter lie to him? The idea of going out with him was unendurable. "Jack," I said, "some other night. Tonight I have a headache."

His eyes turned cold. "Okay," he said. "But you won't mind if I drop around to the bar by myself, do you?"

It was the first time in our marriage that he'd ever suggested doing such a thing. I swallowed hard before I said, "Of course, I don't mind." I minded terribly, but I'd have minded his staying home, too, with the wall between us.

When he came in very late, I pretended to be asleep. But I was in misery.

The next morning I realized that since Janie had used the money, she'd have to write her grandfather a thank-you note. When I told her about it, she sat down and wrote a nice one.

An answer came back by return mail. An answer that said Janie's grandfather would love to meet the polite little girl who had written the note. Could she and I have dinner with him downtown the following Wednesday?

I was going to say no, but I made the mistake of telling Janie.

"Oh, Mom," she said in an awed voice, "I've never had dinner in a restaurant before." She was so excited that I weakened, and when I weakened, she was the one who worked out a story to tell Jack.

"Dad," she said, facing him on Monday night, "the girls in school are giving a mother-daughter dinner on Wednesday. Can Mom and I go?"

"How much are the tickets?" he asked.

"Don't worry about them," Janie said. "I babysat twice last week, so I'll treat Mother."

"All right then," Jack said.

How easily she lied! I felt guilt tearing me apart, and I promised myself that on Wednesday I'd explain to Mr. Dowling as tactfully as I could that we could never have anything to do with him again.

But I didn't count on Janie and Mr. Dowling getting along so wonderfully.

We met in his office. The salesmen and the receptionist greeted us warmly, and Mr. Dowling gave me orchids and Janie gardenias.

"Pick any restaurant you like," Mr. Dowling told Janie.

She shyly picked a restaurant she'd read about and in a few minutes we were headed there in a cab.

At dinner, Mr. Dowling ordered Janie two appetizers because she couldn't decide between shrimp and clams, and as we waited for our order he talked about Janie's school and about schools in general.

"You seem to know a lot about schools, Mr. Dowling," she said.

"Well, we sell lots of pencils to schools." When he talked about business, I noticed, his voice always cooled a bit.

Janie was staring at him wide eyed. When the waiter brought the shrimp and clams, she tasted both and decided she didn't like either of them, so her grandfather ordered her a fruit cocktail. When it stood in front of her, large and frosty, she asked Mr. Dowling in her direct way, "Grandpa, why doesn't Daddy like you?"

The question had been bothering me, too, even though I shot Janie a shocked look for asking it.

But Mr. Dowling didn't seem upset. "Your granny was jealous because I met many women in my business," he said. "She set Jack against me."

Although I thought it was rather mean of him to talk to Janie that way about her grandmother, I had to admit that it could have been true.

After dinner I was about to tell him we couldn't see him again when I heard him say, "Peg, I'll bet this child's never seen a circus. How about letting me take you both next week?"

And then Janie was pleading that she wanted to go.

I thought back to the way Gran had always wanted to do things for me. How could I deny this man the pleasure of making Janie happy? I wouldn't go myself, but I just couldn't keep Mr. Dowling from seeing Janie. "I can't make it," I heard myself saying, "but I don't see why Janie can't go."

Before we left, Mr. Dowling slipped a bill into my hand. When I got on the subway I saw that it was a hundred. I spent it on things Jack had be slow about noticing—kitchen curtains, a new garbage pail, towels, a jacket for Michael.

The following Wednesday I told Jack a lie about where Janie was. I tensed as I lied, feeling our wall harden. Jack went out that night, and

25

Janie came home before he did. She ran into our room and told me all about the circus. Her grandfather had sent her home in a taxi and paid the driver extra to make sure she got in safe. Then she proudly showed me a check from her grandfather for some summer dresses.

Spring passed into summer, and Janie began seeing her grandfather regularly. As he did more and more for us financially, she and I both lied to Jack. When she began to spend three afternoons a week downtown, we told Jack she'd been helping girls who'd flunked math and that she was paid for the tutoring. Janie had always brought home perfect grades in math, so it sounded believable.

And Janie told me about all the good times she was having at her grandfather's. He'd taken her to the circus three more times; Tad Brown had bought her ice cream; the receptionist had taken her to the city. And so it went. It was worth a strain with Jack, I told myself, to give Janie some glimpse of a normal childhood.

One evening in August, as I started the supper dishes, Jack came into the kitchen and said abruptly, "Peg, the summer tutoring is taking too much out of Janie. I think she should stop it. The extra money isn't worth it."

"What do you mean?" I asked guiltily.

"I mean she's losing weight," he said.

I wanted to say that she couldn't possibly be, not with all the good food she was getting. "Of course she's not losing weight," I snapped.

"Have you given her a good look lately?" he asked.

I thought I had. That very night I'd noticed she was wearing a lovely green sweater her grandfather had given her. Maybe I'd been looking so hard at the sweater I hadn't looked at Janie.

I went back into the dining room where she was finishing her milk and cookies. She did look thinner, and she was just playing with her food.

"She's getting into her teens," I told Jack. "Girls do odd things with their weight at that age. Some puff up and some slim down to almost nothing."

"Well, I still think she should quit tutoring and get more rest," Jack said. "Now I've got to go out. I promised some friends I'd drop in at the bar for a few beers."

"Can't you stay in one night?" I snapped.

"Maybe tomorrow," he said. "I promised."

"All right. Go ahead!" I savagely scoured a pot.

When he'd gone, Mrs. Kootz knocked at our door. When I let her in, she hedged and hedged and then she sat down and told me what she'd come about. She told me about the dark-haired waitress in the bar Jack kept going to.

"She has an apartment a few blocks away," Mrs. Kootz said. "She was talking to me yesterday. She said she felt sorry for Jack when he'd come in night after night and drink beer there. She started asking him up to her place. Now, there's talk that they do more than drink beer up there. I hate to hurt you, Peg, but for your own good. . . ."

She hated to hurt me. She'd just torn my heart out of me. That night I lay awake and wondered what to say to Jack, but I couldn't find an answer. I couldn't even talk to him about it because it had been so long since I'd talked to him about anything. The next night, when I faced him at the table with the children, I couldn't bring up anything more personal than the weather.

Janie went on losing weight. The circles under her eyes deepened and her cheeks were drawn. One afternoon, a week before Christmas, I told her worriedly, "Janie, you're spending too much time with your grandfather. You've got to stay home more."

"It's not that, Mom," Janie said. "It's the schoolwork. It's fierce with graduation coming up. I'm studying too hard."

Of course, it was the schoolwork, I thought. She was having fun with her grandfather, and fun could never harm a thirteen-year-old child.

But that night, when Jack came home, his eyes flashed angrily. "I thought you were supposed to be tutoring in math," he said to Janie.

Her eyes got frightened. "I am," she said.

"I just met your teacher," he shouted. "Miss Hughes said you need tutoring in math yourself. Said you hadn't opened a book this fall."

"That's not true," she said sulkily. "She told you that because she doesn't like me. I'm helping four of the kids in math. I make four dollars an hour."

How convincing she is, I thought guiltily. Then Jack's words sank in. Miss Hughes had said Janie hadn't opened a book—and Janie had told me she'd been studying too hard. I'd taught her to lie. Had I taught her to lie to me? The idea was so terrifying that I just sat and stared at my food.

"You haven't been helping other kids and you haven't been studying," he was shouting. "Just what do you do with your time, spend it on corners with boys?"

"I spend it in the library studying," she snapped back.

"You'll tell me the truth or I'll beat it out of you!" Jack roared, standing up. "I think you're meeting a boy on the sly. I want to know who he is."

"I'm not meeting anyone," she screamed. "You've got a wicked mind and I won't listen to you anymore." And then she grabbed her coat and ran out.

I wanted to defend her to Jack, but I couldn't—not without

telling him the whole story. Michael began to cry then, and Jack threw down his napkin, got his coat and walked out, too.

Much later, long after Michael and the baby were in bed, neither Jack nor Janie had come back. Janie was undoubtedly crying on her grandfather's shoulder. But if she'd lied to me, a small voice whispered, what was she doing?

She'd grown up in the past few months. As time passed, I grew more and more scared. Finally, all at once, I couldn't stand any more. I ran over to Mrs. Kootz's and got her out of bed.

"Mrs. Kootz," I said, "can you give me the address of that waitress at the bar?" She found it for me.

"Could you—could you sit with Michael and the baby for a while?" I pleaded.

She put on her robe and crossed the hall.

As I ran through the cold, silent streets, I could scarcely believe it was less than a year since I'd told the lie about the coat.

When I got to the apartment, I rapped on the door and in a little while the girl opened it. She was plain looking, but I was too upset about Janie to care about the girl. "Is Jack here?" I gasped.

She didn't answer, but I pushed past her and walked in. Jack was there, drinking beer. "What is it?" he asked when he saw my face.

"It's Janie." I was sobbing. "She hasn't come home yet."

He left the girl immediately and together we went into the street. I felt closer to him then than I had in months, even though I'd just found him in another woman's apartment. "Oh, Jack," I wept, "it's all my fault." Then the whole story tumbled out. About the first lies and the more recent lies. My lies and Janie's. All about his father.

As he listened, Jack's face got whiter and whiter. Finally he leaned against a storefront and said, "My father's always been a big-time narcotics pusher."

I almost fainted. I had to hold onto Jack for support. Then he was saying tonelessly, "When I was a kid, Mom and I found out he did business with school children. He sold trick pencils with the heroin in place of lead. We kicked him out of the house and told the police, but when they got to him he'd been tipped off and he was caught with ordinary pencils. The cops have never been able to prove a thing on him."

Ordinary pencils. Like the green and red and yellow ones I had hidden in the kitchen drawer. Narcotics. Dear God! But it made sense. Those two salesmen were shady.

"Jack," I cried as the thought jabbed me with a piercing pain, "Janie's always down there, always with him and those young men who work for him."

Jack's voice was still dazed. "He's always had young pushers working for him. He wouldn't dirty his own hands with the stuff. You say Janie's always down there?"

"She's been pale, underweight," I was sobbing. "Oh, Jack, if they've got her taking drugs. . . ."

He sprang into action then. His eyes were as terrified as mine as he flagged down a cab and ordered the driver to take us to his father's house.

"He'll be living in the same big house," Jack muttered. "The same big house, the same filthy business. Oh, Peg, why didn't you trust me when I told you he was no good?"

I couldn't answer. I was crying too hard.

The rest of that terrible night will always be blurred in my memory. But I remember Jack's banging on the door of the house and making the sleepy maid show us to his father's room. I remember him turning on all the lights in the room and roughly shaking the man in bed.

"Wake up," Jack shouted, "and tell me where my daughter is, or I'll kill you!"

His father sat up and stared at him with frightened eyes. "Jack," he said, "I don't know where she is. I don't know!"

Jack grabbed his throat. "I mean it," he said. "If you don't tell me, I'll kill you."

"Let me go," Mr. Dowling muttered, "and I'll tell you."

As Jack backed off, Mr. Dowling said, "She's at a party at Tad's apartment." He gave us the address. "But it's an ordinary party, Jack. You don't think I'd let my grandchild go to one that wasn't."

"If it's not ordinary," he said, "and she's been hurt in any way, I'll be back to kill you. I swear to God I will!"

We crashed the party. But the kids there neither knew nor cared. I'll never forget my first sight of those dead-looking boys and girls sitting woodenly on chairs, on the couch. The room was thick with smoke. Sickening, sweet-smelling smoke. I smelled the strange odor, and then I saw my Janie lying on the rug, her eyes half closed.

We dragged her out of the apartment and carried her to a cab. In the frightful days that followed, when we had her examined by our doctor, we found out how lucky we were. Her grandfather hadn't been a complete monster; he had loved Janie in his way. He had been good to her, and he'd told his pushers not to let her know what their business was.

But Tad had told her all about it; he'd introduced her to marijuana on the sly six months before, and Janie had lied about it to her grandfather as she'd lied to Jack, as she'd lied to me. After it was all over, she told us that Tad had promised to start her on heroin the following week.

There's not much more to my story. Jack had his father arrested, and it was Janie's testimony that put him in jail. Some people said it was unnatural for a son to turn his father in, unnatural to make a child testify against her grandfather. But I know we did right. We had to protect the children who would have been his next victims.

Fortunately, our Janie's not an addict. Tad and Brent are both in jail, and now Janie spends her time with her school friends. But when she's an hour late from school and she tells me she stopped for an ice cream or visited a girlfriend, I look into her eyes and wonder if she's lying. Once you show a child how easy it is to lie, it's hard to ever trust again.

As for Jack—well, it's all over between him and the girl from the bar. He never went back to her apartment, but he did go to see her just once more at the bar. He told me that he felt he owed her an explanation. She wasn't mad, he said. After all, there wasn't anything to be mad about. It wasn't love that had brought them together, just loneliness and need.

Afterward, he told me he loved me—that he'd never love anyone else. But he didn't ask my forgiveness. I know he felt his was the lesser sin.

And he's right. I began it all—the pattern of deceit and lack of faith. And I'll suffer longest in repentance for the rest of my life.

The End

SEX ON THE
LOVE BOAT!
A charming steward made me his mate

"Hi, Kendall. What can I help you with today?"

"Hi, Molly. Travelers' checks again. Could I have five hundred dollars' worth in twenties?"

"But didn't you just take a trip last month?" I asked.

"I sure did. That's what this trip is all about," she said excitedly. "Last month I went on a cruise and met a fabulous man. Now I'm going to New York for the weekend to see him." She smiled. "We travel agents get around, you know."

"I guess so," I said, shaking my head. This is the worst part about my job at the bank, I thought, selling travelers' checks to people going all over the world while I'm hopelessly stuck in Los Angeles. I counted out the number of checks and gave them to Kendall to sign.

Looking at her, I wondered why it couldn't be me—just once— traveling, having new experiences, and meeting exciting men. Kendall was about my age, but she had a varied and interesting life, while I just plodded along from day to day, going to work, going home, going out with Matt.

I sighed. "Tell, me, Kendall, are ships as romantic as they seem on TV?"

"Oh, there's romance. I'm not sure I'd call it 'love,' though, if you know what I mean." She winked.

"Are cruises really expensive?" I asked.

"Not so bad. I'll tell you what—stop by the agency on your lunch hour and I'll give you some brochures. They'll have all the prices."

"Okay, I will," I answered. "Of course, I can't really go on a cruise, but it couldn't hurt to look at some pictures, could it?"

The travel agency was right next to the bank. I'd passed it many times. I usually stopped to look at the posters and to wish, but I'd never been inside. I kept telling myself that, on my salary, it was ridiculous to even think about a trip. But it would be fun to look at brochures.

When I walked in, Kendall smiled and motioned me over to her desk.

"Here, Molly. These are all one-week cruises. Have a look at them and give me a call. I'll be back in the office Tuesday."

Suddenly, I felt a little embarrassed. I didn't want to give her the wrong impression.

"Kendall, I don't know if I should take these or not. I can't afford to go on a trip right now. I'm really just dreaming, I guess."

"Hey, don't worry about it. Lots of people dream for years about a trip. Maybe that's half the fun. So take these and enjoy looking at them. I won't be mad if you don't go."

"Okay, thanks. Have a good weekend in New York."

"You have a good weekend, too."

"Oh, I will, I guess. But while you're out on the town in New York, my boyfriend and I will probably be watching television."

She laughed. "That can be fun, too."

"I suppose," I said, not very convincingly.

When I got on the bus that night, I settled back in my seat and pulled the brochures from my purse. I gazed at pictures of blue oceans, handsome couples walking hand in hand on pure white beaches, tables of food, and tanned bodies lying in a circle around swimming pools. Why couldn't I, just this once, do something like that? So what if it wasn't practical. So what?

I'd had a lot of practice in being practical. "You have to set a good example for your sisters," my mother would say.

"I'm sorry we can't afford a new dress for you, honey," my dad would say, "but Janie needs shoes, and Ingrid needs braces." It wasn't that they hadn't wanted me to have things; it was true that we hadn't been able to afford much. And, being the eldest of four sisters, I'd always been asked to sacrifice, since I'd been considered old enough to understand. Most times I hadn't minded having to give up some things in favor of my sisters, or being given more responsibilities than they'd had, but sometimes I'd wished I didn't have to be the one to baby-sit, or to help around the house.

Now, I wanted my life to be more like the books I read and the movies I saw, but there just didn't seem to be any way to make it happen. Listlessly, I stuffed the brochures back into my purse.

In the apartment, my roommate, Monica, was packing. Her parents live in Sacramento, and she was flying up for the weekend to visit. Even Monica gets to go somewhere, I thought, watching her throw things into her suitcase.

"Oh, Molly, I almost forgot! Matt called. He said he has to work late tonight and won't be over to pick you up until about eight-thirty."

"It doesn't matter," I said, flopping down on my bed. I stared up at the ceiling. "We'll probably just go out for pizza and beer, anyway."

Monica stopped packing and looked at me. "Molly, are you feeling all right? You sound sort of down."

"I'm fine. I'm just feeling a little dull, I guess. I mean, there's nothing to look forward to in my life. Here I am, twenty-two years old, and all I do is go to work, come home, clean the apartment, and go out with Matt

32

on Friday and Saturday nights. I want something more out of life."

"Like what?"

"Like this." I pulled the brochures from my purse and handed them to her. I told her about Kendall coming into the bank, about how she was always going somewhere, and about the man she had met on the ship.

"A cruise? It'll cost you a fortune! Why don't you and Matt go to San Diego for the weekend if you're so bored?"

"Because I don't want to go with Matt. I want to go someplace exotic, someplace where I'm not just plain old Molly Evans. I want to meet exciting, sophisticated men! I have eighteen hundred dollars in savings, and the bank will give me a personal loan for the rest."

"It's taken you years to save that money, Molly. You can't spend it all on a silly trip! And what about Matt? How would he feel? He's a wonderful guy, Molly."

"I know he's a wonderful guy, and I guess I love him. I don't know, Monica. He's just so . . . predictable."

"I think you're crazy, but I can't argue with you or I'll miss my plane. Take my advice, and don't say anything to Matt about this tonight. Maybe you'll get over it by the morning. I'll see you Sunday night. Cheer up, girl!" she said, closing the apartment door behind her.

Maybe it was a crazy idea, but why not do it? I could afford it if I could get one of the cheaper cabins. And I could get a loan and pay it off when I came back. What was I saving my money for anyway? I started to feel better as I thought about it, imagining myself on some beautiful beach, without a care in the world.

Matt arrived right at eight-thirty with a big bunch of white daisies.

"I'm sorry I'm so late, honey. We were really swamped today," he explained.

"I understand," I replied halfheartedly. What is wrong with me? I thought. Any girl would be thrilled to have a guy like Matt. I was really proud of him. He'd been working as a garage mechanic since high school, and eight months ago he and his friend Paul had opened their own shop. They were both working pretty hard, but it was beginning to pay off. Matt was only twenty-five, and he already had his own business. What was more important, I knew he loved me and was honest and sincere. So, what was wrong with me? Why wasn't I happy?

"Molly, you know I love you, don't you? Honey, it takes time and hard work to get a new business off the ground."

"I know. It's not that. I don't know what's wrong with me. I think it's the rain. I've been depressed all day. Let's just go get that pizza now, because I bet you have to go to work tomorrow, don't you?"

He nodded. "Molly, I'm doing this for us. As soon as I get on my feet I want to marry you. I want you to be my wife."

"Oh, Matt, it's too soon to talk about that!"

"Not too soon for me."

"We've only known each other for four months!"

"But I love you, and that's good enough for me."

"Matt, it's just too soon."

"I want you to think about it, Molly. I want to set a date," he said, looking at me very intently.

"All right, I'll think about it," I said, avoiding his eyes. Why tonight? Why does he have to bring up marriage tonight? It was as if he could sense that there was something wrong. We were both pretty quiet during dinner.

Back at my apartment, Matt held me tightly and kissed me over and over, and I felt comfortable and secure. But where was the thrill? Where was all the excitement I'd read about? It was as if we were an old married couple already.

All I could think about that weekend was the cruise I was going to take. I tried to imagine what it would be like to visit all the exciting places the ship went . . . to not know from day to day what would happen, what I'd see or who I'd meet.

Matt's proposal to marry him had just made things worse instead of better. If I married Matt, my life would be set. I felt I could see my whole life before me: I'd probably work in the bank for a few more years, then we'd buy a little house, and then I'd have babies and grow old. I'd never be free. Matt would never do anything exciting. I had to take that cruise; I had to take it before life passed me by!

I called Kendall first thing Tuesday morning and told her I wanted to go as soon as possible.

"I don't know, Molly. Normally, you have to book space six to eight weeks in advance for these cruises. Sometimes there are cancellations. Look, give me a couple of days and I'll check around and see if I can find something. I'll give you a call."

"Please try, Kendall. I really want to go."

"It sounds like it." She laughed. "Those brochures really did their job."

"Yes, they did. By the way, how was your weekend?"

"All right. I've got another call now. I'll get back to you as soon as I can. Bye," she said.

Her weekend in New York with a fabulous man had been just all right? I guessed she was used to that kind of life. What I wouldn't give for just a sample!

In the meantime, I didn't say anything to anyone about my plan. People noticed that I was a lot more cheerful, though. I could hardly keep my mind on work, with fantasies of strolling on a moonlit deck going through my mind.

Finally, on Thursday, Kendall called.

"Well, I found something. The ship sails a week from Friday. The cabin is A-43, and it's twenty-two hundred dollars."

"Twenty-two hundred dollars!" I gasped.

"I'm afraid so. That's the only thing they've got left. And I'll need the money by tomorrow afternoon. Since it's such short notice, the steamship company has to have their money right away. Can you come by the office tomorrow?"

"I—I guess so," I stammered. "Sure. I'll be there tomorrow." Twenty-two hundred dollars! I should've realized that the cheapest cabins would be the hardest to get. That meant I'd have to borrow at least six hundred dollars so I'd have some money to spend. And I couldn't afford to buy any new clothes. Monica was right—it was crazy.

There I go being practical again, finding all these reasons why I can't go, I pointed out to myself. But I will go; I'll do it somehow. And I won't tell anybody until after I've given Kendall the check. Then nobody can talk me out of it!

Since it was winter and I still had a week's vacation coming, I didn't have any trouble getting the time off. Also, the bank was pretty good about giving personal loans to employees, and they let me have the loan with no trouble.

By noon on Friday, I had everything taken care of. I walked into the travel agency feeling lighter than air. Kendall said she'd call me the following week after the tickets came, and that was all there was to it. So that's how the other half lives, I thought.

I was on a cloud all afternoon until I got home and thought about how I'd tell Matt. But I felt sure he'd understand. And, if he doesn't, too bad, I thought defiantly. He doesn't own me. He can't tell me what to do. Besides, it was already done.

Monica didn't have a date that night, so I decided to fix dinner for the three of us and tell Matt with Monica there. I'd pretend it was no big deal, that I just needed a vacation.

At dinner that night, I casually brought up the subject of my vacation. I told Matt that Kendall had come into the bank and said they'd had a cancellation for a cruise, and that, since I'd been interested in the one she'd gone on, she had asked me if I wanted to go. I told him that I had just impulsively said yes.

I think Matt saw right through my story, but he didn't say anything. He just stared at me while Monica mumbled about how she thought I was foolish and couldn't I get my money back. I guest Matt knew that I'd told him in front of Monica to avoid talking alone with him about it, so he just ate quietly and said he had to leave right after dinner because he had to work again this Saturday.

"Matt, will you take me to the airport next week?" I asked as he started to kiss me at the door.

"Sure, Molly."

"You're not upset about my going, are you? Matt, I've never even been out of California! I want to do something exciting."

"You have to do what's right for you. If you want something as badly as you seem to want this cruise, then, well, I guess you'd better go."

I didn't say anything. He kissed me gently and said good night.

Monica finally decided to stop hassling me about my decision to go on the cruise, and we spent the weekend going through her clothes to see what I could borrow. We also went shopping for a few inexpensive things. By Sunday, I was all packed and ready.

On Wednesday Kendall called to say my tickets were there. She laughed at my excitement when I picked them up, and made me promise to call her as soon as I got back so we could have lunch and she could hear all about my trip.

Matt took me to an inexpensive, but nice little restaurant for dinner Friday night before I caught my plane, but I was so excited that I could hardly eat. I hardly listened to Matt either; my head was so full of fantasies about the coming week. Finally, looking kind of pale, he said we'd better get started for the airport. At the airport, he held me and kissed me tenderly.

"Molly, be careful. Don't do anything foolish. Remember I love you very much, and I'll miss you."

"I'll miss you, too, honey," I answered, but I was unable to hide the excitement I felt, and I suddenly felt ashamed. But I really didn't think I'd miss him.

As I walked down the ramp to the plane, I turned to wave one last time, but Matt just gave me a forlorn little smile. This is silly, I thought. It's only for a week. Besides, he's so busy we hardly see each other during the week, anyway. But I guess we both knew that it was a week that could change my life.

The plane arrived in Miami early the next morning, and we toured the city for a few hours before they took us to the ship. Even though I was exhausted when I finally got in my cabin, I was much too excited to take a nap.

The cabin was a lot smaller than I'd thought it would be, a lot smaller than it looked in the pictures. My excitement started to fade a little as I wondered if I'd spend seven lonely nights in the tiny room. But that was crazy. There were hundreds of people on the ship, and I'd noticed some pretty handsome officers when I came on board. I'd start mingling soon.

I showered and washed my hair, but for some reason, my hair

dryer wouldn't work. It took a long time for my hair to dry naturally, and I couldn't go out of my cabin with it wet.

I sat for half an hour staring out the porthole, thinking about all the fun I was missing. Then there was a knock at my cabin door, and a short, balding man introduced himself as Stan, my cabin steward. He told me that if there was anything I needed I should just flip the switch next to my bed and he'd come.

"What I really need is a hair dryer that works," I said desperately.

He smiled and told me that what I needed was a converter so that my dryer would work on the ship's current. In minutes, he was back with the converter. Overjoyed, I rushed to do my hair and make it down to dinner by eight-thirty.

Dressed in a long green dress of Monica's, and with my hair finally presentable, I felt like Cinderella going to the ball. Imagine me, Molly Evans, on a ship in the middle of the Caribbean!

But there were no princes at my table. There were Lorna and Ingrid, both in their seventies, and a middle-aged couple with an adolescent son, Grover, who kept gazing at me adoringly all through dinner.

Where are the tables with the other single people my own age? I wondered. But as I looked around the dining room, I realized there weren't a lot of people my own age on the entire ship!

Lorna and Ingrid invited me to have a drink with them in the bar after dinner, but I told them I was just too tired. I ran down to my cabin, fighting back tears. To think I'd taken out a loan for this!

At breakfast the next morning, Lorna and Ingrid asked if I wanted to go with them on a tour of the island we would stop at today, and that time, I quickly agreed. I was beginning to get lonely on that ship full of people.

The island was beautiful; it really did have glistening white beaches. I began to enjoy myself. Lorna and Ingrid were really nice women, so lively and happy, and they'd traveled so much that they really knew how to get around. At least I'd see some things, even though my heart sank at the thought of how much just sightseeing was costing me.

That night I accepted their invitation to go to the bar, and we had an after-dinner drink and watched people dance. Nobody asked me to dance, however, even though there were quite a few officers milling around. I saw Lorna and Ingrid exchange glances as if they knew how I was feeling. After about an hour I excused myself and went to my cabin. I was foolish not to bring a book. I turned out the light and tried to sleep.

We docked at another port the next day, and again, Lorna and Ingrid and I took a tour. I tried to console myself by saying that at least now I knew that things aren't always what they're cracked up to be. Though that thought was small consolation for the twenty-two hundred dollars I'd spent for the week that was going to change my life.

That night, after dinner, I went to the bar again—more to kill time than anything else. I didn't want to face the inside of my cabin until I was good and tired.

Just as Ingrid was about to show me pictures of her grandchildren, she and Lorna suddenly broke into broad smiles and looked directly over my shoulder. I turned. Standing right behind my chair was one of the young officers. I gazed at him in disbelief. Maybe it was the uniform, but at that point, I thought he was the most gorgeous man I'd ever seen.

"I heard you ladies were aboard again, but I've been so busy I haven't had time to find you," he said to Lorna and Ingrid. "Say, don't you ever tire of being aboard this old tub?" he said, laughing.

"Why, dear—how could we ever tire of it with you here? Judd, this is our new friend, Molly. Judd's a ship's officer, dear, and has been on our last two cruises. So you see, we know him very well."

I smiled up at him, trying to appear worldly, but feeling very jittery.

"It seems I've been so busy I've even missed seeing you, although I don't know how," he said to me. Then he took my hand and raised it to his lips, kissing it softly as he winked at me. I was speechless. All I could do was continue to smile at him and gaze into his beautiful eyes.

Judd asked if he could join us, then bought us each a drink. I was actually glad Lorna and Ingrid were there, because they talked on as I tried to regain my composure.

Finally Lorna poked Ingrid and said that they'd better run off to bed because they had another big day coming up tomorrow. By this time I'd gotten some of my confidence back, and as Judd made no move to leave with them, I didn't mind seeing them go.

Judd suggested we move over to the large, overstuffed couches, where the sounds of the band were muffled and we could talk. As soon as we got comfortable his first question startled me.

"Now, tell me, Molly, just what is a beautiful girl like you doing on a cruise like this without her guy?"

"I, uh, well," I stammered, and finally just told him that I wanted a vacation from my dull life back home and that that included my boyfriend.

"So, there is a boyfriend back home."

"Yes."

"I expected as much. Is it serious?"

"Well, yes . . . I don't know."

"Ah, then I still have a fighting chance?"

"What?"

"A fighting chance," he repeated, smiling.

Was he teasing me? He looked very serious. All I could do was murmur, "I guess so."

"Good," he said, taking my hand. Then he started asking me all sorts of questions about my family and about what I did for a living. And he started telling me about his life, too. He was so fascinating, and so different from anyone I'd ever known. This is it, I told myself, as my heart beat with excitement. This is what I want in my life.

Almost before I knew it, the band stopped playing, which meant it was two a.m. already! It seemed like just minutes since we'd sat down together. Almost as if Judd could read my mind, he said, "Molly, I don't want the evening to end."

"Oh, Judd, neither do I!"

"Let's walk on the deck. The sea is so beautiful in the moonlight."

We were the only people on the deck. I pretended we were on our own private yacht in the middle of nowhere. We held hands and walked in silence for a while. I didn't miss talking; it was enough just having him near me. It's crazy to feel this way after only a few hours with a man, I told myself. But I couldn't help it. Maybe he was the man of my dreams!

We stopped at the bow in some shadows, and Judd turned toward me. He silently took me in his arms and kissed me like I'd never been kissed before. He pulled me closer, stroked my hair, and then ran his hand along my back. I melted in his arms, unable to pull away or think about where this could lead. All I wanted was to be in his arms, with his lips on mine.

Finally, he stepped back, sighed, and looked at me for a long moment, as if he were thinking about something. "I think we'd better go in now, Molly," he said in a flat voice.

"Judd, is something wrong?" I asked, bewildered. One minute he was so tender, and now he sounded almost angry.

"No, no. Certainly, not with you. It's just that—well, it's crazy, but after these few hours I'm beginning to care for you a great deal. And, you see, one of my cardinal rules is never to get personally involved with any of my passengers. At best we'll have four days left, and then you'll fly home to your boyfriend, and I'll be left here on the ship, missing you.

"Most people think it's a very glamorous life we lead on these ships, flitting around the world, but I can tell you, it's very lonely. People come and go and nothing lasts, so I make it a rule to do my job and not get involved."

"Judd, a lot can happen in four days. It doesn't have to be like that. Let's not think about the end of the week."

"Okay, Molly, we won't think about it. I'll pretend we have a lifetime. Let me show you the island of Dominica tomorrow, darling. It's a beautiful place. Say you'll spend the day with me, Molly."

"Oh, yes, Judd—yes."

He kissed me then, softly and gently, and then walked me down to my cabin.

39

That night I sat on my bed gazing out the porthole at the stars, feeling the ship rock gently, and thinking that it was a wonderful, exciting world after all.

The next day, Judd and I toured the whole island and then went to a secluded beach where we played like kids in the sand, swam, and, yes, held each other and kissed as the waves lapped around our feet. It was all so perfect. I felt like an actress in a wonderful love story that would never end.

After dinner I met Judd in the bar, and we danced and talked and again went walking on the deck. Suddenly, Judd turned toward me and took my face between his hands.

"We've been together all day, Molly, and still I don't want to let you go. Come to my cabin with me. Be with me tonight."

As I looked at him it was as if a dark cloud passed over me, and in my mind I saw Matt as he'd looked at the airport. Good, honest Matt smiling a sad good-bye at me. But wasn't Judd the man I wanted? Wasn't he the man of my dreams, the man I'd come all this way to find?

"I don't know, Judd," I said weakly. "It's all happened so fast. I just have to think about it."

"Any other time you'd be right, but, Molly, we have so few days left!"

"I know, but. . . ."

"All right," he said. "I won't pressure you. I want this to be as much your decision as mine. But we've only two more days—and nights."

He told me that he was on duty the next day, but that I was to go ashore with Lorna and Ingrid and have a good time and he'd meet me in the main bar after dinner. He kissed me at the door to my cabin and left.

That night I tossed and turned, wondering what I should do. Somehow, I hadn't thought about where all this was leading. It had been so much like a movie I guess I thought the screen would just go dark when it came to sex. But this was real—the real world. I did want Judd but I just couldn't push Matt from my mind.

But what if Judd was in love with me? I'd heard of people meeting and instantly falling madly in love and getting married. What if I were denying something that I'd never again find in my life? But every time I thought of Judd making love to me I'd see Matt's face. How could I do that to him?

Finally, I fell asleep.

The next day I had a splitting headache. Lorna and Ingrid seemed worried about me until I told them that it was just a bad hangover. They both laughed and told me that that was what vacations were for, at least at my age. I missed Judd, but my mind was in turmoil.

That night he wasn't in the bar when I got there, so I sat with Lorna and Ingrid. I kept looking around anxiously. Finally, Judd showed up, looking very grim, and quickly led me out on the dance floor.

"Darn, I've got duty tonight!"

"But I thought you had evenings off," I said, stunned.

"Normally I do, but one of the other officers is sick so I have to work. I'm on in about fifteen minutes, and it's for the whole night. My darling Molly, we'll only have the last night together. And I think I'm falling in love with you."

"What?" I exclaimed, not believing my ears.

"I think I love you, Molly."

"Hold me. Just hold me, Judd."

We danced until the song ended. Then he kissed me and was gone. Gone. That left us just one more night. My last night before going home. Now what would I do?

I spent a sleepless night and came to the decision that if Judd loved me, then there was nothing stopping us, because I loved him. He was everything I wanted in a man; he was handsome, charming, yet sensitive and loving. I was a fool to have wasted all those other nights. Four days, four months, four years—what did it matter if two people were in love?

At breakfast, I was exhausted, and Lorna and Ingrid teased me about burning the candle at both ends. Our last port was a good place to shop, they said. I decided not to take a tour but to just go into town and shop since I realized that I hadn't bought any presents yet, not even for Matt. I spent the morning poking around shops and finally found some nice inexpensive gifts. But I was so tired I decided to go back to the ship and lie on deck in the sun.

I changed into my swimsuit and walked up on deck. First I stopped at the poolside bar to get lemonade. I leaned against the bar and looked around the deck to decide where I wanted to sit. A couple of the deck chairs were backed up so close to the bar that I couldn't help but overhear the young couple sitting in them. I couldn't see their faces, but I could see that they were holding hands. I smiled when I heard the guy say, "I love you, Makenzi. You know that, don't you?"

I guess when you're in love you want to think that the whole world is also in love, I thought, as I stood there eavesdropping.

"Last night with you was so wonderful for me, darling, so special," the guy continued. "You know, most people think that the life I lead is so glamorous, so exciting, but in truth, it's very lonely. Normally, I don't get involved with any of my passengers, but you—I just can't explain it, you're so special!"

My stomach suddenly tied up in knots. The voice, the words—but

I couldn't be sure—I couldn't see his face. Maybe it wasn't Judd.

The woman laughed and stood up.

"I know. You love me and every girl on this boat. That's part of your job, isn't it? To keep us happy? Now let's go cool off."

He laughed and jumped up and raced after her to the pool. And there was no mistaking it—it was Judd. Tears sprang to my eyes as I turned to go back inside.

"Are you all right, Miss?" I heard the bartender ask, but I ignored him as I ran back into the ship and to my cabin.

Such a fool, why am I such a fool? I felt my face flush just thinking about the lies Judd told me. How could he, how could anyone act so sincere and still be lying?

I lay on my bed, sobbing. At least I'd be off the horrible ship tomorrow, and I could stay in my cabin until then. I'd have the steward bring me something for dinner. But then I reconsidered. Judd was going to be waiting for me in the bar as usual after dinner and I would meet him! Someone should tell him off. I wondered how many hearts he'd broken over the years. No, I'd see him and then I'd tell him exactly what I thought of him.

Judd was waiting for me in the bar when I got there. It was all I could do to bring myself to talk to him.

"Ah, Molly, my darling," he whispered in my ear as we were dancing. "I missed you so much today."

"Did you?" I asked. "And I missed you, Judd," I said stiffly, but he didn't seem to sense anything wrong.

"Why don't we go out on deck where it's cooler?" he suggested.

I hesitated before agreeing. He's definitely not to be trusted, I thought, but I'm safe enough with him as long as other people are not too far off. "Why don't we walk down here?" I said, leading him toward the scene of the conversation I'd overheard earlier in the day.

"Why? The poolside bar is closed now. Anyway, my cabin's in the other direction." Then, "We could go there now, Molly," Judd said softly, his voice thick with desire.

He tried to kiss me, but I turned from his embrace.

"Why don't I show you around a bit, for a change?" I replied. "This must be an important landmark in your life aboard ship." I pointed to the two deck chairs where I'd seen him earlier. "How many seductions of gullible and lonely women have you launched from this site?"

"What are you talking about? What's wrong with you?"

"Why, Judd, I was just referring to your many conquests. Surely you must be proud of all the women you've had—and I do mean had!" I retorted nastily, my voice beginning to shake with rage.

"I don't know what you're talking about. In fact, I think you're quite mad."

"Oh, I'm mad all right! You see, Judd, darling, I was on deck this afternoon. I heard you talking to your friend. I heard you telling her how much you loved her, how lonely your life is, and what a wonderful night you had last night. Did you 'work' hard, my dear? How dare you play games with people that way! You know what you are? You're a creep. You're a waste!" I was screaming all the anger of my broken dreams at him, but he remained as cool as a cucumber.

"Oh, now, wait a minute, sweetie!" he retorted. "What did you come on this cruise for anyway, for real life? No—but for romance and excitement in one lousy week! You females are all alike; you think Prince Charming is going to come riding up on a white charger and whisk you off and make everything exciting and wonderful in your life, don't you? Dearest, I assure you, if love were that easy, it wouldn't be worth having in the first place. No use my wasting any more time with you—I'm going to go find Makenzi. At least she knows she's playing a game. But you, my pigeon, are a fool—and that's no lie!"

"You're no better than a. . . ." But I could no longer find words. How could he say such things to me when he was the one who'd been so cruel? I fled from his mocking smile, wishing desperately that I were home.

As I passed the bar where Judd and I had first met, I couldn't resist looking inside for a moment. It seemed so magical in the beginning, I remembered. It seemed too good to be true—and that's exactly how it turned out. So much for finding romance and excitement on a cruise! I thought bitterly.

"My, what a face! Did something you eat disagree with you, dear? I was just saying to Lorna a few minutes ago I thought I noticed a bit of an undertaste in the salad dressing tonight. Really, it's shocking how the standards of service have declined on these cruise ships. All these chemical additives they put in food nowadays—you never know what you're eating! Would you like an antacid tablet?" Ingrid's voice broke into my thoughts.

"Hush, Ingrid," Lorna cut in. "You always were blind as a bat. Can't you tell that that fool, Judd, has just broken the poor girl's heart?"

"Well," Ingrid said, sniffing indignantly, "I would hardly think that someone as inconsequential as Judd could break anybody's heart."

"Some people just don't remember what it's like to be young," Lorna stated. "Really, dear," she said as she turned to me, "we should have warned you about him. But you seemed such an intelligent young woman—much too smart to be taken in by the sort of pseudo-romantic claptrap he peddles."

"A perfectly charming young man in his own way, of course. But you cannot take him seriously," Ingrid added.

I murmured my thanks to both of them, and headed off to my cabin.

On the long flight home the next day I thought about my experience with Judd. I had to admit that some of the things he'd said were true. He could only fool me because I had wanted to be fooled; I wanted love and life to be easy. If I'd been bored before, it was nobody's fault but my own. I guess I'd just gone along expecting to meet somebody who would make my life exciting, rather than face the fact that my life was my own responsibility. That's why I had been expecting so much of Matt, and why I was dissatisfied when he couldn't live up to my expectations. I realized now that I'd never even made an effort to think of fun things for us to do, but had always left that up to Matt, as if it were his job to make me happy.

When I got off the plane, Matt was waiting there for me. He looked faintly surprised when I kissed him quickly on the lips. I guess he expected either a big kiss or no kiss at all. "Matt," I began, a bit nervously, "I've got to talk to you."

His face fell. "I knew it. When's the wedding?"

"Oh, Matt, it's nothing like that! It's just that I've finally realized that though I've been expecting you and everyone else to make my life exciting, I'm really the only one who can do that."

Matt looked a little stunned, then said slowly, "Where does that leave us, Molly?"

"I don't know for sure. I hope we will always be friends. I like you a lot, Matt, but I'm not ready to settle down the way you are. I've been so bored lately, and I've been secretly blaming you for that. But it wasn't your fault.

"I've been thinking about this all the way home on the plane. There is nothing wrong with you, and there is nothing wrong with me. But I really do need to do more with my life than I have been. Maybe it's even that I need more excitement than you do. All I know is, I have to find out.

"I've decided that, first of all, I'm going to see about getting a job that really interests me. I was thinking of maybe taking some night courses in accounting at the community college. They've got a career counselor there, too."

"You really seem to have this all figured out. Maybe I should take a cruise now and get my life together," Matt said in a sarcastic tone of voice.

"No, Matt, your life's okay. And I want mine to be, too. I still want to see you, if you want to see me, but I think we should both be seeing other people as well." I hesitated then. I did want to be friends with Matt. "What do you think, Matt? Should we still date each other?"

He sighed. "I don't know, Molly. I guess so. I don't understand you though."

That was six months ago. I'm in an accounting course now, and my boss at the bank is very impressed with my new enthusiasm. I feel confident about myself, too. I know that, once I get enough training, if I'm not able to move up in the place where I now work, I can always look for a better job somewhere else.

Matt and I still see each other occasionally, but for the last two months I've been steadily dating Mark, whom I met in my accounting class. He's teaching me how to horseback ride, which is a lot of fun, and he also loves to dance as much as I do.

I've been pretty happy lately, and, I think, I'm more self-sufficient than I used to be. And you know what? I don't envy anyone else their jobs, their trips, or their lives anymore. I like my life, and it gets better every day!

The End

I'LL STAND
BY MY MAN!

When the letter came, Adam and I were alone in the house. The family—Mother and my stepfather, Keith, and Gramps, and Uncle Will—had gone to the lake to open up the cottage for the summer.

Adam was lying on the sofa. "In about ten minutes," he complained, "my boss will be picking me up for that job in Summerville. I won't see you for two whole days."

"In three weeks," I said, "we'll be married, and you'll probably get tired of seeing me."

He grabbed for me, and then I heard the mailman. "The mail," I said, ducking away. "You get it, Adam."

"You're the boss," he said. He dropped a kiss on my head as he went.

He came back with his hands full. "All these dinky little envelopes," he said. "They must be answers to the invitations."

I took half the stack and began to open them. "Accept, accept, reject," I read to Adam. "And here's an advertisement: 'Dear Newlyweds'—and here's another—a bank check for one thousand dollars made out to Mrs. Adam Muldoon! Just what we need!"

"Sure is," Adam agreed. "We could build a house instead of starting out in that crammed-up apartment. Cristina, what is it?"

I was staring at the check. "Adam, it looks real!" I gasped.

"It can't be," he said. "It's just one of those sales gimmicks." He took the check, examined it, and held it to the light. "It does look real!" he admitted. "Could your folks or your grandfather?"

"No," I said, bewildered, "they've already helped with buying the furniture."

"Well, it's sure not from my folks!" he said. "Where's the envelope?"

Frantically, we pawed through the discarded envelopes until we found the plain long one with the Chicago postmark, addressed to Cristina Muldoon. There was no return address, but inside was a single folded sheet of paper with a few typed lines:

Dear Cristina and Adam, it said. With my earnest good wishes that you have a long and very happy life together. Mark Wilson.

"Wilson," I said blankly. "I don't know any Wilson."

"Isn't Mark Wilson your father?" Adam asked.

I stared at him. Yes, of course! Mark Wilson was my father. But

I never thought of him as my father. That is, I hardly ever thought of him at all.

"But he wouldn't do this!" I cried, dropping the note. "He doesn't even know I'm getting married!"

"Couldn't his folks have told him?" Adam asked. "They know, don't they?"

"Yes," I said. "Mother sent them an invitation, but we don't expect that they'll come to the wedding. And this, it's just crazy! I was five when Mother divorced him, and he's never sent a dime, or a note, or even a present at Christmas, for fifteen years! What is this, conscience money?"

"I never knew you were so bitter about him," Adam said. "You never mentioned him."

"Why should I?" I asked. "He was just dead to me. I know that they split up over another woman, and it almost killed Mother. He's never given a sign that he knows I'm alive."

"Maybe he's trying to make up for it now," Adam said. "Maybe he couldn't send money before. Maybe he had too much pride to write, or to send some little present, when he couldn't keep up his financial obligations to you. I'm not trying to make excuses for the guy, honey. I'm just saying that you don't know the whole story, and it's not fair to condemn him right off."

Adam was right. It wasn't fair. And a purely greedy thought crept in: We could certainly use the money!

I'd never wanted for anything. Gramps, retired now, had had a successful plumbing business. Both Keith, my stepfather, and Uncle Will, who had come back to live with the family after his wife died, had always been quick to give me anything I wanted. Right after high school, I'd got a good job at Carter's gift shop. But now that Adam and I were budgeting and cutting corners, trying to stand on our own feet, one thousand dollars looked awfully big.

"We really could start our house," I said, and stopped, remembering how Mother had looked after the divorce.

"I'm scared about telling Mother," I said. "I'm afraid she's going to be terribly upset."

"But she'd want what's good for you, Cristina," Adam said. "And we've gone out of our way to consider your family. We changed our wedding plans. We took the apartment here in town to be near them, instead of the place that would have been more convenient to my job."

"I know," I said, giving him a kiss. "You've been wonderful."

With a little pang, I thought of the wedding he and I had wanted— just a few people at the church on an autumn afternoon. I'd even had a darling dress picked out for it. But then the family had wanted an evening affair—a white gown and veil and all the trimmings.

47

Outside, a horn honked. Adam started up, grabbing his overnight bag.

"That's Frank," he said. "I can't keep him waiting."

I sprang up for a quick goodbye kiss. "What will I do?" I asked. "How will I tell Mother?"

"Wait," Adam said. "You don't have to say anything right away. We'll talk it over when I get back tomorrow night."

I was momentarily reassured. He kissed me extra hard and hurried out.

Hearing the truck start up, I felt so alone and uncertain again. I ran to the door, crying, "Adam!" But he had left.

It was wrong for me to want to call Adam back. Frank was doing him a favor, taking him on that weekend job. Frank was a building contractor, and business had slowed down lately, another reason for me not to refuse my father's check.

When Adam told me not to say anything until he got back, he didn't realize that my not telling Mother right away might only make matters worse. I'd never kept anything from her before. It would certainly look peculiar if I waited a day or two to tell her about anything as astonishing as a present from my father.

I couldn't begin to guess how Mother would feel about it. My father's name hadn't been mentioned in our house for years. Long ago, I'd wondered about him, overhearing Gramps talking about him to his friends.

"That man dragged Joy and the child all around the country," Gramps had said. "They lived in dumps in construction camps, and he was furious when she wanted to come home and visit her folks. When she went back after she'd been out here with the baby for a few months, he had this girl."

Another little girl? I had wondered at the time. But even then I'd known that I mustn't ask Mother. Little as I was, I sensed how terribly she'd been hurt.

When I was in high school and starting to date, Mother had offered to talk about him, as if she felt that it was her duty. For her sake I'd politely changed the subject. I was no longer the least bit curious about him. He was just a name from the dim, distant past. His parents, my Wilson grandparents, lived in the same city with us. I didn't know them, either. Mother exchanged cards at Christmas with them, and that was all.

All my growing-up years I'd had Gramps and Uncle Will, and then my stepfather, Keith, whom Mother dated for years and married when I was in high school. Certainly I had never missed my father. And now he had sent me a thousand dollars for a wedding present! If only all the family hadn't gone to the lake! If only Gramps or Uncle

Will had stayed at home. I'd always been able to go to them for advice.

Then inspiration struck me—Cousin Lisa! Mother and her cousin Lisa were the best of friends. After Mother's divorce, they had worked together for years at the tea-company office. Cousin Lisa had never married. She was one of those cool, collected women who had an answer for everything.

I flew to the phone and called her. "Cousin Lisa, may I come to see you right away?" I asked as soon as she answered. "It's terribly important."

"Cristina, I'm sorry, but I was just leaving for the office, some extra work I have to do," she said. "What is it, dear?"

I told her. For a long moment there was dead silence at the other end of the wire. Then she gasped. "Mark Wilson did that!" she said. "I can't believe it!"

From the tone of her voice, I couldn't tell whether she was pleased or horrified.

"What should I do?" I begged. "What should I tell Mother?"

"It's so strange," she said.

"You mean I shouldn't take the check?" I asked.

"Oh, I don't know!" She sounded as if she were wringing her hands. "After all, he is your father. But, Cristina, remember this: It's your mother who's taken care of you all your life. All the years she sat next to me in the office, punching that keyboard and worrying about your having a cold and putting in overtime so she could buy you a new coat—she did it, Cristina, without any help from him!"

I hung up, my stomach jumping with apprehension. If the check could throw even Cousin Lisa into a tizzy, it was going to shatter Mother. As for the money, I felt better and worse about accepting it. Worse, because Cousin Lisa had made me feel that to take it would be disloyal to Mother. On the other hand, since my father had never lifted a finger for me, why shouldn't I get what I could out of him?

At five o'clock, I was getting dinner and watching tensely for the family to come home. Uncle Will drove in first, Gramps riding with him. They got out and began to unload gear and a string of fish. Mother and Keith drove in right behind, and just what I'd hoped for happened. Keith and Uncle Will went to the basement with the fish, and Mother and Gramps went upstairs to change.

Mother didn't even look into the kitchen, only called, "Cristina? I'll be down in a minute to help with dinner."

"Fine!" I called back, and went down to the basement.

Keith was already busy with the scaler. "Hi," he said. "See what we caught?"

I hardly looked at the fish. "Listen," I said. "I want to talk to you, but Mother's not to know. Look what came in the mail today."

49

"My hands are scaly," Keith said. "Hold it closer. Whew! A thousand bucks! Looks like old Mark is trying to be a right guy!"

"Twenty years too late," Uncle Will said. He'd taken it all in over Keith's shoulder, and his eyes were stormy.

"How can I tell Mother?" I asked. "Or shouldn't I tell her?"

Uncle Will went back to cleaning fish, his lips set. Keith stared at me with troubled eyes.

"How can you not tell her?" he said.

"Uncle Will, what do you think?" I asked. I'd always been his pet, but now he wouldn't even look at me. His glance crossed mine as he reached for another fish, and it was like a knife flash—as if I'd become an enemy.

I went upstairs on dragging feet. Gramps was settled in the front room with the evening paper. Mother was in the kitchen.

Later, I promised myself. I'll tell her later, when we're alone.

I put on an apron, and the envelope in my pocket crackled.

"Mother," I said, "I got a wedding present today."

"Another one!" she exclaimed. "You'll spend your honeymoon writing thank-you notes."

"From my father," I said. "I mean, from Mark Wilson." I took the envelope out of my pocket.

Her face sort of buckled.

"A thousand dollars!" Her voice was a stunned echo of Cousin Lisa's. "Mark did this?"

"It's all right," I said. "I won't accept it if you—"

"Won't accept it? Why not?" she asked. "He's your father! If he wants to—"

Footsteps pounded on the stair, and she whirled and made a quick motion as if to tuck the papers back into my pocket. Then Keith and Uncle Will came in. Uncle Will slapped the fish down on the drain board and scowled at us.

"Oh," Mother said in a deflated voice. "She told you."

"Did you have anything to do with it?" Uncle Will blazed at her. "Did you get all soft and write him some crazy letter?"

"You know I wouldn't!" Mother cried.

And for the first time in my life, I saw easygoing Keith angry. "Shut up, Will!" he said. "You know Joy had nothing to do with it!"

Gramps came into the kitchen then. "What's going on here?" he demanded.

Then they were all talking at once, Gramps thundering above the others. "What's this money for?" he kept shouting. "Does he think we can't take care of her now, when we've had her since she was a baby?"

"Grandstand gesture," Uncle Will cut in. "It's supposed to make us forget things like that dump they were living in in Norfolk."

"Forget!" Gramps snorted. "Like the winter Joy came to see us in a coat as thin as cheesecloth!"

"We'd been living in Florida," Mother said, but her murmur was lost in Gramps's shouting.

It was like that all through dinner. Fifteen years of peace, of my father's name being so seldom mentioned that it had taken me a moment to realize that Mark Wilson was my father. And now the walls echoed with his name. Even the check that had started it all was forgotten as they dug up old grievances. I tried bringing up the points that had seemed so sane and right when Adam had mentioned them.

"Maybe he's trying to make up for things," I said. "Maybe he couldn't send money before."

"Don't worry, he's done all right," Uncle Will grated, glaring at me. "He had money enough for a fancy—" He stopped.

A fancy lady, he meant. But I wasn't supposed to know about it, even now.

Keith finally put an end to the discussion. As soon as I'd set coffee on the table, he got up, saying, "Joy, we're late for the first show. Come on."

And Mother said, "Don't you want to come with us, Cristina?"

I did want to—anything to get out of the house. But I couldn't have borne sitting through a movie right then, so I stayed home.

Quiet settled after they'd gone. Not the usual, comfortable evening quiet, but a sullen stillness. Uncle Will watched television in the back parlor. Gramps was in the front room with the paper.

I did the dishes, and then I went in to kiss Gramps good night, a little ceremony that always pleased him. That night it didn't please him, though. Instead, he jerked his head away so that my kiss landed near his ear.

I went upstairs and threw myself down on my bed, aching for Adam, wishing we were married and I was out of this house forever. The house where I'd been so happy, where I'd been the petted and adored little girl in a family of adults—I felt like an intruder in it now.

I heard Gramps go upstairs to bed. And much later, Uncle Will. Then came the sound I was waiting for, Mother and Keith coming home. Keith went into the kitchen for coffee, and Mother came upstairs. I hurried down the hall to her room. When she saw me, she turned and opened her arms, and I went into them.

"Oh, Mom!" I choked. "Why did he have to send that awful check? I didn't want anything from him!"

"But why, Cristina?" Mom drew back to look into my eyes. "I've never wanted you to feel bitter about him. It was all over long ago, and I don't hold any grudges. I even thought of sending him an invitation to the wedding, but then thought that Will and Gramps might, well, you saw how they were tonight. And you can't blame them. They can forgive an insult or injury to themselves, but never to anyone they love."

"You mean you think I should keep the money?" I asked. "You don't care?"

"Not a bit," she said. "I'm glad he sent it."

I went back to my room feeling that a great weight had rolled off my heart.

I could keep the money. It was all right with Mother, and Adam would be so tickled.

Then a cold, unpleasant thought struck me: Mother would want what was good for me, Adam had said. Was that why she was acting happy about the money now?

I thought about all the years she'd never mentioned my father, how she used to get all shut up tight within herself when outsiders mentioned his name. We had one picture of him—just one—a snapshot in an old album, left there as if someone had thought there should be one picture of my father. The pages were smudged where other snapshots had been torn out.

The picture that was left showed my mother and a fair-haired young man on a beach, with a toddler swinging like a monkey between them. The three of them were laughing. No one had ever told me that it was our family picture. I just knew.

No, Mother couldn't possibly be pleased about the check. She was just pretending, for my sake. Keeping it would only mean trouble. If we put it into a house, every time Gramps and Uncle Will looked at the house, they would be outraged. It would be a constant reminder to Mother of the unhappy past. I would have to send it back the first thing in the morning. On the other hand, I'd better wait until Adam came home. I ought to at least tell him about it before I put it in the mail.

The next day dragged. No one mentioned the check. The silence was almost worse than the uproar of the night before. Twice Gramps started to dress for church, and twice he changed his mind, stamping downstairs, muttering something about "facing people"—as if disgrace had fallen upon his house. Uncle Will went bowling in the afternoon and came back as grimly silent as when he had left. Keith took Mother for a ride. They asked me to go with them, but I had to refuse. I wanted to be at home in case Adam came back early.

We were finishing a barbecue supper in the back yard when I heard Adam's car on the street. I hurried around the house and caught up with him on the front steps. In the dimness of the porch, he hugged me tight.

"It's good to be back," he said, "but I'm glad we went! A fellow came over to look at the work we were doing, and now he wants us to do a whole string of jobs for him over in Summerville. It sure was a load off Frank's mind."

It was a load off my mind, too. With business picking up, Adam couldn't possibly object to my returning my father's check.

He went on excitedly about the new job, and then he broke off, saying, "Honey, you're not listening. Is anything the matter?"

"It's that check!" I said. "Adam, we'll just have to send it back! The family is all upset."

"You mean you told them?" he asked.

"I had to," I said. "I got to thinking that it would be worse if I put it off. And then Cousin Lisa said—"

"Cousin Lisa?" Adam cut in. "Where does she come into this?" I told him everything that had happened while he was away. He listened, his face troubled and sympathetic.

But his lips tightened when I finished with, "So you see, we just can't keep the money. Gramps and Uncle Will would never get over it."

"Listen, Cristina, I won't begin to guess how your mother feels about your dad's sending the check," Adam said then. "But I know this, if she thought you passed up that much money on her account, she'd feel darned bad. As for the rest of the family, what business is it of theirs?"

I opened my mouth, and closed it, speechlessly. None of their business when they'd raised me, fed me, loved, me?

"You're twenty years old," Adam went on, "and it's time you made some decisions for yourself. This is strictly between your father and you. Whatever he's done in the past, he's trying to do a nice thing now, and it would be pretty small not to give him a chance to do it."

"Then if it's between him and me, I don't want the money!" I cried. "It's made so much trouble."

"The check didn't make the trouble, Cristina," Adam said. "The trouble was already there. You know your mother lets the family run her, well, that's none of my affair. But the family has to run you, too, and us, our wedding plans, the apartment we took to please them. I let that go, figuring they wouldn't have so much to say once we were married, and I thought the issues weren't worth fighting over. Maybe they were. Maybe I should have stood my ground about all of it. But I know darned well this is important. You know it isn't the money. It's slapping down a guy who's trying to be nice to you."

Oh, it hurt, Adam's jumping on my family, practically calling me weak!

"Who's trying to run me now?" I cried. "You are! Trying to make me take money I don't want—"

"Because your grandfather and your uncle don't want you to have it!" Adam finished for me. "You bet I'll run you, if it means keeping you from doing something you will always regret!"

I wouldn't listen. I ran and got the check and my pen.

"You know so much, you can handle it!" I said. "I'm making the check over to you, and you can thank Mark Wilson for it, or throw it in the river! Just don't ever mention it to me again! I wouldn't touch it with a ten-foot pole!"

Adam's hand closed hard over mine. "No, you don't, Cristina!" he said. "Stop being childish. You can't wiggle out of it this way—"

"So you're here, Adam!" Gramps said suddenly. In our excitement we hadn't heard him come around the house. He saw the check, and his face reddened. "That's right, Adam!" he said. "You make her send back that filthy money!"

"I don't think it's filthy," Adam said, and I quaked. I'd never seen anyone stand up to Gramps. "I think she'd be wrong not to take it."

"She needs money so bad she has to take it from that man?" Gramps thundered. "Never! Not a penny. I'll give her money, a thousand dollars, dollar for dollar."

"It isn't the money!" Adam said. "Cristina can spend it on clothes or put it in the bank and forget it. The money isn't the point. The point is, this guy's made a decent gesture—"

"What do you know about it?" That was Uncle Will, coming around the house now, Mother and Keith behind him. "Decency! You don't know what he did!"

"I don't care what he did in the past!" Adam snapped. "All I know is that there's nothing wrong in Cristina's accepting a gift from her father. Whatever he did years ago, he's trying to make up for it now. I don't think anyone has a right to deny a man that chance!"

"We're her family!" Gramps roared. "This is none of your business! She'll do as we say!"

Adam's voice was suddenly deadly quiet. "I'm about to be her husband, and it is my business," he said. "We'll do what we think right, and not what someone else tells us. Right, Cristina?"

I didn't know what to say. Adam sounded so sure, so right. A man should have a chance to atone. But how could I turn against my family?

"Cristina?" Adam prompted.

I shook my head, unable to speak. If I could only have time to think!

"Cristina?" Adam said again, and then he stomped off the porch.

"Oh, Cristina!" Mother moaned.

I raced down the steps and flung myself into Adam's car.

"You can't go!" I told him. "I'm not going to lose you!"

"You bet you're not!" he said, taking me in his arms, and his words were as fevered as the kisses that flamed between us. I wanted to belong to him forever, no matter how everything turned out.

"Let's go away tonight, elope," I begged. "We can still go through with the big ceremony later."

"Oh, no!" Adam groaned, all but pushing me away from him. "I think we've both gone nuts. That wouldn't settle anything. I meant what I said, Cristina. You've got to make up your own mind."

"I already have," I told him. "I just want to forget the whole thing, and the only way to do it is to tear up the check and forget it ever happened."

"That's it then," Adam said, and somehow, I was out on the curb. He started the motor and leaned over to look at me. "If you should change your mind, you can let me know," he said. "After, of course, you've told Cousin Lisa!"

He put the car in gear, and I didn't try to stop him. Through all my turmoil one cold, clear thought stood out: It was better to find out now, before it was too late, that we could never get along.

Clear, cold thoughts are no comfort when your heart is breaking and you're tied up in knots of fear. Adam would back down, I told myself. But there wasn't a word from him. I went to work mornings and came home nights to the growing piles of wedding mail that were beginning to look like a mockery. Why open it, when there might not be a wedding?

"Don't worry," Mother said at first. "Adam loves you. He won't let this stand between you."

Gramps and Uncle Will said nothing. But it was a different silence from their glooming over the check, not so much sullen as subdued, as if this greater catastrophe had made the check take second place in their thoughts.

Just once Gramps grumbled, "If that fellow only cares about money, Cristina is better off without him."

No one said anything, and Gramps looked abashed. We all knew that Adam didn't care about the money.

Mother began to wear the lost, haunted look I remembered from years ago, after her divorce, a look that I caught on my own face whenever I glanced in a mirror.

"Call Adam, Cristina," Mother begged. "Don't let pride stop you. He's right, you know. He just doesn't understand people like Will and Gramps."

"Pride!" I choked. "If it were only that!"

I was willing to concede that Adam might be right—the only decent thing to do was to accept the check and thank my father. But if Adam had to do what he thought was right, I had to do what I thought was right, and after all the trouble it had caused, I didn't feel right about keeping the money. I'd have to return it—but nicely, with appreciation and a tactful explanation.

Or I could return it in person! Chicago was only an hour away. It was a terrifying notion, but it was tempting, too, since it was the last thing Adam would expect me to do. He'd know that it would take all the courage I possessed, and surely he couldn't blame me if, after talking to my father and forming my own judgment, I returned the check. If he did—well, that was the way it would have to be. I was tired of being pushed around—Adam telling me one thing, the family another.

Maybe I wouldn't have had the nerve to go through with it, but on Friday there was still no word from Adam, and my boss gave me the afternoon off because he owed me some overtime.

So that's how I found myself at the station, buying a ticket for Chicago. I'd called my Grandmother Wilson from the store, shaky about doing it because I had never spoken to her before that I could remember.

She went to pieces when I asked her for my father's address. "You're going to send him an invitation!" she cried. "Cristina, I've prayed that you would. He won't come—he wouldn't embarrass you. But it will mean so much to him! It's the Dunber Company. Wait, and I'll get his home address."

I said hastily that I didn't need it, that I was using a business phone. I thanked her and hung up, shaken because I'd upset her. I couldn't go through with it, I told myself. I just didn't have the nerve. But an hour later I was on my way, still scared to death and remembering belatedly that I hadn't even told Mother that I was leaving the store for the day.

In Chicago, I called the Dunber Company. It turned out to be a construction firm, and it was a little comfort to know that my father and Adam were in the same kind of business.

"That would be Mr. Wilson, our purchasing agent," a girl's voice said over the wire. "Who's calling, please?"

"Cristina, his daughter," I said.

And then came a strange voice—my father's voice—saying, "Cristina, this is a surprise! Are you in town?"

"Just for the day," I said. "I'd like to see you."

"I'm tied up here for a while," he said. "Where are you?"

I told him, and he said, "You're clear across town from me. Would you mind taking a cab to my house? My wife works, and we have no children. We'll have privacy. Have you cab fare?"

I said that I had, and he gave me the address. It was a double house, he said, and his next-door neighbor had an extra key and would let me in.

I was beginning to think the cab ride would never end when the taxi turned into a block of neat double houses. My father's house was the neatest of all, with a walled garden at the side. I walked up the steps, my heart pounding. Then a flare of anger stiffened me. After all, it was my father's fault that I was here—he'd got me into this! I rang the neighbor's bell, explained who I was, and she let me in my father's door.

Inside, everything was comfortable and nice. At one end of the room was a desk, with a framed photo of my Wilson grandparents, just like one my mother had packed away in a box of old pictures. And—my heart gave a lurch—there was a tiny framed snapshot of a toddler on a beach, fat legs swinging above the sand. Only in that snapshot the grownups had been cut out. I saw only their hands, holding the baby's hands.

That's when it hit me—it was my father I was waiting for. For years he'd been only a name to me. And that morning he'd been a strange voice over the phone. But when I saw my picture on his desk, he became a real person to me for the first time.

I wanted to turn and run, but it was too late. A car stopped outside, and a man came up the walk. Then I was shaking hands with him. He was a blond man going gray, but still young looking, and his eyes were bright, almost as if with tears.

"Cristina," he said, his voice husky. "I never expected this! It was good of you to come."

I recoiled a step at his emotion.

"Maybe it isn't good," I said. "I came about this." I took the check out of my bag and put it on the desk. "I—I can't accept it."

His brows went up. "Why not?" he asked.

"Because it's made nothing but trouble!" I burst out. "The family's all upset and insulted and furious."

"Your mother, too? She called it an insult?" he asked.

"Oh, no," I said. "She tried to smooth things over. She said you'd meant well and—"

"I can hear her," he said. "In fact, I have heard her many times. Your mother's a thoroughbred. The trouble was, she needed plow-horse stamina."

"Stamina?" I cried. "When you left her to bring me up all by herself? When she worked and took care of me and you never gave a sign that you knew I was alive?"

His jaw dropped, then clamped tight in a smile.

"Cristina, sit down and rest the weight of that chip you're carrying on your shoulder," he said. "Do you mean to say your mother had to work to support you?"

I was speechless with astonishment. Then I exploded, "She didn't have to work to keep us from starving, if that's what you mean! But she wouldn't let anyone else carry her responsibilities!"

"A matter of pride," he said. "Pride was a luxury I couldn't afford. Now you listen, Cristina. I'm not going to dig up the past, but there are some things you should know. When your mother divorced me, I had nothing to say. She had been at home with her family more than with me. We hadn't been together enough to have much of a marriage, and I'd met a woman who didn't mind moving wherever my job took me until such time as the job would let me settle down.

"So your mother held all the cards, and she set the terms: full custody of you, no support, and so forth. She was within her rights, but I was still burned up, because none of it need have happened. We could have been together. There need never have been another woman if—well, never mind. It galled me that your mother could walk out, shrug me off, and take the only thing that still meant anything to either of us—you. I told my lawyer I wanted the right to support you, and I wanted my visitation rights. He knew your mother and her family, and he talked some sense into me."

He stopped, cleared his throat, fished in his pocket for a cigarette, and then forgot to light it.

"What my lawyer said amounted to this," he went on. "That you had more family, even without a father, than a lot of youngsters have—your grandparents, your uncle, and your mother. You had security, always a couple of cars in the garage, a house in town, and the place at the lake. Any money I sent wouldn't have meant a darned thing. In fact, from the way they all felt about me, it would probably have been returned. Am I right, Cristina?"

I couldn't answer. Everything he'd said was true. But it wasn't the whole truth. Suddenly I remembered how—how uplifted Mother had seemed about the check. Mother hadn't been pretending after all! She'd really been glad.

"You could have made Mother feel better!" I said.

"I wonder," he said. "Do you think any reminder of me—whether it was a regular check or just a gift at Christmas—could have come into that house without all the old bitterness coming with it? What do you think?"

I couldn't think, remembering the way his one gift, the check, had torn our family apart.

"I doubt," he said, picking up my thoughts, "that any amount of good deeds from me would have made me a good guy. I did what my lawyer said was the biggest favor I could do you—I stayed out of your life completely."

"Then why did you send that?" I asked, pointing to the check.

"Oh, that." His tone was carefully light. "For two reasons: One,

I was indulging myself. It was to make up for a lot of things—for the toy shops I walked through, never buying anything, for the frilly clothes and the dancing lessons and the sodas and the first party dress I never paid for, for a fat, blue-eyed baby who was all smiles and curls, who used to run and throw her arms around me when I came home at night."

He broke off and picked up the check, his hand not quite steady. My own throat was choked tight. I didn't know him, I kept telling myself fiercely. I hadn't seen him for so many years that I couldn't even remember what he was like. I wasn't going to burst out crying over him now!

He held out the check, saying apologetically, "I realized that whatever I did might make trouble, but I hoped that it might be welcome in the general excitement and good feeling over your wedding."

I shrank back. Maybe it was the choked-down tears that spilled over in helpless fury. Adam—our wedding—what wedding? I'd come all this way and got nowhere. I was more confused than ever.

"I can't take it," I said. "I don't need a wedding present if there isn't going to be a wedding."

"Oh?" He drew in his breath sharply, "You and your Adam quarreled over this?"

"What else?" I exploded. "And I'd already had enough quarreling! The family all in a storm over it."

"You talked it over with the family first?" he asked.

I didn't have to answer. He knew.

"Well!" he said, his eyes boring through me. "In that case, I'd say that Adam is a very lucky young man."

I gasped. This from my father, who a moment ago had practically had me crying over him!

"He's very lucky," he went on, "to find out in time that his bride-to-be won't ever really belong to him. And he's a smart young man if he won't have you on those terms. It'll save you both a lot of heartaches."

I could only stare at him. Adam was smart to let a stranger come between us?

"I told you there were two reasons why I sent that check," he said. "You already know one of them. The other was that I wanted you two kids to have something of your own. I didn't think you'd consider me part of your family, and I wanted you to have something that had come from neither your family nor from his, but that would be yours alone, together. Because, although you don't seem to realize it, Cristina, when you get married you and your husband are a family by yourselves. Or you should be. He's still got his parents, and you have yours, but the two of you together come first. You work things out, not with somebody else, but with each other. If it isn't going to be that way, you'd better not get married at all. Do you understand me, Cristina?"

"But—" I cried, and then I found that I had nothing to say. Because I was facing not only my father, but Adam as he had been that last night I'd seen him, the night he had asked me to side with him against my family. Was that all he had wanted—for me to be on his side? Was it that simple, and that important?

A new family—Adam and me. All my old loyalties would become secondary to my loyalty to my husband. "Forsaking all others." I'd heard the words all my life. Now, for the first time, I began to understand what they meant.

I looked up at my father, and caught something anguished and unguarded in his eyes that turned my heart over. He wasn't talking only about Adam and me, but about another couple—himself and my mother. My father hadn't come out and said so, but the family must have done a lot toward breaking him and mother up. They wouldn't have liked mother living far away from them, especially in places that weren't always comfortable. They must have kept after her about how bad it was for the baby—and Mother hadn't been strong enough to stand up to them.

"I don't want to turn you against anyone," he said. "I know how much your family loves you, and you them. But you and Adam come first. If the two of you decide to return the check, I'll understand. But I won't take it from you alone. You've got to do it together."

"Thanks, Father," I said. The word "Father" slipped out, but I wasn't sorry that it had. His face changed. Quickly he made a little ceremony of putting the check back into my bag, his head bent, his fingers barely brushing mine as he snapped the clasp. When he looked up again, clearing his throat, I had my own face straight.

"Thank you for coming to see me," he said. "It was more than I dared hope for, Cristina. And give my best wishes to your mother."

I don't remember how we parted, only that it was less a parting than an unspoken understanding that we would be seeing each other again. He put me into a cab—he had an errand farther out and couldn't drive me to the station himself—and I rode away feeling the brush of his lips against my cheek.

On the train, I cried a little. I didn't know why. Maybe it was for my mother and my father. Maybe it was because my heart was so full that something had to spill over. My father had given me a lot more than a check for a wedding present. I had something much more precious than money to take back to Adam now—something that would stay with us for all the rest of our lives. If he would only listen and forgive me!

When the train pulled in, I ran to the telephone booth at the station and called Adam. His voice was a little guarded at first, until I'd told him what I'd done.

"I'm at the station, Adam," I said. "I just got in from Chicago."

"Chicago?" he asked.

"Yes," I said. "I went to see my father, to thank him for the check."

"Hold everything, honey," Adam said then. "I'll be right there to pick you up."

Five minutes later, Adam and I were holding each other tight, and I was laughing and crying at the same time. It was so wonderful to be back in his arms!

We got into his car, and as he drove me home, I told him all about what happened in Chicago.

"You did the right thing, honey," he said. "I'm very proud of you."

"Gramps and Uncle Will won't be so proud," I said.

He threw me an uncertain glance. "Do you care?" he asked.

"No," I said. "All I care about is you and your opinion of me. From now on, you're the one who counts."

Facing Gramps and Uncle Will wasn't nearly as hard as I'd thought it would be. They ranted and raved a bit, but I told them that I did what Adam and I thought was right. I pointed out that it was our problem, and ours alone, and that we had the right to handle it any way we saw fit. After that, they calmed down, and though they sulked for a few days, I knew that they respected me for what I had done.

By the time the wedding rolled around, they were both their old selves again. Gramps was the one who gave me away, and just before we walked down the aisle, he squeezed my hand and said, "You're a good girl, Cristina. You'll make Adam a good wife."

I smiled at him and squeezed his hand back. We both knew that I had already taken the first step in the right direction.

The End

FOUR MISSING CHILDREN!
Will the community forgive us?

Four days before Christmas, I decided we had to leave Woodlawn and go home. I had just left Doctor Sills's office. He had asked me whether I intended having my baby in Memorial Hospital, here in Woodlawn. I was nearly eight months along. It was time to make arrangements.

I hadn't been able to tell him the truth—that I didn't know where I would be a month from now. I had simply nodded and allowed him to go ahead with the arrangements. Now I was scared. Where would we be when the baby came? I walked along the gaily decorated streets toward our room at Mrs. Haine's rooming house. Woodlawn was the farthest south we had been during the two years of our wandering since leaving Herrington. The Christmas season here was warm, it didn't feel like home. I was used to cold weather.

Mrs. Haine called to me from her sitting room as I started up the stairs. "Come have a cup of tea with me, Mrs. Dowling." Her wide lips were stretched into a broad smile above her double chin. I knew she suspected something was wrong with Lou and me. In the three months that Lou and I had lived here, she had tried to learn our secret under the pretense of friendliness. I shook my head. "No, thanks, Mrs. Haine. I'm very tired this afternoon. I think I'll go to our room and lie down for a while."

She looked disappointed, but she nodded. "You get your rest, dear. I understand. The holiday season can be so exhausting."

Up in our room, I took off my blouse and lay down on the brass double bed, drawing the blanket up around me. Such a tiny room, I thought. The sun was setting, and the shadows in the room were deepening. The baby kicked out. He's alive, I thought. My baby's alive and soon he'll be born. Oh, Lou, darling, please take us home. Please. . . . Mrs. Haine woke me by tapping on the door. "Telephone, dear. It's your husband." It was dark. I groped for the light, then put on my skirt. Downstairs, Mrs. Haine was holding the receiver. When I put it to my ear, I heard the noise of machinery. Lou was working on the construction of a new school gym on the other side of Woodlawn.

"What is it, honey?" I asked. -

"I'll be working late tonight, Heather." He sounded very tired.

"How late?" I asked.

"I don't know for sure. We have to finish pouring the cement for the back wall while the warm weather holds. I thought I'd better let you know, so you wouldn't wait to eat. I'll grab a bite here."

"All right," I said.

"Are you feeling better?" Lou asked, his words nearly drowned out by the noise.

"Yes. Lou, I've got to talk to you."

"Okay, later. I've got to eat and get back to work."

After he hung up, I noticed Mrs. Haine still standing there. "Your husband's a hardworking man," she said. "How come you never settled down in a place of your own?"

"We had a place of our own once," I told her.

"Oh? When? Where was it?" she asked eagerly.

"A long time ago and very far away," I said. I ate alone that evening in the diner down the street. I hardly tasted my meal. I was thinking about that home we had once owned. I was remembering Herrington as it had looked two Christmases ago—snow-covered and cozy. Lou and I had owned a small farm then. He clerked in the hardware store in town and worked the farm as much as he could on weekends and evenings. One of the things we did every year was to take the children from town on a sleigh ride two nights before Christmas. We always took the same route from Cushing's Corner to the Danbury place, then through the fields and across the lake, coming back along the old wood road. A couple of days before this particular sleigh ride, Lou checked the ice on the lake to make sure it was safe.

That night it warmed up and snowed heavily, but the evening of the sleigh ride was clear and cold. At Cushing's Corner we picked up fifteen children and started out. It was a fine ride until we were halfway across the lake. Then there were loud snapping sounds, and the sleigh lurched to one side. A whole area of water had opened up beneath us. The sleigh plunged in, dragging Cinnamon, our horse, with it. Lou and I fell into the water with most of the children. Some of them, the lucky ones, were thrown clear onto the ice. I could hear their shouts and the screams of the others who were in the water.

"Heather!" Lou shouted. "Pull them out!"

In the dark confusion, we managed to pull seven squirming, frightened children to the safety of the edge. I counted heads, then counted them again. "There are only eleven, Lou!" I cried. "I only count eleven!" Lou was still in the water. He swam around the sleigh. I could hear him moaning from the cold, breathing in short, frenzied gasps. He found one more child but didn't have enough strength left to pull the small, motionless form out of the water. I helped drag the child up onto the ice. We knelt down and recognized little Dexter Graham. He was dead.

We had no chance left to find the other three. There were eleven children on the ice who needed immediate attention. I could tell from the growing silence that shock and cold were gripping them tightly. I shook Lou. "Come on! We've got to get them to the Danburys'. We've got to get them warm." Somehow we managed to get all eleven children to the Danbury farm. After that I must've collapsed because I was on the way to the hospital when I woke up again.

It was two days later before old Doctor Jansen would let me go home. By then, men from town had recovered the other bodies. Deedee Thorne and Archie Lewellen, both ten, and little Hector Sanchez, who was nine, the same age as Dexter Graham. All the other children were well. And in Herrington, my husband, Lou, was called a murderer. It was the waitress who snapped me out of my thoughts there in the Woodlawn diner. She was standing over my table.

"Will you be having dessert, Ma'am?" she asked impatiently.

"No." I paid my check and hurried outside. There I paused. I didn't want to go back to the room. I decided I'd walk over to the gym site and wait there for Lou. I had to tell him we must go home.

It was over a mile to the field. As I came close, I could see Lou in the glare of the floodlights slowly pushing a wheelbarrow of cement up the long, narrow ramp. Suddenly the wheelbarrow tipped and Lou stumbled. For a horrible second I thought he was going to fall off the ramp, but he caught himself just in time. Some men in a group near me laughed, and I felt angry tears burn my eyes. "Kind of lightweight for wheeling cement, ain't he?" one of them sneered.

Lou started down with the wheelbarrow for another load. His face in the sharp light near the cement mixer looked pale and exhausted. It was too much for him, but I knew he wouldn't stop, not until the job was done, no matter how much the other men laughed at him. In the private hell of his guilt, hard work was the only way he knew to drive away the ghosts of those children. He blamed himself for their deaths. "It was my fault, Heather," he would tell me so often. "The warm weather and the heavy snow weakened the ice. I should've known. I should've checked it again. Why didn't I, Heather? Why didn't I check the ice again?"

When they had wheeled up the last of the cement, Lou picked up his lunch pail without a word and headed for the car. I slipped out of the shadows and joined him. "What are you doing here, Heather?" he asked. Cement dust was in his hair and caked on his face, making him look even paler.

"I got lonely," I answered. "I didn't want to go back to the room."

We reached the car, and he opened the door for me. "It's too far, Heather. You shouldn't have walked all that way."

"Walking is good for you when you're pregnant," I said.

He drove slowly out onto the street. "Did you see a doctor today?"

"Yes." I took a deep breath. "Lou? You have to understand what I'm going to tell you. We've got to go home."

"Back to Herrington? No."

"Please, Lou. I can't have my baby in some strange town. We can't raise a baby in a furnished room. We can't go on living this way."

"We can't go back to Herrington. They hate us there."

"It's been two years. Surely, they won't feel that way now."

"After what I did? We can't expect them to forgive, Heather. Never." And then as he was parking the car, he said, "Maybe we can go to some other town, a nicer one. We could rent an apartment. We have enough money."

"You promised me that before we came here, and before that in Cleveland, when I found out I was pregnant," I told him. "I want to go home, Lou." That night while he slept, I lay awake thinking. I tried not to disturb him, for it wasn't always this easy for him to get to sleep. He had to make himself very tired first.

It was Dex Graham who really drove us out of Herrington. It was his son, Dexter, we had pulled out of the water too late. Dex Graham was a widower, and Dexter was his only child.

The other parents, Mr. and Mrs. Spencer Thorne, Chaz and Aggie Lewellen, and Mr. and Mrs. Ed Sanchez, hated us, too. But not in the way Dex Graham did. The others had more children, their loss wasn't as overwhelming as Dex Graham's. He was the one who branded Lou a murderer for not checking the ice after the storm. And the whole town, sharing the grief Graham and the others felt, called Lou a murderer, too. It got so bad, we dreaded going to town. The hostile stares, the whispers, the simmering hate were more than either of us could bear. Then Lou was fired from his job in the hardware store because nobody would do business with him. He finally found a job in a town, twenty miles away, yet even there the ugly story spread.

Dex Graham started drinking heavily. He used to wait for us to come to town and then would follow us around, yelling awful things at Lou. One Saturday afternoon he cornered us in Dyer's drugstore. He was very drunk. He grabbed Lou and pushed him against the counter. "Come on, murderer!" he shouted, his strong, beefy face a beet red. "Swing at me, so I can kill you!" Lou silently straightened up and took my arm. We started for the door. "You killed Dexter!" Graham screamed. "You should've known the snow would weaken that ice. You should've known it wouldn't be safe for a whole sleigh load of kids. You should've gone out there that day and checked the ice. You hear me, murderer? You listening to me?"

Before we could get outside, Graham spun Lou around and hit him hard in the face. Lou staggered back, blood trickling from his nose. "Leave him alone!" I cried. "He tried to save them all! He nearly drowned! Oh, leave him alone! Please!"

"Come on, Heather," Lou told me. He didn't argue or try to fight back. That night Lou and I went to see them all. We went from the Thornes' grocery store to the Lewellens' big house to the little shack near the freight yard where Ed Sanchez lived with his wife and four children. Lou apologized to each of them. He told them he would be sorry until the day of his death, and that he would pay them back in any way they wanted.

Spencer Thorne just stood by his counter and stared, saying nothing, his eyes cold with anger, his big hands clenched at his sides. His wife, a tall, thin woman who wore her hair pulled back tightly from her forehead, told us to leave. "We never want to see you again!" she said. "Get out of this store!"

Chaz and Aggie Lewellen, who had once been our close friends, wouldn't even let us into the house. They made Lou say his words on the steps, then shut the door in his face.

Mrs. Sanchez cried, and her husband, Ed, a little man with black hair and deep, dark eyes, stood embarrassed in his cluttered living room. "We are not liked here," he said over and over again. "Hector was our oldest. He was so smart. He was going to be a fine doctor someday, and then people would've had to like us." Tears suddenly rolled down his face. "I cannot forgive you, Mr. Dowling. For what you did, I cannot forgive you."

The next day, Lou told me we were leaving. We sold the farm at a low price to the local real estate man, and left the following week. I rolled over in bed in our furnished room in Woodlawn and then sat up. I stared through the window at a Christmas tree in the vacant lot across the street. For two years we had wandered from town to town, from job to job, from furnished room to furnished room. I had given up all hope of ever having babies, but in Cleveland, in June, I found out from a doctor that I was pregnant. I was so happy, so sure this would be the wonderful thing that would change Lou.

At first he promised we would find a nice town and really settle down, in an apartment of our own, or maybe even a house. But we continued our wandering. From Cleveland we went west to Tulsa, Oklahoma, then back east to Maryland, and then south, where Lou found this construction job in Elwood. He couldn't keep his promise. Day by day, the guilt got a stronger hold on him, slipped its fingers deeper into his soul. As soon as the newness wore off each new place, we moved on. Lou couldn't leave his guilt behind, and he couldn't find any remedy for it in any of the places we ran to. He couldn't escape by running away, but he couldn't stop trying.

"Why do we keep on?" I said aloud.

Lou stirred beside me. "What is it, Heather?" he asked softly.

"You can't keep running," I said, crying now. "We have to go back. Otherwise we'll be running all our lives. Don't you see, Lou?"

"No. We won't go back. We'll find another town. A nicer one. You'll see."

When I finally fell asleep, I dreamed of Herrington. I dreamed that Lou and I did go back, and the people there had forgotten their hatred. They welcomed us. When I woke up, I nearly cried. The dream had seemed so real. But the gray light of morning showed me the same small room.

But I had an idea. In the dream Lou and I had given a Christmas present to each of the families we had hurt—to the Thornes, the Lewellens, the Sanchezes and even to Dex Graham. I couldn't remember what those presents were, but somehow, they had made up for what we had done. And that was the answer. After Lou left for work, I went to the bank and drew out our entire account of fifteen hundred dollars. We could give Graham and each of the three families three hundred dollars and still have something left over. When Lou came back to the room late that afternoon, I told him my idea. . . .

"Don't be foolish, Heather," he said. "We can't give them money and expect that to make them forget."

"Maybe it won't make them forget, but it will show them we want to pay them back for what we did. They'll see how sorry we are. They'll have to let us live in Herrington again."

Lou slowly shook his head. "You're thinking with your heart. Heather. You want to go back, so you're willing to try anything. It wouldn't work. We can never go back to Herrington."

"What are we going to do then?" I asked angrily. "Wander from town to town the rest of our lives?"

"We'll find a nice town, someplace we can settle down. I promise you."

I shook my head. "That's not good enough, Lou. You've promised me that before. If it was just the two of us, I'd follow you anywhere. But we have to think about the baby now. I've got to have a real home for the baby."

"We'll have one," he told me.

"I don't believe you," I said, tears burning my eyes. "You're afraid to stop running. But it's no good. Don't you see? You're running away from your guilt, but it's inside you all the time, and you can't get away from yourself. Also, you can't start living with yourself again until we go back and face those people. Maybe if they forgive us, you can learn to forgive yourself."

"They won't," Lou said in a low voice. "I'm going back. If you won't come, I'll go by myself. My baby is going to be born in Herrington."

67

"You don't mean that, Heather," he said. "Come on, we'll have supper and—"

"No, eat without me. I'm going to start packing."

I turned to hide my tears and when the door closed behind him, I lay down on the bed and let myself cry.

The next morning I bathed, dressed, and took my packed suitcase out of the closet. Lou was sitting up on the edge of the bed. "Why do you have to go back there?" he asked desperately.

"Because it's home and it's where we belong," I said. "It's where our baby belongs. I was born there and my parents are buried there. You and I were married there and lived there together for six years. If that doesn't tell you why, then nothing I say ever will."

"You're really going?"

"Yes, I'm really going. Good-bye, Lou. Kiss me?"

He got up and kissed my mouth. I turned and fled out to the hall. Mrs. Haine was outside her door picking up her newspaper. She turned and watched me come down.

"Wait, Heather!" Lou shouted. He ran down the stairs and took my suitcase. "All right, we'll go back together."

I hugged him happily. "You'll see, honey, it'll work out. It's been two years. When we give them the money, they'll understand that we're sorry. They will, honey."

He didn't say anything. I looked at him and saw in his eyes the pain that had been there so long.

After breakfast Lou went to the construction company's office to quit and arrange to get his pay. In the meantime I packed his clothes, so that by ten o'clock we were driving out of Woodlawn on the start of our long journey north.

We drove all that day and stopped at a motel after dark. Lou tossed and turned most of the night in the twin bed next to mine. Long after midnight, when he was still unable to sleep, I crawled in with him. Just before dawn he cried out and sat straight up in the bed, gasping for breath.

"Take it easy, honey," I said, holding him. "It was just a dream."

He shook himself and lay down again. The light of morning was just beginning to show dimly through the window blinds. "It was the same dream," he said softly. "We might as well get up and get started. I can't sleep anymore." We got dressed. Lou didn't have to tell me about his dream. It was always the same—the sleigh ride, the accident, the attempt we had made in the icy water to save all the children. In this dream Lou saw the four children drowning, yet still could not save them. He always woke up in terror.

We ate breakfast in a little coffee shop near the motel, then drove on. By now there was snow beside the road, and the morning sky was gray with storm clouds.

"It will be Christmas Eve tonight," I said. "When will we get to Herrington?"

"We should be there before dark." I knew he was dreading our arrival in Herrington, but I told myself over and over that this was the only way. If Lou could find forgiveness there, then he would have a chance to forget what had happened. I knew what really counted was whether or not he could someday forgive himself for his mistake. Yet I also knew that before he could forgive himself, the people he had hurt would have to help him. As long as he knew they hated him, he was trapped with his guilt.

We reached Herrington just at dusk. There was a foot of snow on the ground, and new snow was lightly falling from the heavily clouded sky. The Christmas lights along Main Street and in the store windows cast a lovely glow on the snow. We stopped in front of the Herrington House, the small hotel Jesse Martin kept open all winter for the small trickle of skiers who drifted through town.

Tom Wiley was behind the desk. He seemed surprised to see us, but he didn't ask us why we were back. We unpacked in our room, took showers, and then went down for supper. The dining room was closed after the summer season, but Mrs. Martin kept a small restaurant going in one corner of the building.

We took a booth and ordered steaks. The place had been noisy when we came in, but now it was suddenly quiet. We knew every person there, but no one spoke to us. They stared at us. . . .

"We shouldn't have come," Lou whispered to me.

The waitress brought our meal. One of the boys started the jukebox, and the tension seemed to ease a little. I reached over and patted Lou's hand. "It'll be all right," I told him.

Lou shook his head. "No. They haven't changed. They haven't forgotten. They still hate us."

"Do you have the money?" I asked nervously when we were finished eating.

"Yes."

Outside on the street it was snowing harder. "Who shall we see first?" I asked him.

"It's your show, Heather," Lou said shortly. "You run it."

We got into the car. "Let's go see Chaz and Aggie," I said. I took a deep breath. Now that we were here, I was scared. The Lewellens' house was lighted up with red electric candles in every window, and from the living room shone the many colored lights of a tree. We rang the bell. It was Chaz who answered. He was in his shirtsleeves, a bunch of silver tinsel in one hand.

"May we come in?" I asked.

He backed away. "I never expected to see you two again," he said. "Come into the living room."

We followed him inside. Aggie was standing by the tree. Her mouth sagged slightly at the corners when she saw us. "Hello, Heather, Lou," she said faintly. "The kids are out shopping. We were just getting a start on the tree."

A silence settled down over us. I looked at Lou. "What do you want?" Chaz asked. Lou pulled out his wallet and counted out three hundred dollars. No, I thought. Don't do it that way. Explain how it's been for us these last two years.

"We want you to have this money," Lou said in a low voice. "It's not much, but it's all we can give. We want you to take it because we're sorry for what happened. We have to prove that to you somehow," he added desperately.

Chaz looked at Aggie. He didn't put his hand out for the money. "We don't want it," Aggie said. "What do you think your three hundred dollars will do? Buy us back Archie?"

"No," I said. "Please try to understand!"

"Get out!" Aggie said angrily. "Take your money and get out of here!" Lou tried to pass the money to Chaz, but he wouldn't take it, either. "You heard my wife. I don't know why you two came back, but if I were you I'd leave again. Right away."

He showed us to the door, then slammed it shut behind us. Lou didn't say anything as we walked to the car. When we were seated, I turned toward him. "They may not all be like Chaz and Aggie," I said. "She always did have a bad temper."

"Who do we go to next?" Lou asked.

"Dex Graham."

"You're crazy if you think he's changed."

"Let's go anyway. Honey, I know this is torture, but what else can we do?" Graham's house was completely dark when we got there. "Maybe he's asleep," I said. We went over and knocked loudly on the door several times. Finally a window opened in the house next door.

"Who's there?" a woman called.

"We're looking for Dex Graham," I told her. In the darkness I couldn't see her face.

"Most likely he's out," she said. "At Lucky's Café or in Kingston at the Garden Room. He don't stay home much. Drunk all the time, ever since his boy drowned. Terrible thing."

We hurried back to the car. A cold wind was sweeping the snow down the street. "Ed Sanchez," I told Lou.

There was one candle showing in the single upstairs window. Ed met us at the door. "Mr. and Mrs. Dowling!"

"May we come in, Ed?" I asked.

"Well, okay. But please be quiet. My wife is sick."

The light inside was dim, I saw a vague shape on the couch lying motionless under a pile of blankets. Several children were huddled around a small kerosene stove.

"Who's it, Ed?" Mrs. Sanchez called from the couch.

"Just some people. Go back to sleep."

He looked at us and waited.

"We came back because we had to," I began softly. "We've been all over the country, but we've never been able to forget what happened. We-we want to live in Herrington again, but we can't unless you and the others will accept us."

"Who's it, Ed? What do they want?"

"You shouldn't have come," he whispered. "We were forgetting. We were closing off the place in our hearts that belonged to Hector. Now you bring all the pain back."

"I'm sorry. We don't mean to."

"You!" Mrs. Sanchez had sat up on the couch and was staring at us. "Why are you back?" she cried. "Why don't you leave us alone?"

"Please, go," Ed begged us. "Please. She mustn't get upset, the doctor said."

"Ed," I said. "Ed, listen to us."

"Please, Mrs. Dowling, go now."

He held the door open and we went out. Behind us we could hear Mrs. Sanchez sobbing. "W-we didn't even get a chance to give him the money," I said.

"I put it on the table," Lou said.

But before we could get into the car, Ed ran out after us, waving the money. "Here, take it back! Take it back!" he yelled above the wind.

"No, keep it, please," I told him. "We want to make up for what we did, and this is the only way we can."

"No, no!" He pushed the money into my hand. "We don't want your money. It isn't right, Mrs. Dowling. It's a sin to take money because someone is dead."

He backed away. "Your wife's sick, Ed," I pleaded. "Take it, please, take it."

"No!" He turned and ran back into his house.

We stood there in the cold with the wind whining forlornly through the telephone wires above us. "Come on, Heather," Lou said. "Get in the car."

We went to the Thornes' home next. The moment we were inside the kitchen above their store, I knew we had made another mistake. Spencer and his wife stood staring at us coldly. "Well? What do you want?" he demanded.

I told them everything. I knew it was hopeless, but I tried anyway. When I had finished, Lou took the money out again and put it on their kitchen table. "We don't want it," Spencer said.

"You have a lot of nerve," Mrs. Thorne said. With trembling hands she scooped up the money and gave it back to Lou. "Our Junie would be twelve now. Do you think your filthy money can make up for her loss?"

"It was an accident," he said softly. "Won't you people ever believe that?"

"What do you want us to do?" Mrs. Thorne cried. "Let you give us your money? Let you buy our forgiveness? Is that what you expect us to do?" Her voice rose to a pitch of shrillness.

"Come on, Heather," Lou told me.

Mrs. Thorne grabbed my arm. "I see you're with child, Mrs. Dowling," she said. "Well, how would you like it if I killed your baby? Would you feel like forgiving me?"

Lou pulled me outside. On the way back to the car I started crying. "Stop it, Heather," he said. "You'll make yourself sick."

"I don't care! Why do they have to be so cruel? We didn't mean to hurt them."

"I told you it wouldn't work. We should've never come."

"I'm sorry, Lou. Oh, please, I'm sorry." It was my fault. I had forced him to come home, and now it was worse for him than ever. I hadn't helped him. I had only hurt him more.

"We'll leave tomorrow," Lou said. "We'll find a nice town and settle down." He meant it now, but I knew if we left Herrington again, it would be to go back to our life of drifting from empty town to empty town. Lou could never stop running, not as long as this guilt kept its hold on his soul. You can't buy forgiveness, I thought. We had tried and failed.

As we drove slowly along Main Street, we passed Lucky's Café. He stopped the car and opened the door.

"Want a drink, Heather?" he asked.

"I don't know."

"Well, I do. Go back to the hotel and wait for me."

I got out and followed him in. I couldn't leave him alone. The café was crowded. We took a small table near the front, and Lou ordered two highballs. We were neither of us used to much liquor, but he kept ordering drink after drink for himself. "Don't you think you've had enough, honey?" I asked him finally.

"No, not yet," he said. "Go back to the hotel, Heather. I'm going to get drunk this once, and you don't have to sit there and watch me."

"I'll stay."

The noise and laughter got louder and more frenzied as the night wore on. Just when it was that Dex Graham came in, I don't know, but suddenly he was there, swaying over our table, an ugly scowl on his face. "I heard you two were back," he snarled. His face was red and bloated, and his hair entirely gray. The two years of drinking had aged him.

Lou reached into his pocket and threw three hundred dollars down on the table. Everyone around us stopped talking. I heard a woman gasp.

"See that money?" he said thickly. "That's your blood money. Take it."

I tried to grab his arm, but he was already up on his feet. He stood there unsteadily, his face only a few inches from Graham's. "You hate us!" he shouted. "You all hate us! I made a mistake any one of you could've made. If I could give my life to bring back even one of those children, I'd gladly do it. You don't know how gladly I'd do it."

He threw the money into Graham's face. "Take it! Spend it on more drinks for yourself. Hating me won't bring your son back, but go ahead if you think it'll help you. Hate me! Heather and I'll be gone in the morning. You'll never see us again!"

Graham didn't even look at the money. His eyes were bright with fury. "I'll kill you!" he yelled. He swung his fist at Lou's head. The punch caught him in the throat and sent him sprawling back over his chair. "I hoped you'd come back someday," Graham raged. "Now I'll make you pay. I'll make you pay for killing my boy!" Before Lou could get up on his feet, Graham had pulled out a knife and was slowly advancing toward him.

"Stop it!" I screamed. I looked around wildly but no one made a move to help us. They just stood there and watched. Lou scrambled up. His face was pale and dripping with sweat. He was no match for Graham, but he didn't run.

"Stop them!" I begged. "Please, somebody stop them!"

Again, no one moved except for Graham and Lou, who circled each other slowly. Graham swung the long, thin blade in a vicious arc at Lou's throat. He jumped back at the last second, tripped on a table and fell to his knees. In the next moment or two everything happened at once. Graham sprang at Lou with the knife. I grabbed for his arm to stop him. He tried to push me away and, when he couldn't, he pulled himself loose with a violent twist and started to swing in with the knife. At the same instant Lou tried to knock me out of the way. I was falling when I felt a sharp, tearing pain in my stomach.

I must've screamed, and yet I couldn't hear a thing. The room was spinning around me, dark red and far away. I felt a terrible burning heat inside me. My baby, I thought. Oh, my baby! How long I was unconscious, I don't know. There were moments that might've been dreams voices, sounds, Lou's face swimming above me. Then blackness swirled up around me again.

When the darkness finally cleared, I found myself lying in a hospital bed. A nurse stood beside the bed. "My baby," I cried. "What happened to my baby?"

The nurse went to the door and said something to somebody outside, then came back and tried to soothe me. "Your baby is all right, Mrs. Dowling. A fine little boy."

But I didn't believe her. When the doctor came in, I begged him to tell me the truth. "That's the truth," he said gently. "Your baby's in an incubator now, but he's doing fine. We had to deliver him by Caesarean section, Mrs. Dowling, because of your injury, but the baby wasn't hurt."

In the great flood of my relief, I closed my eyes. When I opened them again, the doctor had gone. "Get some sleep," the nurse ordered me. "You need it. You've lost a lot of blood."

I must've slept, for later I heard her calling my name. "Your husband's here to see you, Mrs. Dowling."

I looked up and saw Lou. His eyes were red and puffy and he needed a shave, but no one in the world could have looked handsomer, to my eyes, at least. The nurse went out and closed the door softly. "Is my—is our—son really all right?" I asked. He nodded. "He's fine. I was so scared for you, Heather, I thought I'd go out of my mind. Why did you go after Graham? It was crazy."

"I love you," I said.

He smiled. "I've been doing some real thinking, Heather. I don't know why I was so blind, but now I see exactly what I've been doing to you. Maybe I can't stop remembering and hating myself, but from now on you're coming first in my life. I swear it, honey."

He kissed my hand, and I started to cry. "Don't cry, please don't cry anymore," he pleaded. "I'll make it all up to you. I'll make a real home for us. We'll find a good town to settle down in and we'll never move again."

"It was my fault," I told him softly, "my foolish idea. I shouldn't have forced you to come back here. I-I guess I've failed you, Lou. I haven't been able to help you."

"Shhh," he whispered. "That's all over now. You're the one who counts now, you and our son."

But I knew he'd never be able to forget those dead children. I felt so hopeless. "What time is it?" I asked, trying to break the mood.

"It's Christmas afternoon. They wouldn't let me come to see you before." Suddenly the door opened, and three men came in. With a shock I recognized Ed Sanchez with Spencer Thorne and Chaz Lewellen right behind him. The nurse ran in after them, with the doctor right next to her. "You'll have to leave at once," the doctor said sternly.

"Wait, Doctor, we only need a minute," Spencer said. "Please."

"No, it's out of the question. Mr. Dowling is the only one allowed in here."

Lou stepped back from the bed. "Let them say what they want to," he said bitterly. The doctor looked at him and then at me. I nodded.

"We had to come," Ed Sanchez began. "When we heard about what happened, when we heard you might be." He took a deep breath. "We were so sorry. We—" He stopped and turned and looked at the others helplessly.

Chaz Lewellen broke in nervously. "What he means is we want to say we're sorry. We want to apologize. We've all acted like, like I don't know what. Like animals, I guess." He looked at his hands and then back at us. "Graham must've been out of his head to do what he did. Thank God, he's in jail now where he can't do any more harm, even to himself."

"We're ashamed," Spencer said stiffly. "You hurt us with your carelessness, Mr. Dowling. We hurt you both with our anger and our need for revenge. What we did was so much worse than what you did. Because what we did was deliberate. We want it all to be forgotten now."

"What Graham did woke us up," Chaz said.

"We don't want to be like him anymore. We let him tell us what to feel for too long." He tried to smile. "Move back to Herrington if you still want to. There won't be any more hate."

"Yes, yes," Ed Sanchez said eagerly. "You tried to buy our forgiveness and we were angry all over again. Now, we give forgiveness to you, because we're ashamed."

"Okay, now all of you get out of here," the doctor said, herding them back through the door. When they were gone, I looked up at Lou.

"Will we move back?" I asked.

"If you want to, we will." He leaned over and kissed me.

"It'll be a second chance," I told him softly. "That's all we ever wanted."

"Yes, I know." He straightened up and smiled at me. "Now sleep, honey. You want to get well again soon."

I smiled back at him. There was something in his eyes and in his voice, something new and strong. I knew that this was our second chance and that we would make it this time—together.

The people we had hurt and who had hurt us were sorry, just as we had been sorry for two long years. They were ready to forgive us. Our baby son was alive. From now on, the past would be dead for us. The future was bright with hope.

The End

HE MARRIED ME
FOR MY MONEY!
And brought me anguish

I have always been terrified of being alone—alone in the world, with no one to care for me and watch over me. Alone in my heart.

When my mother died, I was only six—not yet able to understand or fight my paralyzing grief. I turned to my father for comfort and love. Then, one day, I realized I could lose my father as suddenly as I'd lost my mother. I became frightened—I'd be all alone then. I'd have no one to comfort or love me.

Daddy was a truck driver. He made enough money so that we lived well, and I never lacked for anything. I learned to be a good cook and housekeeper—but not how to dance and play, not how to judge the motives and character of others. After graduating from high school, I stayed at home instead of going away to college. I dreamed of getting married one day, but that seemed very far away.

And then, one winter day, Daddy's truck skidded and he was killed instantly. My old childhood nightmare had come true: I was alone!

Daddy had left me everything. With the insurance money, I had $250,000. When I went to the lawyer to sign for the money, old Mr. Henry suggested I enroll in business school so I would learn to manage my finances. Keeping busy, he said, would be the best balm for my grief. I heard him, but all I listened to was the sickening pounding of my own heart, reminding me: You're alone.

The first six months after Daddy's death, I lived mechanically. I was sure I'd never get over my loss. Then, that summer, I met John Marks.

John was alone, too. That became our bond. He talked to me often about his hopes and ambitions. He sold cars at a used car lot, and hoped to be his own boss someday.

I never stopped missing Daddy, but with John I felt less alone. And then, one night, he said, "Casey, I've had a better job offered to me in Sterling." My heart froze. Sterling was at least a hundred miles away.

"Will you take it?" I asked faintly. If John went, I'd be alone again.

He came to me, tilted my chin up and said, "Will you go with me, Casey? I hated to say anything so soon after your father's death, but this new job changes things. Will you marry me? I'd try hard to make you happy, Casey."

We were married a week later. The day before my wedding, I went to the cemetery. I put flowers on Daddy's fresh grave, and on Mother's settled one. I smiled through tears as I whispered, "I'll be all right now. I'm not alone anymore."

Before we left for our new home John had me draw out all the money Daddy had left me. "It'll be easier to just put it into my account, which you're now on anyway," he explained. "I want to keep our finances simple."

We drove to Sterling in Daddy's old car. We rented an inexpensive furnished room until I could find an apartment. But all the apartments were very expensive. The rental market was booming.

Every night I told John what I'd seen and he'd say, "We can't afford that, Casey! Not if we want to live on my pay." For a while I was hurt by his anger, but then I remembered that John was inclined to worry a good deal about money.

One evening several weeks later, John was all excited when he came home. "I've got a surprise for you, sweetheart!" he exclaimed. He caught me in his arms and whirled me around. "We just bought a house! Why pay a landlord when we can have our own place? Your money wasn't doing anybody any good."

"You mean, you bought a house with Daddy's money?" I gasped.

"Wait until you see it!" he said, and whisked me down to the car. All the way to the house he talked while I listened, fighting a sense of betrayal, telling myself John knew best.

But when I saw the house, I felt cold all over. It was big, old, and neglected. "John," I said, "I wish you hadn't. You should have asked me."

"You talk as if I'd stolen your money," he said. "I invested it for you, for us." He was glaring at me, then abruptly his face softened and he put his arms around me. "Honey," he murmured, "we're married. There's no yours or mine, everything is ours!" Ashamed, I kissed the tip of his chin.

He laughed and said, "The place sure looks a mess now, but we'll fix it up."

We moved in, but getting the house fixed was too costly. Months passed, and still the most necessary things hadn't been done. That winter, icy drafts blew through the old house because we had no storm windows, yet John told me I must keep the thermostat very low to save fuel oil.

John was always complaining about how much money we spent. In every other way we got along perfectly, so rather than quarrel with him I tried not to even let the subject of money come up. In March, when I realized I was going to have a baby, I was almost afraid to tell John because of the expense. But I did, and to my joy he was glad—

although he did say, "Babies cost money, honey. We'll have to go slow on some of the things we were planning." So I let him persuade me to consult the free clinic doctor instead of one of the higher-priced obstetricians.

Dr. Chilton, an old man, merely took my blood pressure and pulse every time I went to him and said heartily, "You're getting along fine, young lady, just fine."

But Dr. Chilton was wrong. The memory of my labor is a confusion of pain. I felt as if I'd been torn in two. And it was days before I saw my little girl, who was being kept alive in an incubator. I had another doctor now, a specialist. From Dr. Haley, I learned that both the baby and I had almost died. Yet when John visited me he seemed chiefly concerned with the hospital expenses.

Little Patsy and I were able to go home at last, but we were still far from well. The specialist warned me that Patsy was anemic and would need frequent checkups. As for me, I was to follow a strict diet and check with him if I didn't gain weight.

In the weeks that followed, Patsy seemed to improve somewhat, while I became steadily worse. Finally, I was ordered back to the hospital for complete bed rest. John protested. He said we had no money. I could rest at home. I didn't see how I was going to get much rest with a sick baby, but I agreed.

John lectured me on expenses that night. So I cut down on heat, food, and warm clothing. I cut everywhere it was possible, but still John complained.

So, to save even more, I stopped going to the doctor altogether. My decline was rapid. Normally weighing about a hundred and twenty pounds, I had gone down to ninety by the time Patsy was three months old. My eyes looked like holes burned in a plaster mask. My hair was lifeless and dry. I cried easily and I was so weak I couldn't lift tiny Patsy.

John was angry because I was sick. He said I wasn't trying to get well. I never talked back to him. I tried to rest as much as I could. I'd get up at six in the morning to give Patsy her bottle and fix John's breakfast. Before John left I'd have him lift Patsy out of her crib and put her on the big bed. I'd then climb in beside her and stay there all day. We kept each other warm, and saved on fuel oil.

One thing I wouldn't compromise on was Patsy's weekly visit to the pediatrician. One night the doctor said, "Your wife isn't regaining her strength, Mr. Marks. Has she seen Dr. Haley lately?"

"Of course," John lied.

"They're all alike!" he fumed after he had hustled me out of the doctor's office. "Looking for a fee! Haley probably gives him a kickback. Well, from now on, Patsy goes to Doc Chilton for her shots!"

John's angry decision and the certain impossibility of arguing him out of it drained away the last of my reserve strength. In our room, I fell across the bed with my coat still on.

I fell asleep, but I couldn't have slept more than a few minutes before John was back. "Look at you," he said angrily. "Going to bed in the same clothes you wore outside. No wonder you're sick." He grabbed me roughly. "Sit up and take those clothes off." He practically ripped them off.

I sat on the bed clutching a wrinkled old flannel nightshirt to myself. Then John got into bed with me. I stiffened in alarm. I hadn't let John make love to me since my return from the hospital. He'd wanted to several times, but he hadn't insisted when I pleaded that I wasn't ready. Now he pulled me roughly against him.

"Please, John," I begged. "I'm not well."

"It's four months since you had the baby," he said, "and you haven't let me touch you."

"Please," I moaned. "Tomorrow. Just wait another day." He sealed my protesting lips brutally with his own. He was too strong, too ruthless to resist. Afterward, he fell into a heavy sleep. I lay awake staring at the ceiling. I had to face the truth: John did not love me. No man who loved a woman would be so brutal. Then I acknowledged another painful truth: I'd married John to escape the loneliness I'd dreaded all my life. But I'd found no happiness in marriage. I had nothing at all—except my baby, who was also weak and sick. Tears trickled down my cheeks. Then suddenly I told myself: Patsy deserves a chance. I'll get well for her sake. I'll be strong, and I'll make her strong.

As if my decision had given me strength, I fell asleep, a deep, sound sleep. The next morning I felt better than I had in weeks.

From that day on, I did get better. I rested as much as possible. I had no washing machine, so I told John to take his things to the laundry mat—I couldn't wash and iron them with all the laundry I had to do for Patsy. He gave me a sour look, but did as I said. And he moved all his clothes from our closet and dresser into the room we had once planned for the baby.

We went on living together all through that freezing winter. Slowly, I got better.

It was as if my anger against John, my bitter disappointment, nourished me. Then in March, Patsy was very sick. Even John was frightened by her high fever. She coughed in helpless spasms, and her skin was a pale blue.

In my worry, I did something I knew John would never permit. While he was at work one day I called a taxi and took Patsy to the pediatrician. I had money enough only for the taxi, and I didn't know whether or not John would ever pay the doctor, but I was desperate. The pediatrician discovered that Patsy's heart was badly enlarged. My baby was gravely ill—she might not live. I couldn't believe it. Not Patsy, not the person I loved more than anyone in the world! I was frantic.

John was furious at me for going to the pediatrician. Nor would he agree to let me consult a heart specialist. But I insisted until, finally, John threw a blank check at me. The next day I took Patsy to a clinic for X-rays and an electrocardiogram.

Three days later the report came. It was a death sentence! Not only was Patsy's heart enlarged, but it was deformed as well. No operation was possible. She might live for several years—she might die tomorrow. There was nothing that could be done to save her.

That night I wept in John's arms. In despair, I turned to him for comfort, even though he'd failed me so often. He was shaken and frightened. "There's only one thing we can do," I said. "We can make Patsy happy while she's with us."

In the days that followed, John spent a lot of time with Patsy, and she responded to it. She'd smile and gurgle and wave her arms in delight. One Sunday evening he volunteered to bathe her and put her to bed, and he was gone so long I finally went upstairs to see if he needed help. He was sitting on our bed with Patsy in his arms, twisting her curls around his finger. And when he heard me and looked up, I saw tears in his eyes.

Sudden hope filled me. Maybe there was still a chance for our marriage. Maybe this tragedy would cure him of his selfishness. I put my arms around him, and he whispered, "Casey, sweetheart, I'm sorry, let's try to get along better together."

"Oh, we will!" I cried softly. "I never wanted it this way. I've been so lonely!"

"So have I. I know it's been tough, honey, trying to get along on what I make, but someday things will be better. I'll have my own place, and you won't have to scrimp and save."

"I don't mind that," I said, "if only I feel all right, and know you love me."

"I do," he said. He kissed me and then both of us stood looking sadly at our baby.

For a few days John and I were happy, but then things worsened again. Sales were slow, so he fretted about expenses. The temperature was zero. I begged him to push up the thermostat, but he refused. To keep Patsy warm, I moved her into John's room to give her the benefit of the sunlight.

One afternoon I heard her choking and ran to her. To my relief, I found she had only vomited. I glanced around for something to clean her up with, and then pulled open the top drawer of John's dresser. I pulled out an undershirt and a twenty-dollar bill fell to the floor from it. Puzzled, I wiped Patsy's face and put her on my bed. I walked back slowly, thought for a moment and then began going through John's clothes.

I found bills tucked into rolled-up socks, inside a sweater and underneath a pile of shirts. Tens, twenties, even fifties. I counted up to four thousand dollars, and stopped. My head was spinning, and a fire burned inside me.

All this money—hidden—while John's child shivered and sickened in a cold house. No wonder John spent hours here with the door closed. He must have been fingering this money, gloating over it, loving it!

This was what John loved, not me, not even Patsy, but money. I was still standing there, stunned, when I heard the downstairs door close. John called my name, and I answered, "I'm in your room!" Standing rigidly, the money strewn at my feet, I waited for him. He gave a hoarse cry and fell to his knees, gathering up the scattered bills with shaking hands.

He raised his head and threw me a look full of hate. His hands never stopped their frenzied fumbling. "You had no right," he said in a choked voice. "This money, it's mine." Tears were running down his cheeks.

The sight touched off hysteria in me, and I bent over him, screaming, "What kind of man are you? Because of you, Patsy will die! You wouldn't let me keep her warm!"

He had all the money now, and stood up, clutching it against his chest. "Her heart was bad from the time she was born."

"You don't know that! It could have been her sickness! You're a beast, a cheap bastard!"

"I was saving it for you," he said. "I thought I'd need money to help you get well!"

"Liar!" I spat. "You don't care whether I live or die. You saved this money from my blood, from Patsy's heart." Then I pulled out the bottom drawer and dumped its contents on the floor. More money fell out. "I'll never forgive you!" I cried.

Again he was on his knees, picking up his money. Suddenly, he looked up at me. "I had a box of old books," he said slowly. "Where is it?"

"I was cold a month ago." I had guessed his secret. "The books made me a warm fire, John."

He screamed. "You burned my books? There was money in them!"

"It was a nice fire," I said.

He came at me like an insane man, and hit me again and again until I lost consciousness.

After a while I opened my eyes. Somehow, I knew John was gone, and had taken the money with him. I knew I might never see him again, and I didn't care. I gave Patsy her bottle. Finally I went to bed and slept.

I was awakened in the morning by the doorbell. When I opened the door a policeman was standing there. "Mrs. John Marks?" he asked. "I'm afraid I have bad news. Your husband has committed suicide."

"No," I said, instinctively certain that John would never commit suicide while he had money.

The policeman handed me a note that had been found in John's car. It was very short: "Dearest Casey, After last night, I don't want to go on living. Please forgive me. Your John."

"He's run away!" I said bitterly. "He's alive." I told the policeman about the money. He agreed that John might not be dead.

Days passed, and still no trace of John. I didn't grieve. I had the sour knowledge that he had put money ahead of his sick child. When my plight became known, a local social worker came and suggested I might be able to board foster children. I seized upon the idea, and before long I had four children besides Patsy to care for.

I got money each week for each baby and after the way I'd lived with John, the supplemental income made me feel rich. The foster children were lively, healthy kids ranging from three months to three years in age. The old house rang with laughter. Best of all, their presence seemed good for Patsy. She was gaining weight, and her color improved. I dared to hope again that she might live.

During the summer I made a new and comforting friend. Unable to leave the house with five children on my hands, I ordered my groceries by telephone from the local chain two blocks away. When the owner, Rich Cambric, heard about my foster children he began delivering the orders himself. Then extra oranges and milk were appearing in my box. When I protested, saying I had no way to pay back his generosity, he replied, "Invite me to dinner some night."

He came and played with the children while I cooked dinner. He said, "Someday I want a dozen of my own." Then I told him about Patsy's illness.

Rich's eyes held infinite sympathy as he said, "You're about the bravest person I've ever known."

More and more, I depended on Rich—for practical help, and for companionship, too. At Christmas he gave us a tree and all the ornaments it needed, and gave all the children presents—but the nicest doll was for Patsy. She loved the lights and caught the excitement and gaiety from the older children.

If this should be the only Christmas she ever knows, I found myself thinking, I'll always be glad it was so lovely for her and grateful to Rich for making it so.

After putting the children to bed, we talked and then fell silent. I felt tenseness growing between us. Suddenly he took my hand. "Casey," he said, "you can't go on like this. You need someone. And I'd like to be that someone. I love you. Don't you know that?"

My eyes filled with tears. Yes, I'd known it. No one could be so good, so kind and generous, unless he loved you. "I love you, too," I said at last. "You're the finest person I've ever known. But what can do? I'm not free."

"I'll get a lawyer. I want to marry you, darling," he said.

But the information he brought back from the lawyer was disheartening. In our state, disappearance was grounds for divorce after seven years. Until then we were helpless. My hatred for John grew. Though he was gone, his cruelty still pursued me, depriving me of a husband and cheating Patsy of a father.

Rich and I went on as we were. He came to my house nearly every evening, and always on Sunday. Sometimes he would kiss me, and each time our yearning need for each other was stronger.

And all the time I worried more about Patsy. She gained hardly any weight, and still had the bluish pallor. Then, one windy spring day, the door of her room blew shut with a slam. It startled her so she began to cry in terror. I picked her up, but she kept crying and gasping for breath. Her little body stiffened in my arms, her halting arm dropped limply, and she was gone. Hours later, when Rich found me, I was still holding her.

Rich took charge of everything. He called the funeral home and children's services, to ask them to make other arrangements for my foster children. He lifted Patsy from my arms while I fought and begged him to let me hold her.

He supported me at the cemetery, beside the small white coffin, and caught me when my knees gave way. He brought me home and put me to bed. And at the love and compassion I saw in his face, I began to cry.

Rich," I sobbed, "I tried so hard to keep her, but she's gone, and I'm alone."

"Don't cry," Rich whispered. "You're not alone. I'll never leave you." With gentle hands, he took off my outer clothes and gave me a nightgown. He tucked me into bed and brought me food, and when I'd eaten it he turned out the light and took me in his arms.

I remembered a time when my husband had done these things. But there was one difference. Throughout that night, Rich held me, asking nothing more. But somehow his touch was healing, and when morning came, in a surge of emotion, we took our love and I believed it was right—righter and more beautiful than it had been with John.

From then on, we lived together as man and wife. Rich kept his apartment, but most of the time he stayed with me. When I was well enough I went to work for him in his store. For about a year our love was nearly perfect. The year in which the dream hid the reality, the year before we faced facts and accepted the knowledge that people in the small-town neighborhood referred to us as "that couple," and that people had stopped buying from him.

The inevitable reaction came. We worked harder at hating those who hurt us than we did loving each other. Rich lost weight, bungled the cash receipts, got edgy with the help, and finally came the day when he shouted abusively at me over a simple mistake I had made.

When the store was closed and the others had gone home, Rich said sadly, "Darling, I'm sorry. I don't know what makes me so cross with everyone."

But I knew. Rich was clean and decent. He was desperately unhappy living in sin and shame, even with the woman he loved.

I sensed that his feelings toward me were changing, but I tried to ignore that realization. He was still tender with me, but more and more often restlessness drove him from me evenings after supper. If I lost him, I'd be alone again, more alone than ever. I tried to fight my fear, tried every way I could to make Rich want me more. Seven years isn't forever. As soon as John is declared legally dead, Rich will marry me. Seven years! I seethed in my bitter hatred for John. Would Rich wait?

I knew he might not the first time I met Donna Victor. She was young and lovely, and had a spontaneous laugh. She came into the store often, and Rich always waited on her. Once, I saw something when their eyes met.

A wave of fear swept over me. I walked home, fighting it. I mustn't start imagining things, I told myself. Rich was pleasant to all his customers.

When he came in for supper I scanned his face, trying to read the thoughts behind it. My attempts at conversation fell flat, and suddenly, I heard myself crying in desperation, "What's the matter with you tonight, Rich? Why don't you say anything?"

He seemed to come back from far away. "What? Oh, I'm sorry. I was thinking about the store, I guess."

A few evenings later he was half an hour late for supper, I remembered that Donna Victor hadn't come into the store while I was there. Might she have come later, just before closing time? And might Rich have walked her home? I tried to tell myself I had no cause for jealousy, but if there was no cause, why was Rich so cold to me now?

I still hadn't dared to speak on the afternoon I walked into the house and heard the telephone ringing. I picked it up, and a man's voice said, "Mrs. Marks? This is Sgt. Riordan."

Riordan, that was the detective I'd talked to after John's disappearance. I felt suspended in midair.

"A man answering your husband's description was murdered in Annapolis, Maryland. We can't be certain—he was known there as Jake Martin—but everything fits. He owned a used car lot and the name is similar. The Annapolis police think he's your husband. It was probably a robbery killing. There was a rumor that he kept large sums of money on him."

I told the detective I would go to Annapolis to make positive identification. I looked around the room—cozier and more homelike now than it had been when John lived with me. There was no sorrow in my heart, only a tremendous relief. Now I was free to marry Rich.

I called Rich at the store. "Rich, you know what this means!"

He said very quietly, "Yes, of course. I'll be home as soon as I can."

Slowly, I replaced the telephone. Now, for the first time since the detective's call, I remembered Donna Victor. But she didn't mean anything to Rich! He loved me! All he wanted was for our love to be sanctified and made clean, so we could hold our heads high and have the children we both longed for. Clinging to that thought, I went into the kitchen and started supper.

When I heard Rich's step on the back porch I ran and threw myself into his arms. He held me, and for a long moment we didn't speak. Then his arms relaxed, and holding me a little bit away, he said, "Casey, we mustn't get our hopes up. This may not be your husband at all."

"It is!" I said wildly. "I know it is!"

"Yes, well. . . ." Dropping his hands, he turned and took a few steps. "I don't want you to be too disappointed if—"

There was a silence, and I felt fear clutch me. "You want us to be married, don't you, Rich?"

"Of course!" he said too quickly. I went closer to him, looking into his face.

"Rich," I breathed, knowing it had to be asked, "is there anybody else?"

Something flickered far back in his eyes. Then he cried, "No! Oh, Casey!" And he caught me to him, pressing my head against his shoulder. I couldn't see his face. "How could you think that?" he said hoarsely. He kissed me hard.

It had been weeks since Rich had kissed me like this. He did love me and want me for his wife! There was no one else—no Donna Victor—and if there were, I'd make him forget her when we were married and living a normal life, with friends and children.

"Now you'd better catch a train to Maryland as fast as you can," he said.

Eagerly, I agreed. He helped me pack. There wasn't time to

think—and when I was on the train the memory of his good-bye kiss, his smiling face outside the car window, blanked out my doubts.

Late the next day I was in the Annapolis morgue, looking at John's corpse. "Yes," I said weakly, "that is my husband." I swayed a little, and an officer supported me. Then I made arrangements for a funeral. Rich and I had decided that if the man in Annapolis was really John, there was no reason to bring him north for burial. I went to a hotel and stayed there until the next afternoon, when services were held.

I sat near the casket with my head bowed. Now, for the first time since I'd heard of John's death, I thought of him instead of myself. He had been cruel to me—he had neglected me and denied me his love— but now I pitied him. The love for money that had been his ruling passion had been the cause of his death. I had married John knowing nothing of him, knowing only that I feared loneliness.

What had I learned from my miseries with John? Even now, as I buried the man I'd married so unwisely, I realized that I'd learned nothing. I was about to make the same mistake again. I was going to marry again for the same twisted reason that made me marry the first time. I was afraid of being alone.

This time I cared for the man, but was it love or gratitude and habit? I cared for him, I trusted him, but I didn't love him with my soul, as a wife should love her husband.

Rich was good, decent. He'd honor his promise; he'd marry me because he felt responsible for me. But it was not love, and Rich had known it for a long time. Rich loved Donna Victor. I knew it as only a woman can know. Still, he would marry me out of duty.

The black funeral car was driving back to the city. In a few moments I would be leaving Annapolis, leaving John and the part of my life that he symbolized. I felt so alone again, small, unwanted, and alone—even though I was going back to Rich to be married. I was facing a bleak future: A marriage that had little chance of success. Alone in my hotel room, minutes later, I cried to myself, "But I must marry Rich! I'm afraid not to. I'm afraid of having nothing to lean on."

"You'll have less than nothing if you marry him," some inner voice said. "You'll have misery and grief, because he doesn't love you or want you."

"I'm afraid," I whimpered aloud to the empty room. And then I realized that unless I faced my fear alone, it would never leave me. With Rich I might know a few months or years of security, then heartbreak and misery would surely come again. And again I would be terrified and lonely, with only the guilty knowledge that I had knowingly hurt a man who had been good to me.

Through the long hours of the train trip, I sat thinking. For the first time I forced myself to plan my own life, to force myself to do the right thing. When I reached Sterling I went right home and called Rich. He sounded cheerful and happy.

He came in soon after seven. He kissed me—a long, welcoming kiss—and then we ate. I told him about the trip and the funeral. At last we had finished eating, and there was a little silence before Rich said, "We'll get married soon, then?"

I drew a deep breath. "No, Rich, no."

He stared at me and frowned in a puzzled way. "No? I don't understand."

Looking straight into his eyes, I asked, "Rich, does Donna Victor know about us?" I saw the name strike him. I saw the pain in his eyes.

His eyes held mine a moment longer, and then they dropped. "She knows," he said. He sounded ashamed, and I didn't want him to be ashamed.

"Go back to her," I said quickly, strongly. "Tell her it's all over with us. Ask her to marry you. That's what you want, and I know it."

"I can't do this to you." His face was twisted with pain. "I can't leave you alone."

I went to him, and laying my hand lightly on his shoulder, I said, "I'm not giving you a choice, Rich. It's best for both of us. I want to learn to depend on myself. You made me very happy, but it was the wrong kind of happiness."

He was still, thinking, and then he pressed a kiss on the back of my hand. "God bless you, Casey," he said.

"Good-bye, Rich." I took my hand away, and he stood up. "I'm going out now," I said. "I'll be gone about an hour. Will that be long enough to take your things away?"

He nodded. As I turned to go, he held one hand out toward me. But I didn't stop, and he let it fall.

After I had walked for an hour, I came back to the house. He was gone. I threw myself across the bed and let the tears come. But it was for the last time. I don't weep any more.

I sold the house for a good profit, rented a small apartment, and took classes in business administration. The newspaper carried the announcement of Rich's marriage to Donna. It hurt, but not as much as I had expected.

After getting an office job, I quickly made new friends. I learned something: The more I became interested in people, the more they gravitated toward me. I learned that the shroud of loneliness repels people rather than attracts them.

My days had purpose and meaning and then, a year ago, I met another man. We became good friends, we came to know and understand and appreciate each other.

It was mutual emotion—something I'd never shared with John or Rich. I'm married to that man now, my second husband. Second? No, to me my darling will always be the first—the first to love me, and be loved by me, forever. On our wedding day he whispered, "You're such a wonderful girl. I'm so lucky, so grateful you're mine."

A "wonderful girl," he called me. I pray he will always think that. I'm not wonderful, I know that, but I am so much wiser than the lonely, frightened girl I used to be.

The End

I TAMED THE
NEIGHBORHOOD BULLY!

I sat motionless in the hospital anteroom, waiting. Terry was taking the first plane home, and soon he'd be here. He'd take my hand and he'd say, "Don't blame yourself, honey. Everything's going to be all right." That's what I had to believe he'd say, so that I could go on being married.

In a little while, Dr. Devlin would come out from the children's ward, and he'd smile and say, "Marlena, they're going to recover." That's what I had to believe he'd say, so that I could go on living.

Dr. Devlin had spoken to me earlier. "Marlena," he'd said, "go home with Mrs. Foley and wait for Terry. I'll call you if there's any change."

What home? My home was here where my babies lay. My mind blazed with hatred as I glanced across the room at the woman who'd been keeping her own vigil. Why was she there? In all the time we'd been at the hospital, I hadn't spoken one word to her. I couldn't. She was Chauncy's mother, and it was her fault that I was there now.

I wished that I had never heard of Molly Foley or her son. Why hadn't I listened when Esther tried to warn me? Why had I refused to believe that Chauncy was beyond my help?

Esther was the first of my neighbors to call when Terry and I moved to the Maplewood development. I was unpacking dishes from a barrel, and Terry was busy putting the beds together and trying to keep the boys out of mischief, when she rang the bell.

I whisked off my kerchief and went to the door.

"Hi, I'm Esther Biggs, your neighbor from across the street," she said. "I know you're going crazy getting settled, but I wanted to welcome you to the block and ask if your children would like to come over to our yard and play with my two."

"That would be wonderful," I said, smiling at the little boy and girl who peeked out at me from behind their mother's dress.

I called Stevie and Paul and they ran into the kitchen and stopped short at the sight of strangers. "Stevie is six and Paul is three," I said. "Say 'hello' to Mrs. Biggs and her children."

The four children eyed each other shyly. Then Esther's boy said, "I got a swing in my yard. Want to see it?"

That broke the ice, and the children went off with Esther, chattering happily.

Esther kept my boys at her place for the entire afternoon, and she invited them again the next day. Terry and I were able to do all our work in a hurry with them out from underfoot.

"Esther's terrific, isn't she, Terry?" I asked. "Things are a lot easier all around with her so friendly."

"Just don't overdo it," he cautioned. "It's not good to get too cozy or too obligated right off the bat. The kids love to go over there, though, and that's a good sign. If the kids approve, then I do."

The next day, Esther came over again. She said that she was giving a tea in my honor and that she had invited most of the women on the block to meet me.

"Oh, Esther," I protested, "you don't have to go to all that trouble."

"What trouble?" she said. "It's a good excuse for a get-together. When I moved in, no one came to welcome us or to give me a hand, and I'd rather make it easier on you. Maybe it will wake some of them up and teach them how to welcome strangers."

I poured coffee for us and sat down, eager to discuss the tea.

"By the way, Marlena," Esther said, "They're a pretty good bunch here with the exception of one. You'll hear about her sooner or later, so you may as well be prepared."

Here it comes, I thought uneasily. Neighborhood gossip.

"Normally, I wouldn't run someone down you haven't met yet," Esther went on. "I'd rather you made up your own mind about her. But—"

I moved restlessly in my chair, feeling sorry for the unknown woman. "What about her?" I asked.

"Well, it isn't so much Molly Foley we object to as her nine-year-old boy, Chauncy," Esther said. "He's a holy terror—and dangerous. The boy is simply beyond help, Marlena. He's a bully and a sneak and always in trouble with the police."

"Really, Esther," I said, feeling my way. "I can't believe that a child that age can be so bad."

Her manner cooled slightly. "Take my word for it, Marlena, he's dynamite. He's not allowed in any of the yards around here and is forbidden to play near or around my children."

Underneath the coolness, I got the message. Esther was warning me that if I encourage Chauncy Foley in any way, I could count on being put into the same class as Mrs. Foley.

"Tell me," I pressed. "Is it Molly who's coloring your opinion, or is it all Chauncy?"

"Molly isn't to blame too much," she said. "I don't hold her completely responsible for Chauncy's actions. Ever since he was little, he's been a handful for her. Her husband deserted her when she became pregnant. She's been working off and on ever since to support Chauncy. Between that and what her boyfriend's give her, she manages."

"What a shame!" I said. "Is that why her husband took off, because she fools around?"

"No," Esther said, "Before Ed left, Molly was a good kid, crazy about him and tickled about the baby coming. But he wasn't the type to be tied down for long. After he left, she went to pieces. She sees to it that Chauncy's fed and clothed properly, but outside of that, the boy's strictly on his own. He has been since he was old enough to toddle."

That evening, I filled Terry in on the neighborhood news. "I don't think that it's fair for all of them to gang up on a child that age," I said. "Esther as much as told me that if I don't think the way the rest of them do around here, I'm out. That could make it rough on our boys if they forbid theirs to play with them. I just don't know what to do about it."

"That's my girl, looking for trouble before it finds her," Terry said. "When the time comes, you'll know what to do. Why worry about a boy you know nothing about?"

"He needs help," I insisted. "He's a misfit, so people ignore him. I can't help but worry about him."

"All right, then worry about him," Terry said, mussing my hair. "As for me, I've got some pictures to hang. Come on and give me a hand."

The next afternoon, I met the rest of my neighbors at the tea. I was surprised to find that most of the women were elderly. No wonder they object to Chauncy, I thought. They're over the hill where noisy boys are concerned.

At first, everyone was a little uneasy, and stilted small talk filled the room. Then Kirsty Pernel, one of the few young wives, brought up the subject of the Foley family, and every woman snapped to attention.

"I'm considered to be a good, Christian woman," old Mrs. Fannie said, "but when it comes to that Foley boy, I feel like the devil's own."

All afternoon, the women gossiped and exchanged the latest stories of the family they disliked so intensely. I listened to all their accounts, and then I began to get annoyed.

"Has anyone ever tried to befriend that boy or correct him when he does wrong?" I asked. "You can't just chase a child away and expect him to learn anything from it. Couldn't it be that the more you criticize him and exclude him, the worse he acts, just to get even with you? He must be a terribly lonely child." I faltered as I watched their friendliness disappear.

Esther glared at me. "We've lived here a long time, Marlena," she said. "I know that you think we're hardhearted, but listen for a while

91

and see if you don't change your mind. You've got children to protect, too. So please listen carefully." She turned to Mrs. Miller. "Tell her about Billy, Jennifer," she said.

Jennifer turned to face me. "This happened three years ago, when my Billy was only two and a half, but I still get chills when I remember it," she said. "Chauncy came by my place while we were having a cookout. Well, I could no more sit there at that picnic table and ignore that child's face any more than you could. He never said a word, just stared in at us, the hate in his eyes blazing. I finally weakened and told him to come in and have a hot dog.

"He's as polite and as mannerly when he talks to you as you'd be to your husband's boss, but I should have known better. I let him stay and play with Billy, who was in his playpen. Chauncy seemed so normal and so friendly, I was disarmed.

"Later on, I started clearing up and went into the house for a garbage bag. The next thing I knew, Billy screamed something awful. I ran outside. The playpen was empty, and Chauncy had taken Billy and left him on the grate of the barbecue pit. I nearly fainted when I found him. His overalls were scorched, but, thank God, he wasn't burned.

"I had murder in my heart that day, and if I'd had Chauncy there that minute I would have killed him." Her voice trembled with remembered emotions. "I calmed Billy down and tried to cool down myself before I went over to Mrs. Foley's house.

"Molly listened to my story and never said one word to me. She called Chauncy in and proceeded to smack him around, and never a whimper out of that boy. I tried to stop her, but she went right on beating him. She stopped long enough to say, 'Satisfied? Now get out!'

"I've had enough of the Foley family to last me a lifetime. If that boy comes near my house again I'll call the police, same as everybody else."

Jennifer's story triggered fantastic accounts of Chauncy's behavior pattern. The list was endless. Chauncy had broken windows, bullied children on their way to school, and turned in a number of false alarms at the fireboxes.

I went home feeling strangely frightened and disturbed, but underneath, I was more convinced than ever that Chauncy needed my help. I love children, and I was especially partial to boys, with two of my own. Chauncy Foley might be a menace and a problem child, but I couldn't just turn my back on an unhappy human being, and that's all that boy was. Surely love and simple kindness could set him straight.

One week later, I caught my first glimpse of Chauncy. As I started to hang out a sheet on the clothesline, I found myself looking straight into his narrowed eyes. He was lounging against our apple tree in the backyard.

I don't know how long he'd been standing there watching me, and though he was absolutely motionless, I knew that he was ready for flight.

I stared right back at him for a minute. He was a handsome boy with blond hair and those piercing eyes.

"Hi, Chauncy," I said finally. "Come on over and help me carry this basket inside."

The expression on his face remained the same, but he came over. He picked up my clothesbasket and waited for me to lead the way to the basement.

"I'm Stevie and Paul's mother," I said. "You can call me Marlena. My boys are away today, visiting with their grandmother."

I put the laundry things down and turned back to Chauncy. "I've heard you've got nice manners," I said, smiling. "Aren't you ever going to talk to me? I'd like to be your friend."

A trace of a smile at the unexpected compliment flickered across his face, but he continued to stare at me.

"Come on up and have a snack with me," I invited. "I'm dying for a cup of coffee. Come on," I urged as he hung back.

"Okay," he said, and followed me up the stairs. He stayed just long enough to bolt his milk and cookies, then he thanked me politely and left.

"Well," I told myself as I lit a cigarette, "not bad the first time around. I've praised him and fed him. Now I'll see what happens."

Later on, when I went out with my second load of wash, I caught my breath as I stared at the back screen door. Someone had slashed the screening with a knife, and that someone could only have been Chauncy. I was stunned at the unwarranted show of destructiveness, but I rallied long enough to make a mental note. So much for the milk-and-cookies routine, I thought.

That night, I told Terry about the afternoon. "Why, that little monkey!" he exploded. "I'd like to give him a ride on the end of my foot."

"No, Terry," I said. "He's had enough of that from what I've heard."

"I'm warning you, Marlena," Terry said. "Don't encourage that kid. He's no good."

"Terry, please!" I said. "I've got to try. The screening isn't that expensive. He's testing me to see how much I'll take. I can't explain it, honey, but I've got to reach that child and I will."

Chauncy stayed away for four days. On the fifth day, he reappeared. He was curious. He had expected us to follow up his act of malice, and when everything had remained quiet, he had come to investigate.

I smiled to myself and went to the back door. "Hi, Chauncy," I called. "Where have you been?"

He eyed me warily, his eyes going beyond me to the screen door. I followed his gaze. "Kind of senseless, wasn't it, Chauncy?" I said. "Don't do anything like that again. Well, come on in. The boys are upstairs playing. Go on up and meet them."

Chauncy spent the afternoon playing with my boys. He was so good with them that I couldn't believe that he had tried to harm Jennifer's baby. I listened to the talk as I went about doing my housework. I was impressed by Chauncy's intelligence. Where he was sullen and quiet with me, he chattered to my boys constantly and kept them laughing. He invented new games with their old toys and was patient as he explained the new rules.

At the end of the afternoon, I told Chauncy it was time to go home. His face changed. He got up quickly and left before I could invite him back for the next afternoon.

A few minutes later, I went downstairs, almost afraid to look at my new back door. I sighed with relief. The door was just fine. But, oh, when I looked out into the yard at my tulips! Every head had been cruelly snapped off!

Why, Chauncy, why? I thought. Why do you hate so hard?

Chauncy had had a fun-filled afternoon for a change, and when I had ended it, he had struck back. Well, I had a whole summer to work on him. Flowers could be replanted. It was Chauncy's soul that needed to be encouraged to blossom.

Once again, Chauncy followed the pattern and stayed away for a few days. Then suddenly he was back knocking timidly at my door.

"Hi," I said. "Come on in. By the way, you picked my flowers kind of short last time, didn't you?"

He had the grace to blush, staying only long enough for me to tell him that the boys had gone out for the day with their dad, but when he left, I breathed a small prayer of thanks. Nothing had been harmed. This is progress, I told myself.

Later on that night, I planned an outdoor supper. I asked Stevie to go up the street and invite Chauncy and his mother over. Stevie came back almost immediately to tell me that Mrs. Foley had gone out but that Chauncy would be over. In ten minutes, he arrived. He'd put on a clean shirt and slicked down his hair for the occasion.

I introduced him to Terry, and right from the start he took to my husband. He followed Terry around from barbecue pit to picnic table, and when the boys begged Chauncy to play ball with them, he shook them off impatiently, turning his attention again to Terry.

Terry, in turn, treated him like an adult, and Chauncy responded. When Stevie and Paul argued about who would pour water over the hot coals, Terry said, "You boys are too young to play near any kind of fire. Chauncy's the oldest, so he gets the job."

A look of understanding passed from the man to the boy, and Chauncy beamed his gratitude.

I was amazed. With no effort at all, Terry had won him over. Evidently, Chauncy had been starved for male companionship, and Terry's acceptance was what he wanted and needed.

After the picnic, I told Terry how happy he'd made me by being so friendly to the boy.

"Well, if he's going to be around here so much," he said with mock seriousness, "he'd better know right off the bat who's boss."

From that time on, Chauncy was always around. His attachment to all of us grew stronger. He'd come around in time for breakfast and stay for dinner. I wondered how any mother could neglect her son the way Mrs. Foley did. She never called or checked up on him, and some days my nerves grew frazzled when Chauncy teased the kids or took them over to the empty lot without telling me.

One morning Terry and I had planned to take the boys on a swimming party. For once I hadn't invited Chauncy along. There were times, I felt, when a family should be alone.

I was embarrassed, though, when I looked out my window and saw him standing there against the apple tree. Evidently he'd heard the boys talking about the outing and was waiting for us out there. I didn't like the idea of being responsible for someone else's child when it came to swimming, but how could we all pile into the car and leave him standing there with that bathing suit and towel rolled up under his arm?

I motioned to him to come in. "Better go home, Chauncy," I said, letting my voice trail deliberately, "and get permission to go with us."

His eyes brightened, and he waved a five-dollar bill in front of my nose. "I already did, Marlena. My mother knows you wanted me to go. You meant to invite me, didn't you?" he said.

"Well, sure," I agreed helplessly. "But you'd better stay right around when we get to the lake. I don't want any accidents, you hear me?"

"I will. I will," he promised. "I know how to swim anyway."

Once there, I was glad that Chauncy had come along. I've never seen a child that happy. He splashed in the shallow water with Paul and built sand castles for him. He spent an hour with Stevie, teaching him how to float. When he was tired playing with the boys, Terry took him out to the raft and taught him to dive.

Chauncy's voice rang out excitedly over the water from time to time. "Marlena, Marlena! Watch this one!" he'd call.

At the end of the day, we gathered up our three tired boys and started the long drive home. My heart swelled with affection for Chauncy as I watched him make room so that my little ones could stretch out. Chauncy's energy had been spent constructively that day, and he was at peace with the world, and best of all, with himself.

In all the time that Chauncy had been coming to our house, Esther had avoided me. She'd phoned only once to tell me to send her children home if Chauncy came around. I had been honest with Esther and told her that all the children were welcome in my yard as long as they behaved, but if she preferred it that way, I would understand and hope that she would be as understanding of my views, too.

I wasn't worried about losing Esther's friendship. Once Chauncy was acceptable to the rest of the neighborhood, she would accept him, too. I was sure of it. Then I'd work on cementing our relationship. Right then, though, Chauncy's needs were uppermost in my mind.

On the days that my boys went over to Esther's yard to play, Chauncy would go with them only to be turned away at the gate. Then he'd revert to the old Chauncy. Complaints poured in to me instead of his mother. Chauncy had turned over somebody's garbage. He had taken a lawn mower and thrown it into somebody's backyard swimming pool.

I referred all complaints to Terry and let him handle them. He would take Chauncy down to the basement those times and read him off. Chauncy would listen quietly, his head bowed, the knuckles on his hands white. He never denied any of the stories that came back or tried to lie to us, but he did apologize.

"Terry, I'm sorry," he'd cry. "I don't know why I do those things, either. I guess I'm just rotten the way everybody says. Give me another chance, please."

My heart would go out to him those times, and we'd give him another chance. Chauncy really cared when he upset us, and he tried hard to stay out of trouble. I guess it's easier to live up to a reputation than to live it down.

One thing was certain: Chauncy was getting too dependent on us and too attached. I found out just how much the day I came home late from my dental appointment.

The dentist had decided to pull my tooth, and I was delayed getting home. My face hurt, and the boys had been cutting up all afternoon. When I reached home, I found a highly indignant group of neighbors and a police car in front of my house.

Esther came out to meet me, her face red with anger. "I watched that boy try to crawl in through your window," she stormed, "and when he couldn't get in, he threw a rock through it. I called the police. Now, Marlena, this is the last time I'm going to keep an eye on your house or interfere in any way and also the last time I'm coming over here. I've told my children that they're not to step foot in your yard, and I'd appreciate it if you'd keep yours home." She stalked off, her back rigid with tension.

I turned to face the officer who was holding a defiant Chauncy. "It's been a mistake, Officer," I said, my eyes on Chauncy's face. "I'm not pressing any charges."

I opened the door and pushed Chauncy in ahead of me. "Now, young man," I said. "I've had it for one afternoon. You are going to work around here with Terry until you earn enough to pay for the damage you've done today. Is that clear?"

Chauncy's chin trembled, and tears flooded his eyes. "You told me you'd be here today, and you weren't," he cried. "You didn't care about me, and I wanted to fix it so you'd remember next time."

Chauncy poured it all out that afternoon. How he felt the first time he understood that his father hadn't wanted him—hadn't even waited around until he was born to see whether he'd like him or not. How he hated the men who came to take his mother out, how he resented his mother working when the other kids' mothers were home, how half the stories circulating about him weren't true, and how his mother never stood up for him.

This was his moment of truth, and I questioned him. "Tell me about Billy Miller," I said. "What really happened that day? Jennifer said you tried to burn the baby. Tell me now, and tell me the truth."

"She didn't believe me, and you won't either," he said. "I wasn't going to hurt him. He wanted to see the barbecue pit, and I carried him over to show him. I dropped him by mistake when he wiggled. He started to scream, so I ran."

"You should have stayed, Chauncy, and picked him up and taken him to Jennifer. She would've understood."

"She would've told my mother," he said.

"Okay, Chauncy," I said. "I believe you. But that's all in the past now. From now on you are going to be perfect. Do you understand? The first time I hear anything at all about you that I don't like, you are not going to come back here again. Is that clear?

"And another thing," I added. "Between us, we're going to make this neighborhood sit up and take notice. I can't do it by myself. I'm going to force you down their throats, and you're going to taste good.

"For a beginning, you're going to go over to Esther's with me, and we're going to set her straight. She's been too nice a neighbor and friend for me to lose over an ungrateful boy. Now march, Chauncy."

Esther took a lot of convincing. She was an active church member, and I reminded her of Christ's love of little children. Finally, she gave in.

"I know I've got rocks in my head, Marlena, but I'll give Chauncy one more chance for your sake," she said. "The next time he steps out of line, you've both had it."

"Thanks, Esther," I said. I pushed him out ahead of me. "Now, Chauncy, for heaven's sake," I said, "go home and help your mother or something. My mouth hurts, and I'm going to bed."

I went home exhausted but happy. I felt that I had won a small victory. If Chauncy could be included in the neighborhood birthday parties and outings, he'd have a fair chance of growing up to be a decent person and not just another juvenile delinquent with no respect for others.

A month passed, and to my great delight and pride, Chauncy kept his word and was a model boy. He acted better than my two did.

August came limply in and left soggily, and Chauncy spoke eagerly of returning to school in September. "I want to get good grades," he said, "so you and Terry will be proud of me."

"We're proud of you now, honey," I said. "There are so many good reports about you from everyone. I can't tell you all the nice things I've heard about you."

"I don't care about the others," he said. "Just you and Terry and the kids." He hugged me tight and then he blushed to the roots of his hair. "Marlena, promise me you'll never go away from here," he begged. "Don't ever leave me."

I thought carefully before I answered. "How can I promise a thing like that?" I said. "Circumstances change. Things beyond my control might happen. Don't worry about it, though. If we ever have to move, it will be because of Terry's work, but it won't change anything. We'll always be good friends, Chauncy."

His muffled answer frightened me. "If you ever go away, Marlena, I'll—I'll do something awful. I'll die."

I pushed him away from me and gripped his shoulders hard. "No, you won't. You cut that out, Chauncy. What a thing to say!" I scolded. "Don't ever let me hear you say that again. You're a good boy, and you don't need Terry and me to be that."

He refused to be consoled. "Promise me, Marlena. Please promise it now!" He started to cry in earnest.

"All right, all right," I said. "I promise. Now cut out the storm. I don't mind the wind, but the rain!"

The day after Labor Day, Chauncy came over early to pick Stevie up and start him off on his first day of kindergarten. Stevie was excited to be going to school at last just like Chauncy. He, in turn, was like a mother hen, straightening Stevie's bow tie and inspecting his fingernails.

"Just like he was my brother, huh, Marlena?" he said.

September passed quickly and uneventfully, and then it was October. The boys gave a Halloween party in our basement, and

98

Chauncy supervised all the preparations. He was so terribly happy that I cried over it.

Thanksgiving came, and Mrs. Foley accepted my invitation to dinner. Terry took the boys to a football game, and Molly and I had a long chat. She told me how pleased she was at the change in Chauncy.

"These so-called 'good' women," she snorted, "harmed my boy more than Ed did. They were always complaining. What did they want me to do? Put him in a cage or something?"

I told her how fond we'd become of Chauncy and asked permission for him to spend part of his Christmas vacation with us. Even though she lived just down the street from us, I thought that Chauncy would enjoy sleeping over on Christmas Eve and sharing in the fun.

"He'd be tickled to death," she said, "and it would give me a chance to go visit with a—a friend."

I understood, and I was relieved that it had all been arranged so simply. The afternoon before Christmas, I sent the three boys to the corner lot to pick out a Christmas tree. While they were gone, Terry came home full of excitement.

"Guess what!" he crowed. "My first big promotion. Three hundred dollars extra each week, and we're off to New York State on the fifteenth of January."

"Why, Terry, how wonderful!" I squealed. I ran into his arms and kissed him. "I'm so proud of you, darling!" Suddenly, I remembered and drew back. A small knot of fear replaced my joy. "What about Chauncy?"

"What about him?" he answered, laughing. "Here I tell you my good news, and the first thing you do is worry about how Chauncy's going to take it. What about me? I live here, too, remember?"

"You don't understand," I said. "I promised him." I told Terry then of the private talk I'd had with Chauncy months back.

"For crying out loud, Marlena," he said. "You've been darned good to that boy, but I'm getting kind of tired having you worry about him all the time. He's not your child, honey, will you please remember that?"

I guess the stricken look on my face softened him. "All right, if you're so worried about telling him, then leave it to me. Now give me a kiss. It's Christmas Eve—I want to celebrate."

That night I smiled as I watched my four men decorate the tree, but my heart was heavy. Chauncy was so happy, his face lighting up each time he stepped back to approve the decorations. I caught Terry's eye and motioned to him.

He came over and bent down to kiss me. "What's up?" he whispered.

"Don't tell Chauncy tonight," I said. "Wait until tomorrow, please."

"Okay, doll," Terry said. "Now come on and hang some tinsel. Hey, Paul! Stop throwing it on. Watch the way Chauncy does it."

Christmas morning finally came. The boys came whooping down the stairs, rapped loudly on our door, and scrambled into the living room.

After all the gifts had been opened and admired and the boys were playing happily with their new toys, Terry signaled to me. My eyes were glued to Chauncy's face as Terry broke the news.

"I've got a big promotion, boys, something I've worked for a long time," he said. "It means we'll be leaving here, but it won't be for quite a while. I'll go along first."

Chauncy paled. His eyes swung from Terry's face to mine. He stared at me accusingly.

"Chauncy," I said, "listen, please—"

"You promised! You promised!" he said.

"Now look, Chauncy," Terry cut in. "This can't be helped. I've been counting on you to be the man of the house after I've gone."

Chauncy's answer was clear and direct. He rushed out of the room and out of the house.

"Go after him, Terry," I begged. "Molly's away. There's no one home at his house."

"No, Marlena," he said. "He's got to work this out alone. He'll get over it. He'll come back."

Terry was right. A half-hour later, a tear-streaked, sullen Chauncy was back.

"You left so suddenly," Terry said, "you didn't give me a chance to tell you the rest of my news. No matter where we go, we'll expect you to spend your summers with us. I'll fix it up with your mother. I'll send you the fare, and I'll meet you when you get in. Won't that be something to look forward to, boy?"

Chauncy's face remained guarded. "You say it now, but you won't do it," he said. "You're leaving on purpose. You're tired of having me hang around. You want to get rid of me."

I put my arms around him. "No, Chauncy. No," I said. "You're like our own boy. We'll never forget about you, believe me."

Terry and I talked to him for over an hour, reassuring him of his place in our lives and hearts. Chauncy was quiet, too quiet, and the look in his eyes haunted me.

Even Esther understood a little of what I felt when I confided my news and my fears to her the next day.

"Help him, Esther, when we're gone," I pleaded. "I feel terrible about it, and it's all my fault. Maybe he was better off before when he had no friends. We're breaking his heart now."

"Don't worry, Marlena," she comforted me. "You've been good

to him and for him. Better than I've ever been. Sure, I'll keep my eye on him. He'll be fine."

Early in January Terry left, and I worried even more. Chauncy stayed away from me for days on end. He came over occasionally to see if I needed anything, but he wouldn't stay for dinner or play with the boys. He was on my mind constantly. I couldn't forget his threat. I tried to shake off the feeling of dread, and I wondered how I could prove how much I cared about him.

Finally, I hit upon a plan. One afternoon I spotted him walking down the street, his head carefully averted from our house.

"Chauncy!" I called. "Come here a minute, please."

He turned toward me obediently and headed over.

"Chauncy," I said. "I have a big favor to ask. Tomorrow I have to go to the real-estate office and sign some papers. Will you stay with the boys after school?"

"You mean just me?" he asked.

"Well," I said hesitating, "if you'd rather I asked Esther—I just thought you might want to do it for me. The boys have missed you lately, and I'm confident you can handle them."

Chauncy's face was unreadable, but the next moment he was telling me, "Why, sure, Marlena, I'd be glad to."

The next day a feeling of uneasiness nagged me, but I shook it off. "What's the matter with you?" I chided myself. "You told him that you trusted him. Now prove it!"

For a fleeting instant, I thought of Terry and what his reaction would be to my leaving the boys in Chauncy's care. I pushed all thoughts of him aside and tried to reassure myself. Chauncy cared about my boys. He'd take good care of them and himself, too. Terry wouldn't have to know.

After some last-minute instructions to Chauncy, I set out. "I'll call you when I'm ready to leave, and you can all walk up to the bus stop and meet me," I said.

I kissed thy boys good-bye and reached for Chauncy. His arms tightened around me convulsively.

"Well, Chauncy," I said. "That's some send-off! Be good. I'll be back soon."

My dealings in town took longer than I thought. I glanced at my watch and was surprised to see that it was past suppertime. The boys would be hungry. I hurried to the nearest phone to call home and tell them that I was on my way.

My first premonition of danger flashed through my mind when no one answered the phone. I told myself that the boys had grown impatient and had already gone up to the bus stop to meet me.

I deposited more change and rang Esther's number. Her line

was busy, and my annoyance grew. I was too impatient to try again. I hurried out of the booth and caught the bus back.

I was in time to see a police car careening down our street, its siren shrill and terrifying. My heart turned cold as I watched the car pull up alongside the fire trucks farther down the street. No! I screamed inwardly. No! Not my house. Please, God, not my house!

Fear lent speed to my legs as I flew down the street. I screamed my terror as I rushed madly into the crowd lined up in front of my house, scattering them, fighting the hands that reached out to pull me back.

"Let me go!" I screamed. "My babies are in there!"

And then Esther was there, pulling at me. "They're not in there any more, Marlena," she yelled. "They got them out. Come on. They're in Hillside Hospital. I'll drive you there."

On the way, Esther told me what she knew. She said that she'd seen Chauncy running from my burning house. . . .

He left my boys to die! I thought later as I sat in the hospital waiting room.

With a start, I realized that Molly Foley was talking to me.

"Chauncy came home to get his homework," she said, her voice choked with emotion. "When he got back to your house, it was on fire. He ran back to get me and told me to call the fire department. He raced out the door, and I ran out after him. I could see the smoke pouring out of your house, and I called in the alarm. Then I ran to find Chauncy. I got there just in time to see him break a window in the cellar. I yelled for him to come back, but he climbed in and disappeared. I tried to follow him, but the firemen came and stopped me. My poor baby!"

"You mean Chauncy's here, too?" I asked. "But he ran away—"

Molly went on as though she hadn't heard me. "It was an accident! My Chauncy was crazy with fear when he came to get me. The firemen said defective wiring caused it."

I gripped her arms. "Molly!" I cried. "I thought Chauncy started it!"

She stared at me blankly, and her eyes swept behind me. Dr. Devlin had come into the room. He was smiling.

"Well, ladies, the worst is over. A few superficial burns, and a lot of smoke poisoning, but thanks to your son's quick thinking, Mrs. Foley, they'll be all right in a day or two. Chauncy told me all about it, and he's anxious to see you, Marlena," he said, turning to me. "You, too, of course, Mrs. Foley," he added.

"Thank God," I breathed as we hurried down the corridor to the boys' room.

I kneeled down beside my boys and kissed and hugged them.

They were full of excitement, both trying to tell me about the fire at once. I quieted them down and walked over to Chauncy's bed. Molly moved over to make room for me.

"Marlena," Chauncy whispered, "I only left them for a little while. I'm sorry."

I smiled through my tears. "Tell me, honey. What happened?"

Chauncy said that he played with the boys for a while after I left. Then he made them both lie down and take naps. When he was certain that they were both asleep, he went back home to get his schoolwork.

When he returned, he saw the smoke pouring out of the basement windows. He tried the door and found that he'd accidentally locked it behind him. He raced home to get help, and then back to my house. He broke the window and crawled in, fighting to see through the smoke.

He fought his way upstairs, roused the boys, and tried to get them back downstairs. When he found that his escape had been cut off, he herded the screaming boys into the upstairs bathroom. He wrapped wet towels around their heads, soaked down their clothes, and made them lie down on the floor. That's where the firemen found them, huddled together, Chauncy's arms flung protectively around my sons.

Tears were streaming down my cheeks, and Chauncy reached up to pat my face. "Don't cry, Marlena," he begged. "I'm sorry."

"Darling, I'm crying because you're such a brave boy, and I'm so proud of you," I said. "I'm the one who's sorry. . . ." I left the words unfinished. Chauncy would never know that I had doubted him—not if I could help it.

Terry flew back that night, and he stayed with me until the boys were out of the hospital. Our house had not been badly damaged, so we were able to move back in in a few days and supervise its repairs. Terry had found a new home for us in New York, and in a month we were on our way.

Chauncy came down to the station to see us off, and as I watched him, I wondered how I could ever have doubted him. It was my boys who cried that day, not Chauncy. Stevie and Paul hated the thought of leaving him behind.

"Why all the tears?" Chauncy said. "Gee whiz! It's not like you were leaving forever. I'll be with you in a few months for Easter vacation, and a few months after that, I'll be there for the whole summer. So you better be good. If you're not, your folks will tell me."

"We'll be good," they promised.

"You, too, Chauncy," I said, hugging him close.

He looked me straight in the eyes. "You know I will be, Marlena," he said. "Even if you're not here, I want you and Terry to be proud of me."

"We'll always be proud of you, Chauncy," I said. "No matter where you are, you'll always be our boy."

I watched Chauncy as the train pulled out until he was just a little speck on the platform. I had no need to worry. He had been brave because he loved my sons. He would be good because he loved my husband and me.

The End

MY LOVE RIVAL GAVE ME THE GREATEST HAPPINESS OF MY LIFE

Why wasn't I aware of what happened to me? Why was it so hard to face the truth about myself? Let me begin on the day my cozy little world collapsed around me. It was a lovely Spring morning and I was in high spirits as I fixed breakfast. Ronnie and I had a happy marriage—he'd been made full partner in the tool manufacturing company he'd worked at since high school. We were financially secure and we had a lovely home. It was going to be a perfect day!

Ronnie came in the kitchen, still in his robe, fresh from his shower. I enjoyed the look of him, so trim and handsome at twenty-eight, my age. I smiled at him. "Good morning, hon! Did you sleep well?"

"No, I didn't—I had too much on my mind. Don't bother about breakfast for me, Meg—I want to talk to you."

"What about coffee?" I poured a cup for him, one for myself, and sat down. Strange, he didn't want breakfast—it was usually an important meal for him. He looked very serious, but Ronnie always looked serious. He usually didn't talk much and I wondered what he had to say that was so important.

"How long have we been married, Meg?" he began.

"You know," I said, "almost nine years—our anniversary's coming up soon."

"Are you happy?"

"Sure," I said. "Shouldn't I be?"

"I don't think you're really happy, Meg. You're fooling yourself— hiding your real feelings. I've been miserable for a long time, too—not that you've noticed. I hate to tell you this, but I think we should live apart form while. I want a separation."

I thought he was joking. "Stop kidding, Ronnie. You know I have no sense of humor in the morning!"

"I'm not joking, Meg."

As he stared gloomily at his coffee cup, I searched frantically for answers. Why was Ronnie acting this way? Was he going through an emotional crisis? He'd been moody lately. Was it because we had no children? Ronnie had been disappointed about that, but hadn't mentioned it in a long time.

I thought he was satisfied with his life. He loved his work to the point of being a workaholic, spending long hours at the plant. I didn't mind—my life was centered around our big, beautiful home. I was

105

always busy. I did all the gardening. I painted and redecorated. I loved to sew things for the house. I kept it sparklingly clean and polished.

Suddenly, the harsh reality of his words began to sink in. "Ronnie," I said fearfully, "I thought you were happy. I've done my best to be a good wife to you!"

"Have you, Meg?" he asked bitterly. "The tragedy is, you really believe that!"

Of course, I believed it! I'd always been a good wife. I rushed to defend myself. "Maybe if you'd spend more time with me, and take some interest in the house and garden, you wouldn't have these feelings!"

"Well," he said, "that's the first time I've heard you complain about my long working hours. I'm sure the average wife would be angry at me for being away from her so much, but you haven't minded at all, and at work, I can at least escape from my unhappiness. The house is your first love, Meg. I'm just incidental. You don't want me around. You don't need my help—you want to do everything yourself, as if you're trying to prove something. We don't even talk to each other anymore—you're always too busy. You don't care about me. I'm just someone who pays the bills. It's not enough. I want to be loved as a man and as a husband!"

He stood up. "I'm late for work now. I'll be back tonight to pack my things. I'm sorry if I hurt you, Meg, but we both deserve more out of life than we're getting!"

He strode out of the kitchen, leaving me utterly destroyed. When I heard the front door close after him I walked out into my garden, hoping to find some comfort there. But all that beauty meant nothing to me now.

I was in such incredible pain. Ronnie's devastating announcement had cruelly exposed all the old, empty feelings I'd tried so hard to hide. I'd had two dangerously complicated miscarriages during the early years of our marriage, and had never become pregnant again. I'd gone to pieces, three years ago, when my doctor gave me the final verdict: I could never have a child.

Ronnie refused to consider adoption. For a long time my need for a baby was unbearable. I cried when I saw mothers with young children, and I dreamed at night of a little child running toward me with outstretched arms.

Eventually, I accepted my childlessness. Now that old, barren feeling was back again. I felt a wrenching anger at Ronnie. He'd done this to me! He didn't want me anymore. Why?

His attitude toward me must have changed when he learned I could never have a child. All this time, he'd considered me only half a woman. Oh, he'd hidden his feelings very well, but that had to be the reason he was leaving me. I couldn't accept any of his other complaints!

A voice broke into my thoughts. "Hi, Meg!" My neighbor, Mindy, peered at me over the fence. "Enjoying your garden?" she asked. "You should, considering all your hard work." She saw the dazed expression on my face. "What's the matter, Meg?"

I was far too upset to talk to Mindy or anyone else, and besides, it was painful to hear her two little girls playing in her yard. "Ronnie just left," I said, "and I didn't sleep well. I think I'll go back to bed for a while. See you later, Mindy!"

I walked slowly back into the house, feeling like a terrified child left all alone in the world—deserted, abandoned.

I'd never been on my own before. I'd gone directly from my parents' home to this home, and being a wife and homemaker was my whole life. I had no family to turn to now. I was an only child, born when Mom and Dad were in their forties. Both of them were dead.

I did feel close to Jillian Forte, the wife of the owner of the plant where Ronnie worked. She and her husband, Casey, an older couple, had always treated Ronnie and me like a son and daughter. Casey had even made Ronnie his partner. I'd talk to Jillian when I got myself together.

I threw myself on the bed, trying to think rationally. Something had triggered Ronnie's sudden request for a separation, but what? He'd been spending even longer hours at the plant lately, and working weekends. He said it was because of a backlog of orders. I had a frightening thought: Can there be another woman? The idea was outrageous, yet my suspicions deepened. By now, my wounded pride had fanned the flames of resentment and I was thinking clearly.

I'd met Alexa, the girl who worked in Ronnie's office—the only girl in that small plant. She was a beautiful girl, about twenty-two, a divorcée with a young child. Ronnie often spoke of her admiringly. Suddenly, I knew. It was Alexa!

With that thought, I went dead emotionally. Mercifully, I sank into a deep sleep, slept for hours, and awoke in a much better state, refusing to believe Ronnie had really meant what he said. . . .

I lived with my hollow hope all day, praying Ronnie would change his mind and not leave. We could work things out, I told myself. Tonight, I'd be warm and affectionate, telling him how much I loved and needed him. But when he arrived silent and grim-faced, and immediately started packing his suitcases, I knew my pleading would be useless.

I confronted him. "Be honest, Ronnie—you've found someone else, haven't you?"

He flushed angrily. "Of course not, Meg! Can't you believe that your behavior is the reason for this mess? We can't go on like this—we're ruining both our lives!"

I stared at him accusingly. "It's Alexa, isn't it?"

"Alexa?" he asked in amazement. "Where'd you get such a ridiculous idea? I have no interest in Alexa other than feeling sorry for her. You wouldn't want her problems! She's not well, her husband deserted her, and she has a four-year-old son to support. No, Meg, she has nothing to do with my need to get away from you!"

Oh, no? I thought bitterly. A picture of Alexa flashed into my mind—a beautiful young girl—a blond, plastic doll, with that helpless, fluttery look men love.

"It's her!" I burst out angrily. "I know it! Don't try to deny it!"

He shook his head sadly. "How can I get through to you that I'm not interested in Alexa, or any other woman? I still love you, Meg, but I can't live with you."

"You can't fool me, Ronnie! You stopped loving me when you found out I couldn't have children. Why don't you admit it?"

His voice rose in anger. "That had nothing to do with it! It's you who has changed! When you got the news from the doctor, you turned into an unhappy, frustrated woman. I kept assuring you that I loved you as much as ever, but you didn't listen. You withdrew from me. When I make love to you, you're cold and unresponsive. We don't share anything anymore—all you talk about is the house, the garden, the new drapes, all your big plans to turn the house into the showplace of the neighborhood!"

That enraged me. "It isn't true! You're just inventing an excuse to be with that girl!"

He looked at me pityingly. "I feel sorry for you, Meg. You have such a low opinion of yourself as a woman. Why don't you consider what's happened to us? We're living completely separate lives. You've even isolated us from our friends. You're not the warm, loving girl I married!"

Why, in the heat of anger, did I say things I didn't mean? "Excuses! All excuses! All right—get out! Go to Alexa!"

He shrugged his shoulders, resignedly finished his packing, and left. I had an awful feeling my marriage had ended. I had to talk to someone! I·called Mindy and asked her to come over. "Can you leave the children with Bill? I'd like to see you alone."

"Be right there!"

As soon as she arrived, I began to cry hysterically. Mindy and I had gone through a lot together as friends and neighbors—she'd understand.

"What on earth happened, Meg?" she asked anxiously. "Are you ill?"

"No, not physically. It's Ronnie—he's left me!"

"What do you mean, left you? He wants a divorce?"

"He says a separation, but I'm sure he has divorce in mind!" I blurted out all of Ronnie's accusations. "What do you think of that, Mindy? He tried to justify his behavior by accusing me of letting him down. I hate him!"

"You don't mean that, Meg," she said. "You're striking back at him because you're hurt and angry."

I wasn't listening. "It's so unfair, Mindy! Our marriage was exactly the way Ronnie wanted it. All these years, I've tried to please him in every way. Now he's turned to another woman!"

"Another woman?" she asked incredulously. "Who?"

"Alexa, where he works. She's a young girl with a four-year-old son. Ronnie tried to tell me he only felt sorry for her, but I don't believe him!"

"I don't understand any of this," said Mindy. "Bill and I have been your close friends for many years, and Ronnie's an honorable man. You must be mistaken!"

"I'm sure it's Alexa," I said wildly. "I haven't done anything to spoil our marriage, except not give Ronnie the children he wants—and she already has a son!"

"Honey," Mindy said in a worried voice, "you're hysterical, and not making sense. Be careful—remember what happened a few years ago."

I knew what she was talking about: that terrible time after the doctor told me I'd never have a child. Everything seemed distorted, as if I were looking at life through a flawed glass.

"You don't have to remind me," I said, "but I didn't break down. I came to terms with—with my childlessness."

"Did you?" she asked. "I wonder. I'm your friend, Meg, and I've watched you over the years. I think you felt so empty and inadequate that you made a conscious decision to prove your worth as a woman by being the super-perfect housewife. Your home certainly puts mine to shame!"

It was uncanny how she was probing into thoughts I'd buried long ago. "What am I going to do, Mindy? I'm so heartbroken and confused."

"Think about what Ronnie said, and be honest with yourself. You haven't lost him yet, and for heaven's sake, don't do anything foolish! Both of you need time to think."

"Do you think he'll come back to me, Mindy?"

"Ronnie still loves you, dear, and where there's love, there's always strong hope."

Ronnie called the next morning to tell me he was staying with Casey and Jillian Forte. That infuriated me! Jillian Forte was my friend. I'd counted on her being my confidante! Now that avenue of friendship was closed to me, all she'd hear would be Ronnie's version of our breakup. I had too much pride to call her.

"I'm sorry I lost my temper with you last night, Meg," Ronnie was saying, "but your accusations about Alexa hurt me deeply. Take a good look at your behavior the last few years. That's the reason for our unhappy marriage."

I didn't listen to him—I was too caught up in anger and distrust. Alexa—it had to be her. As the days passed, I got even angrier at Ronnie. I realized how dependent I'd been on him. He was an old-fashioned man, never wanting me to work, believing a wife belonged at home. Loving him the way I did, I'd agreed. I'd dedicated my life to Ronnie, and he'd abandoned me, leaving me completely unprepared to face life alone. It was so unjust!

After that, I didn't want to see anyone. I even asked Mindy to leave me alone for a while. I was like a wounded animal, retreating into a cave to lick my wounds. My self-esteem was destroyed. I kept myself feverishly busy, emptying and rearranging drawers, cabinets, and closets; cleaning and polishing the house until my hands were raw.

Working in the garden helped. It brought me close to nature and the feeling of birth—the birth denied me. I couldn't bear to go into my sewing room; it brought up too many sad memories. Originally, it was planned to be a nursery. Why, oh, why, had I been denied the joy of having a child?

Ronnie had stopped calling me, and told me why. "It's too upsetting to listen to your accusations about Alexa," he said. "Just send the bills to me and there'll always be enough money in our checking account for you to use."

All this time, a rage of jealousy was building up in me. My mind fastened on Alexa as the sole reason for my unhappiness. She was young, beautiful, had a son for Ronnie to father, and she could give him the children he wanted. I was distraught with jealousy, grief, and anger when I decided to see Alexa and have it out with her.

I followed her after she left the plant one evening. She picked up a little boy at our church's day-care center, did some marketing, and went home to an apartment. After a few minutes, I knocked on the door. A wave of embarrassment washed over me when she answered.

Ronnie had told me she wasn't well, but I wasn't prepared for her appearance. She looked so pale and tired. A little curly-haired boy clung to her skirt. My face turned red with guilt and shame. I had no business being here! I wished I were a thousand miles away!

"Why, Mrs. Miller," she said, "what a surprise! Please come in."

I sat down on the couch, fighting my feelings. "You've never met my son, Peter, have you?" she asked. "Peter, this is Mrs. Miller."

He ran over to me with a peculiar little hitch in his leg. Alexa saw the question in my eyes. "Peter has a slight malformation of one hip," she said. "It can be corrected by surgery, but not until he's ten years old. It doesn't bother him."

I felt so tender toward this dear little fellow. I gathered him up in my arms and he clung to me. She was astonished. "Well, that's quite a tribute to you, Mrs. Miller! Peter's usually very shy with strangers."

"He's a wonderful little boy," I said.

"He is, indeed, and a great comfort to me. I don't know what I'd do without him. Did you want to see me about something?"

I felt so awkward and ashamed I didn't know what to say. She sensed why I was there. "I was sorry to hear you and Ronnie had separated," she said, "and I hope you don't think I had anything to do with it."

I stared at her dumbly.

"It's not too hard to understand your state of mind," she went on. "I know how it feels to be rejected. My husband deserted me after Peter was born. At first, I was sure there was another woman, but I finally realized he was afraid of responsibility."

"I'm sorry," I said, "I—"

"Ronnie and I are just friends, Mrs. Miller. All the men in the plant, and their wives, too, have been very kind to me. I don't know the details of your separation, but I do know Ronnie loves you very much, and I hope you work out your differences."

I started to cry. I felt like such a hateful, suspicious wretch. I'd never bothered to find out anything about Alexa, or lifted a finger to help her, and now she was being more gracious than I deserved. "I'm sorry for coming here." I sobbed. "I feel like such a failure!"

Peter was still clinging to me, staring wonderingly at my tears. "Don't cry," he said. "What's your name?"

"Meghan—but my friends call me Meg."

"Am I your friend?" he asked.

"You certainly are, darling," I said. I dried my tears and held him close.

Alexa smiled. "You sure have a way with children," she said. "You don't have any of your own?"

"No, I can't have children." I had to get away from that subject. "Ronnie told me you've been having some health problems. What's the trouble?"

"Oh, everyone worries too much about me. It's nothing serious. I've been anemic all my life and I get tired, that's all."

"Have you seen a doctor recently?" I asked.

"Not since I moved here three years ago. I don't like going to doctors."

"You should take better care of yourself," I said. "At least have a doctor check you over."

"I'm okay! I watch my diet, take my iron pills, and I'm fine!"

She didn't look fine to me, and I wanted to help. "If there's anything I can ever do for you, Alexa, will you call me? I'd love to take care of Peter anytime you want me to."

"Thank you," she said. "I'll remember that. I could use a good friend."

On the way home, I was so full of guilt and shame that I decided to tell Ronnie about my foolish act and apologize to him. It was time I started being honest with him and myself. I called him. He was still at the plant, as usual. He was furious when I told him what I'd done.

"Alexa was wonderful to me, Ronnie," I hurried to add, "She understood how I felt; she knows I'm sorry and I'm ashamed of my suspicions. Please forgive me!"

"I'll have to think about it," he said, hanging up abruptly.

He called back in ten minutes. "I'm embarrassed by what you did," he said. "It's typical of your self-destructive behavior, but at least I hope it's helped you to take a clear look at yourself."

"I noticed Alexa didn't look well," I said, "and I suggested she see a doctor."

"Everyone's tried to get her to a doctor, but she's very stubborn."

"I told her if she ever needs a friend, to call me," I said, "and I mean it, Ronnie!"

"Well," he said, sounding unconvinced, "it's been a long time since you've gone out of your way to help anyone."

"I know," I said earnestly, "and I want to change. I realize I've been selfish and self-centered."

"I've been thinking, too," he said. "Maybe I haven't been fair to you, insisting that you stay home. Would you like a job? Would that make you happy?"

The thought of facing the job market terrified me—I had no skills. But this was a big concession for Ronnie, and he had a point. I was beginning to understand why I'd been so obsessive about the house. It was my way of blocking out hurt and anger over being childless, insulating myself against the pain. A job might help change that. "I'll think about a job," I said, "but what I really want is to have you home with me. Won't you please come back, Ronnie? I need you!"

"I'm sorry, Meg," he said. "I can't do that. My unhappiness has been building up for years, and it's impossible to get rid of my bad feelings so quickly. I haven't made up my mind what I want to do."

He sounded cold and indifferent. I had an awful feeling Ronnie never intended to come back to me—he was thinking about divorce!

The days that followed were the loneliest and most miserable of my life. The whole house had a deadly stillness about it. I wandered around the silent rooms, lingering over each piece of fine grain wood furniture I'd polished to a brilliant sheen, and all the little treasures I'd had such fun collecting. They meant nothing to me now. I couldn't sew anymore. I didn't even go into the sewing room. I was so depressed that I didn't want to see anyone, not even Mindy, though she dropped by every day. I tried to think about a job, but couldn't hold a thought in my head for more than a few seconds.

When the front doorbell rang one morning, I almost didn't answer it, but I did. It was Jillian Forte. When I saw her sweet face, grey hair, and her look of loving concern, I burst into tears. "Jillian, thank God you're here!"

"Why didn't you call me, Meg?"

"I felt that Ronnie staying with you had driven a wedge between us, and you'd be on his side."

"Rubbish! Nothing's changed between you and me. I still think of you as a daughter, and I'm on your side."

"Has Ronnie talked to you about me, Jillian?"

"Not too much. I waited to talk to you, Meg, to give you time to get over the shock of Ronnie's leaving, so you and I could talk sensibly. I've been concerned about you for a long time."

"Why didn't you say something?"

"I tried to, but you wouldn't listen. In a way, I'm glad Ronnie's brought everything out in the open by this separation. Now you have a chance to face the truth of what happened to you."

"What did happen, Jillian? I'm so confused I can't even think!"

"Let me tell you about myself, dear—maybe that will help. Have you ever wondered why Casey and I have no children?"

"Yes, but I didn't think it tactful to ask."

"I had a hysterectomy in my twenties, right after Casey and I were married. It made me bitter and depressed. I'd read somewhere that a marriage without children was like a night without stars, and I bought that whole false bill of goods. I felt like an empty shell of a woman, unattractive and undesirable."

"Oh, Jillian!" I exclaimed fervently, "I understand. I have the same feelings. I haven't felt like a real woman for so long!"

"My poor husband had a terrible time with me," she went on. "I became cold and withdrawn. I stopped seeing my friends. I tried to fight my emptiness by insisting that everything be perfect around the house. I wouldn't tolerate even a speck of dust or anything out of place, and Casey couldn't relax at home for fear of disturbing the perfection I demanded. He began escaping into his work, just like Ronnie."

That didn't sound like Jillian and Casey. They were such a happy couple. "What did you do?"

"Fortunately, I came to my senses and saw what I was doing. I was shutting Casey out of my life and keeping myself so busy I didn't have time to think."

I recognized so much of myself in Jillian's story! I'd behaved the same way, sacrificing Ronnie to my frustration and self-pity. "How were you able to change, Jillian?"

"I stopped being a perfectionist. I made Casey my first priority. I showed him in every way how much I loved and needed him. I realized there were plenty of children in the world to love, and began working with underprivileged kids. It's called the law of compensation, dear, letting your pain at having no children of your own work for you. And it does work! Now, Casey and I share an interest in a lot of young people. We consider the plant employees our family, with a special place in our hearts for you and Ronnie."

I was ashamed of myself as I listened to this warm-hearted friend. "What should I do, Jillian?"

"It takes insight and courage to change attitudes, Meg. Having something nurturing and rewarding in your life would help. I have a suggestion. I'm on the board of trustees of our church. Have you ever been through our day-care center? It's your church, too, isn't it?"

I flushed remembering how I'd followed Alexa when she picked Peter up at the day-care center. "I've never been in the center," I said. "In fact, Ronnie and I stopped going to church years ago."

"I know, dear, and it's too bad. But marriage is made stronger by spiritual values. We have volunteers at the center on a daily basis, but there's an opening for a paid worker five days a week, and I've been asked to find someone. I suggest you take the job. It'll make you feel good about yourself to be helping children and earning money at the same time. Why don't you come over there with me now, and see how you like it?"

I had grave doubts about my ability to do the job, but it appealed to me, and I agreed to go. I met Mrs. Thompson, the woman in charge. She explained that the children were all preschoolers from single-parent homes, where the mothers, and sometimes the fathers, had to work.

"It's much more than a baby-sitting job," she said. "We need a warm, caring woman who loves children and can help me supervise them. Let me show you around."

The day-care center was behind the church, consisting of an office, two large rooms designed for children, and a playground. I felt a tug at my heart as I watched the youngsters playing on the swings and slides, and heard their happy, excited little voices.

Then I saw Peter. He saw me at the same time and ran toward me. "Meg! Meg!" he cried.

"You know Alexa's boy?" asked Jillian in surprise.

I felt so ashamed. That dear little boy remembered me from the day I'd confronted his mother with my jealousy. "Oh, yes," I said, picking him up and kissing him, "we're friends!" I turned to Mrs. Thompson. "I'll take the job—how soon can I start?"

That was the beginning of a positive change in my life. I felt so needed at the center, caring for those little ones. With his sweetness and charm, Peter quickly entwined himself around my heart. I often chatted with Alexa when she picked him up—she was a lovely girl!

It had been many weeks since I'd heard from Ronnie. It was as if he'd dropped completely out of my life. The day-care center was a big help, but it couldn't satisfy my hungry yearning for Ronnie. I loved him so much, and at night I cried myself to sleep. I was so afraid I'd lost him forever.

I came out of the day-care center office one afternoon, and was shocked to see Ronnie leading Peter out of the playground. Ronnie saw me, looked away quickly, put Peter into his car and drove off, leaving me hurt and bewildered, with many painful questions. Why had Ronnie deliberately avoided me? And why had he picked up Peter for Alexa—he never had before! They looked like father and son! Ronnie was lonely and vulnerable. Alexa was conveniently nearby and tempting. Had he turned to her, after all? I rushed over to Mrs. Thompson. "Why did my husband take Peter?"

"Oh," she said, "you weren't here when he brought Peter in early this morning. He said his mother was ill."

I hoped Alexa's illness wasn't serious, but my sympathy for her was overwhelmed by my irrational panic. The situation was worse than I thought. Ronnie had always felt sorry for Alexa. She needed him—he needed to be needed—and need must have ripened into mutual love. Dear God, I had lost him!

Jillian Forte came to see me that night. She could see I was under a strain, but I was afraid to tell her what was upsetting me so. Jillian was such a trusting soul—she'd never believe it!

"Meg," Jillian said quietly, "did you know Alexa's in the hospital? Did Ronnie tell you when he picked up Peter this afternoon?"

That shocked me to my senses. "No," I gasped, "he didn't tell me. What's wrong with her?"

"She called Casey and me last night asking for help. Ronnie came with us and we found her in bad shape, short of breath with heart palpitations. We took her to the hospital, and Ronnie took Peter back to our place."

"Is it serious, Jillian?"

"All we know is she's very ill. They're doing all kinds of tests now."

My eyes stung with tears. I'd been such a witch with my insane suspicions! "Can I see her?"

"No, dear. She's in intensive care; no visitors allowed. I'm here because, on the way to the hospital, Alexa begged me to ask you to take care of Peter until she's well. She said he loves you dearly. Will you do it, Meg?"

I felt so grateful to Alexa for entrusting me with her little son. "Oh, yes, Jillian. I love Peter!"

"I'm glad. You'll be giving of yourself and you need more of that in your life. And, by the way, I talked to Ronnie about your having Peter. He said it was up to you."

Ronnie! How did he really feel about my caring for Peter? He might not like the idea at all, but it was a risk I had to take. I loved that little boy, felt so tender toward his mother, and I'd learned, through the day-care center, that helping others was my salvation. "Where's Peter now?"

"He's asleep at my house. I'll bring him to the center in the morning, and you can take him home with you tomorrow night."

That little boy was such a blessing to me, giving me the will to survive without Ronnie. I kept him close to me—it was vital that he felt secure and loved. He slept on a cot in my bedroom and I was with him all week at the day-care center. Over the weekends, Mindy's two little girls played with him, and Mindy and I spent enjoyable hours together. "Meg," she told me, "you look great, but it worries me that you're so attached to Peter."

"I'm mindful of that," I said. "When Alexa's well again, I'll follow Jillian Forte's example and find a lot of children to love."

Alexa's condition worsened steadily, and her doctor called in a couple of specialists. She was not allowed visitors or phone calls, but since I was taking care of Peter I was permitted to call her once a day with news of his activities. That cheered her up. We'd developed a warm, close relationship—she was like the little sister I'd never had.

A few days later, Jillian came to see me at the day-care center, her face red and tear-stained, and with devastating news about Alexa. Since she had no family the doctor had summoned Jillian and Casey to the hospital.

"Oh, Meg," Jillian sobbed, "Alexa has leukemia. She's going to die! Oh, why do people refuse to see a doctor when they're first aware that something's wrong?"

"I don't know," I said, my voice shaking. "Maybe they're afraid of what the doctor will find. How long does she have?"

"They're not sure—anywhere from a few days to a month."

"Does she know?"

"Yes. She insisted on hearing the truth. I've talked to her and she's accepted it. Now she wants to see you, Meg. She says it's urgent. Go ahead, honey. I'll take your place with the children."

116

I was shattered when I saw Alexa—so thin, pale, lifeless.

"Thank you for coming, Meg," she said with a little smile. "I know I don't have long, and I'm very concerned about Peter. I don't want him to end up in a foster home."

She held out her hand and I grasped it, too overcome to speak. Her eyes were pleading with me.

"Meg, please adopt Peter. You love him and he loves you. Even if Ronnie doesn't come back to you, I still want you to have my son. Will you adopt him?"

I held on to her hand tightly, my eyes filled with tears. "Of course, I will, Alexa—and I promise I'll always love him and take good care of him."

She lay back against the pillow with a gasp of relief. "One thing more, for my peace of mind, Meg. Please see a lawyer immediately and have legal papers drawn up for us both to sign. Do it now, Meg—I don't know how much time I have."

She closed her eyes in exhaustion. I left, trembling with shock, grief and confusion. I didn't even know a lawyer. I needed Ronnie's help. I drove over to the plant. He was surprised to see me—we hadn't communicated in months. I cried as I explained my reason for being there.

"I hope you have no objection to my adopting Peter," I said, "but with or without you, Ronnie, I want that little boy! Will you arrange for me to see a lawyer right away?"

Casey had already told Ronnie about Alexa's terminal condition, and he was staggered by my decision to adopt Peter. "Aren't you reacting too emotionally, Meg? Are you sure this is the right thing to do?"

I faced him squarely. "I know you've always been opposed to adoption, Ronnie, but this is important to me and if necessary, I'll raise Peter by myself. Will you help me?"

He picked up the phone, watching me intently as he dialed, then spoke to someone. After he hung up, he wrote on a piece of paper and handed it to me. "I've set up an appointment for you with the plant's lawyer. Here's his name and address. He'll see you right away."

I'd hoped Ronnie would come with me but it was apparent he didn't intend to do so—he looked so stern and disapproving I gritted my teeth and drove over to the lawyer's office and waited while legal papers were prepared. The lawyer went back with me to the hospital. Alexa and I signed the papers and he witnessed them.

"Will this take care of Meg adopting Peter legally?" she asked anxiously.

"Absolutely," the lawyer assured her, "getting the court's approval will be a simple matter. Your son is safe."

"Then I'm happy," said Alexa, smiling at me. "I don't care what happens now."

From that point on, I stayed with Alexa. The doctor arranged for a room where I could sleep. Jillian, bless her heart, arranged for a substitute for me at the center, and she took care of Peter. My heart overflowed with love for Alexa—I just wished there was more I could do for her.

The doctor permitted visitors now, and she was eager to see all her friends from the plant. One by one they came. Alexa was deeply moved. "They're all so kind, Meg, but you're the one I feel closest to. You're a wonderful woman, and I'm at peace knowing Peter will be safe with you."

Three weeks later, Alexa was gone. Casey, and Ronnie were there with me. I was near collapse, and they all insisted I go home, they'd take care of the arrangements. I drove to the day-care center, picked up Peter, and took him home. I sat quietly for a long time, holding him close, mourning for Alexa, for the end of such a beautiful young life.

I realized Peter would have to be told—otherwise, he'd think his mother had deserted him. I figured out how to tell him in a gentle, uplifting way. I held him in my arms, kissing him and stroking his hair, as I explained that his mommy was in heaven now and that she'd love him forever. Holding him very close to me, I told him I loved him dearly, and I'd always take care of him. Tears filled his eyes, and he seemed to understand. After that, he wouldn't let me out of his sight.

After Alexa's funeral, I was too depleted, mentally and physically, to do anything but care for Peter and fix meals. I hadn't done any housework in weeks, but that didn't seem to matter. Just how important was it in view of the life and death struggle that had been going on?

I thought a lot about the way it used to be with Ronnie and me, when we were so much in love. How I'd loved sleeping in his strong arms! What a fool I'd been to treat him so badly! Now I'd lost him—our marriage was over. I had to accept it. We'd been strangers for months, and the few times I'd seen him recently, he'd been cold and distant.

When Ronnie called the next morning saying he was coming over, I had a feeling of foreboding. When I opened the door, he looked tense. He came in, ruffled Peter's hair, and asked him to go outside and play.

We sat together on the couch. He was uncomfortably silent, while I stared vacantly at the dust on the mahogany coffee table, acutely anxious, fearful of what he was going to say. Was our marriage finished? Would he ask me for a divorce?

His first words were not reassuring. "I wanted to talk to you before this, Meg, but because of Alexa, the timing wasn't right."

I didn't like the sound of that—had he held back on giving me the bad news while I was so involved with Alexa?

"Go ahead, Ronnie," I said, "tell me what's on your mind."

"Well," he said, "I don't know quite how to begin. When we split up, I felt so hurt, angry and rejected, I couldn't think straight, but lately, I've been more clearheaded. Now I know what I want." He hesitated, as if he didn't quite know how to continue. I waited with fear and apprehension, not having a clue as to what he was thinking.

He started to say something, changed his mind, and leaned over to the coffee table. Using his index finger, he began to write in the thick dust. I bent over to take a closer look. Ronnie Loves Meg? That dusty table, with its clear message of love, was a beautiful sight to me!

"Ronnie," I gasped, "do you really mean it?"

He took my hand and smiled at me, the first smile I'd seen on Ronnie's face in months! "I do, darling—I'm sorry it took me so long to admit, but you know how stubborn I am!"

He looked deep into my eyes. "I love you and I respect you for what you've done," he said earnestly, "giving so generously of yourself to the day-care center, to Peter and Alexa. You're a warm, compassionate woman, Meg, and I can't live without you. May I come home?"

I answered by throwing my arms around him. We kissed—the first loving kiss we'd shared in so long! I felt like a real woman again, cherished and desired! We clung to each other, savoring every delicious moment of our reconciliation.

Then he gently freed himself. "Can we go outside now, and see our son? You will let me adopt him, Meg?"

He saw the question in my eyes. "I've changed, too, sweetheart. It was unfair of us not to adopt a child. I could have been much more loving and understanding. Will you forgive me?"

I kissed him again. "Ronnie? It wasn't your fault—I was wrong all the way. I love you—it's a new beginning for us—and of course you can adopt Peter! He's our son!"

I thought of Alexa so often, when Ronnie and I were back together, blessing her for enriching my life and teaching me that the secret of happiness is in giving of yourself to others.

Now, our marriage is a loving, sharing experience in every way. Thank God we learned the truth about ourselves before it was too late!

WRITER'S NOTE: It took me a long time to write this story, and longer to get up the courage to send it to you. Now I have wonderful news! I'm pregnant! I couldn't believe it at first, and then, in view of my medical history, I wasn't sure I could carry my baby to full term. But I'm six months pregnant, and the doctor assures me that everything's normal, and I'll have a healthy baby. If possible, Peter is even happier than Ronnie or I am. He has ordered a sister or a brother. "I don't care which," he says, "as long as it can play baseball!"

The End

MY HOLY AFFAIR

It was time to get back to my café for the evening rush. The place would be crowded tonight. Friday nights were always busy, with the beer-drinking longshoremen celebrating the end of another grueling week on the docks.

Still, I lingered on the deserted pier where I always came to think things out. With a long, sad sigh, I looked into the murky water sloshing against the rotted planks. And when a foghorn sounded in the distance, I wanted to cry.

Running the café hadn't been so bad for my folks. The love and respect they'd felt for each other had made the rough, sleazy— sometimes brutal—atmosphere of the docks bearable. But for me there was no love—not real love, not the deep, enriching affection Mom and Dad had shared. For me there were only men like Jeff Simmons.

Shivering, I turned up the collar of my coat and looked at the imitation gold necklace Jeff Simmons had given me last night, my twenty-fourth birthday. Holding up my hand, I saw the jagged nail, part of which had broken off when I'd clawed him in self-defense later in the evening.

"You little bitch!" he'd shouted after I scratched him. "Those hungry eyes of yours tell me you want loving as much as me. Who do you think you're kidding?"

And it had started again, the sickening fight we'd carried on for years. Jeff didn't want a wife and home, just a sordid affair. When I tried to tell him we could have a decent marriage, he wouldn't listen.

"We're waterfront people, baby," he said. "It's a lousy life, but we're stuck with it. Seeing a priest and signing a scrap of paper won't make it any different. So why fight me?"

The thing was, I was secretly losing the fight. Maybe Jeff was a far cry from the kind of man I dreamed about, but he was the only man interested in me. And I wanted love so desperately—any sort of love—that it was becoming hard to refuse even a moment of lust.

Turning away from the water, I reluctantly started back to the café. I knew Jeff wouldn't give up until he had mastered me with his passion, just as he'd mastered the job of loading the freighters and steamships on the docks. I also knew with a dreadful certainty that if I ever gave in to him, it would be the end of me.

Through the darkening haze ahead, I could see the red neon sign of the café. The café had been a part of my life as long as I could

120

remember. Even when I went to high school, I'd waitressed there in the afternoons, while Mom handled the griddle from her wheelchair and Dad handled the rowdy longshoremen or merchant marines who tried to date me. I'd loved Dad a lot, but Mom, frail as she was, had been my strength and anchor. It was her fondest dream that I get away from the waterfront after graduation. But the dream never came true.

The paralysis that had crippled Mom's legs had weakened her lungs, too. After my graduation, her strength gave out and I had to take care of her. Then when she died a year later, I was suddenly like a rudderless ship, floundering in a tide of heartache. Soon Dad withdrew into his own world of despair with booze, leaving me to run the café.

Sometimes Dad pulled himself together and helped me, but mostly he prowled along the dock like a bedraggled old scarecrow. About nine months after Mom died, a big crane, lifting two-ton crates onto a freighter, suddenly dropped its crushing load on the dock. Dad was too drunk to hear the warning shouts, or maybe, without Mom, he just hadn't wanted to go on facing the bleakness.

I had to go on, though, so I hired a full-time waitress, Kristy, and a part-time assistant, Dominic. Dominic took over for me three nights a week. I could've sold the place instead, but I guess I was afraid to venture out into a strange world. Besides, the café was the only thing of my parents' I had left to cling to.

Pausing outside the café now, I drew in a deep breath of night air, the last fresh air I'd have until I closed up at midnight. Then my hand found the doorknob, but before I could turn it, another hand reached for it out of the shadows. Automatically I braced myself for a fresh pat on the backside or a crude wisecrack. But all I heard was a man's voice murmuring, "Excuse me." Then the man politely opened the door for me.

"Why, thank you," I said, catching a glimpse of him as I walked inside. He was a tall, thin, dark-haired young man in a shabby jacket.

"Erica, it's about time you came back!" Kristy whined when I slipped behind the counter. "These clowns have been running me ragged. Hey, who's the tall hottie?"

The young man had taken one of the empty booths in the back. Kristy grabbed her order pad and walked toward him, her broad hips swaying in perfect time to the blaring jukebox strains.

"Hey, Erica, we played the piece just for you!" Frank Guerrin shouted. "Looks like Jeff got a real lesson last night, judging from those scratches on his face."

I felt myself redden as I flipped four hamburgers on the griddle. But I didn't say anything or act as if I'd heard. Long ago I'd learned to let the customers' wisecracks bounce off me. Let them say what they wanted to. Who cared what a bunch of bums thought?

Still, tonight my stomach knotted as the teasing continued. Maybe it was because of the soft-voiced stranger who had, for one shimmering moment, treated me like a lady. Somehow I didn't want him to hear the usual wisecracks that were hurled at me. When I looked over at his booth, though, I saw he was having problems of his own with Kristy. She kept bending over him, her low-necked blouse revealing her cleavage. But he wasn't interested. He did his best to look away from her, his face red.

Suddenly I became angry. I knew Kristy was the lure that attracted male customers to my place, but I didn't want her bothering this wholesome type. So I threw a hamburger on a plate, filled a cup with coffee, and walked quickly to his rescue.

"This must be your order," I said, giving Kristy a little nudge. Then I told her to take care of two sailors who had just walked in. The man looked relieved when she flounced away. Then he glanced up at me with the clearest gray eyes I'd ever seen.

"Listen, I can't afford the hamburger," he said. "And I guess I shouldn't take up a booth just for some coffee."

"Sit still," I said. "The hamburger's on the house. If you like it, maybe you'll come back. I can use all the new customers I can get."

An appealing smile tugged at his mouth as he reached for the plate, and I couldn't seem to take my eyes off him.

"I've been looking around for a job," he told me between hungry bites. "Do you know anyone I could see about work? I'll take anything."

I almost laughed, because I'd taken a good look at his hands. Not a callous! He had the smooth, white fingers of a businessman, or a professional man, or maybe even an artist—but never a longshoreman!

"Unless you belong to the union, you probably won't have a prayer around the docks," I said gently as he finished his meal.

He put a dollar under his plate—his last one, probably—and stood up. I felt a little jolt when his warm hand closed briefly around mine. "You've been very kind. I'm grateful to you."

As he started to leave, the expression on his face grew strained. I'd seen the same bleak look on little kids' faces when they'd been challenged to a street fight they couldn't possibly win.

"Wait!" I called after him. "I know someone who might help you—Jeff Simmons. He's kind of a boss around here. Maybe if I ask him, he can find you a place. Where are you staying?"

He looked at me gratefully. "At Mrs. Henry's rooming house. My name is Max Parson, by the way, and. . . ." He lifted his hands in embarrassment. "What can I say, but thanks again?"

From you, a smile is enough thanks, I thought as he found his way apologetically through the jostling crowd. I couldn't help feeling protective toward him. He probably didn't even know that years ago Mrs. Henry's rooming house had been a notorious bordello and that Mrs. Henry—most of us called her Old Rita—had once been a madam.

I dreaded asking Jeff for a favor, but later that night after serving him a steak and a beer and giving him a long kiss while we danced, I spoke to him about Max Parson. He said he could give him a job as checker. I hated myself when I saw the smirks on the other guys' faces as I danced cheek-to-cheek with Jeff. But if it would help Max Parson, it was worth it!

Max was hired the next day, and in the weeks that followed, my heart skipped a beat each time he came into the café. He always chose the off-hours, when there were few customers and I could have a companionable cup of coffee with him. Soon I found myself doing little things to please him, such as buying a new blue dress because blue was his favorite color. In my eagerness to please Max, though, I began to annoy Jeff.

"This dump's turning into a ladies' tea shop!" Jeff complained the day I ran out of doughnuts. I'd ordered fewer doughnuts than usual, so I could stock up on the light, flaky coffeecake I knew Max would prefer. "The next thing you know," Jeff continued "they won't let you in here without a tie!"

Kristy screeched as if Jeff were the funniest guy on earth, and he looked at her with new interest. Once, that would have made me jealous, because with all his faults, Jeff had been all I'd had. But now I had a new friend. Now there was someone who listened to me when I talked about my hopes and dreams and problems.

Now I had Max.

"You never speak about yourself," I told him once during his afternoon break when we strolled along the pier.

He smiled his shy, endearing smile. "I'm just an ordinary guy."

"But you're not!" I insisted, as he picked up a pebble and skimmed it across the water. "I know one thing for sure—you never worked with your hands before. When you came here, there wasn't a callous on them. You know what I think? I think you're hiding a deep, dark secret, Max Parson!"

I linked my fingers through his, smiling teasingly. But he didn't smile back. He pulled his hand away instead, and I saw his fingers tremble as he ran his hand through his hair. "Let's talk about something else," he said. "All right?"

"All right, Max," I said quietly. But I was more curious about him than ever.

After that, we talked about other things during our strolls on the pier—Old Rita's bouts with the bottle, the peace pickets who'd shown up at the dock the week crates of ammunition were shipped to Iraq, and of course there was always Snowflake.

Snowflake was a seagull Max had found on the dock one day, her wing broken at the tip. Risking Jeff's anger, Max had taken a few minutes off to bring the bird to me. Together we made a crude splint and nursed her back to health. The afternoon we took Snowflake out of her box and set her free, I wanted to cry.

Max tried to comfort me. "She's meant to be free, Erica," he said, as our pet became a mere speck on the horizon. "God, how I wish I could feel as free as those birds in the sky!"

There was such anguish in his eyes, I felt a vague, terrible fear. "Max, why aren't you—"

"I have to get back," he said abruptly. Then he was gone.

Max, why aren't you free? my heart called after him. And as I headed back for the café, my heart asked another question: Why don't you ever look at me, really look at me, the way a man looks at a woman?

Yet it was Max's very restraint that made me respect him. His strength of character made him more of a real man to me than Jeff and the others could ever be. Still, I began to hope that we'd grow closer someday, that I'd know the wonder of his lips touching mine. And the more I thought about Max, the more intolerable Jeff's attentions became.

One Friday night Jeff swaggered into the café with a dark look that told me he'd been drinking.

"Hey, Erica!" he yelled. "Come here, baby. I wanna talk to you about our date for the union dance tomorrow night."

Everyone had been talking about the dance for weeks. It was the biggest social event on the waterfront, with a live band, hot food, and enough free beer to keep everyone drunk for a week. With all my heart, I'd hoped Jeff wouldn't ask me, but now he was doing just that and, typically, at the very last moment.

"You wait on Jeff," I whispered to Kristy. Max had come into the café, too, something he seldom did when the place was crowded, and I didn't want him to think I was still Jeff's girl. "I'll take care of the booths," I added.

But there was no subduing Jeff. He strode over to me and grabbed my arm. "I said I wanted to talk to you about the union dance!"

"I don't have a date for the dance with you," I said. "Now let me go."

Someone snickered. Someone else said, "Tell him off good. Atta girl!"

Jeff's eyes glinted, then a slow smile spread across his lips. "You mean you want us to have our own private party, baby? Well, now, that suits me just fine!"

I was conscious of the silence all around us now, the rapt attention and the smirks making me feel like an animal performing in a circus cage. "I mean I've got another date for the dance!" I lied. "So just drop it, will you?"

Jeff's mocking laugh grated on my nerves. "That so? Who's the lucky slob anyway? You, Steve? Or Frank over there? Willy? Speak up, or maybe he's a ghost, huh?"

Suddenly Max's voice cut across the crowd's raucous laughter. "The young lady has a date with me."

Wrenching free of Jeff, I walked over to Max's booth and sat down. He was unusually quiet. Even after the normal din started again, Max didn't have very much to say. As far as I was concerned, though, he'd already said enough and I thought my heart would burst.

The next evening, I looked through my closet like a nervous schoolgirl going on her first date. I finally chose a simple blue dress. Jeff would've hated it because it wasn't flashy enough, but when Max arrived I saw a look of approval in his eyes.

"I've brought you a flower for your hair, Erica," he said, handing me a small florist's box. "I hope you like it."

Tears blurred my eyes as I opened the box and saw one perfect camellia. "It's the most beautiful flower I've ever seen!" I gushed. "Oh, Max, please pin it in my hair for me. I'm all thumbs, I'm so excited."

He smiled as I moved closer, giving him two bobby pins. And for an electric moment, after he fastened the flower in place, his hand lingered gently on my cheek and I saw a flash of longing in his eyes.

So you're attracted to me, after all, I thought before he quickly turned away. But why do you keep fighting it?

The union hall was already crowded when Max and I got there. Colored spotlights circled the dance floor, and along the bar people stood four deep, shouting for beer over the blast of the music.

"I hope you're not sorry you brought me here, Max," I said when we'd found a table. "I know you were kind of roped into it."

He toyed with his untouched beer. "I'm glad I brought you. But I'm not much of a party type, and when it comes to dancing, well, I've got two left feet."

"How about letting me be the judge of that?" I said, standing up and pulling him onto the dance floor.

He held me like a fragile glass doll, and as my hair brushed against his cheek, I thought, I love him!

"You're a wonderful dancer," I said softly. "Just wonderful!"

He looked at me as if I'd paid him a fantastic compliment. After that, the evening flew by like a marvelous dream.

Hours later, when I saw Max stifling a yawn, I said, "Come on, take me home and I'll fry us some ham and eggs."

"Oh, no, you won't!" he said. "You worked at the café all day, and you're not going to do any more cooking."

A funny, thrilling feeling went through me. There he was, worrying about me. And here I was, concerned over him, wishing he'd gain some weight, wanting to fuss over him the way a woman does with the man she loves. The way a wife does with her husband!

The very thought of being Max's wife left me so shaken that I didn't notice Old Rita swaying drunkenly near the bandstand until Max stiffened beside me.

"Come on, Rita!" someone hooted. "Let's see you shake that thing!"

Too drunk to be aware of the cruel laughter around her, Old Rita hoisted her skirt high and started to dance. Soon she was being pulled from one pair of rough arms to another until finally she collapsed in a heap against a table.

Max, his face white, walked over to help her. But two other men had reached Rita first and were taking her home. Max followed them outside. A few moments later, I found him standing in the shadows of the building, still shivering in horror at the cruelty he'd seen.

"Max." I touched his arm. "Old Rita always gets this drunk when there's a party or a dance."

"But it was awful," he choked, "with everyone tormenting her." He let out a long breath. "Oh, well, I suppose it doesn't matter."

But as he bent his head on the way home, I saw that to him it did matter, for there were tears running down his cheeks.

I lay sleepless most of that night in my apartment above the café, thinking about Max Parson. What kind of man was it who could live the hard life of the waterfront jungle and yet have a heart big enough to feel deep compassion for a derelict like Old Rita? But there were no answers in the darkness, only the beat of my own heart crying, I love him, I love him, I love him!

I kept daydreaming about Max all through Sunday. But Monday I had other things to think about, because I knew there'd be trouble on the docks when a new group of pacifists arrived to protest the loading of a troop ship that was going to Iraq.

Frank came into the café late in the afternoon, his cheek bruised from a picket sign some kid had thrust at him. "Them liberals are bad enough," he complained. "But now we got a bunch of religious fanatics, to boot. Call themselves conscientious objectors, no less. It's enough to make you give up religion!"

I served him his hamburger, then heaped on an extra helping of French fries when he gave me a woeful look. "You don't mean that, Frank. Everyone knows you go to church with Nancy and the kids."

"Yeah, six o'clock Mass on Sunday and me usually with a head as big as Old Rita's must've been yesterday. Your friend Parson always looks in good shape, though." He took a few bites, then went on. "If the altar boys don't show, Parson goes right up there and serves for Father Manson himself."

I was a little surprised, since I hadn't gone to church in months and Max had never mentioned that he went. And yet, it all seemed to fit somehow.

"He's some kind of weirdo, if you ask me!" Kristy piped up.

"No one asked you!" I flared in his defense. Yet I couldn't help feeling hurt because Max had told me so little about himself. I longed to share his worries and dreams and hopes and to become so close to him that he could never let me go. I had to break down the strange barrier separating us! But how?

I was still brooding about it early that evening when Max stuck his head in the door.

"Want to take a walk?" he asked.

"You know you don't have to ask twice!" I told him.

Controlling an impulse to slip my arm through his, I walked out to the deserted pier with him. There we paused to watch a passing ship in the harbor. "Wouldn't it be wonderful to sail away on it, Max?" I asked. "And just keep going forever?"

"Forever," he echoed hoarsely, "into eternity."

I looked up at him, trying in vain to read his thoughts. "You're very religious, aren't you?" I suddenly blurted out. "But I never even knew you were a Catholic until Frank told me he saw you in church."

"Why doesn't he mind his own business?" Max snapped in a way that was very unlike him.

"And why does it make you so angry to have me know anything about you?" I demanded frantically. "Why won't you let me get close to you?"

He moved away then, but I plunged on. "If I could only understand you! You've never touched me or tried to kiss me—yet I know you're attracted to me. Oh, Max, aren't you human?"

For a long moment, his eyes searched my face. "Yes, I'm human," he said. "Heaven knows, every time I'm near you I feel more human than I ever dreamed I could be."

"Heaven knows. But I don't!" I lifted my face to his, my eyes brimming with tears, hoping desperately he'd kiss me.

And he almost did. His arms closed around me, and the earth seemed to tilt as I heard the throb of his heart against my ear.

"Erica—Erica—" he moaned. Then he made a sound in his throat that was almost a sob.

"I love you, Max!" I whispered. "Oh, Max . . . I love you."

He moaned my name again before he gently pushed me away.

"No, don't be in love with me," he added in a strained voice. "There are plenty of other men for a girl like you. I—I can never marry you."

The sting of his words made me flinch, and I turned away from him. When I turned back again, he was gone.

I walked for hours, too stunned to mind the cold, too numb to even cry.

I can never marry you. I can never marry you.

The cruel refrain tore through me again and again. How foolish I'd been to think I could ever deserve Max Parson's love. He'd been kind to me, yes, but it was only out of pity—the same sort of pity he felt for Old Rita. I might as well accept the truth. I'd never rise above the grime of the waterfront. I'd never be anything better than Jeff Simmons's girl.

Max didn't come into the café for nearly a week after that. In an attempt to push him out of my mind, I let Jeff take me to the movies on my next night off. After he brought me home, I pulled his head down to mine, kissing his lips eagerly, so the hurting memory of the lips I'd never kissed could be erased forever.

"You feel good in my arms, baby," Jeff said, grinning. "You've been out of them too long." His lips crushed against mine again. "Wised up about that loser Parson guy, huh? I could've told you he's not for you."

At the mere mention of Max's name, I felt a new ache in my heart, and I wanted to be alone. "It's—it's late, Jeff," I said. "You'd better go."

For once, he didn't try to fight me. But before leaving, he said, "Don't make me wait too long, baby. We've wasted enough time as it is."

Maybe Jeff was right. Maybe I was wasting time. Maybe the passion he offered me could turn into love if I gave it a chance. What was I saving myself for, anyway—more emptiness and loneliness? If I wasn't good enough for Max, why shouldn't I turn to Jeff? In the next few days, I tried to make up my mind. I'd almost decided to give in to Jeff the day another troop ship was being loaded and a third group of demonstrators appeared. Somehow, this group seemed more rebellious than the others, and even inside the café I could feel the tension that was mounting outside.

"I'm missing all the excitement," Kristy said when we heard muted shouts late in the afternoon. "Why wait to read about it in the papers? I'm going out."

Before I could stop her, she put on her coat and bolted out the door, and an inner urgency made me close the empty café and follow her.

Others were running toward the wharf, too. I saw the peace pickets being pushed away from the restricted area by burly longshoremen. Then Jeff grabbed one of the hand-painted signs and tore it up.

"I was in Afghanistan," he bellowed, "and I'd fight again now. I'm warning you—you losers—get off my dock!"

The longshoremen moved forward threateningly, and the pickets backed off uneasily. And someone near me muttered, "I hope those kids have got enough sense to go away now."

But suddenly a young boy carrying a bottle jumped on top of a crate. His head was shaved and the veins in his neck stood out like ropes. "Stay!" he commanded the others. Then he turned to Jeff, screaming hysterically, tears running down his anguished face. "We want an end to all killing now! Peace—peace—no more war!"

The other pickets moved back in, taking up the chant and waving their signs with renewed fervor. "No more war!"

"Shut up!" Jeff shouted, glaring at the boy who was standing on the crate. "You punks haven't got a chance to stop our work," he warned. "So why don't you wise up and get the hell out of here!"

The boy stared back defiantly at Jeff, opening the bottle he was carrying. "I'll die for my convictions if I can't make you listen any other way!" he shrilled, pouring the contents of the bottle on his clothing.

When I caught a strong whiff of kerosene, I cried out, "Jeff! Stop him!"

"Shut up, Erica!" he yelled, his rough hands keeping me from running forward "The kid's just bluffing." Then he turned to the protestor. "Go ahead, kid, light a match! I'm daring you, do you hear?"

I looked wildly around me, praying for one sympathetic face. But everyone—even Old Rita—was jeering at the boy.

"We're waiting!" Jeff goaded. "Go to it, kid, so we can get back to work!"

For a horrible moment, there was an ominous silence. Then the boy quickly pulled a matchbook from his pocket. Seconds later a cry of pain cut through the air as long fingers of flame began to devour him.

Several people screamed.

This time I managed to wrench away from Jeff, ripping off my coat as I ran. The boy had rolled off the crate onto the dock, his screams blending with the crackling flames that enveloped him, blackening his hairless head.

"Someone please help me!" I shouted, trying to put out the fire with my coat.

I was sobbing so hard I didn't see the tall figure pushing frantically through the crowd. I didn't see him until he fell to his knees to fight the fire. It was Max. And it was Max who put the flames out with his bare hands, then cradled the unconscious boy in his arms.

"He's dying," he said hoarsely. When no one moved, he stared furiously at the gaping crowd. "Someone call an ambulance and the police!" His voice had deepened with authority. "Right away!"

Several men ran for help and most of the crowd backed away, while Max murmured to the boy. At first I couldn't believe my ears; he was speaking words that only a priest had the right to say. But Max couldn't be a priest! Then, through my astonished tears, I saw his burned hand make the sign of the cross over the still figure. ". . . in nomine Patris et Filii et Spiritus Sancti," he was saying. He had given absolution to the boy.

At that moment, the world seemed to stop. I stood up shakily, thinking, No, no, no! But as Max slowly rose, his eyes meeting mine, I knew it was true. I was looking at a priest!

I can't remember what happened next. I must've told Kristy to take charge of the café. Then I must've gone directly to my apartment. But the first thing I actually recall is sitting on the edge of my bed. I sat there for hours, my mind a blank. I didn't come out of my numb, trancelike state until long after midnight when I heard a thud at the door. I opened it to admit Max. His hands were bandaged.

"Will you take a walk with me?" he asked. "I want to talk to you."

"All right," I said.

As I put on my coat and we started downstairs, I thought, Now the agony of loving him really begins. And I wished I were dead.

Automatically our feet guided us to the deserted pier where we'd almost kissed once. We remained there, talking all through the night. For the first time since I'd known him, Max spoke about himself.

He told me how much he'd loved his mother, who became a widow when he was only a small baby. "As I grew older, I realized I was her whole life," he said. "And she was everything to me. She worked to the bone to give me a good home. Then when I was thirteen, she became very ill. And I thought, Why, after all her misery, does she have to suffer sickness, too? She was in bed for nearly two years and she never complained, not once. But she didn't smile either, unless one of the priests came. Then she shone with a wonderful inner peace."

He sighed softly. "Though I was just a kid, I wanted desperately to make her happy, the way the priests did. And when I asked her what she thought of my becoming a priest, you should've seen the glow on her face."

He paused, then continued slowly. "My mind was made up. She died when I was fifteen, and at her deathbed I promised to become a priest. Years later, after I was ordained, I chose to remain in the cloister of my order. You see, I was afraid to go out into a world I missed more and more every day. And then one morning, the sister of a dying priest was allowed to visit her brother at the monastery. I didn't even see her face. I just smelled the faint scent of her perfume as we passed each other in the corridor."

He turned away from me. "That's when I began to have doubts about myself. But it wasn't just a woman I yearned for, it was life itself—the sound of crowded city streets, kids playing baseball, a sandy beach on a summer day. How I wanted all that again! And how I prayed to be free of my yearnings!

"But when my yearnings continued in spite of my prayers, I finally went to my superiors and asked to go out into the world again."

I drew a shaky breath. "And the vow of celibacy?" I asked unsteadily.

He seemed to be struggling with himself as he answered. "I could've proven I was pushed into ordination against my will because of that rash promise to my mother—and given up the priesthood entirely. But I didn't want that. I felt that after I'd been in the world a while, I'd go back." His eyes swept over my face, then closed in pain. "But now I don't know anymore."

I put my hand against his face. "Max, do—do you want to be free to marry?" I faltered.

"How can I answer that? When I'm with you, I want you very much. But then, when I think of never being able to offer Mass. . . ."

The catch in his voice told me even more than his words. And much as I wanted him, I knew the agony that might be his if I asked him to give up his priestly vocation for my sake. The decision must be his and God's.

"Erica, I—" Max began tenderly.

But I put a finger to his lips. "Don't say anything now," I said. "Go back—for a year. And then, when your heart has told you what to do, I'll be waiting right on this pier for your answer."

Through my tears, I saw him make a helpless gesture with his bandaged hands. The first rays of dawn had just filtered through the misty sky, and far above us a seagull gave a mournful cry. I raised my head to watch the bird's progress over the gray-blue water, knowing that Max would be gone when I looked down again.

Let him come back to me at the end of the year, I often prayed in the weeks that followed. And each evening I walked to the deserted pier, half hoping to find him there. Then I cried a little and returned to the café, where I worked in a daze.

Finally after several months, there were no more tears to shed, and a deep peace settled over me. I was able to sleep once more and keep my mind on the café. And though I knew Max might never marry me, I cherished the knowledge that he had loved me. Now I would never again be tempted by someone like Jeff. And to my amazement, just thinking of Max gave me the strength to sell the café and the courage to start a new life away from the only world I had ever known. A new life with fresh hope.

I bought a small lunch counter on the other side of town and rented a pleasant apartment not too far away. But even as I plunged into a new life and made wonderful new friends, I kept remembering Max. Every day I scratched one more day off the battered little calendar I'd kept since he left.

Then at last, the year of waiting was over. When Max and I had made our date, we hadn't mentioned a specific hour. But I was strangely confident that we would find each other on the pier—though I wasn't at all sure what his decision would be. I closed my lunch counter on the appointed day, and in the afternoon I made my way back to the deserted pier. I stood there for more than two hours before my hopes of meeting Max began to fade. And then as a thick fog closed in on the harbor, I waited some more.

When I finally heard footsteps behind me, every nerve and muscle in my body tensed with renewed hope. It must be. It has to be!

"Erica?" a familiar voice called.

Slowly, very slowly, I turned toward the tall, lean man who was all but hidden by the fog.

"Oh, Max," I choked. "Is it really you? I can hardly believe it."

"I can hardly believe it's you," he said. "It's wonderful to hear your voice again, even though you sound—different."

"I am different. So much has happened! I sold the café and I have a new business now—and wonderful friends—everything I've always dreamed of! And all because of you!"

"I'm glad," he said, and I strained to see him more clearly. "I prayed for you, for both of us."

He was closer now—heartbreakingly close—and for the first time I saw that he was dressed completely in black, except for the white collar around his neck!

"It was wrong for me to think I could ever be anything but what I was destined to be," he continued. "And I was destined to be God's alone—a priest."

"But that was just a rash promise! You said so yourself!"

"I thought so. But I was wrong. Now I know God instilled a true desire in me." Max's hands closed around mine, his beautiful, sensitive hands.

God has so many priests loving him, I thought resentfully. Why must He have Max, too?

Then I looked down and saw that the hands weren't those I remembered. They were ugly, misshapen, scarred, and I recalled how they'd fearlessly fought the flames of death, then blessed a dying boy. They were Christ's hands now, doing His work through Him and with Him and in Him. And for a brief, bittersweet moment, I lifted them to my tear-streaked face.

"Good-bye, Erica," Max said, as I left him. "God loves you."

I walked along the docks, passing some of my customers from the old days. But when no one spoke to me or called my name, I realized with surprise that they didn't recognize me. I was a changed person. The brooding girl, trapped by loneliness and despair, was gone forever.

I lifted my head high. Thanks to Max, I had escaped from the waterfront at last. I had been reborn. I had hope and decency and a future. Suddenly Max's parting words came back to me.

Why, yes, I thought wondrously as the fog lifted and the first stars appeared, God does love me!

The End

THE SOFTER SIDE OF
MY MACHO MAN

The evening had been like a dream—until the car refused to start. A candlelit dinner by the lake, waiters in tuxedos, more forks and spoons than I knew how to use, and a seven-course dinner. Jacob had won dinner for two at the company football pool, and Dylan's was one of the nicest places in town. I was overjoyed when he chose me as his date. There wasn't a single girl at Alexander Electronics who didn't have her eye on him, me included.

I was the newest person there, hired to work the switchboard. I'll never forget my first day on the job. The girl who was supposed to train me, Sarah Dennison, spent most of the day in tears! The reason, she explained, was Jacob Peterson, who had dated her twice only to move on to another woman.

"Stay away from him, Abigail," she'd warned me. "He's the type of guy who uses women to build up his ego. He doesn't care about anyone except himself."

At first, I assumed there was just a little bit of sour grapes in Sarah's assessment, but nonetheless, I gave Mr. Jacob Peterson a wide berth. Besides, I got the same story from several of the other girls. The electronics plant was the largest in the area, and had nearly fifteen hundred employees. Many, like me, were straight out of high school. So what if his bedroom eyes made my heart do flip-flops, and set into motion countless butterflies in my stomach. So what if his smile made my mouth go dry?

As a woman who'd always had luck with guys, I figured a good-looking one like Jacob was the last thing I needed. So, whenever he came around, I did a commendable job of masking my true emotions, and usually managed to feign a highly convincing indifference. Still, I jumped at the chance to accompany him to Dylan's, a restaurant that had always been beyond my means.

I tried telling myself that I'd only accepted because I wanted to see how the other side lived. But, deep inside, I knew I was falling fast and hard for Jacob and couldn't put on my cool, aloof act much longer. Sarah, who'd quickly recovered from Jacob and was currently dating an engineer, told me my indifference toward Jacob was probably what had prompted him to ask for the date. She'd warned me to be on guard, but one look across the candlelit table into his glowing eyes, threw my caution to the wind.

I continued to admire his ruggedly handsome profile while he fiddled with the ignition on his car.

"Darn," Jacob muttered. "I just had this thing tuned up last week. I don't understand the problem. They charged me an arm and a leg, too. These mechanics all seem to think they're brain surgeons."

"You mean you don't tune your own car?" I asked.

He gave me a funny look. "No, I've never had time to get into automotive work. Getting my degree in business management was a full-time job." I guess I must have really seemed surprised because he continued. "Why? Do you tune up your own car?"

"Sure, I always have. My brothers taught me everything I know. Try the ignition again, I have an idea." Jacob turned the key, looking at me as though I'd just asked him to do something outrageous, like rob the corner grocery store or stand on his head.

"Well, Ms. Mechanic?" he said sarcastically. "What's your diagnosis?"

"I don't hear the fuel pump. Since everything sounded so good on the way out, I think you blew a fuse. Do you have any spares?"

He stared back in utter amazement. "I don't think so," he finally admitted, his voice low and sheepish.

"If you just had a tune-up, the mechanic should have changed the fuses and put the extras in your glove compartment. A lot of them do that."

"And I suppose you worked in a garage, before trying the switchboard for a change of pace."

I already had my hand in the glove compartment. Sure enough, I found three small metal boxes of tiny glass fuses. "This ten-amp should do it. Open the hood latch." I took the tiny flashlight attached to my key ring, got out, and replaced the fuse.

"Give it a try!" I yelled to Jacob.

The engine purred like a contented cat. "I don't believe this," Jacob muttered. He sounded miffed and relieved at the same time. "Do you mind explaining now?" he asked as we roared away from the parking lot.

"Sure. You see, you aren't getting any power to your fuel pump if—"

He cut me off. "That's not what I meant. I want to know how you came to be such an expert on cars. I know they let girls into auto shop now, but you have to admit, diagnosing that problem took some pretty fancy thinking."

"Oh, no! It was really pretty simple!" I saw the hurt look on his face and tried again. "I mean, simple if you've seen the problem before with a fuel-injected engine."

He cast a frown in my direction and said nothing.

Feebly, I went on. "I have six brothers. I'm the only girl in the family. I got my first car when I was sixteen, because I needed it for a job on the other side of town. I used to hang around my big brothers all the time when they worked on their cars, so I usually knew how to handle mine whenever something went wrong. When I didn't, I just asked one of my older brothers to troubleshoot for me. It's a good skill to have. Do you have any idea how much mechanics charge these days?"

"Believe me, I know."

"Well, maybe I can show you how to tune this baby up sometime!" I offered brightly.

His frown deepened. "Thanks for the suggestion, but I don't think I have the time to learn. I'd rather pay someone else. There's a new position as project manager opening up at the plant. I'd love to have it," Jacob confided.

"Oh, you don't have to pay! I'll do it for. . . ." I quickly perceived that, for some reason, my generous offer was being taken in the wrong way, and I let the matter drop.

Jacob didn't have much else to say, either. I suppose the long silence must have seemed awkward to him, because he attempted some small talk as we neared my family's house. "How do you like those outdoor tables they installed at the plant?" he asked.

"They're okay," I said rather glumly, hurt by his standoffish attitude.

He parked the car. "Well, maybe I'll catch you there sometime. I think they're great."

I lingered until it became apparent he had no intention of walking me to the door. "Sure," I said. "Thanks for dinner, Jacob. I've always wanted to see what Dylan's looked like."

"Don't mention it. Thanks for fixing my car."

"Oh, I didn't really fix it! I just. . . ." My voice trailed off. "You're welcome. See you Monday."

I raced upstairs to my bedroom, and collapsed in tears. Fortunately, Dad was already asleep and Michael, my fifteen-year-old brother, was watching TV in his own room. If anything, I thought resentfully, Jacob should have been grateful instead of acting like I'd just beaten him at arm wrestling ten times in a row. If it weren't for me, he would have had to call an emergency towing service. One of my brothers had once worked for the only twenty-four hour towing company in town. Joshua told me then that many of the drivers were young and inexperienced and couldn't handle simple problems, meaning Jacob would have wound up having the car towed into a garage, where the mechanic would have charged a hefty minimum fee for a two-minute job.

What did he expect me to do? Sit there like an idiot waiting for the tow truck, just so I wouldn't step on his delicate male ego? Besides,

I saw nothing wrong with a woman understanding cars. I grew up surrounded by dozens of them. Matthew and Ethan, my two oldest brothers, used to supplement their income from building boats by buying old heaps, and restoring them to mint condition. Many was the time that I earned a few dollars here and there during grade school by running down to the corner auto store, and picking up parts they needed. The owners, both men, thought I was cute, with my flowing braids and grease on the tip of my nose.

I just thought of myself as an ordinary kid, making money by helping her older brothers. Frequently, the owners would infuriate me by asking complicated questions about cars in front of the other customers they knew well. They always laughed and got a big kick whenever I got the question right, which was most of the time. They thought they were being real funny, and I felt like they were making fun of me.

Once, at the age of thirteen, I came home in tears, provoked by this situation. I was dying of embarrassment because a cute guy in my eighth-grade class happened to be there with his older brother. They all joined in the merriment, laughing as though I were some kind of a stand-up comedienne. Matthew, my oldest brother, patted my head and sat me down at the kitchen table. He encouraged me to be proud of myself and my skills, and not let any "grease monkeys" intimidate me.

This may sound odd, but Matthew was the closest thing I had to a mother while growing up. Mom died when Michael was only two months old, leaving behind a total of seven children. She was hit by a drunk driver while waiting to cross the street. The man was so out of control that his vehicle actually came up onto the sidewalk. I was only two years old then and really don't remember her. Once in a while, a vague image comes to mind, but I think it's really just based on things my brothers and Dad have told me.

The drunken driver had had his license revoked a year earlier because of a similar accident in which a teenage girl was fatally injured. In other words, Dad didn't collect any insurance money because the man didn't have a policy. Dad took on an extra job, in addition to the one he already held selling used appliances. At nights and on weekends, he clerked in a drugstore. He hired a series of women to baby-sit and do housework, but they never seemed to stay long. I guess there were too many kids, and Dad couldn't really afford to pay top wages.

As soon as Michael started kindergarten, he stopped hiring outside help and let our older brothers run the house. Michael attended a day-care center because kindergarten was only half a day. I would go straight from my second-grade class to the day-care center after school and Matthew, who was a high-school senior then, would pick us up in his car and take us home. Sometimes Ethan or Andrew, two of my other brothers who were also in high school and had cars, would come instead.

The oldest brothers were responsible for most of the cleaning and cooking, although Michael and I helped out as much as we could. Gradually, we came to assume more work around the house, as the older boys married and left home. I can bake an apple pie or cook a great beef stew as well as fix cars. But all my life, I've been bugged by guys who only want to see my domestic side.

I cried until all my tears were gone, and drifted into a restless sleep, thinking gloomily that I'd probably wind up spending the rest of my life living at home with my father.

The next day, Jacob didn't do anything to relieve my fears. He walked by me twice. The first time, he nodded curtly and the second, he acted like I was The Invisible Woman. It was a glorious sunlit day, and Sarah and Ashley, the other girl who works the switchboard, insisted upon dragging me to the outside tables. They wanted to hear all the juicy details about the previous evening.

"Did he try anything?" Sarah asked pertly. Ashley giggled, and munched her piece of the foot-long submarine sandwich we were sharing.

"Not even a good-night kiss," I answered truthfully.

"You're kidding!" Sarah shrieked. "At least I got that far."

"Good for you," I said dryly.

"Hey, what happened?" she asked, more serious now.

I didn't care to go into the gory details. "Nothing. We just didn't hit it off, that's all."

"Well, did you like Dylan's?" Ashley wanted to know.

"It was gorgeous," I confessed. To fend off further questions about Jacob, I launched into a lengthy description of the elegant restaurant.

"Geez, I wouldn't have even the right dress to wear to a place like that," Ashley remarked. "The best thing I have is my senior prom dress, and that's out of style already. And it sure wouldn't be worth buying something new for a guy like him."

"I didn't. I borrowed a beautiful dress from Emma."

"Who's she?" Ashley asked. Sarah continued to scan the tables for interesting men.

"My sister-in-law. Ethan's wife. Thank God we're the same size." I went on to describe the strapless, deep-blue crepe dress.

Sarah interrupted when I got to the part about the flared hemline. "There's Mr. Wonderful," she whispered. "He's with that new girl from manufacturing."

Since the day was so lovely, all of the outside tables were occupied. I shifted around slightly so I could just get a peek at them. The new girl was staring up at Jacob with adoring eyes, and he was scanning around for an available table. My heart sank when the people right next to us vacated theirs. Jacob and the girl made a beeline for it, passing our table on the way.

He greeted each of us by name, speaking to me last. "How's it going, Abigail?"

"Fine. Nice day, huh?" I swallowed the rising lump in my throat and managed to sound extremely pleasant and carefree.

"Fantastic. See you all later." He cupped the girl's elbow and escorted her to the table.

Her saccharine-sweet, high-pitched laughter grated on my nerves while I tried to finish lunch. Jacob was speaking in a quiet, low tone, so I couldn't really hear what they were discussing.

"I'm getting out of here," I whispered to Ashley and Sarah. I had my back turned to them. Ashley filled me in on a scene I could easily imagine.

"I can see why. Boy, is Mr. Wonderful really lapping it up. We'd better all leave before we get too nauseated to take calls."

We returned to the switchboard. For the next two weeks, the pattern continued between Jacob and me. We were polite, but never really friendly. I saw him a few more times with the girl from manufacturing, and after that, there was another new girl. Frankly, I couldn't understand my own emotions. Just what did I see in this womanizer? There was simply some inexplicable essence of him that touched my heart and kept me from sleep on many nights.

I got the shock of my life after one such long sleepless night when I plugged into a line on the board, not expecting anything unusual. "Alexander Electronics," I said automatically.

"Hi there, sweetheart," came the sexy voice.

That really didn't rattle me. I've had lots of guys flirt like that before. "How may I help you, sir?" I replied stiffly.

"By going out to dinner with me tonight. Maybe we'll see a movie afterwards, if anything good's playing."

At that point, I recognized his voice. "Jacob?"

"Who were you expecting?" he teased.

"You'd be surprised by the weirdoes I get on this board."

"Nothing about you would surprise me, Abigail. Are you busy tonight?"

Since he had been so unfriendly lately, I briefly considered making up an excuse, but my heart dictated otherwise. "No, I don't have any plans. I'd love to go out with you." I needed to know what to wear. "Jacob," I asked hesitantly. "Do you have a place picked out?"

139

"How about Dylan's again? You seemed to enjoy it before."

Not anymore, I thought. It evoked too many painful memories, and besides, since the dinner would be coming out of his pocket this time, I didn't want Jacob paying so much. "I did," I hedged, "but to tell you the truth, all the attention from those fancy waiters made me feel a little uncomfortable."

"Me, too," he admitted readily. "And since I have to wear a suit to work every day, I hate getting into one at night. Have you been to that new rib place on Seagate?"

We agreed to go there, and I spent the rest of the afternoon on cloud nine. Of course, I got a lot of teasing and well-intended advice from Ashley and Sarah.

"You're going to wind up getting hurt," Sarah predicted. "I can tell you're trying to deny it, but you really care for this guy, don't you?"

"How can I? We only went out once," I said, evading the truth.

Ashley had something more upbeat to add. "Maybe he really cares about you, too. I swear, Abigail, every time he walks by, he can't get his eyes off you. And I haven't seen him with that new girl for at least a week."

"Oh, big deal!" Sarah muttered sarcastically. "Who knows what Mr. Wonderful has going for him outside work. Be careful, Abigail."

I took her cautions to heart, but that didn't do much to quell the rising anticipation inside me. Even Dad and Michael noticed my excitement that evening while I waited for Jacob to arrive.

"At least I'll be home to meet him this time," Dad said, giving me a playful wink. "This young man is going to have to be something pretty special to pass muster for my little girl."

"Is he the same idiot who didn't know where the fuse box was on his car?" my younger brother asked.

In a moment of weakness, I'd poured out the entire story to my sister-in-law Emma, when I'd returned her dress. I guess she must have told my brother, who in turn broadcasted it to the rest of the family. "If you mention that to him, I'm going to kill you, Michael," I warned.

"Oh, don't worry. I won't blow it for you. I'm just curious to see what a guy that stupid looks like."

I shot him a murderous stare and stood to examine my outfit once more. I had decided on maroon corduroys and a nice ivory-colored pullover sweater, since this morning's sun had given way to a brisk breeze. Like the teenage brat that he was, Michael raced to the door when the bell rang.

"She's over there," he said, jerking his thumb toward me.

I heard Jacob's resonant laughter. "Well, is it okay if I come in?"

"Sure." Michael shrugged and stepped aside to let him enter.

My heart lurched against my ribcage. As hard as it was to believe,

Jacob looked better in his snug-fitting jeans and Western shirt than he did in the suits he wore to work. Not that he wasn't handsome in the other clothes. These just almost took my breath away.

"Hi. I'm ready," I said shyly. "I'd like you to meet my dad and brother before we leave, though." I made the introductions. Michael was his usual, unimpressed self, but I could tell Jacob had made quite an impression on my father.

Jacob must have felt likewise about Dad, because over dinner, he remarked, "You really have to hand it to a guy who raises seven kids on his own."

"Yes, my father's quite a man," I said proudly. I realized I knew virtually nothing about his home life. "What did your father do?"

His smooth brow creased. "As little as possible. He was a drunken bum who ran out on us when I was two."

"Two! I was two when my mother died," I confided.

He reached across the table for my hand. "What happened, Abigail?"

I lowered my voice. "She was killed by a drunk driver."

"Geez, I hope it wasn't my father."

It was a bad joke and neither one of us laughed. "No, the time differences would be off," I said at length to fill the heavy silence. "Were there any other kids in your family?"

"Yes, one. I have a sister who's fourteen months younger than me. She was just a little baby when he took off."

I sipped my iced tea and urged him to go on about his family life. "Did your mother ever remarry? Dad never did, you know." The bitterness in his laughter shocked me. "My mother must hold a world record for that. She's had at least four different husbands, maybe more. I've lost count. They were jerks, one and all. When I was thirteen, I had to kick one out of the house for molesting my little sister. She was barely twelve then."

I squeezed his hand in compassion. "How terrible that must have been for all of you. How did your mother react?"

"She was too drunk to notice for a few days. When I told her, she didn't believe me, but said it didn't matter anyway. She had her eye on another man she'd met at some bar."

I was beginning to understand more and more about Jacob. Undoubtedly, his life experiences had soured him on the subject of marriage, which was probably why he played the field so much. Also, I concluded, he must have spent a lot of time taking care of his mother and little sister, and wasn't used to women like me, who tended to be highly independent.

My intuitions were proven correct as the evening wore on. Hand in hand, Jacob and I took a long walk on Park Avenue. We compared childhood experiences. He made me realize how fortunate I'd been, even though I'd lost Mom at such an early age.

We also discussed other far more pleasant topics, such as the electronics plant, and our outside interests. We had a lot in common— mystery novels, old black-and-white science-fiction films, and classic rock 'n' roll from the sixties.

"Then it's settled," Jacob said, smiling into my eyes.

We were standing in the doorway of Capri's Bakery. The store was closed, but pleasant sweet scents wafted into the night air. "What's settled?" His face was inches from mine. I felt like I could hardly breathe.

"We're going to see that old Lon Chaney movie that's playing at the Seaford Theater." His hands moved to my waist. "I bet you've seen it a hundred times."

"I have, but never with you," I whispered boldly. Just then, his lips met mine in a tender kiss that quickly escalated to something far more intense. Longingly, I leaned against his body.

Jacob was the first to withdraw. "That's about all of you that I can take in a public place, lady."

I was too moved to speak. Silently, I took his hand and we walked to the Seaford, which was two blocks over. In all honesty, I have to say I couldn't concentrate on the movie. With Jacob's arm around my shoulder and our hands locked together, I had other things on my mind. Like love and "happily ever after."

Once back at my house, we shared several impassioned kisses in the front seat of his car before I decided it was time to say good night. Knowing my bratty brother, he was probably observing the scene from inside. Besides, after the slow start, things were moving all too quickly now. I'd never been intimate with a man before, and I didn't want the first time to be with a playboy who was dating me for only the second time. Breathless, and longing for the warmth of Jacob next to me, I congratulated myself for my cool thinking as I drifted into a contented sleep.

Things were different between us at work after that date. We began to meet every day for lunch, and usually saw each other three or four times a week outside of the job. Ashley and Sarah were amazed when our relationship happily entered its third month.

"Sometime you're going to have to give the rest of us lessons," Ashley teased one day when the board was slow.

"I still don't know about that guy," the more cautious Sarah contributed. "I think you're headed for Heartbreak Hotel."

"Maybe," I admitted practically. "But I can't let that prevent me from seeing him now."

"In other words, you're in love," Sarah said, sounding none too thrilled by the prospect.

If she were any other girl, I may have thought she was jealous, but I knew her well enough to know Sarah was truly concerned about me. "I've been thinking a lot about that. I really don't know."

"You're just afraid to admit it to yourself, I bet," Ashley speculated.

"That's fine, just don't admit it to him," Sarah advised seriously. She paused to take a call. "Well, speak of the devil. It's Mr. Wonderful himself."

I picked up the line. "Hi."

"Hi yourself, beautiful. How's your day going?"

"A lot more exciting now." We'd met for lunch two hours ago, but it seemed like ages now. "How's your day going?"

"Routinely. Look, I completely forgot about the company picnic on Saturday. I don't want to go—they're usually so boring—but I feel I should. I'm still bucking for that promotion. It'll be a good opportunity to be around the people who will be making the decision."

"Oh, you mean kiss-up?" I giggled.

Jacob laughed back. "Yeah, right on. But, keep it under wraps, sweetheart. You'll go with me, won't you?"

"Sure, I'd love to." Jacob explained that the picnic was held at a nice city park near the lake, and that we didn't have to bring anything. The company hired people to barbecue burgers and steaks, and cater the rest of the meal.

"Hey, Jacob just told me about the picnic!" I yelled excitedly to Ashley and Sarah. "It sounds like fun! Why didn't you guys tell me sooner?"

"Because it's a drag," Ashley told me. "None of the younger single workers go. It's usually the older, married people who attend."

"It's a pretty dull event," Sarah added. "However, it might be fairly exciting in your case, what with a hunk like Jacob around and all."

Unfortunately, things didn't work out quite that way. It wasn't fun for me at first. Jacob immediately abandoned me to seek out the company of his male colleagues. I was left alone in the company of women I either barely knew, or had never met. At nineteen, I must have been the youngest person there—of the employees, at least. Many teenagers, a few nearly my age, had accompanied their parents to the event.

I don't have any problems in getting along with older women, but in this case, I was bored stiff. Their favorite topics of conversation seemed to be the new grade school that had just been built on Ocean Street, and the rising cost of real estate in the area. Frankly, I didn't care about either. Also, it seemed like whenever I tried to make a polite effort to join the conversation, they ignored me.

After a while, I started to feel self-conscious about my appearance. It was a glorious, sun-filled day, and I'd worn a halter top which bared my tanned midriff. Jacob had teased me that my shorts were bordering on indecent, but I knew that wasn't really true. They covered everything that needed to be concealed quite nicely, but they did fit a bit snugly. All those extra visits to restaurants with Jacob had added a few pounds to my figure.

When I became too restless to sit still any longer, I decided to leave the table. Lunch had already been served, and I was more than slightly perturbed when Jacob didn't reappear, forcing me to eat with a bunch of rowdy kids and other strangers. I found him sitting at a table, which had been hidden from my view by a grove of ornamental plum trees.

Jacob and four or five other men I recognized from work were playing draw poker. I went over to Jacob, standing behind his chair. The table was piled with colorful red, white, and blue chips. I had no idea if they were playing for real money or just for fun. Jacob patted my arm, and the other guys all said hello. They seemed very intent upon the game. He had a good hand, but he blew it by throwing the jack away and asking for three more cards. Christopher Buckley, Jacob's direct superior, took the pot with a royal flush. Mr. Buckley was grinning from ear to ear.

"Nice pot," I congratulated. "That mountain of chips makes the last one I won look like an anthill."

Jacob jerked his head around, a frown slashing his face.

"You play poker, Abigail?" Mr. Buckley asked, his eyebrows raised.

"Sure, since I was a little girl." All of the men, except Jacob, got a big hoot out of that and started laughing. "My older brothers taught me," I added. "There are five of them." The men kept laughing at me, and Jacob's sour expression didn't change.

"Well, are you any good?" William Edwards wanted to know. He worked in personnel, and had interviewed me several months back.

"I guess," I replied modestly.

Mr. Buckley let out another howl of merriment, which was echoed by the other men. "Okay, gents, let's deal the little lady in. Her boyfriend can use a few tips from an expert."

I suppose I should've had the good sense to refuse, but their chortles were making me see red. I wanted to show them a thing or two, and besides, I'd had a dull, boring afternoon. Mr. Buckley and Mr. Edwards scooted apart and pulled up a chair. They dealt me in. Playing poker is a game of chance to a high degree, but it also involves skill and practice. I had plenty of both. During all those long evenings when Dad worked late, I had often joined my brothers in a friendly game. We used to play for buttons, or sometimes pennies.

144

Lady Luck was on my side for that first hand. I had three deuces, and asked for two more cards. I came up with four of a kind, all twos, but they took the pot. Like most beginners, Jacob had made another poor decision by exchanging most of his cards for new ones. I noticed with rising pride that the smirks were fading from the other men's faces. Their patronizing grins were entirely gone an hour later, when most of the chips on the table had mysteriously migrated to my side.

"Those brothers of yours must be mighty fine poker men," Mr. Buckley said.

"They're okay." At first, Mr. Buckley and the other men had appeared annoyed with me, but now it seemed as though I'd won their respect. "There was a period of time when we couldn't afford to have the TV repaired. We did a lot of card playing then."

"You must have," he said cordially. "I hate to quit when I'm behind, but the ladies are going to kill me if I don't get busy on the games for the kids. I'm in charge of that this year. I'll tell you what, Abigail, sometimes we play Friday nights at my house. Would you like to come over sometime?"

"Oh, sure!" I blurted out, never dreaming that one of the most important men at the plant would invite me to his house. Believe me, there wasn't anything romantic about it. He was fat and fifty, and happily married with three kids, and I was head over heels in love with Jacob.

"Good, I'll have my secretary call you. If you can find time to give your boyfriend here a few lessons, he's welcome, too."

Mr. Buckley slapped Jacob on the back and started laughing. The other men joined in and made a few choice remarks to Jacob, who sat there grinning broadly, but I could tell it was a forced effort. He looked like he was ready to explode. The thrill of victory suddenly soured. I was speechless when all the men, Jacob included, opened their wallets and started counting out bills.

"What's this for?" I stammered. They all shoved the money over to me!

"Hey, I thought you were a pro," Mr. Edwards said. "You won. It's yours."

There must have been two hundred dollars in front of me, if not more. The worst part was that at least half of it had come from Jacob's wallet! "I thought we were playing for fun," I murmured, my face hot with embarrassment.

"We were. Money and fun. That's the way it goes," Mr. Buckley said. "Thanks for the game, Abigail." With that, he and the other men left to join their wives and children, but not before they teased Jacob a little more.

Jacob and I were alone at the table. I counted out nearly a

145

hundred dollars. "Here, honey, take this back. I can't possibly keep your money. Honestly, I thought it was chips only, or a nickel-and-dime game. I never expected this."

His face contorted into anger. "Nice going, high roller. You hang onto that. You won it fair and square," he muttered savagely.

"I'm sorry, Jacob. They invited me to play. I didn't ask in. Besides, they hurt my feelings when they started laughing at me."

He stood, pounding his fist on the table. "Laughing at you? Who cares if they laugh at you? Do you realize that you just succeeded in making me look like a complete idiot in front of the people I was trying to impress?"

"I didn't mean to," I said, fighting back tears and my own anger.

"Who cares what you meant! Don't you ever think about anything besides showing off all your unusual talents?" he demanded.

I leapt to my feet, hands on both hips. "Don't you ever think about anything besides making yourself look good all the time? About building up your male ego?" I didn't let him intimidate me one bit. As a girl who grew up with five older brothers, I was used to holding my own in arguments with men. I never once backed down from them, and I wasn't going to let Jacob scare me now.

"I'll see you later," he ground out. "Much later."

I looked up and saw the girl he used to date—the one from the company picnic tables whose name I didn't even know—staring at us in open curiosity. "Fine with me. Why don't you go see her?" I said, jerking my head toward the girl. "I bet she doesn't know the difference between a poker chip and a cow chip!"

"Yeah, but she sure knows how to treat a man."

With that, he actually strode off and joined the other girl! Fighting back tears, I walked slowly to the bus stop. There was no way I could return in Jacob's fancy car.

I spent the evening hovering around the phone, praying Jacob would call and things would be all right again. He didn't, and I had too much pride to go crawling back to him. Dad and Michael knew I was upset. They both tried to help, but I wanted to be alone.

"Did you get in a big fight with Jacob?" Dad correctly surmised.

"I really can't talk about it now, Dad," I told him.

Awkwardly, Michael placed his arm on my shoulder. "Don't worry about it, sis. All my friends think you're a total fox. You'll have lots of other guys coming around."

I was touched by his efforts to comfort me. "Michael, do you remember that dirt bike you're saving for?"

He looked puzzled. "Of course, I remember it. It's all I think about. Why?"

I went upstairs and retrieved my purse. Michael and Dad were spellbound when I dumped out the wadded bills. "Here, you can have this. I won it at the picnic."

Michael's eyes bulged. "I can have it? There must be a thousand dollars here!"

I smiled a little. "No, but there's two hundred and twenty-four."

"Close enough! Sis, are you sure? I mean, this is a lot of money."

"I'm sure. I don't want any part of that money." On the verge of tears, I retreated to my room and cried myself to sleep.

Predictably enough, Jacob didn't call the next day, nor did he have anything to do with me at work. The story about how I'd beaten the guys at poker was all over the plant. Ashley and Sarah had even teased me about it, although they dropped the subject when they saw how miserable I was.

"If it's any comfort to you," Sarah said one day when we were alone in the rest room, "my boyfriend said Jacob is as miserable as you are. Ryan said he mopes all the time."

"I bet he has that dizzy girl to console him," I sobbed bitterly.

"No, Ryan said he's not seeing anyone. He also said his work is suffering. He can't seem to concentrate on anything since he lost you," she related.

"Lost me! He dumped me!" I wailed. Sarah rested her hand on mine. "Look, Abigail, I hate to come to Mr. Wonderful's defense, but maybe you should meet him halfway. He was really bucking for that job, and you did make him look like a jerk in front of all the top guns. Ryan said everyone is still teasing him about it. Jacob takes it well, but I have a hunch he's really hurting deep down, not just because of the promotion, but because of you. Give Mr. Wonderful a break."

Just then, another woman, someone I barely knew, entered the rest room. I hastily said good-bye to Sarah and raced into a stall. I've always hated for people to see me crying. Finally, I composed myself enough to finish the day. By the time the clock struck five, I'd come to a decision. Hands trembling, I rang Jacob's office. I'd heard through the grapevine that he was working late nearly every night.

He was stunned to hear my voice. "Jacob, is that you?" I asked when he didn't say anything.

"Yeah," he said in a dull voice.

I couldn't quite make out his tone. "I think we should talk."

"I'm listening." Now, he sounded distant and removed.

My stubborn pride rose, but my love prevailed. "Not like this. Not on the phone. And I don't want to meet you at your office. I'll be at your apartment in an hour. Meet me there if you want to talk." Quickly, I hung up.

I had never been to his apartment for the simple reason that I knew what would happen not long after I crossed the threshold. I'd been putting off lovemaking, because I wanted the first time to be special. As much as I loved Jacob, he'd yet to utter the magic words, "I love you." And I was well aware of his aversion toward marriage, and his past, which included countless women. I didn't know what lay ahead, I only knew I had to tell him what was in my heart while I still had the courage.

I drove home, showered, and changed my clothes. I didn't pay much attention to my outfit, choosing the first things I saw in the drawer—an old pair of jeans and a worn blue T-shirt.

I almost laughed when Jacob answered the door wearing nearly the identical outfit, except his T-shirt was a little darker blue. "You have great taste in clothes," I tried. My heart went out to him. The poor man looked completely exhausted.

"So do you. Maybe we should go to Dylan's," he replied, his smile very tired.

"They'd kick us out the back door."

He invited me in. "Somehow, I find the idea of anyone kicking you out of anywhere extremely difficult to grasp."

"Jacob. . . ." Unexpectedly, he took me in his arms. His lips found mine. "Jacob," I uttered again, gasping for breath. "I came to talk." I could feel his heart pounding against mine through the thin material.

"I only have three words for you, Abigail." His eyes burned bright in the dimly lit room.

The air felt trapped in my lungs. "If it's 'Get out of here,' I'm going to die."

He kissed the tip of my nose, his arms locked around my waist. "That's four words, nincompoop."

"Jacob, please. Don't tease me, not now." I moved my hands along his back, reveling in the firm, rippling muscles.

"Okay. I'm sorry. It's just that I'm not very good at this. I've never said it before. I love you. I want you to marry me. I've been miserable without you." He let out a deep breath and grinned. "There, did I say it right?"

"Oh, yes! No one could have said it better! I love you, too. You have no idea how miserable I've been!"

"If it's a fraction of how miserable I've been, then it's a lot, sweetheart. Go call your father and tell him you won't be home tonight."

"Jacob! I can't do that! I'll call and say I'll be very, very late. He'll fall asleep and be gone for work before I'm home."

His lips brushed across my forehead. "No bed check?"

"No bed check. Dad raised a very independent girl, remember?" I tried to conceal my serious tone, but I knew we still had a great deal to work out.

"Do I ever! I hear about his independent, unusual girl every day at work! Oh, by the way," he added casually. "I got that promotion today."

"You did! I'm so happy!" I squealed in delight. After I calmed down, I suggested we talk.

"Later," he said, snuggling against my hips.

"But, Jacob."

"No buts. I know what we have to discuss and you know what we have to discuss. We'll do it over coffee in the morning. Not now." He kissed me soundly on the mouth.

"Definitely not now," I said when I came up for air.

After a long, tender, and passionate night of lovemaking, Jacob and I talked. We discussed big words like tolerance, understanding, and mutual respect. It's hard to remember who had the most apologies, me or him. Jacob decided he wanted a break from work before tackling his new job, so we made plans for an immediate wedding ceremony and honeymoon.

With Jacob's encouragement, I left the switchboard a few months after our wedding, and interviewed for a job in manufacturing. My experience with cars transferred well into the tiny electronic components the plant produces. Soon, I was working at much higher pay. Jacob and I are saving for our first home now, and deciding when to begin our family. We are two strong-willed people and everything hasn't been perfect. We've had several fights, but each one seems to bring us closer together. We're learning people can be independent, but that a good marriage involves a lot of give and take. Every day I pray that I'm giving as much as I take.

The End

THE LITTLE TRAMP
WHO RAN OUR HOME!

Gene drove the car skillfully through the late afternoon traffic while I relaxed at his side. I glanced at his handsome face, and the smile he gave me was dazzling. His eyes sparkled—the look in them made me tingle all over.

We'd known each other since high school. By the time we graduated from college we both knew there'd never be anyone else. Our parents wanted us to wait a few years before marrying but we were determined. And it had worked. We were still in love after five years of wedded bliss. Even now—in the car going home from work—Gene's nearness excited me. . . .

We both had good jobs in the same bank, but not on the same floor. Unless we met for lunch we didn't see each other all day. And I could hardly wait until we met after work and started home.

Our home was about five miles outside the city limits—almost rural—and we loved it. Sometimes, before starting our late dinner we'd take a swim in the pool, make love, and just lie peaceful and happy in each other's arms.

"What are you thinking about? You have the most idiotic grin." Gene's deep voice broke into my thoughts as his hand caught mine, sending thrills of delight through me.

"I'm not going to tell you—you'll only make fun of me."

Gene laughed, showing his even white teeth, his eyes crinkling at the corners. My very bones melted. "Erica, you're as transparent as glass." He laughed as he pulled the car into our driveway.

"Oh, no, I hope not," I answered while getting out of the car. Before we could say more, a taxi screeched into the drive. A man in a Navy uniform bolted out and crushed Gene in a bear hug. Then it was my turn—I felt like my ribs were crushed.

"My God, you two look wonderful." Slapping Gene on the back, he continued in his merry voice. "Marriage sure is good for you. Gene. I never saw you look better, but then, I imagine pretty Erica has something to do with it."

"Vince! It's good to see you! You haven't written for over a year—we were wondering where you were." Gene hugged his younger brother again. As they laughed into each other's eyes, I couldn't help seeing the love they shared.

Vince was younger than Gene, and after their parents were killed in a plane crash, Gene was a parent as well as a brother to Vince. But no matter how hard he had talked, Gene couldn't make him go to college. Then when we were married, Vince had enlisted in the Navy. This was the first we'd seen him for over a year.

"Say, do I sit here all day?" My jaw dropped as I stared at a young sexy blonde in tight jeans and a sleeveless sweater getting out of the taxi. She had on high-heeled shoes and she swayed slightly. "Say, honey, aren't you going to introduce me?" She caught Vince around the waist as he paid the driver, and the taxi sped away.

Turning back to us, Vince's face was as shining and proud as at a child's first Christmas.

"Gene, Erica, I want you to meet my wife, Winnie." Vince's arm was around her and he looked so happy.

"Hello, Winnie," I said, and taking her hand I pulled it through my elbow and started up the walk. "When did all this happen? I'm so happy for you both." I was chattering like an idiot, but I couldn't help myself. It was such a shock. No word for over a year—and now this bombshell!

I could hear the murmur of the men's voices behind us as I led Winnie into the kitchen.

"Please, sit down. I'll mix drinks before I change. Gene and I usually have a cocktail before we eat. What would you like?" I stood at a loss in front of the refrigerator, watching her cross her legs and light a cigarette before she answered.

"Champagne will be fine for me. Vince taught me to drink the bubbly and it spoiled all other drinks for me." She laughed tipsily and looked around the kitchen. "Vince sure is wonderful to me. Anything I want, he gets it almost before I ask." Looking me up and down with her blue gaze she murmured, "He said you were a good looker," as her eyes traveled over me again and then through the door into the spacious dining room. "He said you and his brother make lots of money." She blew smoke through her nose as she studied me.

Well, I thought, as I opened the bottle of champagne, she sure isn't coy. I couldn't imagine why Vince didn't see through her before he married her. My God, anyone with half a brain could spot her kind! Then I chided myself severely. Stop it, Erica! This is Vince's wife, and if he's happy and satisfied, why should you care? After all, they'll probably be here only a short time, so be pleasant, make them welcome.

My mind was whirling with all kinds of questions as I cut ham and cheese and placed raw vegetables on a snack platter. Vince and Gene had come into the kitchen, opened cans of beer, and were talking and laughing a mile a minute. Winnie had gotten up and draped her arms over Vince's shoulders. She leaned against him so he had to talk over her blond head. I thought it crude, but it seemed to make no difference in the men's conversation. Occasionally, Vince kissed Winnie's bright curls and she snuggled closer.

I slipped from the room and went upstairs. Changing into slacks and a cool cotton blouse I suddenly felt old and prudish. Then I caught sight of my reflection in the mirror and laughed aloud. Erica, you idiot, why should you be jealous? You're ten times prettier than Winnie and more poised and mature. And God knows that pretended childlike innocence of hers will soon wear thin. Surely, Vince will come to his senses before long. And then what? After all, they're married! Well, it's Vince's problem, not mine, or so I thought then.

Days went by, and each evening when Gene and I got home we could see Vince and Winnie frolicking in the pool or lying on chaises drinking champagne. Or at least she was. Vince always had a beer. Each time I left work and met Gene to start home, I prayed silently that a note would explain their departure and we'd have our home to ourselves again. But no such luck. The drive home had always been a very pleasant time for Gene and me. Now we rarely talked, and it seemed that every time he did ask me something I was rather gruff in answering. If I answered at all, mostly I just said, "I don't know."

Our happy evenings and late dinners became a burden for me. It seemed like cooking for four was so much more tiring than fixing a meal for two. Winnie, of course, never helped with a thing. Sometimes, Gene helped, but then Vince would be in the kitchen, too, and our intimate moments were spoiled. Besides, if the men stayed too long with me, Winnie's petulant voice called for more drinks or someone to rub her back.

Before Vince and Winnie came, Gene and I would accept invitations from our friends once a week, and always had a party of our own over the weekend. Now we stayed home. I missed the talk and banter of our own crowd.

Not that there wasn't talk now. Gene and Vince never quit. And believe me, I really enjoyed seeing them so happy—I just felt so left out! Winnie couldn't go anywhere without a portable radio that blared incessantly. Unless she was smooching Vince or drinking champagne, she just sat and hummed along with the radio. How did she put all that booze away and still keep her looks and figure? I wondered for the twentieth time.

And then, four weeks after their arrival, we came home and found a suitcase and Navy bag on the porch. Vince and a tearful Winnie were cuddled on the wicker loveseat.

"What's all this?" Gene's voice was full of concern. I remained silent, hoping. I didn't speak, afraid my voice would betray my real feelings.

Vince detached himself from Winnie and approached Gene. "Can

I talk to you alone a minute?" They wandered down the path bordered by flowers and came to a standstill beside the pool.

Trying not to sound so happy and relieved, I asked Winnie if I could get her something to drink. Thank God this would be the last bottle of champagne I'd have to open for her. As I took the tray to the porch, a taxi came into our drive. As Vince and Gene approached the drive, She started crying wildly and threw herself into Vince's arms.

Gene walked over to me, and, putting his arm around my waist, whispered, "I'll explain later, sweetheart."

With Winnie clinging around his neck, Vince leaned over and kissed my cheek. "So long, Erica, you've been great." He wrung Gene's hand again, detached himself from Winnie, and got into the taxi alone. As it sped away, I had the overwhelming desire to throw myself on the walk and scream and kick.

Winnie collapsed into Gene's arms. He helped her into the house while I stood in dumbfounded silence. Suddenly, I felt as old as time, and my feet dragged like lead as I went into the house. Gene was coming out of Winnie's room as I reached the top of the stairs. I could hear her sobs and felt no pity, and no guilt at myself for being so heartless.

Inside our room, I walked to the window and stood, stiff with anger, looking out. Gene came over and put his hand on my arm. "Erica, let me explain."

I threw his hand off and walked away from him. I suddenly sat down on the bed. I'd no strength left in my legs. "How long, Gene? How long will she be here?" My voice was toneless and harsh.

"Sweetheart, only till she can find an apartment."

"But I thought they gave up on living here. Vince said he was taking her along to San Diego where they could live on base."

"Honey, it's only for a little while." He came over and tried to take me in his arms. I pushed him away and walked over to the window. "Gene, did you know before today? I mean, that Winnie would be staying?"

"Well, Vince had asked. But it's only temporary, sweetheart, I swear."

"I don't care if it is temporary—I should have been consulted. I live here, too, you know."

"Honey, I know you do, but honestly, when he first asked me, I thought he was kidding." Gene was walking the floor, running tanned fingers through his blond hair. He stopped and faced me. "Then later he said to forget it, he guessed he'd take Winnie with him. Then when he mentioned it again, I thought it best not to say anything to you until he and Winnie made up their minds."

Gene spread his hands in a helpless gesture, his face looked drawn. "Erica, what do you want me to do? Throw her out? Say no to Vince for the first favor he ever asked of me?"

I turned away and stared out the window, so angry I was afraid to say anything.

"Besides, honey," Gene continued when I remained silent, "his leave has been cut short. He's being sent on some mission that he volunteered for several months ago, before he married Winnie. That's why he took me aside down there—he wanted me to explain to her after he left."

"I don't give a damn about that." My voice was quaking with wrath as I swung around to face him. "You'll have to get rid of her. I won't live in the same house with her and you can't expect it of me."

"For God's sake, Erica, why not? True, she isn't your idea of a great lady, but she's only a kid. Vince thought you could, well, he said being around you might change some of Winnie's ways." Gene's voice trailed away and he looked at me, his eyes pleading.

"If he wants her changed, why did he marry her in the first place? And I don't have time to babysit. In case you didn't notice, I work every day and my evenings are taken up being a champagne waitress."

"Oh, for heaven's sake, forget it! I'm sorry I promised Vince. I'll start looking for an apartment for Winnie tomorrow." Gene was tearing off his jacket and tie, throwing them on a chair. Then he went into the bathroom. I could hear the shower running as I boiled in silence. As I turned back to the window I caught my reflection in the vanity mirror.

I stared in horror. My face was flushed and hard, my brows drawn in a frown, and my lips pressed in a thin line. Altogether, it made a distasteful picture. For a moment, bitterness and despair flooded through me. Why? Why? We'd been so happy! And next year we'd been planning on a family—our own child. Now, hundreds of dollars out of our savings had been spent on steaks and champagne, and God knows where it will stop. Why must our plans be put on hold to accommodate someone else, why? I can't bear it, I just can't bear it!

And yet, if I went on like this—being hard and unforgiving— would Gene ever forgive me? What if I had a brother, and Winnie were his wife?

Gene came out of the bathroom with a large blue towel wrapped around his waist. As always, I felt a thrill of desire sweep through me. "Gene, I'm sorry. Will you forgive me? I'm being unreasonable, I know." I sat on the edge of the bed watching Gene get clean clothes from the bureau. "It's just that we had such great plans of our own." My voice drifted into silence as I felt the anger drain away from me. God, why did I have to love and want him so much? I lowered my eyes.

I didn't know he'd crossed the room until his hand tilted up my chin. Our eyes met, and suddenly we were smiling, then laughing. Then I was reaching up and pulling him down onto the bed. His lips were buried in my hair, muffling his words. "Sweetheart, I know, believe me. I don't like this any more than you do. But he's my only brother, Erica, and I love him. I couldn't say no."

His arms crushed me. "I know it isn't fair to you, but I was hoping you'd understand."

I put my hand across his lips. "Gene, please don't say any more. It's my fault—I should have been more receptive to Winnie instead of being so jealous."

His laughter rang out and my whole being rejoiced. "You, jealous of Winnie? My God, Erica!" His laughter choked him and he lay on the bed in helpless mirth. For the first time in weeks, our lovemaking was spontaneous and fulfilling. Afterward, we lay in contented repose. While Gene slept, I kissed his moist brow and wished this moment could last forever.

But as hard as I tried, I couldn't get Winnie into a receptive mood to any of my proposals. She had no interest in cooking or cleaning. Reading was a "bore," shopping and the hairdresser's were a "drag."

I'd never seen anyone with such aversion to the words "look for a job." To Winnie, employment meant getting a tan beside the pool while drinking champagne and listening to the portable radio blaring in her ear. I had to admit to defeat and I took my frustration out on Gene. The bitter words brought no release to me and only a baleful look to his eyes. Each evening he retired to the study earlier and earlier, saying he had piles of work to do.

Knowing Winnie's type, it wasn't any surprise when she started getting restless. One evening as we were having coffee on the patio, she asked Gene if she could borrow the car.

"Sure, Winnie, if it's all right with Erica."

"Of course," I murmured. A dread I couldn't explain swept over me, but I kept quiet. I went into the kitchen, put our remaining dishes in the dishwasher and started it. Looking out the window, I saw Winnie talking to Gene. Her red lips were smiling as she reached up to caress his cheek with her hand. I couldn't hear through the closed window, but I didn't have to—I saw Gene reach for his wallet and hand her some money. A veil of red drifted across my eyes and the blood was pounding in my ears. I caught the back of a chair for support as I tried to control my racing emotions. One look at my face was all Gene needed when he came into the kitchen.

"Erica, what do you want me to do?" He came close, but didn't touch me. "We won't miss the few dollars I gave her, and let's face it, it can't be much fun for her, either. Evenings here haven't been pleasant."

"And I suppose that's my fault. But you see, Gene, I just don't have much time to entertain you and Winnie. I've already given up our leisure time by the pool to tidy up the kitchen after she's been popping corks and soiling glasses all day. Then I make our meal, which, of course, she can't help with, and go over my own papers from the office. By then it's almost bedtime. If you like, though, I suppose I could hire a three-ring circus to perform for you and Winnie each evening." My words were clipped and sarcastic.

"Really, Erica, that's beneath you. Do you dislike her so much? She's only a child, you know. Give her a break."

"She wasn't too much of a child to get married! And children don't swill booze all day and want to run around all night. My God, Gene, can't you see through her?"

"Erica, I'm not blind. I'm just trying to keep some kind of peace here till Vince gets back. I thought with her away we could have a few hours to ourselves. Darling, let's not quarrel. I hate it when we bicker." Gene took me in his arms and rocked me gently. The sweetness of his embrace drove the anger away and I yielded to his kisses. After all, an evening alone with Gene, in our own home, was too precious to be wasted.

Once Winnie got a set of car keys she was never home evenings. Most of the time she'd be gone when we got home from work. Sometimes, she waited to ask Gene for money. It made my blood boil, but I kept quiet. At least we could have our drink and swim and relax beside the pool again.

But somehow it wasn't the same. Both of us knew we were only trying to hide our fears and misgivings under a banter of chatter and play-acting. As we lay beside the pool, our hands touching, I knew we were thinking the same thoughts, but neither of us had the nerve to put it into words.

Where was Winnie? What was she doing? It was always past two a.m. when we heard her climb the stairs. Should we interfere? After all, she was living in our house, using our car, our money. She never brought any friends home and I hated myself for what I was thinking. But I wasn't going to risk spoiling my time with Gene by quarreling over Winnie.

Vince had been gone for five months when things got so bad that Gene finally lost his temper. It was about two-thirty a.m. on a Saturday. We'd been home from a party since midnight and were sleeping when drunken voices woke us. Hastily, I pulled a robe around me but Gene stalked into the hall in his pajamas, fury written all over him. Snapping on the light we saw a man trying to help Winnie up the stairs. They were both drunk and laughing, taking turns drinking from a bottle.

"What the hell is going on, Winnie? Who is this man?" I'd never heard Gene speak so harshly.

"Oh, hi. Want a little drink?" Her voice was high and slurred. She stumbled as she tried to take another drink while climbing the steps. Gene caught her and held her steady while he confronted the man.

"Just who are you? And who the hell do you think you are to be bringing Winnie home in this condition?" Gene set her on the steps and started down toward the man. The stranger backed down, holding out his arm to ward Gene away.

"Look, mister, she was at the party—couldn't let her drive—not so good at driving myself." He laughed drunkenly. "But you should be glad I got her this far. She sure makes a party, though." He stumbled backward and bumped against the door. Turning, he wrenched it open and bolted into the darkness.

Winnie had passed out. Gene picked her up. As he passed me on the way to her room, I noticed her green pallor and the messy state of her clothes. Too bad Vince can't see her now, I thought.

Half an hour must have passed before Gene came back to our room. I just could not force myself to go and help him. I was too disgusted. Bitter words were on my tongue but the look on his face stopped them. "Is she all right?" I asked, half ashamed.

"Yes, I guess so. I never saw anyone so sick from drinking." He sat down on the bed and passed his hand across his face.

"Gene, what are we going to do? I think you should get in touch with Vince. He ought to know."

"Good Lord, Erica, no! This would kill him." He lay back on the bed, his arm across his face. "I'll talk to Winnie in the morning."

"That's what you said before, but it never happened. Frankly, Gene, I'm fed up with this." I was walking the floor in agitation. "If Vince wants to be married, then let him make a home for his wife. Why do we have to put up with this?"

"Erica, it's late. Let's not quarrel tonight." He reached up and snapped off the light. I could hear his sigh as he rolled onto his side. I took off my robe and lay down beside him.

"Darling," his voice sounded tired, "I promise, tomorrow we'll talk, all three of us." He drew me close. "I thought at first she'd settle down. I don't mind Winnie not working, but she could be helping you more." He kissed my cheek tenderly. "You've been wonderful, sweetheart, and there were times when I admired your self-control because I knew you wanted to lash out at her. I know she's young, and lonely without Vince, but tonight was the end. I won't have her running around on him—not while she's living here. And from now on, no more money and no more using the car."

The next morning, Gene and I got up late and had a leisurely breakfast. We didn't mention Winnie and the night before. After reading the Sunday papers, we rode our bikes and it was almost noon when we got home. Winnie still hadn't made her appearance.

"I'll see if she's okay while you make some iced tea. But remember, honey, not too sweet," he said teasingly, as he brushed the back of my neck with his lips and left the kitchen. I smiled to myself as I fussed about, making the drink, not too sweet—one tablespoon to a quart was too much sugar for Gene.

I wasn't really watching the time, but after a lengthy absence, I became worried and went in search of Gene. He wasn't in our bedroom and I couldn't believe he was still trying to arouse Winnie. Nevertheless, when I stopped before her door, I heard Gene's voice raised in anger. Stepping inside, I saw him helping Winnie out of the bathroom. She looked ghastly. I helped get her to bed and brought a cold washcloth for her head. I glanced at Gene's face and saw he was white with rage, his lips closed in a tight line.

"What is it?" I asked.

He walked to the windows and stared into the bright late morning sunshine. Keeping his back to me he said tonelessly, "Winnie's pregnant."

"Oh, my God!" I sank into the nearest chair and covered my face with my hands. For a minute I wanted to kill her. How dare she shame Vince and abuse the hospitality of our home? The slut! I ran from the room, slamming the door furiously, hoping it hurt her already-aching head.

I was beside the pool before I came to my senses. Where was I running to? And why was I even running? It wasn't my problem. Or was it? Could I have prevented this outrage by being more loving toward Winnie? No matter now—this had to be faced squarely, and immediately. My first thought was to call Vince home. This was something you couldn't write in a letter. But we hadn't heard from him for over four months. If Winnie received any letters, she didn't share them with us.

My mind was whirling so fast I felt dizzy. I kicked my shoes off and sat on the edge of the pool, my feet dangling in the cool water. I don't know how long I sat staring into the blue depths trying to calm my rage.

Gene finally came out of the house with a tray of drinks—not my iced tea—I guess he knew we both needed something stronger to steady our nerves.

"Oh, Gene, how could she?" I blurted out. "Did you call Vince?"

"No, I didn't." Taking a long sip, he sat down on a chaise close by. "Winnie told me Vince's on some secret assignment. Her letters go to his commanding officer's office and are forwarded. Vince can't send any messages out at all."

"Do you believe her?"

"Yes. I just got off the phone, and everything she told me was confirmed. If you remember, Vince tried to tell me something when he left Winnie here—we just didn't believe him."

"That's no excuse for her behavior," I said angrily. "It's not fair that we have to bear this burden. Doesn't she have any family we can get in touch with?"

"I don't know. But I wouldn't do that anyway. I feel kind of responsible for her. I thought I was being good, getting her out of our hair. It seemed so easy, a set of keys, a little money. . . ." Gene got up abruptly and paced back and forth.

"Gene, don't start that. You're not going to make me feel guilty. Anyone could see she was a tramp. How on earth Vince ever married her is beyond me, and the quicker we get rid of her the better." I stopped in horror, wishing I could take the words back. Gene's face was white and stricken, and suddenly, I was sobbing uncontrollably.

"Forgive me!" I covered my face, tears running through my fingers. "I just hate her for doing this to Vince, hate her for upsetting our peaceful existence when we were so happy." I looked up and met his eyes. "What are we going to do?" I said tearfully.

He pulled me close, cradling me on his lap. "I don't know, Erica, but we've got to stop bickering." His lips caressed my wet cheek, his breath fanned my face. "We can lick anything as long as we stick together. I can't stand it when we quarrel. I love you so, sweetheart. Help me find a way till Vince comes home."

His arms held me tight and I could feel his heart beat. A warm tide of love washed over me. I felt ashamed. I knew if it had been my family, Gene would have supported me—I had to do the same for him—no matter what my feelings toward Winnie really were.

"I'm sorry, darling. I let my anger get out of hand. I shouldn't have said those things." I was sitting up, mopping my face with Gene's handkerchief.

"It's all right, Erica, it's my fault, too. I should have given Winnie more of my time, made her feel more at home, more like one of the family." His hand brushed my hair back from my forehead. "Just giving her a car and money to get rid of her. No wonder she feels like a poor relation!"

Well, she is, I thought to myself, then flushed with shame for being so unfair.

It didn't happen overnight, but slowly, a change did come about. I think Winnie knew she'd gone too far this time and Gene really meant what he said. Her condition left her weak and helpless, and she knew she needed us. Also, I think she was scared, and why not? She really was just a child, only nineteen. Somehow, she seemed to cling to me and I couldn't understand why. After all, I'd been cold and heartless, but her eyes followed my every move when we were in the same room.

After her morning sickness passed, she was constantly peeking over my shoulder in the kitchen. I thought it was because her appetite was coming back.

"Winnie, would you like me to make you something special?" I asked kindly.

"Oh no, Erica, I just like watching you. I used to cook a lot, long ago." Her voice fell silent and for a minute she was lost in thought. Then she smiled. "But you do it so much different." Her voice was bright again.

"Would you like me to teach you?"

"No, I guess not, but I could try something, and see if you and Gene like it. On my own, I mean." Her face was flushed and she appeared so shy.

"All right, Winnie. If you need anything that isn't here, tell me and I'll get it." Popping the casserole in the oven I asked, "When did you cook a lot?"

"When I was still home. I was the oldest. I have three brothers, Mom died—" Her eyes were sad and it was the first time she had ever mentioned a family. Again, she drifted into memories.

"And," I prompted her.

"Well, I just did all the cleaning and cooking. Pa was always drunk, hitting or kicking us." For a minute, she was rebellious again, then she started to set the table for me. "Anyway, I ran away. Tomorrow I'll fix supper. I'll surprise you." The smile she gave me was sweet and sincere, and for a minute, I could see how Vince had lost his heart. She didn't talk about her past anymore, and I thought it best to let it alone.

Since the day she'd told Gene about her pregnancy, there'd been an uneasy truce among the three of us. Gene had really raved, telling Winnie off in no uncertain terms. But for all his abuse, she had remained still and silent and downcast.

When the tirade had passed over Winnie's head and the tears flowed down her pale cheeks, Gene had stared at me helplessly and walked out of the house. And then, to my horror, Winnie had turned to me—me, the one who'd been cold and, yes, cruel to her. Her eyes had been pitiful as she had begged me to let her live with Gene and me until she could think what to do.

She wanted to explain how everything had happened, but I stopped her, feeling compassion for her for the first time. She was so young and if I had been more like a sister instead of a shrew, maybe I could have helped her protect herself against aggressive men.

But were they to blame? Winnie was very forward. What if the man had been a gentleman? But when a young, lovely woman invites advances. . . . My mind was so tired, and no amount of regrets would change the facts, so for the sake of peace, we all started to play a dangerous game of pretend.

160

I came back to reality as Winnie finished with the table. "Erica, could I ask a favor of you?" Her voice was low and timid.

"Of course, dear." The endearment had slipped out unconsciously, but with unexpected amazement I found I didn't want to take it back.

"Well," she stammered, "I can't very well look for a job now, so I thought, if it's okay with you, I could help more around here." Her eyes met mine squarely. "Time goes so slowly." Tears filled her eyes. "It's so painful to think all the time." I could hardly hear her. "I don't want to be paid for anything. God knows there's no way I could ever repay you and Gene for what you've done for me already." She straightened up and held onto the chair back. "But it would fill some time, to help, I mean, if it's all right with you."

From then on, Winnie had a meal ready almost every night. And it was good. Not exactly the way I'd have done it, but Gene and I both liked her cooking, and praised her meals truthfully. She also took over the laundry. I'd always sent it out, but she insisted it wasn't any strain and she liked using an automatic washer and dryer.

Although Winnie showed very little yet, I thought she needed something besides jeans and sweaters, so one Saturday while Gene was golfing with his buddies, I took Winnie shopping. Before we entered the mall, she put her hand on my arm, stopping me. "Erica, I know you're being kind because I'm Vince's wife. I also know this is distasteful to you. I just wanted to say I'm thankful and I'll pick cheap things—and somehow, pay you back." Her face was flushed and vulnerable and a wave of sympathy engulfed me.

"Winnie, I don't want to be paid back. I know this is hard to believe, but I want to do it." Our eyes met and held. "I won't lie and tell you I loved you from the start, or pretend I approve of the way you became pregnant. But, somehow, you're becoming the younger sister I never had. And frankly, I'm beginning to enjoy it." Looking deep into each other's eyes, we burst out laughing, and entered the mall like schoolgirls.

Although I didn't know it then, from that day I started walking on dangerous ground. I never neglected Gene—God knows, I loved him dearly and my bones still melted at his touch and our lovemaking was as ardent as ever, but so much of my time was spent now on reading mother-to-be books, talking to Winnie about her plans for the baby, giving her books on names and then giggling over outrageous foolish names to call "him" or "her" or "them." Often, I caught Gene's expression as he watched us. Later, I was to remember the speculative look I saw there.

The hours Gene and I didn't meet for lunch I spent shopping for baby clothes and toys. I'd grab a sandwich and coffee to eat in my office. Over the weekends, Gene helped Winnie and me redecorate the room next to hers for a nursery, all cream and white and pale yellow. Even on rainy days, it looked like the sun was shining through the sheer ruffled yellow curtains. It was like being wrapped in a warm, cozy cocoon. I spent hours alone there, just dreaming about the baby.

A month before the baby was due, Winnie shattered the serenity one evening while we were finishing our meal. Her hands folded demurely on her lap, she looked at Gene and me prudently. "Erica, Gene, I must tell you something. I've written to Vince."

"Oh, my God, Winnie!" My fork dropped on my plate with a sharp clatter. "Why did you do that without consulting Gene or me?"

"Because I knew I'd let you talk me out of it." She held up her hand to stop me. "Wait, Erica, let me tell you. Vince had to know. I couldn't let him walk in here and see me this way. If you'd been counting, you'd have realized his special assignment ended a month or more ago."

She didn't cry, but her lips quivered pitifully as she continued. "What I wanted to tell you is this: I wrote to Vince telling him everything and asking him to make sure he wanted me before coming here. I don't blame him if he never wants to see me again. I did an unforgivable thing, and I guess he thinks so, too, because I haven't heard a word from him."

She wiped away her tears. "I'm getting off the track—what I started out to ask you is, may I stay here until the baby comes? I know I have no right, now that Vince doesn't want me, but I promise I'll get a job and move the minute I can."

"Of course you can!" Gene and I said at the same time. Until Winnie mentioned his name, I'd forgotten all about Vince, thinking it was only Winnie's baby. And, God forgive me, wishing it were mine— thinking that if he never came back. Winnie and the baby would stay with us always.

She got up and hugged us each in turn. "I've come to love you both so much. I can never tell you how grateful I am." She left the room, and I got up to follow, my face stricken.

"Let her go, Erica. She needs a few minutes alone. And besides, I want to talk to you." He caught me around the waist and changed my direction toward our living room.

"I know you'll be angry hearing this, and rightly so, but Vince called me two weeks ago. He'd received Winnie's letter and he was roaring mad." We were sitting on the couch, Gene's hand holding both of mine. "I let him rave. I figured he had every right to blow up. But when he calmed down, and I got a word in, I told him to think about it a while before he came to see Winnie. I said that harsh words and yelling wouldn't change the situation."

Gene's eyes held mine, and his voice was soft and low, as though he were explaining something to a child. "I told him we were going to take care of her until she could be on her own—and much as we wanted to see him, we wouldn't have Winnie upset just now." He stopped and gathered me close. "Did I do right?"

"Oh, darling, I love you so, and you did just fine. But I think you should see Vince. I know how you have missed him." I kissed his lips and said, "We won't mention a thing to Winnie, but call him. Brothers should be together and talk things over. She wouldn't want to keep you apart."

Again I was shoving aside that awful moment of truth, but I just couldn't face reality yet. And then, a few weeks later, Winnie gave birth to a beautiful, perfect seven-pound baby boy, and all our joys were fulfilled.

Tears sprang into Gene's eyes as Winnie asked if she could name the baby after him.

"I'd like to call him Charles Gene. Charles for my father, though most of the time he never acted like one. But also because Charles means 'strong man' and with just a mother to raise him, my son will need all the strength he can get." She smiled as her hand stroked the soft baby hair. "We could call him Little Gene for short."

From the minute Winnie and Little Gene came home and I got my hands on him, he was mine. Never had life been so sweet! If there was a seventh heaven, I was in it—until Gene and I came home one night and found Winnie and Vince in the kitchen with the baby between them.

Vince hugged and kissed me. "Hello, Erica. You look radiant, as usual." He hugged Gene and, of course, they fell to talking and opening beer. My eyes sought Winnie's and suddenly, fear rushed over me as I saw the joy and hope in her eyes.

Gene and Vince were leaning against the sink, facing Winnie and me, and from their expressions, I knew doom was descending for me.

"Erica, I want to thank you for taking care of Winnie." Vince's eyes met hers and they smiled intimately. He came over to me then and took my hands. "Gene told me how great you've been, and Winnie has never been so happy. She always wanted a sister, and you're the best." He kissed my cheek, and then the bomb fell.

"Erica, I've found a furnished apartment in San Diego. Winnie and Little Gene and I are leaving in the morning. I know it took me a while to wake up, but I do love Winnie very much, and I can forgive her. After all, what happened is partly my fault, too.

"Neither of us had grown up, especially me. I should have been a better husband, not left her alone so soon. The Navy offered me a desk job, but I thought. . . ."

Vince stopped and walked away, looking at Gene, and I saw the love and understanding pass between them. "Anyway, I want you to know you're always welcome in our home."

For a minute, all was silence. "Erica, you will visit, won't you?" Vince's voice was full of compassion.

"Of course she will! How could I get along without her?" Winnie came over and put her arms around me. Suddenly, I had the feeling of being treated like a child.

"But, Winnie, you don't have to leave. After all, Vince, it will be lonesome for her in San Diego, not knowing anyone. She can stay here." I'd swung around to face Gene and Vince. "We'd love to have her and Little Gene, wouldn't we, darling?" My hands reached out to clutch Gene as panic raced through my veins.

"Erica, my wife and child must be with me from now on. I did a lot of growing up in the last few weeks, and I know Winnie went through hell these past few months. But that's all over now." He draped his arm across her shoulders and the look they gave each other should have made my heart sing. "Erica, be glad for us. You helped make it possible, you know, you and Gene."

Vince picked up the basket with Little Gene sleeping peacefully inside and the three of them left the kitchen to Gene and me.

For a minute, shock kept me motionless, then I swung on him. "Stop them! Oh, please, don't let them take Little Gene away! What will we do?"

Gene caught me close, pressing my head into his shoulder. "Darling, it's their decision." Then mockingly, "Don't you want to be alone with me anymore? Have I lost out to Little Gene?"

"It isn't that. You know it. But they can't take the baby, he's too little. Tell them!" I was crying now, really scared. "Ask them to let Little Gene stay here until they get settled, that's all. They need a little time alone, don't you see?"

Tears were streaming down my cheeks and I let them fall unheeded. Once I'd cried almost this same way, wanting to be rid of Winnie and her baby, but now everything was different. I loved her like a sister and Little Gene was almost like my own. I clutched Gene's shirt. "We can't let her go. Stop Vince. Please, Gene, do something! Don't you see, I—we can't live without the baby." My words were incoherent and he shook me roughly.

"Stop it, Erica. You're acting like a fool. Stop it, I say!" He shook me again as I tried to pull away from him.

And then I suddenly collapsed against him, my arms going around his neck. He let me sob until no more tears came. Rocking me gently in his arms, his words slowly penetrated through the fog in my mind. I became aware of what he was saying. "Darling, I'm so sorry. I'd have spared you this anguish, but I was powerless, helpless to stop the coming storm, so to speak." His words trailed away as I drew back and looked into his eyes.

"What do you mean?" I demanded, wiping my wet cheeks with my fingers.

"Oh, Erica," he said gently, "I watched you glory in a pregnancy not your own, and knew you were headed for grief. But each time I tried to talk to you, it was like trying to move a mountain. You just shut me out completely. You didn't want to hear the truth."

My eyes looked into his piteously. He drew me close again, kissing the top of my hair tenderly. "You have to accept it, Erica. You must give in with good grace. You wouldn't really want to spoil their happiness, would you?"

He looked deep into my eyes and I saw the love there, and for the first time, I felt a twinge of guilt. "After all, of the three of us, you worked the hardest to make a happy ending. And even though it wasn't the one you planned, don't you think you can be gracious and let them go without a storm of tears?"

We clung together again and my heart almost broke as I heard him whisper, "I love Little Gene, too, darling. It will be unbearable for a while, but it'll also be a joy to have you to myself again. I love you so much."

I was proud of myself the next morning as we said goodbye to Vince and Winnie. As I cuddled Little Gene for the last time. I smothered him with loving kisses, but I held back the tears. And I held them back each day, first out of respect and love for Gene, and then because it didn't hurt as much as I thought it would.

In no time, Gene and I were back in our old routine. True, we missed Winnie, Vince, and the baby, and they were in our thoughts and words frequently. I called Winnie once a week—Gene and I both put our ears to the receiver to listen to Little Gene's first gurgles. When gloom and despair overtook me, I worked off my frustration by repainting the nursery a beautiful azure blue. The woodwork was a sparkling white as were the sheer curtains.

"Erica, are you trying to tell me something?" Gene asked one evening as he caught me rearranging the crib for the tenth time.

"Oh, Gene, I wish I were." I put my arm around his waist, and we looked out the window to the pool. I knew we were both thinking of Vince and Winnie, seeing them again in our minds, frolicking in the pool. And then Little Gene, so soft and sweet.

"Don't cry, sweetheart. You've been so brave these past three months. It's all right. I don't mind as long as I have you." He kissed me tenderly.

"Are you sure? You don't hate me for not being pregnant, do you?"

"Erica, how could you even think such a thing?" He shook me playfully. "I think we're both trying too hard. We should relax more, forget everything." A gleam came into his eyes as he said mischievously, "How'd you like a trip to San Diego? We could stay a while, that is if you—" I stopped his words with a loud smacking kiss, laughter on my lips and joy in my eyes.

"Oh, Gene, when can we go? I know Little Gene will be our inspiration, and it will be so wonderful to see Winnie and Vince again."

"Erica, there you go again, transparent as glass," he said teasingly, catching me around the waist.

"Oh, Lord, I hope not." My voice choked with emotion, and I knew a blush was staining my cheeks as our lips met, but I didn't care.

The End

"COME AWAY WITH ME!"

Hudson was there waiting for me when I stepped off the train at Ciara del Fuego into the hot September desert air. He hadn't changed a bit in the five years I'd been away—the same warm eyes, the same denims and Western shirt that he said add just the right touch to Bensonville's old and only hotel, which he operated. I saw the bright, eager smile that broke out on his face when he saw me, and I knew that when things had settled down a bit, he would propose to me again.

"Melody!" He caught me in his arms for a big hug. "It sure is good to see you!"

"It's good to see you, too, Hudson. As a matter of fact," I added, looking around, "it's good to see the desert again. I missed it in Houston."

Hudson collected my luggage and we climbed into his huge station wagon that had Morgan Hotel emblazoned on the sides.

"How's Grandma?" I asked, getting straight to what was weighing most heavily on my mind.

Hudson swung the car onto the two-lane highway. "She's a crusty old gal for eighty-four," he said with a smile, "but her old bones aren't what they used to be. The arthritis is fierce. She can hardly get around."

"Poor Grandma," I said softly, remembering how energetic she used to be.

"Was that the only reason you gave up your job in Houston and came home—to take care of your grandma?" Hudson asked a little too casually.

I looked at his profile against the plains of the desert that slid by the window. "I don't know," I answered. "I guess I wanted to see you, to try to sort things out."

"I was so afraid you'd find someone in Houston," he said.

I touched his arm. "I met a lot of people and I dated a lot. I'll admit there were one or two guys I was interested in." He glanced at me quickly and I hurried on. "Not in love with, Hudson, just interested in. I guess I decided the city folks weren't for me. Right now, I just want to take it one day at a time for a while."

We pulled off the highway and climbed the short hill into town. The Morgan Hotel stood at the end of the main street, dark brown against the desert.

"The hotel looks good," I said. "How's business?"

"Great," Hudson replied. "Especially in winter. The tourists flock in and eat the home cooking, explore the old silver mines, and visit the history museum and the ice-cream parlor."

167

When we pulled up in front of Grandma's little house, my heart quickened. It had been my home ever since Grandma took me in after my parents were killed in a mudslide that destroyed our house when I was ten.

Hudson brought in the luggage as I ran through the gate and burst in the front door. "Grandma!" I called.

She came from the kitchen, a smile cutting across her no-nonsense face. "Hello, Melody," she said.

I squeezed her tight and kissed her. "It's so good to see you, Grandma."

She pulled away. "Now, you stop your fussing, Melody, and sit down here at the table. You, too, Hudson. I just happen to have some apple turnovers." It must have cost Grandma a lot of time and pain to make those turnovers, but that was like her, always doing for others without complaint.

"You're looking good, Melody," Grandma said. "I can't for the life of me think why you're moving back to Bensonville."

"The city's not for me, Grandma," I said lightly.

"What are you going to do out here?" she asked.

Hudson gave me a significant look. I knew what he was thinking and I dropped my eyes. "I don't know. I'll get a job if I can, maybe at the museum. Mrs. Quentin told me she could use some help if I ever decided to come home."

Later while Grandma was taking a nap, Hudson and I took a walk east of town, climbing up the hills.

Hudson talked about how he had bought the hotel from his dad, who wanted to retire early. The hotel had been in the family for four generations, since it had first been built during the boom days. Hudson was content with the desert life and didn't want to leave.

He and I had grown up together and had begun dating when I was seventeen and he was a few years older. Our dates weren't terribly exciting because there wasn't much to do in Bensonville. There were chocolate sodas at the ice cream parlor, hikes in the desert, and horseback rides together. Sometimes we explored the old silver mines, and sometimes in the evening, I'd sit with him and the guests in the hotel lobby to watch television.

Hudson proposed when I was twenty, but I had a hankering to see the big city, and I didn't know if I was in love with him. In fact, I wasn't even sure what love was. That was one of the things I was hoping to discover in Houston, where I found a job in an office. I'd never experienced the intense passion for one person that I'd read so much about, though, and I was convinced that the kind of love described in books and movies was just make-believe.

I wanted to get married and have children. The memories of my early childhood were happy ones, and I knew that now, at the age of twenty-five, it was about time I settled down.

I looked at Hudson as the lowering sun glinted off his hair. He'd said he loved me, and whatever I felt for him, it certainly included friendship and respect. He turned suddenly, caught me looking at him, and smiled. "What are you thinking?"

"I guess I was thinking about you," I admitted.

His grin broadened. "That I like to hear. Why don't we take a rest?" He drew me over to some boulders and we sat down.

"I told myself I'd give you a couple of weeks to settle in, and then start dating you again, but. . . ." He looked at me, his eyes earnest. "Oh, heck, Melody. It's like you've never been away. I just don't feel I could know you any better than I do now. What I mean is—I still want us to get married."

"I sort of figured you did, Hudson," I said softly.

"Could you live in Bensonville, Melody?"

I nodded. "That's no problem. I love the desert, and if I ever get itchy feet, Houston is only a hundred miles away."

"I love you, Melody," he said, taking my hand, "and I'll take real good care of you." He slipped an arm around my shoulder and slowly brought his lips to mine. The kiss was sweet and gentle, and I could tell he was holding himself back.

He looked at me. "Do you love me?"

"I want to be with you, Hudson," I said. "I like your company, I respect you, and we're good together. I care about you and what happens to you, and I think you would make a good husband and father. I guess that spells out love, doesn't it?"

As I said the words, I realized that that was what my relationship with Hudson was going to be. I knew he had a more intense feeling for me than I had for him, but I also knew that we could have a good life together and that I could be fulfilled. That was a lot, more than most people had. Why hanker after the moon?

Hudson gave a joyful laugh and pulled me into his arms. "That's good enough for me!" He gave me a resounding kiss, then pulled me to my feet and we started the long descent into town.

When I told Grandma the news, she merely nodded. "You don't expect me to act surprised, do you?"

I laughed and kissed her. "Hudson and I will move you into a ground-floor room at the hotel," I said. "That way, I can look after you."

"I'll do no such thing," she said, chin up.

"Grandma," I said firmly, "you need looking after. Please be reasonable."

"I'll be as reasonable as a judge when the time comes," she said. "Right now, I still want my privacy and my kitchen."

The following week, I spoke to Mrs. Quentin and got myself a job at the museum. The pay wasn't much, but the work was interesting and I met lots of nice people.

On Monday, the day the museum was closed, I went over to the hotel. Hudson wanted to show me where we'd make our living quarters.

"I think you're really going to like it, but remember, you can make any changes you want to," he said as he unlocked the door to the three-room suite on the third floor. The rooms were sunny, cheerful, and comfortable, filled with lovely, cozy furnishings.

"Hudson," I breathed, "it's really lovely. I couldn't be happier."

He pulled me into his arms for a long, deep kiss, and I felt I was going to like life with Hudson just fine.

When we returned to the lobby, Hudson introduced me to one of the guests, Ryder Cameron, who was waiting for Hudson to take him on a tour of the silver mines.

Ryder's eyes had a snap to them and they trapped mine for a moment as we shook hands.

The two men invited me to come with them, and as we hiked to the first mine, Ryder told us that he was fascinated by American history and that this was his first visit to our part of the country.

"Where are you from?" I asked.

"Green Bay," he answered.

Ryder was tall with broad, muscled shoulders, and he looked at home in his jeans, cowboy boots, and denim jacket.

"You don't look like a city man," I said. "You look like you just rode up from Arizona."

Ryder laughed. "As a matter of fact, I did. I worked on an Arizona ranch for a year. Now I'm heading on up to Utah for another job. I'm through with cities."

I smiled. "So am I. I just deserted Houston."

Hudson led us into the silver mine then and the talk turned to history.

After a half hour, we returned to the sunlight, and the heat hit us like a blast from a furnace. Back at the hotel, we sat in the lobby and washed the dust from our throats with tall glasses of iced tea. When I got up to go, I asked Ryder how long he was going to be in Bensonville.

"A week or two," he told me. "Then I'll go on up to the gold country before heading into Utah."

"I hope you enjoy your stay," I said. "Be sure to come by the museum. I'd be happy to show you around."

That night, sitting over sodas in the ice cream parlor, Hudson and I set a wedding date for early December. We would have made it sooner, but I wanted time to prepare for a proper wedding in the little church, and Hudson had some business to attend to.

He hoped to get the hotel designated an historical landmark, which would involve a couple of weeks of meetings in Houston with members of the National Committee on Historical Landmarks, plus a lot of forms to fill out. "If it works out," he said, "it will mean a little extra funding for keeping the place up, and I think it will give the hotel added appeal to the tourists."

Two days later, I drove Hudson into Ciara del Fuego to catch his train.

"See you in a couple of weeks," he said, kissing me soundly.

The next day, Ryder came into the museum. "Hello, Melody."

My heart jumped at the sound of his voice and seemed to race for a few beats. I turned to look at him. "You—you startled me."

"Sorry." His smile was as warm as I remembered it. "I've come to take you up on your offer."

The museum wasn't much, just two small rooms with old photographs on the walls, mining tools and equipment on display, glass cases of Indian artifacts, silver-threaded rocks, and a few gold nuggets. There were some old books and yellowing diaries and logs kept by the mining engineers.

I gave him some of the history that Hudson had skipped the other day and answered his many questions. Some of his questions stumped me.

"I've never known a tourist to want such thorough information," I said.

"I told you I'm a history nut. As a matter of fact, I used to teach history in a Green Bay high school."

I smiled. "You're full of surprises."

He smiled down at me with those dark eyes, and my heart started to thump again. I turned away.

"I—I better get back to work," I said.

"It's closing time," he reminded me. "Let me buy you a soda—or we could go to the bar for a drink."

I knew I should be going home to help Grandma with supper, but I found myself saying, "Okay. A soda would be nice."

When the frosty glasses were before us, Ryder said, "Tell me about yourself, Melody. You know I'm a schoolteacher from Green Bay who has chucked it for the life of a ranch hand, but what about you?"

"I'm getting married to Hudson," I blurted out. Then my cheeks burned as I saw a teasing smile light his lips.

"I gathered that," he said. "But there's more to you, isn't there?"

So I told him about my childhood and my folks being killed and

171

my living with Grandma and my working in Houston. "It's not very fascinating," I said. "Now I'm home to get married."

"And live happily ever after?" he asked.

"Of course," I said firmly.

"What happened in Houston?"

"I told you."

"I mean about men," he said, the teasing glint back in his eyes. "A pretty woman doesn't live in Houston for five years without a little romance."

"Not that it's any of your business," I said tartly, "but, well, there were a couple of men, but no one special."

He took a sip of his soda. "Well, there was a very special woman in my life, but just as I began to learn that I wasn't a city man, I realized she was a city girl. So it ended."

"I'm sorry," I murmured.

"Don't be," he answered shortly. "Somewhere in this world is a woman just for me."

I returned his gaze for a moment, and for a split second, I thought I saw the depth and passion of the man in front of me.

I rose awkwardly. "I—I better go home," I said.

"All right. I'll walk you."

I had an impulse to run, but then I scolded myself for being silly. What in the world was I afraid of?

That night, I couldn't sleep. Images of Ryder tumbled in my head. I tried to concentrate on Hudson and his smiling face, but it kept turning into Ryder's rugged, chiseled features. Impatiently, I got up and opened the bedroom window.

What was the matter with me? No man had ever upset me the way Ryder had and certainly not Hudson. Hudson was hometown, Bensonville, comfortable as an old shoe. He was a part of my life and would be until the end of my days. Ryder was a burr under the saddle.

Monday morning, after fixing breakfast for Grandma and making her comfortable, I pulled on my boots and struck out toward the desert hills behind town. I needed to be alone. I was annoyed at Ryder Cameron for being in my life, if only for a few days, and I was annoyed at myself for being annoyed. What difference did it make that I'd met a man who set off sparks? That was all they were— sparks, bright flashes that died in the air before they could start a fire anywhere. I reached the low ridge of the hills and had rounded an outcropping of rock when I stopped short.

Ryder was sitting there, leaning against the rock. His eyes flickered over to me and he smiled.

"Can you imagine—there are people in this world who have never known the solitude of the desert?" he asked.

I didn't answer. When I stilled the jumping of my heart, I was aware of something else—a sixth sense clamoring in my brain. My eyes swept the ground and the bushes, pausing at stones scanning boulders. Then I ran my eyes carefully along the base of the outcropping. I saw what I knew was there.

Gliding slowly toward Ryder in the shadow of the rock, its forked tongue darting, was a rattlesnake, a diamondback almost five feet long. It paused and moved its head from side to side.

"Freeze, Ryder. Don't even breathe," I said softly.

He looked at me steadily a moment before he realized I wasn't playing a game. His body stilled to a statue.

"It's about two feet away from your left hand," I said. "I'll distract it with a stick. When I say so, move out."

Swiftly, I pulled a stalk from a creosote bush and moved toward the snake. Its tongue flickered, picking up my presence. As I circled around, scraping the stick on the ground in front of it, it followed me with its head. I drew closer, threatening it, and it began to pull its long body into a coil. It was turned away from Ryder now, concentrating on me.

"All right," I said softly. "Move."

Ryder pulled his left hand up and rolled into the sun, standing quickly. I threw down the stick and ran back a few steps. Ryder looked at the snake and gave a low whistle.

Suddenly, I was trembling all over.

"You darn fool!" I cried. "Didn't you learn anything in Arizona about snakes?"

In two steps he was beside me, grabbing my shoulders. "Hey, take it easy."

"Don't you know about snakes taking shade by rocks? This isn't Green Bay, you know!" I pushed angrily at his chest.

He pulled me a few yards away from the outcropping and held me tight. "What's the matter with you? You're shaking like a leaf. I should think you'd be used to snakes."

"I am!" I said violently, the tears stinging my eyes. "I was scared that you . . . It was so close. . . ." I was amazed at my own fear, at the thudding of my heart. Then I was aware that he was holding me tightly against his chest, his eyes boring into mine.

"You were frightened for me, is that it?" he demanded.

I wrenched myself from his arms and ran blindly down the slope.

I heard his voice calling, "Hey, Melody! Wait a minute!"

I kept running. Strange emotions tore at me like shards of glass. I'd never panicked over a rattlesnake before, yet I couldn't stop my trembling. It was more like I'd walked into a cage of lions. I heard Ryder start down the hill behind me.

173

My boots slipped and skittered on the rocks. I tore through bushes and kept going. I knew the entrance of a small mine lay ahead, hidden by brush. I slid down the embankment, crashed through the bushes, and let the cool darkness envelop me. I moved a few yards into the dark tunnel, and then leaned against the cold, rocky wall, panting for breath.

As my heart began to calm down, I heard Ryder push through the brush and enter the tunnel. I raised my head and saw him silhouetted there.

"Melody," he said softly. He moved slowly toward me. I had nowhere to run. He stopped a foot away, and we stared at each other through the gloom.

"Melody," he said again, and something in my heart cracked. With a cry, I was in his arms, and we were kissing, quickly, frantically. We sank onto the cool earth and then I was holding him to me, responding with kisses and caresses, caught helplessly in the new emotions that seared me.

"Melody, Melody," he murmured hoarsely.

Everything about him—his touch, his kisses, his voice, his strong arms—were natural, a part of me, and I arched my body against his with all the fierce love that suddenly burned in my veins. All else was forgotten.

Afterward, for a while, there was the sheer sweetness of shared love. He held me against his chest, and I felt a peace I'd never known. His fingers played in my hair. "Oh, God, Melody!" he whispered. "It's taken me thirty years to find you."

I caught his hand and held if against my cheek. "I thought I'd loved, at least a little," I said. "But it was never like this. Never."

"I love you, Melody," he whispered.

"I love you, Ryder," I answered softly, "with every part of me, body and soul."

Then the world came crashing in.

"Oh, Ryder!" I said, a sob catching in my voice. "I'm engaged to Hudson!" The guilt brought me surging to my feet. Hastily, I shook the dust from my clothes, pulling them on quickly. How could I have let such a thing happen? Where was my sense of decency and fair play?

Ryder stood beside me. "Just tell him, Melody. There's no other way."

"I can't," I said. "It's so cruel!"

We moved to the mouth of the tunnel and pushed through the bushes into the daylight. The sun was already far over in the western sky.

I turned in the direction of town, but Ryder held my arm fast.

"Melody," he said, "nothing and no one should stand in the way of what we have. You know that."

"It's odd," I said, trying to feel my way through my confused emotions. "I met you five days ago, and yet I feel I've known you forever. I've known Hudson all my life, but he's a stranger compared to you."

"Then you'll have to tell him. He'll get over it."

I looked at Ryder, the tears standing in my eyes. "Will he? I don't think that I'd ever get over it if I lost you."

He pulled me into his arms and held me close. "Just as soon as Hudson gets back, we'll tell him. Then we'll leave." He held me at arm's length to look at me. "We have so much to talk about," he said, smiling. "I'll be a ranch hand in Utah for a while, but I want to save to buy my own spread. Is that okay with you? Could you be a rancher's wife?"

I smiled and nodded.

"Oh, Melody," he said. "We're going to be so happy."

I kept Ryder's words locked in my heart the next few days. I danced on a razor's edge of emotion—joy and guilt, happiness and anguish, wanting to tell the world yet afraid of the town's grapevine.

Many times I wanted to tell Grandma, but every time the words were on my lips, I drew back. I dreaded her sharp disapproval of my betrayal of Hudson. He loved and trusted me, and I had done something to him that he didn't deserve.

Whenever Ryder and I could snatch precious moments together, we escaped to the cool of the mine tunnel and planned our future or made passionate love.

Grandma wasn't so old and ill that she couldn't pick up vibrations, though. One evening, she sat me down and asked, "Whatever is the matter with you, Melody? You're nervous as a cat."

I looked at her quickly. What did she know?

"Is it getting married that does this to you, child?" She shook her head and smiled to herself. "Well, I expect maybe it is. I guess I just forgot what it was like."

I knelt beside her rocking chair, bursting with the happiness and the wretchedness that filled me. "Grandma—"

"I know, Melody, I know," she said, patting my hand. Then she began to talk. She told me things about her life that I'd never known. I knew she'd been twice widowed, but I didn't know the details.

"My first husband was so much in love with me, but I was too young to appreciate it," she said softly. "I wanted a husband and a home, so I married him. He took sick three years later and died. No long after, I met your daddy's papa. For the first time, I knew what love meant but your grandpa wasn't a very affectionate man."

They'd moved to Bensonville where Grandpa got work in the mines. Daddy was born, and ten years later, a mine accident had killed Grandpa.

Grandma was silent for a moment, then continued, "I didn't want to marry again. I just stayed on here with my memories and the house I shared with John. Your daddy grew up, moved away, and married. But I was content." She looked at me. "It's a contentment I know you'll find, too, Melody."

"Grandma, there's something I—"

"I want to tell you something else, Melody," she continued, almost as though she hadn't heard my anxious words. "I'm glad you're marrying Hudson, not just because he's a nice young man, but because it's like repaying a family debt."

"What do you mean, a family debt?" I asked.

"No one knows this. Your dad didn't even know." Slowly, she told me what had happened. Grandpa had bought the house and the small parcel of land it sat on. It was all paid for by his toil and sweat in the mines. Then Daddy, as a child, had become seriously ill with meningitis. The doctor and hospital bills were staggering, especially for a simple miner. Grandpa had taken a loan from Hudson's father, Curtis Morgan. He had given Mr. Morgan a "quit-claim" deed on the property as security. Then a few months later, he had died in the mine accident.

"I knew about the deed," Grandma said. "I went to Mr. Morgan to say I was ready to leave the property, but he wouldn't hear of it. He insisted I stay. He wouldn't even talk about repayment of the loan." She sighed. "Then when Hudson bought the hotel and other properties from his dad, I went to him and reminded him about the deed. He said he had no intention of closing on the property, either." Her eyes filled with tears. "I've never in my life known people to be so generous." She looked at me. "If it hadn't been for Hudson and his daddy, I wouldn't have had any place to live—I wouldn't have been able to take care of you and raise you."

I was stunned. Grandma and I owed the Morgans our home and our lives together, and I was going to pay them back by destroying Hudson's trust, breaking my promise of marriage and possibly breaking his heart, and running off with Ryder. A cold fist closed over my heart.

"So you see, Melody," she said, "your marrying him will be like a gift. In time, this house and property will be yours and Hudson's—just as it ought to be."

"Oh, Grandma!" I choked.

"There, there, child," she said. "You mustn't take it hard. Just be glad that there's a way at last of repaying the Morgans' kindness."

When I was in bed at last, I lay there shivering. It was a warm desert night, but the shaking racked my body. I couldn't leave Hudson. I couldn't possibly do anything so selfish. I owed him and his family everything.

My heart cried out to Ryder, the only man I ever loved, the only man I would ever love. It was lost now—our love was lost forever.

When I met Ryder in the mine the next afternoon after work, I told him everything. He just sat and looked at me, anguish in his eyes. When I finished, there was a long silence. Then, suddenly, he pulled me into his arms and held me so tightly I could hardly breathe.

"I know you feel you have to do what's right and honorable, Melody," he said hoarsely. He looked at me and smoothed back my hair. "I could say to you, come away with me, anyway. Love is too rare and too priceless to be forfeited, no matter what the reason. I could say to you that Hudson will get over it, and that even you and I will forgive ourselves and forget eventually."

He kissed my lips gently. "But I can't tell you those things, Melody. You have to make the decision. You have to make your life so that you can live it without guilt—and without regret."

The tears spilled from my eyes at last, and I sobbed against his chest as he held me tight.

When I quieted down, he wiped the tears away.

"Hudson is going to be home the day after tomorrow," he said. "I'll wait three days. If you haven't come to me then, I'll know what your decision is."

"Oh, Ryder!" I cried. "I can't do it! How can I ever make a decision like that?"

"Because you're strong, Melody," he whispered against my ear. "Because you have a strong sense of right and wrong. You'll make the decision." Then he added raggedly, "If I lose you, I'll understand, but I don't think I'll ever be the same person again."

We made love then, for the last time. It was selfish, but we both needed it and wanted it so desperately.

When Hudson's train pulled in at Ciara del Fuego, I was there to meet him, and all during the thirty-mile drive back to Bensonville, he talked about Houston and the success of the trip. "It's official," he said, grinning. "The Morgan Hotel is a national historical landmark!"

He didn't even notice that my smile was stiff, that my eyes were red from lack of sleep. I deposited him at the hotel and agreed to see him that night.

I got through the evening all right. I never knew I had that kind of strength. We talked about the wedding and our future plans. I listened to him and I concentrated on his words, but somewhere deep inside me, I felt like a traitor. I was deceiving him in words, in thought, and in previous actions.

I also got through the next day, but that night, I thought I was going to fall apart. Ryder was leaving tomorrow, unless he heard from me. I had already made up my mind to stay with Hudson and marry him. There was nothing else I could do, but my heart was tearing in a thousand pieces.

After dinner, Grandma called me to her and gave me a long look. Then she said, "You never could fool me, you know, not even as a child. Something's eating you alive."

I think if she hadn't said anything, I could have carried it off, but her kind words and tone of voice reached me and I fell apart.

"Oh, Grandma!" I wailed. I threw myself on my knees and buried my head in her lap. "I can't stand it! I don't think I can live through it!"

She stroked my hair, and, gradually, through my sobs, I told her the whole story.

"I didn't mean for it to happen," I said. "I don't think Ryder did, either. It just happened. We love each other so much." I raised my eyes to her. "It's as though we're one person—our thoughts, our likes and dislikes, our hopes and dreams. He's a friend and a lover. He's my whole life, and tomorrow he's walking out of this town and getting on the train, and I'll never see him again."

Grandma was silent as she looked at me, but I could see tears rimming her eyes.

I rose and turned away. "It's all right, Grandma. I'm going to do what's right. I'll marry Hudson. After all, like you say, he's a good man. I'll have a good life with him, but I don't think"—I remembered Ryder's words—"I don't think I'll ever be the same person again."

I sank into a chair in the aching silence.

After a moment, Grandma cleared her throat. "You're a good and honorable girl, Melody. I admire your decision, but for all the Morgans did for us, you don't owe them your life."

I looked at her, my mouth slowly dropping in astonishment.

"Now let me say something," she continued. Her voice was low but clear. "I have loved and I have been loved. But I have not had it at the same time, and I know—I know—I have missed one of the greatest blessings on earth. To love and be loved is the richest joy, the most magical experience any of us can have."

Our eyes held. I didn't dare let a thought or a feeling enter my mind.

Grandma leaned forward in her rocking chair. "Melody," she rasped, "go with Ryder."

The silence was electrifying. Only her words seemed to march in my head—go with Ryder. Then suddenly, all my true thoughts and desires came flooding in. The tears sprang to my eyes, even as a laugh burst from my lips. I ran to her chair and threw my arms around her. "I love you, Grandma!"

I phoned the hotel and spoke to Ryder, and the next moment, I was flying through the night, down to the mine entrance and into his arms.

"Ryder!" I cried. "I'm coming with you!"

What I had to do in the next days wasn't easy. In fact, it was the most painful thing I'd ever done in my life. I told Hudson, and although I saw the hurt on his face, he wished me well.

Grandma, at her insistence, was signed into a retirement community in a small city on the edge of the desert, and her house and land were purchased by the Morgans. They wanted Grandma to have financial security. Even after what I did, they proved their friendship and unselfishness.

I knew that I would be happy with Ryder and his life and our children and our love. I knew I had made the right decision, as painful as it was for me and people I cared for.

Grandma had given me one last gift, and she was right in giving it. If life had offered me contentment and a measure of fulfillment, I would have taken that gladly and been grateful, but life offered me the richest blessing of love returned. I seized it, at last, without fear or guilt or hesitation, and I will thank God for it to the end of my days.

The End

"DON'T LOCK UP GRANDPA!"
We need each other

When my brother Timmy quit school and wrote that he was coming home with a bride, Mom tried to move Grandpa out of his basement apartment because it would be perfect for Timmy and Nina. There was one bedroom, a galley kitchen, and a combination dining-living room looking out at the old apple orchard.

"Just what a young couple needs," Mom said at the supper table. "We'll clean it up, paint it, and get a new refrigerator. They can stay there till they're ready to find a place of their own. Anyway, it'll be better for Grandpa up here where I can look after him. Right, Dad?" she said, patting his hand.

Grandpa snatched his hand away. He had dribbled spaghetti sauce down the front of his shirt, and I saw my older sister Robin smirk. I pinched her under the table.

"You're not getting any younger, Grandpa," my father said. "We can give you a nice room, and you won't have to go up and down stairs."

"I ain't your grandpa!" Grandpa tightened up his belt and pulled on his suspenders. His head shook back and forth. "Nobody's taking my apartment." Then he marched downstairs without saying another word.

"That man!" my mother said, watching him go. Mom could get anyone to do what she wanted, except Grandpa, who was her own father.

Robin made a face at me. "Mother, did Gregg Rogers call me? Did Aimee answer the phone and hang up on him? He said he was going to call me for sure."

"What if I did hang up?" I teased, even though I really hadn't. Robin was so goofy about boys and parties, she wasn't even human, anymore.

"Mother!" she screeched. "Aimee's messed up my date. She's ruined everything if Gregg Rogers doesn't call me!" She always ran to Mom. The big baby!

"Boy-crazy teenager," I said.

"You little pig," she muttered, so only I could hear. Eileen, the baby, began banging her spoon on her high chair, and Nicky, my older brother, drummed on the table with his fingers.

"Stop it, all of you," Mom said. "Aimee, I don't want another word out of you!"

"Don't blame me. She started it! I ought to punch her in the mouth!"

That did it. They all piled up on me. Dad hollered at me to stop talking like a hoodlum, and Mom said, "Aren't you ever going to become a lady?" Robin was happy because I was getting scolded, Nicky grinned mockingly and drummed faster on the table, and baby Eileen made a noise with her lips.

I jumped up and threw down my napkin. It landed in the stewed plums, but I didn't care. I wasn't a lady! I didn't feel like a lady. I didn't even want to be one. I just didn't want to be picked on all the time.

Mom snatched up my soppy napkin. "You leave the table and don't come back till you're ready to act properly," she said. "I'm fed up with your bad manners, Aimee Redmond. Between you and your grandfather, I don't know what I'm going to do."

I stormed out of there, straight down to Grandpa's apartment. He was the only one in the whole house who really cared about me, who wasn't trying to change me.

"Grandpa, are you going to tell them what for?" I said. "You're not going to let them kick you out of your own place, are you?"

"Get the pad and pencil, Aimee," he ordered.

I ran for the pad and pencil Grandpa kept in the kitchen counter drawer. He was always sending Mom messages, which he had me tack up on her kitchen bulletin board. I sat down at his newspaper-covered table. "Shoot, Grandpa. What do you want me to write?"

He looked really fierce with his white hair flopping in his face, and his eyes hidden under his bushy gray eyebrows. Grandpa really knew how to send messages. He could really blister the opposition. A long time ago, before I was even born, he'd been a general superintendent in a big factory. They were always sending messages. Interdepartmental memos, Grandpa called them.

"If you want people to know what you mean," he always said, "write it down in plain English." It was only because his hands were all knotted up and shaky with arthritis that I wrote the messages for him.

The way he was clasping his hands behind him, I could tell he was thinking. "No hard words, Grandpa," I reminded him. "My spelling isn't too good."

"Put this down, Aimee. 'To Whom It May Concern: this house is built on my land, which in a weak moment, I foolishly gave you when you were married. My house is my castle. I will never willingly surrender my apartment!'"

I was having a lot of trouble keeping up with him. ". . . surrender my apartment. Okay."

"You will have to carry me to the old people's home feet first! Now give it here and I'll sign my name. Then you bring it up."

I practically hugged myself with excitement as Grandpa signed his name, Harold Laxton, in his scratchy hand. "There," he said sternly, "post it on the bulletin board so they all see it."

181

I raced upstairs and tacked up the memo. After Mom read it, she got mad at me all over again. "First, I have no intention of putting your grandpa in an old people's home, and second, your spelling is atrocious!"

I didn't care what she said, because Grandpa had his way. When my brother Timmy and his bride, Nina, came, they got my room, and I moved in with Robin. I guess there was nothing else to do but put Robin and me together, but I hated it! She was Mom's young lady. I wanted to go down and stay with Grandpa.

Mom wouldn't hear of it. "You may as well save your breath. You're going with Robin, so get used to it. And while we're at it, that junk in your room is going out."

Mom acted like I was living in a jungle just because I had a turtle, a snake, and a pair of cute little white rats with pink eyes in my room. They were all in cages and I cleaned them every day, but Mom couldn't stand nature. It was only because she was afraid to handle my animals. I saved some of them and sneaked them into Grandpa's apartment; I could never have kept them in Robin's room. The others I gave away.

From the first, Robin told me if I touched any of her stuff, she'd skin me alive. "This is still my room," she said. Who'd want to mess with her stupid cosmetics anyway, or read the crummy books she brought home? They were all about love and kissing. I know, because once I sneaked into her room and peeked at them. It was boring junk!

Timmy's wife, Nina, was just as boring. That first night they came, everyone made a fuss over her at the supper table. Except Grandpa. He was the way he always was. When Mom told him to drink his milk, he growled, "I'm not a baby."

She made Grandpa so nervous he knocked the milk over, and it spilled on Nina. She jumped up as if he'd burned her. Mom scolded Grandpa, "If you'd just sometimes listen to what I told you, Dad!"

Nina only made matters worse, sulking that her dress was ruined. What a baby. She was a great big pain in the neck. And because she was married, she hardly looked at me and didn't even say thank you after taking my very own room.

I didn't understand why my brother married her. He wasn't the way he used to be. I didn't even know if I liked him anymore. He and Nina were always whispering together, little secrets, and planting gooey little kisses all over each other.

Nina said as soon as Timmy got the big job he was after, they were going to buy their own home. "The sooner the better," I said.

Mom made me apologize to Nina, but I didn't know what Mom was sore about. I just was telling the truth. It only proved how she favored Nina. Nina smoked, and Mom hated it as much as she hated Grandpa's pipe, but she never told her to stop smoking the way she did to Grandpa. Mom was a lot more polite with her.

When Timmy was out, Nina locked herself in her room like she was in a house full of thieves. Mom didn't like locked doors. She wouldn't even let us lock the bathroom door. "What if something happens?" she always said.

She told the same thing to Nina. "Dear, you might fall asleep with a lighted cigarette in your hand." Nina said she'd leave the door unlocked, after Mom promised her that nobody opened a closed door in our house without first knocking.

Well, Grandpa sometimes gets a little mixed up. He opened her door by accident. He must've forgotten it wasn't my room anymore. Nina screamed as if a monster had entered her room. Everyone ran; there was poor Grandpa, frozen in her doorway. And there was Nina in her slip and bra, crying to Mom that she'd been lying on her bed reading a magazine when Grandpa surprised her.

"I don't want that dirty old man leering at me!"

"For heaven's sake, Nina, he didn't do it on purpose," Mom said.

For once I thought Mom really stuck up for Grandpa, but then I heard her whispering to Nina that his mind was wandering. "He truly isn't that kind of man, Nina," she said.

You could say that again! I hated that Nina. If she was so worried about who saw her, why didn't she put on some clothes once in a while, instead of walking around half naked all the time? Every time Nicky passed by her in her slip or her nightie, his ears got all red.

I thought for sure Grandpa would send Nina one of his special memos. I knew he was upset the way he kept mumbling "dirty old man" under his breath. But he never asked me to get the pad.

It was right after that day that Grandpa refused to eat with us anymore. What happened was that he always liked to eat the same thing. He didn't like surprises, so Mom made him a hamburger and mashed potatoes almost every night. This one evening Mom served him a Chinese dinner. I heard her telling my father that she couldn't keep up with everything going on in this house and make special dinners for Grandpa, too. But when Mom put that Chinese dinner in front of him, he just sat there staring at it. Finally he got up and said, "I wouldn't touch that glop with a 10-foot pole!" and walked out.

I ate as fast as I could and hurried after Grandpa. He was waiting for me. "Pad and paper," he ordered. "Address it, 'To my daughter, Laura. Subject: food.'" Grandpa cleared his throat. "This is to serve notice that I know you are slowly poisoning me. You want me out of the way. From this day on, I will not eat any food prepared by your hand!"

"But, Grandpa, the food was okay."

"Post it, Aimee," he ordered.

After I put up Grandpa's note on the bulletin board, Mom and

Dad had a big conference. Dad said Grandpa was losing his grip. Mom sat at the table with her chin in her hands just staring off. "He's old," she said. "I know—I'll send his meals down."

I brought the first meal down, kicking at Grandpa's door because my hands were full.

"What's that?" he said suspiciously.

"Food Mom sent you, Grandpa."

"Take it away. It's poisoned."

When I brought the food upstairs and told Mom, she snatched the tray from my hands and marched downstairs again. Grandpa wouldn't even open the door for her. She told him she was leaving his food at the doorstep. He said it could stay there and rot for all he cared. Later I heard her talking to Dad.

"I don't know what to do. What if he really doesn't eat? What am I going to do?"

"He'll eat," Dad said. "But if he keeps up this tomfoolery, he might find himself in a nursing home!"

"Don't say that," Mom said. "He's my father." It sounded like she was ready to cry.

"We can't go on this way," he said. "He's making a wreck out of you. It doesn't make sense."

I was scared. Dad was really serious. I butted right in and said I'd cook for Grandpa. "I could make him his hamburger, Mom, and. . . ."

"You're just a child," she interrupted. "You can't even set the table right." She wouldn't give me a chance. As far as she was concerned, I couldn't do anything.

The next day, Grandpa made me sit down and prepare a list of groceries he wanted. "You tell your mother I want you to go to the store and buy these things."

Grandpa mainly wanted things like cereal, and raisins, and milk, and fruit, too, because his teeth weren't so good. I ran upstairs with the list. Mom looked at it and told me to fetch her pocketbook. "At least he isn't going to starve himself."

Later, Grandpa was out in the yard when Mom was hanging up clothes. "Hi, Dad," she said, but Grandpa acted like he didn't hear her and he moved off to sit somewhere else. She couldn't do anything with him anymore. He wouldn't eat her food. He wouldn't let her in his rooms to clean. He cut himself off from everyone in the family, except me. He was even cranky with me sometimes, but I didn't care. I understood Grandpa. He felt left out, just like I did.

Saturday night, Robin had her party in the basement, and I was playing checkers with Grandpa in his apartment. We weren't bothering anyone. Robin and her friends were as loud as they could be. They sounded like they were right in the room with us. It was making Grandpa nervous. I went out and told Robin to turn down the noise. She accused me of being a spy. Just because one of her stupid girlfriends was making out with a dumb boy on Mom's old couch. . . .

"I wasn't looking at you and your creepy friends," I said. "There's nothing to see, anyway."

"Well, get out then," she ordered.

"I will when I'm good and ready," I said, taking one of the sandwiches she'd made for her friends.

Mom came down and told me not to get in their way. "It's not your party."

"I wasn't spying!" I yelled. "Tell her to turn down that awful noise. Grandpa can't stand it!"

Mom pressed her lips together. "I'm sick of hearing Grandpa this and Grandpa that. There's other people to be considered, too! The music will be turned off in plenty of time, young lady. Now you get along." And she gave me a little push.

I went back to Grandpa and he told me to write a note to my mother. "Memo: stop that screeching, grunting, and rooting around. It's not music. It's a madhouse. Stop them, or I'll stop them."

He sent me upstairs with the note. Mom read it and crumpled it into a little ball. "You," she said to me, "go to bed! I don't want you down there any more tonight."

I pleaded that Grandpa and I were playing checkers, but Mom wouldn't listen. "The two of you together are worse than—than, I don't know what!" she said. The next morning the whole house was in an uproar. Grandpa had broken up Robin's party. He started by banging on the wall, then hitting the window with a stick. Then he'd come running in like a crazy man and chased all of the kids out. "Nobody will want to come here again because I have a crazy grandfather! He ought to be sent away!" Robin cried.

"Be quiet," Mom said. "That's no way to talk about your grandfather."

"Something's got to be done," Dad said. "Can you imagine him chasing those children out of the family room? We're going to have to put him into an old age home."

"It's a wonderful idea," Nina said. "They'll take good care of him."

"You keep out of this," Mom ordered. "He's not your father."

Timmy got mad at Mom for yelling at Nina. Nicky started drumming on the table, and the baby started crying. I was so upset, I ran out behind the shed. I couldn't even face Grandpa, I felt so awful.

Grandpa knew all about their plans. "It's money," he said. "That's all they're thinking about. They want to put me away, then they can search my apartment for the money."

I started to cry because I didn't want to live without Grandpa. He was the only one in my whole family who really cared about me.

"Stop that blubbering," he said, frowning. "I still have a few tricks up my sleeve, Aimee. They think I'm a stupid old man." His hands started to shake, and he sat down in his chair. "We'll go to Arizona. I was there a long time ago."

He told me all about Arizona, where a man could live on the edge of the desert, just the way he wanted, without anyone telling him anything. Then, Grandpa sort of forgot what he was talking about and started poking around in his big pile of newspapers, looking for something he wanted to read.

That same night, there was a fire. It wasn't Grandpa's fault, the way everyone said. He was cooking his hamburger. His hands were knobby and shaky, and it was hard for him to hold the frying pan. Some grease got in the fire and made a lot of smoke. The fire engines came, even though my father had put the fire out. Grandpa's apartment smelled smoky, and it was wet and messy, but it wasn't so awful.

Mom said she was scared half to death, and she put her foot down. She said she wouldn't let him cook for himself anymore, no matter what. She made Dad turn off the gas for Grandpa's stove. "He's going to eat what I cook, or he's going into a nursing home."

Grandpa wasn't the same after that fire. He didn't even protest when Mom came in the next day and cleaned out everything. "Junk yard! Fire trap!" she said, throwing out the newspapers he'd been saving to read. He took it all without a word of protest. He didn't even want to write a note to anyone.

Then Grandpa got sick. The doctor told Mom to keep a close watch on him. That was the end of his apartment. Dad helped him upstairs, and made him lie on their bed while Timmy and Nina moved downstairs into the apartment. Mom got rid of all the animals I loved. She threw out all Grandpa's old pipes, and his black sweater with patches and big sagging pockets, and even the old calendar picture he'd tacked on the wall. The apartment was stripped clean. I could hear Timmy hammering down there, and smell the paint, but I couldn't go down.

Mom ran Grandpa's life the way she wanted to now. She was in and out of his room ten times a day, fixing up his bed, making him eat, or helping him to the bathroom. Grandpa just wasn't himself. One day I came home and found Grandpa sitting in the rocking chair Mom had put in his room. He hated that rocker. "Old woman's chair," he called it.

"Help me up, Aimee," he said. "Let's take a walk."

Mom didn't want Grandpa to go out. But he hung on to my arm and told me to keep moving.

"We have to get away where she won't hear us. She's trying to keep me a prisoner," he whispered to me when we were away from the house. He wanted me to write a memo to the district attorney and another one to the newspaper, telling them that he was being kept prisoner in this house on Abbott Place. Then I knew he was getting better, even though I never wrote the notes. Grandpa said there was no time. They'd almost found his money. If they had, it would have been the end for him. That's why they pulled him out of his apartment. He'd heard them, even though he was sick, ripping up the walls and floors. But they'd never find anything because he had his money safe, pinned inside his undershirt.

"We're going to Arizona, Aimee," Grandpa said. "That's where a man can be free."

He was leaning really heavily on my arm when we got home. Mom said I'd worn him out. She made him get in bed. "You shouldn't have let Grandpa walk around so much," she scolded.

"He wanted to walk," I said.

"He should be in a nursing home," Mom said. "I don't know what he's going to do next. I can't go on this way."

"Nursing home?" I could feel my heart hopping inside me.

"Don't look at me as if I'm sending him to prison, Aimee!" Mom said. "They're not that bad. Sometimes when people get old, they can't look after themselves."

"Grandpa just doesn't like to be bossed around!"

Mom sighed. "I don't want to boss him. He's my father. I only want to do what's right for him."

I was scared. I was sure Mom and Dad had made up their minds. I expected that tomorrow or the next day they would come for Grandpa and all his things. They'd take him away and he'd never return. A nursing home was where they sent you to die. Grandpa told me that.

The next morning, before anyone was up, I crept into Grandpa's room and told him we had to start for Arizona today. We slipped away before anyone was awake. The bus on the corner took us downtown and then we walked to the station. Grandpa handed me a bunch of crumbled bills, and I bought two tickets for Terre Haute, Indiana. I knew we still had a long way to go from there to Arizona, but the main thing was to get away from Springfield.

Grandpa slept a lot on the bus, and I looked out the window. After a while, it seemed to be the same thing over and over—land, and cows, and little towns. I ate some candy bars and drank a bottle of pop, and Grandpa drank some water at one of our stops. Then I must have dozed off, because when I woke up, we were in Terre Haute.

We got off the bus and I went to buy tickets to keep going. The man wanted an awful lot of money to go to Arizona. I only had ten dollars left of Grandpa's money. I went back to where he was sitting and told him we needed more money.

"Money?" he said, like he didn't understand what I was talking about.

"Grandpa, we need it for the tickets to get to Arizona."

He shook his head. There was no more money. He'd given me all his money when we first got on the bus at home.

"What are we going to do, Grandpa?"

"I'm tired, Aimee," he said. "I used to hitchhike all around the country, and I never got so tired. I was young then."

"Hitchhike, Grandpa? That's a good idea. We can do that."

Before we left the station, I bought two candy bars and two sodas. "That's fifty cents extra if you take the bottles outside," the man said. So I made Grandpa finish his soda right there. When I gave the bottles back I asked which way to Arizona.

"You driving?" he said. "Best bet is to stay on Route 40 to St. Louis, then get on 66 and stick with that through the Arizona border. Got that, little lady?"

"Yes, thank you," I said, trying not to show how scared I felt. It sounded like it would take us a long time to get to Arizona.

When Grandpa and I started hitchhiking, it was still light, and we got a ride right away with a salesman who talked to Grandpa while he drove. Grandpa didn't say much. The salesman left us off at a crossroads where there was a diner. "I turn here, old timer," he said. "You go straight ahead."

Grandpa seemed awfully shaky when he got out of the car. I took him into the diner and ordered some bean soup for him.

"What about you?" the waitress said. I told her I wasn't hungry. "My grandfather has a wonderful appetite, though."

"I can see that," she said sarcastically. He hadn't touched his soup. I drank down the soup and put the crackers in my pocket for later.

Then we got a short ride with an old couple. The woman asked me a lot of questions. She wanted to know where I was going with my grandfather, and didn't I have to go to school? I told her Grandpa and I were going to Arizona, that we had relatives there. They took some side roads and left us off in the middle of the country. The fields were cut and stubbly. It was windy and cold and dark. A dog barked at us. I picked up a big stick. I was scared, and worried about Grandpa.

I knew I shouldn't be afraid with Grandpa right there, but I couldn't help it. There were so many funny sounds in the night, and not many houses, and it was darker than I'd ever seen. We walked for a while, but not very fast, because Grandpa was tired, too. After a while, we crept into on old broken-down barn that was full of hay and little animals.

I heard them scurrying around in the dark. I crept close to

Grandpa and shared my soda crackers with him. Grandpa put his arm around me and we both fell asleep on the itchy hay.

When I woke up the sun was shining. Grandpa was still asleep. His nice white hair was tangled, and I knew Mom would be furious if she saw how dirty and mussed up he was. I went outside and there was a beautiful apple tree. I picked some apples from the ground, ate one, and brought some back for Grandpa.

"Grandpa," I said, "I brought you an apple." When he hardly moved, I got scared and shook him till he woke up. He didn't know where he was. I pulled him out of the barn and into the sunshine at the side of the road. He just sat there.

We started walking again. Grandpa didn't say much. I was afraid he was getting sick or unhappy, so I kept talking. We drank some water from a little brook, and Grandpa seemed to feel better after that. I kept worrying about food, though. We stopped in a diner and I had an egg and a glass of milk. Grandpa had some cornflakes.

After we started walking again, I noticed some empty pop bottles thrown in the ditch along the road. That gave me a good idea. I took off my sweater and made a sack out of it. I filled it with empty pop bottles as we walked along.

"They'll get us some change, Grandpa. When we get to the next town, well trade them in and buy you some soup."

We'd been walking a long time when a farmer came by driving a tractor and pulling a big wooden wagon. He stopped. I thought he would be friendly, but he wanted to know what we were doing out here, as though the whole country belonged to him!

"Well, come on! Cat got your tongue?" I looked at Grandpa. He was muttering something to himself. I told the farmer my grandfather and I were going to Arizona. "Arizona, huh? Big plans for a little girl! Hop in and I'll give you a ride. I'm going ten miles down." I climbed into the back of the wagon, and then the farmer and I both had to help Grandpa up. "Your gramp looks sick," the farmer said.

"Oh, no, he's all right. He just wants to get to Arizona."

"Long way for a little girl and an old man to go. Gat any money?"

"P-plenty," I stuttered, trying to hide the sweater full of empty soda bottles. Grandpa fell asleep again as the wagon jolted over the road. I felt itchy and sort of dirty. Mom would have laughed if she knew I wanted a bath.

Thinking about Mom made me homesick. I wondered if anybody missed me, anybody like the baby or even Robin. She was probably glad to have her room to herself again. And Timmy and Nina, what did they care? They never even knew I existed. Timmy had been a super big brother till he went away to school and met Nina. Well, I wasn't going to cry, that was certain.

The farmer stopped near a big gray-shingled house with a faded red barn behind it. A lot of farm machinery sat in the yard. I hopped off the wagon and called Grandpa. He was sleeping. "Grandpa! Come on, wake up. We have to walk now." The farmer came around to the back of the wagon and watched me. I climbed up and shook Grandpa hard. He opened his eyes, but he looked as if he didn't recognize me.

"Your gramp is sick," the farmer said, sounding angrier than ever. "You get in the house, and the wife will let you use the phone. You call your people!"

I started to cry. I didn't want to call. They'd come and put him in a nursing home! I didn't know what he was going to do. I snuggled down next to Grandpa and put my arms around him. His eyes closed and his mouth hung open. The farmer came back with his wife. She was skinny and wearing blue jeans and a gray jacket.

She looked at me, frowning. "Child," she said, "do you want to be responsible for your grandfather's death?" I felt as if I was going to burst. I closed my eyes and my head started to twirl dizzily. I felt so scared I couldn't even speak.

"Child, calm down. Call your people."

I looked at Grandpa again. He didn't look big and fierce any more. He seemed to have shrunk into his shirt. I got up and went with the farmer's wife into her house. I called Mom collect and told her where Grandpa and I were. Mom started to cry and scold me over the phone. Then she talked to the farmer's wife, Mrs. Bowen, and told her she and Dad would drive down to get us.

While we waited, Grandpa lay on Mrs. Bowen's porch glider sleeping. I walked around the farm. In the barn there were dogs, and ducks, and chickens. But I couldn't get very interested in the animals. Then I thought about Mom and Dad, and how angry they were going to be.

I didn't feel good for the rest of the day, and even though I'd been awfully hungry, I didn't eat much of the nice meal Mrs. Bowen made. Grandpa only drank a little water. When my parents came, they thanked the Bowens and then helped Grandpa into the back of the car. He lay down and Mom covered him with a blanket. I got in front with my parents. They still hadn't said a word to me.

When we were on the way, Mom asked me in a sad voice how I could have done such a terrible thing. "Are we so awful to you? Is that why you ran away?"

"I didn't want you to lock up Grandpa in a home! You don't care about him. You don't care about me!"

"Don't care?" my father repeated.

"You don't think about me," I said, "except that I'm in the way, that's all!"

Mom took my hand and held it between hers. "You're part of me,

Aimee. I can't help but love you." She held up her fingers. "Each one of these fingers is like one of my children. I don't think about each one of them every minute, but they're a part of me. It would break my heart to lose even one."

Everyone had been upset, she told me. "Even the baby knew something was wrong and cried all day for you. We all did."

I started crying. We were all squeezed in together in the front seat. I felt crowded, but warm and cozy, too. I cried because I was so happy to be going home. A few days after we got back, Grandpa was taken to a nursing home. Dad had a long talk with me. He said Grandpa was old and couldn't take care of himself any more, and needed the care of nurses and doctors. He needed someone to get him up to go to the bathroom, to see that he ate and didn't hurt himself.

Sometimes I wished we could have made it to Arizona, but maybe it wouldn't have made any difference for Grandpa. If anything had happened to him on our trip, well, I would have hated myself forever. Like Dad said, if you love somebody, it isn't always right to just hang on to him. I get to see Grandpa every week, and he does feel better. I know because he has me writing notes to the doctor and the superintendent of the nursing home. Grandpa still gets real angry about a lot of things that he thinks are wrong, but he doesn't think people are trying to poison him anymore.

Mom and I seem to be getting along as usual. I'm still not enough of a lady to suit her. I still fight with my sister, too, but I don't feel as if she and everybody are against me anymore. We fight and have our differences like any family, but underneath we all love each other. Like Mom told me, we're joined together like the fingers on a hand.

The End

32—AND I CAN'T HAVE SEX!
Mama won't let me

I was what Mama called a "late bloomer"—so late, in fact, that I almost didn't bloom at all. I was thirty-two years old by the time I met Andrew Hart and fell in love.

At first there didn't seem to be anything special about Andrew. He was just another one of the customers who came into the bookstore I ran. A shy man in his late thirties who had only recently started dropping in to browse through the used book section, he usually had little to say. One morning, though, Andrew lingered at the checkout counter after I'd made change for him.

"I wonder. . . ." he began awkwardly. "You see, there's this book I wanted to ask you about, and I hate to take up your time here in the store. I thought that maybe we might go out for a cup of coffee while I tell you about it. I wouldn't keep you very long."

I hesitated, taken by surprise. "Well, I don't know."

"I realize you don't know me," he said hastily, "but I work at Willow's Jewelry Store down the street. Mr. Willow will vouch for me."

Maybe it was because of the eagerness in his eyes I wasn't used to seeing, or maybe it was only because it had been such a long time since a man had asked me out for coffee—or anywhere else. But whatever the reason, I found myself turning the shop over to my assistant, Jess Colt, and accompanying Andrew to the coffee shop next door.

Of course, when we got there, I sat stirring my coffee in silence, unable to think of anything to say. I had never been at ease with men, which probably accounted for the fact that I'd attracted so few dates during my school years and so little male attention since.

But then Andrew plunged somewhat nervously into a description of the book he was looking for, and I soon responded to his interest. Books were probably the only subject that I was completely comfortable talking about.

"You see, I collect books about clocks," he explained. "I'm the watch and clock repairman for Mr. Willow and I rebuild clocks in my spare time. Mr. Willow said I would most likely find the type of book I was looking for in your shop. He said you have the best selection of old books in town."

"My father built up quite a trade in used books. I've tried to keep it up since I took over the store."

"Mr. Willow says you're something of an expert on old books, yourself," Andrew said.

I ought to be! I thought dryly. I had been working in the store since I was a teenager. Of course, I'd had precious little chance to do anything else. But at least when Dad died a few years ago, I was able to take over the store and make a reasonable living out of it for Mama and me.

"I don't know that I'm an expert," I told Andrew, "but I do know where I might find the book you're looking for."

"Mr. Willow said he knew you could find it and that you wouldn't mind doing it."

"Mr. Willow seems to have told you quite a lot about me. What else did he have to say?" I asked.

Andrew gave me a shy sort of smile that lit up his face in a most attractive way. "He told me that your name is Jillian and that you aren't married. But he didn't tell me whether or not you have any family, and I've never seen anyone working in the store who seemed close to you."

"Mama never comes to the store. She knows absolutely nothing about the business."

I could have added that Mama could barely be trusted to make out a grocery list, much less be turned loose in the store. Never having done anything but putter around the house and help out at the church, she was completely helpless where business was concerned. As far as I knew, she had never paid a bill or made an important decision in her entire life.

Of course, that was the way Dad wanted it. He had been the old-fashioned type who believed that it was a man's place to rule over his family and a woman's place to do as she was told. I'm sure that if there had been a son, I would have been left out of the business as much as Mama. But since I was the only child he had, Dad taught me the business. I suppose he realized as his heart condition plagued him more and more that it would be up to me to take care of Mama. It was impossible to imagine her looking out for herself.

"Oh, no," I said to Andrew. "Mama leaves the business strictly to me. She would be more trouble than help."

"I take it then that you live with her?"

"Yes. She couldn't possibly manage alone."

"Then she's lucky to have a daughter like you to look after her," Andrew said politely.

He turned back to the subject of books then, and we were soon deep in conversation. Our coffee break stretched to a half an hour and then forty-five minutes. It was Andrew who regretfully brought it to a close—after I had promised to go out for coffee with him again the next day.

I had coffee with Andrew the following morning. And the next morning, and the next. By the end of the week, our coffee breaks had become a daily affair. When, after a few weeks, he asked me to have dinner with him one evening, I accepted eagerly.

I hurried home after work, excited as a teenager. I had started into the house before I remembered I had forgotten to tell Mama I wouldn't be home for dinner.

"I'm sorry," I said as I walked into the kitchen and saw the table already set. "I should have told you not to cook for me tonight."

Mama was taking the meat loaf out of the oven. She looked up, pink from the heat, and frowned slightly. "I wish you had told me, Jillian. It would have saved me a lot of work."

"I should've called, I know. But I got busy, and it slipped my mind."

"Oh, well, I suppose the food will keep," she said, her displeasure disappearing as she began taking off her apron. "I wouldn't mind a night out myself."

Mama had set her hair that day and looked particularly nice. With a fluff of curls about her face, she looked like a trusting child. Only a slightly plump figure betrayed the fact that she was a woman in her mid-fifties. And as she smiled at me in happy anticipation of what she had taken to be an invitation to go out to dinner, I felt a twinge of guilt. "I'm sorry, Mama," I said uncomfortably, "but I've been invited to have dinner with a friend."

Her happy expression changed to one of disappointment. "I can't imagine what girlfriend of yours would object to my company," she pouted.

I took a deep breath. "This isn't a woman. It's a man."

She looked up at me, startled. "A man! Wherever would you meet a man?"

"He works at Willow's Jewelry Store down the street from our store. We have coffee together nearly every day."

Mama's disapproval turned to concern. "Surely, you're not thinking of going out with someone like that? You can't just take up with a stranger. He could be anything—an impostor, a criminal—no telling what." She stared at me. "Why, he could even be a married man!"

"No, Mama," I said firmly. "There is nothing at all questionable about Andrew. He's a kind, considerate person, and he definitely isn't married."

She gave a loud sniff. "That's what he tells you. It's the oldest trick in the world." Her eyes narrowed suspiciously. "How old a man is he, anyhow?"

"He's only a few years older than I am, and he has been very nice to me. I'm sure you'll like him when you meet him."

Her lips tightened. "I'm afraid I'll have to make my own judgment, Jillian. And I can tell you I haven't the faintest idea of being taken in by some smooth-talking stranger."

I had to struggle with my irritation. Mama was reacting as she always did. She always managed to find something wrong with the men who asked me out—the few there had been. "You're being completely unfair as usual," I accused her. "You're judging Andrew before you've even met him."

"I'm simply making a judgment that you're too inexperienced to make. I expect you'll find—when the truth is out—that this man is married and lying about it. But if he's not, that only makes it worse. Common sense should tell you there's bound to be something wrong with a man nearly forty years old who has never married."

I drew back, stung by Mama's unintentionally cruel words. But what about me? I wanted to cry out in protest. What about a thirty-two-year-old woman who has never married? Is there bound to be something wrong with her, too?

Because it would hurt too much to admit them, I kept my bitter thoughts to myself. I turned away and went to get dressed, refusing to listen to any more of Mama's objections.

Although she was positioned in a chair beside the front door when Andrew arrived, I whisked him away before she could begin questioning him. I was determined not to let her spoil things for me this time.

The evening turned out to be all I had hoped for. Andrew seemed to enjoy himself as much as I did. The restaurant he chose offered pleasant surroundings and delicious food. We took our time over our coffee, finding even more to talk about, wanting more and more of each other's company.

"You're such an easy person to be with, Jillian," he told me, offering me the shy smile I had come to find so attractive. "Usually I find it hard to talk to people."

"I know what you mean," I agreed. "I've never found it easy to make conversation, either."

"I guess that's the difference. I don't feel like you and I are just making conversation. When I'm with you, I feel that I can talk about the things that are really important to me. I hope you feel the same way."

I nodded, too shy to say more, but Andrew seemed satisfied with my response. He made the evening last as long as possible and lingered at the front door when he told me good night. When he asked me to go out with him again on the following Saturday night, my contentment was complete.

I continued seeing Andrew at every opportunity, but I did it in spite of Mama's fierce objection. She tried her best to dampen my interest in Andrew, taking every opportunity to find fault with him.

I couldn't understand her attitude. Although Andrew wasn't handsome or exciting and didn't make a lot of money, he was kind and sweet, and in every way was the kind of man she ought to have approved of. It seemed to me that she should've been glad I had found a fine man to love me, but instead she went out of her way to be unpleasant and try to drive him away. It was as if she didn't want me to have a man of my own.

Andrew ignored her disapproval as best he could, seeming determined not to let it come between us. But I could tell he was becoming more and more impatient as time passed and her unpleasantness to him continued.

One evening when we were at his apartment cooking dinner, he turned to me suddenly and said, "We can't keep on like this, Jillian. We have to get things straight between us."

He drew me down beside him on the sofa and took my hands in his. "You're bound to know by now how I feel about you," he said. "I have to know if you feel the same way about me."

"Tell me how you feel," I said softly.

In answer, he leaned forward to take me in his arms. I went to him eagerly, finding in him an ardor I hadn't experienced until now. He had kissed me before, of course, but never like this. And even more startling was my response to him as I found myself yielding to him with a passion I hadn't guessed I could possess.

He drew away at last and said huskily, letting me see the longing in his eyes, "Now you know how much I love you. I had to find out if you loved me, too."

"Of course, I love you, Andrew," I answered.

He took me back into his arms and whispered, "You can't know how much it means to me to hear you say that. I want to marry you, Jillian. I can't offer you a lot of money, but I can promise I'll do everything in my power to make you happy."

"I'll be happy as long as I'm with you," I told him as I gave myself up to him. I had found the place I had been searching for all my life.

It was almost dawn when Andrew brought me home. I overslept and barely had time for a quick good-bye to Mama before I hurried off to work. But I could read the disapproval in her face, and she was waiting for me, loaded with questions, when I got home that evening.

She barely let me get inside the door before she began. "I would like to know where you were last night, Jillian. I can't imagine what could have kept you out most of the night."

"We were at Andrew's apartment, Mama. The time slipped by."

She gasped, for a moment at a loss for words. "Surely you know that's not a proper place for you to be," she managed to say finally.

"It's Andrew's home, Mama—just as this is mine."

"The two of them are in no way the same, Jillian, as you very well know. I shouldn't have to tell you that you are becoming far too familiar with Andrew," she said sternly. "Don't you see that you may be giving him ideas? After all, he is a man."

Yes, Mama, I thought happily, he's quite a lot of man! Then, unable to conceal my happiness any longer, I blurted out, "It's all right. Andrew and I are going to be married. He asked me last night. He's coming over in a little while, and we want you to help us plan our wedding."

Mama's mouth dropped open, and she had to struggle for breath. "I can't believe you know what you're saying! If you did, you would know that I haven't the faintest intention of taking part in any such scheme," she said when she finally could speak. "My feelings about this man haven't changed."

My smile faded. "You've never given Andrew a chance," I accused her. "You made up your mind at the start to dislike him."

"With good reason, Jillian. I could see him for what he is."

"And what do you think he is, Mama? It seems to me that he has been very nice to you."

"He's been nice to me because he wanted to cover up his true intentions. But he hasn't fooled me. The man is an out-and-out fortune hunter," she declared. "He sees that you have a nice business going, and he has been hoping from the start to get his hands on it."

I felt as if she had slapped me. I had to struggle to control my anger. "Does it seem so impossible to you that a man could want to marry me simply because he loves me?" I said finally. "Am I so hopelessly unattractive that a man couldn't want me for myself?"

She reached out to pat my arm pityingly. "I won't bother to answer such a question because I understand that you don't know what you're talking about. If you did, you would know that I'm only trying to keep you from grief. Believe me—you wouldn't be missing anything if you never married. Being a wife is no picnic, I can tell you."

"That's something I would like to decide for myself!" I retorted.

She shook her head sadly. "I'm only thinking of your happiness. I'm simply trying to spare you a burden you would be better off never having to know about." Her voice dropped and became mysterious as it always did when she hinted at sex. "You would thank me for stepping in if you knew what it was like."

"But I do know, Mama," I cried out rebelliously. "And it's not like that at all! It's wonderful, and I only feel sorry for you if you don't know that."

Mama's face went white. Without a word, she turned away and

went to her room. When Andrew came to the house later on, she did not come out. The next morning, she did not appear to make breakfast, saying only that she wasn't feeling well and wanted to stay in bed.

Three days later, Mama was still in bed. The housework and laundry went undone. She dragged to the table in the evening, picking at the meals I'd cooked. When I brought up the subject of my wedding, she refused to talk about it.

I dismissed her complaints as sulking, and, while I did what I could to help her with the housework, I refused to quit seeing Andrew. It upset me to see her unhappy, but I had found out what love was and had no intention of giving it up.

Andrew and I were together every night, and it became harder and harder for us to leave each other and go to our separate homes.

But as our love for each other grew more impatient, Mama seemed to get sicker. She had taken to bed and apparently intended to stay there. And though I was still convinced that she was only being dramatic, I had to admit to a nagging concern. Finally, I insisted upon taking her to a doctor.

To my surprise, Mama wasn't pretending. The doctor found her to be suffering from a digestive ailment, and her blood pressure was higher than was safe. He prescribed medicine and a diet and told her not to let things upset her. I took her home and put her to bed, feeling guilty and contrite, ashamed of having been so caught up in my own desires that I had neglected her.

"I feel terrible for having ignored her when she was really sick," I confessed to Andrew that night at his apartment.

"You haven't done anything except try to live your own life, Jill," he objected.

"I should have given her time to adjust to the idea of my getting married. She's bound to be terrified at the thought of being left alone."

"But at some point she has to accept the fact that you're a grown woman with a right to a life of your own."

I shook my head miserably. "That's what bothers me, Andrew. If the very thought of my leaving home puts her to bed, I wonder what she'll be like when I'm gone!"

We looked at each other unhappily, the real problem out in the open. I could think of only one solution, one that had been in the back of my mind for some time. Timidly, I suggested it to Andrew.

"I know it would present problems, but there is a way we could get married. Maybe Mama could live with us."

Andrew's reaction was immediate. "No, Jillian; it would never work. Our marriage would be a disaster with your mother disliking me the way she does."

"But she would be different after she saw that she wasn't going to be left alone, that she was going to share in our life."

He shook his head. "She doesn't want to share you, especially with a husband. I would only be a rival to her for your attention, and I honestly couldn't live with the constant bickering and criticism I would have to put up with. I'm sorry, Jillian, but I just couldn't."

I sighed in discouragement as I saw that Andrew was not going to change his mind. "Then we'll simply have to wait to get married. We'll have to be patient and give this time to work itself out."

"It isn't going to work itself out," he insisted. "Unless you do something about it, it isn't going to get any better."

"But what can I do? I can't just desert Mama. I'm all she has."

"You can help her find something to take your place. She's not an old woman, you know. She has years of living ahead of her, and there's no reason why she can't make them useful and interesting."

"But she would be completely helpless alone, Andrew. What kind of life could she possibly have?"

"I don't know, Jillian. Whatever she made it, I suppose."

"You know she isn't capable of making a life for herself."

"Of course she is! That's something we all have to do for ourselves."

I fell silent, hurt by Andrew's unyielding attitude. I couldn't understand his lack of sympathy for Mama and his unwillingness to even try to see things from my point of view. I could see, though, that there was no use in arguing further with him. Our marriage wouldn't have a chance, anyway, as long as he and Mama felt the way they did about each other.

As time passed, things got worse—not better. Although Mama seemed to be feeling well enough, she made no attempt to get back to her former activities. She seemed to have accepted the semi-invalid way of life she had settled into, becoming more dependent upon me than ever. In despair, I watched my wedding date slip further and further away from me.

I was equally troubled by Andrew, as I watched his impatience turn into irritation. Not only with Mama, but with me, too. He complained that I was doing nothing to help our situation, that Mama would never learn to take care of herself as long as I did everything for her.

"She's never going to change unless you make her," he accused me. "You're going to have to insist that she take over her own household and start handling her own affairs."

"But she simply wouldn't know how to. She's never done anything except putter around the house and cook."

"Then she ought to learn. And she never will as long as you take charge of everything."

Although I thought Andrew was being unfair about Mama, I had to agree with him about one thing: I could never hope for a life of my own until I could get Mama to take on some responsibility.

I finally decided that the best way to begin would be to put Mama in charge of her household. She could start paying the household bills and learning something about handling her money.

She complained loudly when I told her of my decision, but she grudgingly took on the task. Andrew, who approved highly of my plan, cautioned me not to interfere or criticize her, but to let her work things out in her own way.

And I tried. I honestly did. I could see unopened bills scattered about her room and it was all I could do to keep from nagging at her to pay them on time. I watched her labor over her check writing, biting my tongue to keep from giving her advice. She would sigh and eye me hopefully, but I didn't offer to take over for her. However long it took, I was determined that for her own good, she should learn how to do this job by herself.

I was determined, that is, until one morning a few months later when she called the store so distraught she could barely speak.

"Something terrible has happened, Jillian! I don't know what to do!" she said on a sob. "I'm here at the bank, and they say I might have to go to jail!"

I hurried to the bank and found Mama in the office of the accounts manager. He looked as upset as she did. "I'm terribly sorry," he said to me, "but I'm afraid we have a serious situation here which your mother doesn't seem to understand."

He took out our account records and I listened, aghast, while he explained what had happened. It seemed that there was no money at all left in our checking account and that checks were still coming in with no money to cover them.

"I've gone over your mother's checkbook with her as best I can," the banker explained. "But she hasn't kept enough of a record to show how many checks she has written. She doesn't seem to understand how a checking account works. I have tried to explain the law regarding checks, but I don't believe I'm getting through to her."

"He says that I've broken the law, Jillian—that they can put me in jail!" Mama wailed.

"Of course they can!" I shouted angrily. "You can't go around writing checks unless you have enough money in your account to cover them! Surely, you can understand that."

Mama dissolved into tears. "I knew something like this would happen," she wailed. "I tried to tell you I didn't know anything about banks, but you wouldn't listen. You made me write the checks, and now I'll be the one who has to go to prison!"

I spent the rest of the morning untangling our bank account. I transferred money from our business account to cover the rest of the checks Mama had written, and the man at the bank promised his cooperation in explaining the bad checks. Mama stood to one side, sniffling indignantly.

When we finally got home, she went straight to bed—and I sank into a chair, defeated. I had been foolish to believe she could accept such responsibility after a lifetime of dependence on others. She was simply too old to learn new ways.

"It's hopeless," I told Andrew that night. "It's impossible to even think of putting her on her own. There's no way she can manage without me."

"And as long as she's with you, there won't be any room in your life for me," Andrew said grimly.

"There could be if you would only be reasonable, but you're as stubborn as Mama!" I cried out angrily. "The trouble is that neither of you will make a place for the other."

"I'll make the proper place, Jillian. I'll do all I can to help you at the store; we can hire extra help so that you can have your time free to give to your mother. She can have the income from the store to live comfortably on—if need be, we can even get someone to stay with her. But I won't agree to letting her live with us. I won't take second place in your life."

"What you're really saying is that you won't make a place for Mama."

"I'm saying I want a husband's place, Jillian. I have a lot of love to give you, but I want a wife's complete love in return. And you'll never be a real wife as long as your mother comes first with you."

"You're being completely unfair," I accused him, cut to the heart by his unsympathetic attitude. "You're asking me to choose between you and Mama when I don't really have a choice. If you force me to choose between you, you know what my decision has to be."

"I hope you don't mean that," he said, "because I can't go on the way things are—being with you but knowing I can't have you. If I can't have you as a wife, Jillian, it would be better not to see you at all."

"You can't mean that," I said, not ready to believe him.

"I do mean it," he replied. "You have only to tell me when you're ready to be my wife and come and live with me. But if it's never going to be that way, I don't think we should see each other anymore. It would be best if we put an end to this."

I barely heard Andrew's words. I couldn't believe he really meant them. I didn't understand until, after several days of not hearing from him, I called him and he refused to see me. "Only if you have changed your mind," he said firmly. "I meant what I said, Jillian."

I cried for hours that night. The next morning, Mama studied my swollen eyes inquisitively, but she contented herself with asking if I would be home for dinner. She didn't comment when I said I would not be going out, but I saw a flicker of satisfaction in her eyes. A wave of bitterness swept over me, along with a feeling that the doors of a prison had swung shut behind me.

The next day Mama was up early and had breakfast on the table when I got to the kitchen. By the end of the week, she was back in her former routine. Gradually we settled into the old, humdrum life we had lived before I met Andrew. Mama resumed her church work and spent long hours chattering on the telephone with her friends, contented now that her life was "back in order." I spent the evenings reading and the weekends running errands.

I suppose the thing that kept me going as the weeks dragged by and I heard nothing from Andrew was the fact that I never really believed it was over between us. I was certain that in time he would change his mind and see things my way. Eventually he would see that living with Mama was better than not being together at all. In the meantime, since he had made it clear he wouldn't see me unless I changed my mind, I made no further effort to get in touch with him. I didn't telephone him, and I went out of my way to stay clear of the store where he worked.

One evening, though, when I left the bookstore and started driving home, the traffic was heavy. I was forced to circle the block and drive past Willow's. I was within a few doors of it when I saw Andrew coming out of the door. My heart began pounding foolishly and I slowed down, hoping he would see me.

Then, as I drew nearer, I could see that he wasn't alone. An attractive, dark-haired girl stood beside him, smiling up at him, while he looked down at her attentively.

I felt shock run through me, and I drove away quickly, not wanting to be noticed now. But I couldn't resist looking in the rearview mirror after I had passed them. I saw that I needn't have worried about being noticed. There was little possibility of that. Andrew and the girl had already started off down the street in the opposite direction, too deep in conversation to notice anyone. I drove on, so distraught I could barely see where I was going, wanting only to get away from the sight of them together.

I drove aimlessly, trying to get control of myself, trying to put the thought of Andrew and that girl out of my mind. Sick at heart, I finally faced the fact that I had lost Andrew. He had found somebody else. There was nothing left for me but Mama and her idle chatter . . . nothing to go home to but a lonely room.

Not really aware of where I was going, I found myself caught up in the flow of traffic moving onto the freeway. Blinded by tears, I could barely see as I pulled out into the moving stream of cars. I didn't notice the car ahead of me when it slowed for the traffic ahead of it. I didn't react until it was too late. I remembered trying to swerve to keep from hitting the car in front of me, feeling a crash as a car rammed into me from behind, and being jolted and tossed about. But then I was aware of nothing until I came to in an ambulance on my way to the hospital.

I came out of the accident far better than I might have expected. Miraculously, I was the only person who was hurt. I suffered a badly sprained arm, a dislocated knee, and a king-sized lump on my head, but none of my injuries were really serious. Even though my knee required surgery and would be weeks in healing, I considered myself too lucky to complain.

The accident did leave me with problems, though. It would be a while before I could walk, even with crutches; it would be weeks before I could drive a car. And in the meantime, there was the bookstore that I somehow had to run.

My assistant, Jess, managed to get through the first few days of my absence, but she could find no one to come in and help her. Jess struggled along for another week before she called to say that she couldn't continue to run the store alone.

"Do you suppose your mother could help out?" Jess asked in desperation. "Just until I can find someone else?"

"But Mama doesn't know a thing about the store," I objected. "She would be more trouble than help, Jess."

"She could at least answer the phone and keep the books in order," Jess insisted. "Anything she could do would be a help at this point."

Although the idea seemed impossible to me, I could think of no other solution. Finally, when Jess kept insisting, I told Mama that she would have to go.

"But I don't know a thing about waiting on customers. I'll only get things mixed up," Mama protested. "I haven't the faintest idea how to work a cash register or make change."

Propped up in bed with my knee throbbing, I was in no mood for excuses. "Then you'll just have to learn how," I lashed out at her. "If nothing else, just go down there and stand around. There's bound to be something you can do to help."

Although she grumbled loudly and I had to order her out of the house, Mama finally gave in and set out fearfully for the store. She dragged in that evening exhausted, complaining bitterly, barely able to open a can of soup for our supper. I could tell when I talked to Jess later on, that the day had been a disaster.

Even so, I sent Mama back to the store the next day. It was the only thing I could do. If nothing else, she could bring the daily receipts to me so that I could keep up with the bookkeeping and paperwork at home. I apologized to Jess, but I told her to put up with Mama as best she could for a little longer.

After a few days, Mama resigned herself to her new duties and quit complaining. Jess's spirits also improved. She even told me they were managing nicely and could get along without extra help. Although I could only wonder how smoothly things were actually going, I took Jess at her word. And somehow we got along until I was able to go back to work. Of course, Mama still had to come to work with me. Since she had to drive, I had no choice. And as long as I was on crutches, we needed whatever help she could give.

To my surprise, on my first day back at work, I found Mama to be of real help, trying cheerfully to do as best she could with whatever Jess or I asked of her. Of course, she spent more time talking than working, but the customers seemed to like it. She had such a pleasant way with them that they didn't seem to mind the mistakes she made.

When she appeared the second morning dressed for work and ready to drive me, I gratefully accepted her help. As we settled into our new workday pattern, I tried not to criticize and she didn't complain. The time passed surprisingly fast until I was able to drive again.

Oddly enough, Mama seemed disappointed when I told her I no longer needed her at the store. She watched wistfully as I set out without her the first morning; that night she was filled with questions about the customers and happenings at the store. The next day she dropped in unannounced and started waiting on customers. When I told her it wasn't necessary, she insisted that I still needed her and continued coming in for a part of each day.

Although I was surprised and puzzled, I accepted her offer of help. After all, it gave her something to do. I didn't suspect that there was another reason for her interest until she sidled up to me in the store one afternoon.

"Would it be all right with you if I didn't eat dinner at home tonight, Jillian?" she asked, eyeing me anxiously.

"Of course it's all right," I said. "But where are you going?"

"I'll tell you later," she whispered and hurried back to the customer she had been waiting on. I recognized him as a Mr. Fleming, a pleasant man in his sixties who went to our church and had been a regular customer for years.

After a lengthy conversation, he left the store, and Mama returned to me to explain. "I told Mr. Fleming I would go to the church supper with him tonight. I didn't think you would mind. We've gotten very well acquainted since I've been working here at the store, and of course, we'll be with people we have both known for years. You know, he really is a very nice man, Jillian—so lonely, too, since his wife died. He lost her about the same time we lost Daddy."

Although I wasn't too sure what I thought about Mama's evening out with Mr. Fleming, I could find no reason to object. But I found myself somehow disturbed by the idea, and it was hard to say which of us was more nervous while she waited for him to come for her.

Mama had taken special pains with her appearance, and it occurred to me that she was really quite attractive for a woman her age. With some misgiving, I watched her leave with Mr. Fleming. After they had gone, I felt as anxious as a mother whose daughter was setting out on her first date.

It was only when I was alone and the house was quiet that I admitted my disgruntled feelings. It was only then that I recognized the irony of the situation in which I found myself. Here I was sitting at home alone while Mama went out on a date.

With the realization, an anger came over me that left me shaking. I had given up Andrew to stay home and look after Mama, and now it was Mama who had run out on me!

As I thought about it, I had to ask myself bitterly if Andrew had been right all along. Was it really a fact that Mama couldn't get along on her own, or was it that she had simply never had a reason to try?

The more I thought about my situation, the more frantic I became. I knew I had to do something, go somewhere, get out of the house. I couldn't just sit there in silence regretting the happiness I had thrown away. In desperation, I threw on my coat and ran from the house. Because I was too upset to think clearly, I let my heart lead me where it wanted to go.

I got into the car and drove to Andrew's apartment. It seemed an eternity while I waited for him to answer the door. I could hear the television set playing inside, and I knew he was there. I could only hope that he would be alone.

When he opened the door, he stared at me silently for a moment. "Jillian?" he said, obviously surprised.

I swallowed hard and gathered my courage. "Yes, it's me, Andrew. I've finally come to my senses. I know you've found someone else now, but I felt I had to see you."

Eagerness came into his eyes, accompanied by confusion. "I don't know what you're talking about," he said. "I had almost given up hope of ever hearing from you, but there has never been anyone else."

"But I saw you with a woman, a pretty brunette—one day when you were leaving the shop."

He looked at me, puzzled. "I don't know who it could have been. The only brunette I can think of is the new saleswoman at the store.

But she's a happily married woman with no interest in anyone except her husband. No, Jillian. There's only one girl I'll ever care for. I just keep wishing that she would change her mind and come back to me." He hesitated and a look of longing came over his face. "Could that be why you're here? Have you come to tell me you've changed your mind?"

"Oh, yes, Andrew. I came to tell you how wrong I was to let you go—and to ask you if it's too late for us."

In answer, Andrew held out his arms to me. All the loneliness of the past disappeared as they closed around me. It was a long time before either of us could speak.

But finally Andrew drew away. "What's happened to make you change your mind?" he asked. "What about your mother, Jillian? What are you going to do about her?"

I nestled close to him and buried my head against his shoulder. "I'm not going to do anything," I said. "I'm going to leave it up to Mama to decide what she wants to do for herself."

Andrew and I have been married for over a year now, and things have worked out even better than we'd hoped. Of course, Mama raised a terrible fuss at first, but since then, she has managed surprisingly well. She's learning, with help from Andrew and me, to manage her household; she comes to work in the bookstore every day and seems to enjoy her work. While she will never be a businesswoman, she has learned a lot about running the store.

She and Mr. Fleming go out together regularly and seem to enjoy each other's company very much. Whether they have considered getting married, I can only guess.

In any event, I don't worry about her anymore. Whatever the future holds for her, I'm confident that she will be able to handle it.

The End

MY HUSBAND'S
UNDERWORLD LIFE!

With nothing on my mind but new curtains, I drove along the winding highway. I was on my way to the farmhouse Jake had bought the previous year. To my husband, the farm was a financial investment. But what a pleasant place it would be, I had often imagined since then, with its lilac hedges, little pond, and spreading meadows, for vacations and holiday weekends.

By then I was tired of Jake's type of vacation. We always went somewhere as guests of some wealthy older couple—like staying with the Fosters on their boat in the Florida Keys or with the Cavanaughs at their mountain lodge. There was always too much partying, alcohol, and flirting with other people's spouses for my taste.

Naturally, too, we couldn't take our daughter, Wendy, on such trips. Jake kept saying she was just a baby, too young to travel, but now that our daughter was in kindergarten I thought she was old enough to feel like she was being deserted by her parents—left behind while they went off to have a good time. My heart grieved at her hopeless sobbing when it was time to say good-bye and leave her with her middle-aged sitter.

If we take our vacations at the farm, I thought, we can have Wendy with us. How she'd love the bird songs, the frogs, and scampering squirrels.

Wendy was a lonely little girl, too quiet, which disturbed me. But Jake wouldn't hear a word about us having another child to keep Wendy company.

The lopsided oak that marked the entrance to the farmhouse lane came into view. Proud of myself that I hadn't gotten lost, since I'd only been there once before, I swung the sleek sports car, an anniversary gift from my husband, into the lane.

The country place. I might never have known Jake was buying it—he tried not to bore me, he said, with details of his financial plans. By chance I was with him that day in the shopping plaza when the real-estate agent caught up with him to say, "Oh, there you are, Mr. Franklin. I've been phoning your office all morning. The perfect country place, just what you're looking for, has come on the market. Want me to take you out now for a look?"

"Fine." Jake had shot me a quick, uneasy glance. "Honey, will you drive the car home? I'll be back in a couple of hours."

"Maybe your wife would want to see the house, too," the agent had cut in. "And it's a beautiful day for a drive in the country."

"I'd love to come along," I said, wondering why Jake hadn't suggested it himself. At the time, I felt he was a little displeased with the agent, perhaps because Jake wanted to surprise me with the place as a birthday gift. Later, though, he had explained he was buying the old farm only as an investment, not for our personal use. When months passed, then, without his ever mentioning the subject again, I realized this was the case.

Well, investment or not, the old farmhouse would be better with some fixing up, I decided, and, as a vacation home, it would help solve the problem of Wendy. So last week when Jake was in bed with the flu, I had sneaked the farmhouse key off his key ring long enough to have a copy of it made for myself.

In the lane, the car bucked and bounced. The real-estate agent's car hadn't bounced like that on that other visit to the farm, but that fact meant nothing to me—then. Nor did it register then that the wide tracks I was trying to straddle, so deeply cut into the mud, must have been made by heavy vehicles like trucks, coming and going.

I just didn't notice any of those things. My mind was on curtains. First the windows would be measured—I'd brought a tape in my purse—then drapes and curtains could be ordered. Next week I would pick out new furniture and have it delivered. Then I'd phone to have the utilities turned on. Of course, the walls would need repainting, but perhaps Jake and I could do that on weekends. But not this month, of course. We were all booked up right now.

Smiling, I parked the little car beside the house. Jake and I working together again! We could relive that happy time when we had been newlyweds fixing up a shabby apartment, enjoying the clean smell of fresh paint and the sense of accomplishment. He had been fast with the roller on large areas, while I had done the detail work with the brush around windows and doors. We had sung bits of songs at each other, played CDs, cooked simple meals on a hot plate, and had made love at any hour.

After Wendy was born, Jake began making good in the insurance business and everything seemed to change overnight. He was gone long hours. Then he said we needed a bigger house in the suburbs where we could entertain, and of course we also needed nice furniture, cars, and wardrobes to match those of our new circle of friends. I never knew how Jake could pay all the bills. Since we'd moved from the apartment, in fact, I never knew just how much money my husband earned a year. He told me not to worry about such things, so I didn't. The most extravagant bills I ran up—with his encouragement—on our charge accounts were always paid promptly; the checking account was never overdrawn.

Gazing at the old house, I suddenly felt chilled. It looked so lonely and deserted—haunted, even. The door hinges had squealed fearfully that day when the real estate agent had swung the door open. But things had seemed pleasant enough then, with Jake's hand on my arm and the agent's bright chatter.

Now, restraining a shiver, I opened the big, weathered door. The hinges didn't squeal now. The door opened noiselessly, as if well oiled. Gingerly, I stepped in.

Boards had been removed from some of the windows and shafts of sunlight filtered into the rooms, revealing that the house was no longer empty. In fact, it looked like a department store. Heaps of cameras and electronic equipment filled the corners. Row after row of TV sets, stereos, and camcorders were in the living room. In the master bedroom, assorted handguns lay on canvas tarps, while rows of rifles leaned against the walls.

That is, all except for one antique rifle. That one was hanging by its leather shoulder strap in a place of honor over the fireplace. I recognized that old rifle with its carved walnut stock: It was a flintlock with an impressive history, the gem of a collection belonging to Richard G. Porter.

I remembered how proudly the wealthy old lawyer had displayed the flintlock at his most recent party, at which Jake and I were guests. I remembered, too, what Jake had said to me while we were dressing for the party that evening. "You get Richard talking about his hobby. You know, give him a chance to impress you with his memory for historical details, which he'll love. Then I'll corner him later about whether the collection is adequately insured. Could be a fat commission for me there." And now ironically, the antique gun had been stolen. I hoped Mr. Porter had taken out insurance on it.

Stolen goods? It dawned on me then that the house I had been mentally redecorating for weeks was being used as a warehouse by a gang of thieves. Shaken, my heart beating fast, I nearly ran from the house to find a phone to call the police. With difficulty, though, I repressed the urge and began to explore the house. I tried to memorize details, as if the loot would all disappear the minute I turned my back, and before the police could see it. That's how I found the clue.

It was in the kitchen. A square, modern safe stood in one corner. Some folding chairs and a card table were arranged in the middle of the floor. On the table lay assorted wristwatches and credit cards, evidently not valuable enough to go inside the safe. And a half-empty pack of gum.

The gum was the brand that Jake liked.

I did run out of the house then. I flew down the lane to the car, and how I maneuvered it back to the highway is a mystery to me. My hands were still shaking when I was halfway back to the city. My husband a thief, maybe even one of a gang of thieves! Our fine clothes, cars, the weekly visits to the hairdresser, the lovely house—all paid for with the proceeds of crime. The man I had sworn to love, honor, and cherish had abused the hospitality of our friends to case their houses for valuables, to study the alarm systems and other home safeguards, returning later to take what he wanted. Sick at heart, I didn't know which way to turn for help.

It may seem I leaped to a hasty conclusion, judging my husband guilty on very slight evidence. Someone else could have left the pack of gum. But there are times when one small clue explains a bewildering series of events. In this case it just made too much sense, explaining things about my marriage that had puzzled me for years.

Where all the money came from, for example. Why it was so important for us to be invited to all the big social events in Rosedale, to attend parties at certain houses, whether I had a headache or not. Why I had to be so well groomed and fashionably dressed, regardless of expense. Why I wasn't allowed to help with the household budget anymore. Why my husband made so many out-of-town trips. Why he worked late almost every evening when we weren't actually scheduled to attend a party.

For hours I drove around the city, wrestling with my shocking discovery. If my husband had yielded to a sudden temptation, or had committed a crime under emotional stress, I would've forgiven him quickly, standing by him with a loyal heart. But I certainly couldn't tolerate his practicing crime as a way of life.

Once when I was a child I had stolen something, and the experience had left an indelible mark on me. It was just before Halloween and I was in the third grade. While walking home from school, some classmates and I found the gate open to the little neighborhood cemetery. We had entered to sit among the tombstones and scare ourselves with spooky stories. A new grave heaped with flowers caught our eyes. My best girlfriend exclaimed, "What a pretty vase someone threw away. I'm taking it home to Mama."

At once the others raced for vases and flower baskets, throwing out the contents on the ground. I headed home with a monstrously ugly gray urn I didn't even want.

Up the street I went, proudly hugging my trophy, and rang the doorbell for my mother to let me in. Down the same street I trotted with the urn a few minutes later, crying, my mother walking behind me in indignant silence all the way back to the cemetery. There I was forced to make tearful apologies to the caretaker and offer restitution. That night Dad spanked me for the first time. Not hard, but the agony of shame and humiliation makes me squirm even now, remembering. Worse, every time he looked at me for weeks afterward, my father would shake his head sadly and say, "Amy, I never thought you would steal."

Restitution was my first concern now. Mr. Porter must have his valuable flintlock back as soon as possible. All the stolen goods at the farmhouse must be returned to the rightful owners. But how could we give back what had already been sold so that Jake and I could live the good life? Naively, I believed I would only have to explain my feelings to my husband, and at once he would reform his ways.

When it was time to pick up Wendy from kindergarten that day, my hands ached from gripping the steering wheel so tensely.

"Mommy, you're not going out tonight, are you?" she asked while we ate supper. Her sweet, wistful expression tugged at my heart.

"No, dear." I smiled reassuringly. "No baby-sitter tonight. We'll watch TV or play games, and I'll tuck you in bed myself." Jake was away on a trip with—as usual—an indefinite return date, but he had urged me to accept an invitation to the Dorchesters' house tonight. Another couple was to pick me up at eight o'clock. Hastily, I phoned to plead a headache and, feeling almost sinful, enjoyed spending the evening at home with my daughter.

The next day I canceled my hairdresser's appointment. The day after that, I canceled a shopping date with my friend, Donna, and skipped my biweekly session at the gym. All my purchases were limited strictly to necessary groceries. Already, I was practicing Spartan economy for the years of hardship and struggle that I knew lay ahead.

As the hours dragged on, my doubts grew. Would Jake listen to me? During our first happy year we had been true partners, but after that he had become the dominant force in our marriage. His strong will and consuming ambition dictated everything about how and where we were to live. My initial protests were overwhelmed and I had yielded, allowing myself to be taken care of "as a wife should be," to quote him. Something inside me had even been rather pleased at being relegated to the status of a child! But no more; my mind was made up. Jake would reform and we would be equal partners again, or I'd seek a legal separation.

Where was my husband now? Off in another city contacting black-market outlets? Perhaps selling Mrs. Farnsworth's pearls that had been stolen last week? And when Jake returned home, would it be only to pick up Mr. Porter's flintlock to deliver to an unscrupulous collector?

Richard and Julie Porter had been kind to us the first year we had lived in Rosedale. They had even gotten Jake accepted as a member of two exclusive clubs. Richard would be the ideal person to advise me in my troubles. Although retired from practice, he was skilled in arranging settlements, discreetly protecting his clients while at the same time seeing that the rules of fair play were observed.

On the third day after my visit to the farm, I dialed the Porters' phone number. I only reached an answering service that said the family was away on a month's vacation. So they don't even know yet that they've been robbed, I thought. That explained why I had heard no news about the burglary.

My need for counsel grew, however, so the next morning after I dropped Wendy off at her school, I headed for Smithtown to consult Dr. Curtis, the pastor of the congregation my folks had belonged to years ago.

Every city has its Smithtown, I guess—a district of busy alleys and quiet streets, weathered, three-story houses with attics, curtained windows with "Room to Let" signs, and a central commercial street of used-goods shops, ethnic restaurants, and dingy neighborhood bars. Irish families settled heavily there during the potato famine, followed by Italians and Slavs and, recently, Syrians, Maltese, Filipinos, and many others. A Smithtown differs from other poor sections of the city in that it possesses a strong feeling of neighborhood, pride in its ethnic diversity, and in its few historic buildings such as a wax museum, a very old church, or the house where some half-forgotten poet once lived.

Filled with bittersweet memories, I drove slowly past the rambling high school where my father had been principal. It looked smaller now, and a broken window needed repair. Detouring next to pass the big house with the vine-covered porch where my parents had lived, I was jolted by the new, garish yellow color of the front door and trim. Sadly, I doubled back to the main street. My father had died when I was seventeen. My mother had lived to see me married and through what she called my "first" pregnancy, hoping for many grandchildren, and then had succumbed to a heart ailment. With her funeral, my ties to Smithtown had been severed and I had not revisited the district since.

There was the little church now, just ahead. But it had changed too much for me to seek help there today. Two girls in flowing saris were selling paper flowers on each side of the doorway, while from the dark interior came a monotonous chant from the congregation. I drove past.

Then the man who ran the shoe-repair shop came into view. Eagerly, I called to him.

"Oh, Mr. Stein," I said, "where has Dr. Curtis, the minister, moved?"

"Gone to the next world," was his answer. "Heart attack, poor fellow." Narrowed eyes, Smithtown's response to outsiders, scanned me closely. "Was there something you wanted, ma'am?"

Clearly I had changed, too; he didn't recognize me. As I hesitated, he added politely, "The congregation's mostly moved to the suburbs, but those who remain meet in each other's houses for Bible readings. I take a bus to St. Nicholas's, myself."

"Thank you." I began to roll up the car window.

"Say," he asked abruptly, "how did you know my name?"

"Why, I used to go to school here in Smithtown." Smiling at him, I drove on.

Impulsively, I parked the car in front of Dorrance's Drugstore, where I had worked as a teenager, and where I had met Jake. The place seemed narrower than before, with a clutter of boxes in the aisles and badly arranged displays.

From behind his glassed-in counter under the sign "Prescriptions Filled Here," the pharmacist, Kevin McCabe—or Mac—frowned at me.

I smiled and waved at him, but his attention was demanded by a red-faced, anxious businessman, shoving a folded prescription at him.

I noticed that Karen Dorrance was in her office, her back to the door as she spoke urgently into the phone about a delayed delivery. Her head, with its familiar unruly hairdo, nodded vigorously.

Automatically, my eyes turned back to the store, appraising customers. If I was a successful, poised hostess now, as Jake was so fond of saying, it was because I had learned at Dorrance's the knack of sensing individual needs—understanding which individuals should be left alone to browse, which ones relied on the clerk's judgment to make choices, and which ones you had to stick close to, chatting in a friendly way, until they made a purchase and left, to keep them from pocketing anything portable.

Sure enough, Mrs. Nichols was taking advantage of the situation. Karen was busy on the phone, Mac was occupied with a customer, and the blond girl who should have been tending the store, my replacement, was combing her hair behind the cash register, looking off into space and letting just anyone browse.

Mrs. Nichols's weakness was cosmetics, especially powder compacts in bright cases, although she never wore a speck of makeup. In a flash, without thinking, I was swooping down on her. "Why, Mrs. Nichols. How nice to see you again," I said. "Is your grandson still winning at football?"

Embarrassment mingling with pride, the woman said, "Who, Wally? He's in the Navy now. Wait, I'll show you the last picture he sent me."

While she was fumbling with one hand in her purse, I firmly rescued the compact concealed in her other hand and restored it to the rack, saying cheerily, "Here, let's put this out of your way. It's the wrong shade for your skin."

213

Just about then, Karen descended on us. Apparently she'd sensed what was going on and ended her phone call. She pressed my arm warmly in passing as she escorted a now meek Mrs. Nichols to the front of the store, helped her to select a tube of toothpaste, and left her at the cash register. The blond girl, ringing up the sale, yawned, oblivious to everything.

Instead of speaking sharply to her, as I expected, Karen rushed back to hug me. "Amy! How good to see you again! If it's work you're looking for here in Smithtown. . . ." She winked to show she hadn't missed my expensive clothes. "Your job is always open for you."

"Thanks, but my husband isn't as tolerant of career wives as your Doug," I said. "How is he, by the way?"

Her face twisted. "I lost him three years ago. A stroke. He was paralyzed for months, so it was a mercy when he slipped away," she said.

"Oh, I'm terribly sorry." I hugged her, appalled at the thought of that good-natured giant of a man lying helpless in a hospital bed. Doug Dorrance had been a close friend of my father's. So both Doug and Dr. Curtis, pillars of strength in Smithtown, were gone now and I hadn't even known, caught up as I was in the social whirl of Rosedale.

Fortunately, Mac joined us then. His customer seemed more flushed than ever as he paid at the cash register, at the last minute reaching for a bag of potato chips. As he left the store, Mac muttered, "There goes trouble."

Quickly, Karen asked, "Forged prescription?"

"No, genuine enough. But he's getting drugs from two different doctors for his angina. I tried to warn him. And that salty bag of chips he just bought is sheer poison to him. As for you, Amy!" His stern gaze switched to me. "What pills have you been popping? You, who were so radiantly healthy and wholesome! Your color's bad and you're a walking skeleton."

My jaw dropped. For a minute I couldn't believe my ears. Used to hearing only compliments from my husband and friends on my slim figure, it was a shock to receive such a slap in the face here in Smithtown, where I had come for comfort and aid. The unfairness hurt, too, because I hated dieting. My strict diet and the relentless exercise classes had been Jake's idea, not mine.

Meanwhile, Mac stepped briskly to the counter. "I was afraid you might be on speed. Staring eyes, hyperactive, twisting and fidgeting every second. Are you sure you aren't taking some kind of pep pill?"

"No drugs at all," I said.

"None of your business anyway, Mac," Karen scolded. "You're part owner of this place now, so try to cultivate a little tact with the paying customers. Besides, I'm trying to lure this gal back to work for me. She gave class to the place. Her displays were eye-catching, the cash register always balanced, and the shoplifting rate hit zero when she was here. What about it, Amy? At a nice raise in pay, of course."

"Sorry, but my husband doesn't approve of working wives." I sighed.

Then I remembered how Jake supported me in luxury, why he wanted me slim and stylish, and I crumpled inside. Again in my mind's eye I saw the old farmhouse with its neat rows of stolen TVs, rifles, the safe—and that pack of gum left behind.

Some of the misery I felt must have shown in my face for Karen murmured, "You poor kid," exchanging a glance with her partner. Mac, his face now kind and gentle as it used to be, said, "Now, Amy, whatever the trouble is, maybe Karen and I can help. What's wrong?"

But I couldn't talk to them about my shocking discovery about Jake. Swallowing, I said, "There's a personal problem, yes. That's why I came to Smithtown today, to consult Dr. Curtis. But never mind, I know what his advice would've been. And I mean to take it."

I knew then that Dr. Curtis would have said, "Don't compromise with evil."

So I found strength and consolation in Smithtown, after all, I thought as I drove home. Dear Karen and gruff, kindly Mac, partners now. What a pair they made. Maybe now that they were both through their periods of mourning, they might marry. As for myself, I knew what I had to do.

That night when Wendy was tucked into bed and I was dealing out a game of solitaire, I heard Jake's quick steps as he entered the house. My heart leaped inside me; I couldn't help it. He was still the man I loved, the only man I had ever wanted. After five years of marriage, we were still lovers.

"What's this I hear?" he asked as he dropped a fleeting kiss on my forehead, then stepped back to eye me in mock severity. "On the street, I ran into Eric, from the gym, and he tells me you've been skipping your exercise sessions. Fat is gross, Amy. Do you want to be obese like your mother?"

Years ago I had never thought of my mother as fat. Like her mother before her, Mother had been considered "a fine figure of a woman" in Smithtown, which still retained old-country standards. Full bosomed, with generous hips and a small waist, had been called a perfect girl by her husband, who liked a woman to be soft and rounded.

I said bluntly, "Jake, I'm giving up the gym and hairdresser—to keep expenses down. We can save on luxuries."

"Save?" He was taking off his tie, and he turned his head to stare at me. "What for? We're in the green now, darling. Lots of money."

"Yes. And I know where it comes from," I said.

"What do you mean?" His voice went flat.

"I went out to the old farmhouse, thinking we might take our next vacation there with Wendy."

"Who have you told?" he asked. "The police?"

"No. I'm no informer." I drew myself up proudly, but inside I was shaken. All along, I guess I had been expecting him to deny it, to say he had no idea how any of those expensive items had gotten inside the farmhouse. But he was guilty—guilty!

"In that case, forget it," he said. "If you love me as much as you claim to, you'll help me get ahead in this world, like a loyal wife should."

"But," I cried, "stealing, Jake? Isn't there some other way?"

"Everybody steals," he said. "From the office or shop where they work, or from hotels where they're guests. Fraudulent insurance claims, juggled books, cheating on the income tax—it's universal."

"Even if you could justify theft that way," I said, "it's one thing to cheat a big company or government, but another thing to hurt private persons—friends who trust you."

"These rich slobs aren't hurting," he said. "They deduct their losses from taxes at the end of the year and collect full value from the insurance companies, too."

"Will the money replace Richard Porter's treasured heirloom?" I asked. "Oh, Jake, give it up. Let the owners have their stuff back from the farmhouse and we'll get by. We'll move to a smaller house—economize."

"No!" he stormed, his face furious. "I won't live like that again. I had enough of penny-pinching with my parents. It was always 'Steve, don't throw that shirt away. I'll turn the collar,' and 'Steve, we can't afford new shoes for you so soon. Your old ones can be resoled. The tops are good.' No, I want new, quality things for the rest of my life. The top, that's where I'm headed. Wouldn't you like to be a multimillionaire's wife?"

For a moment I could not speak. Steve? But my husband's name was Jake. He had told me that his parents had died when he was a baby, a wealthy uncle had adopted him, and his boyhood was divided between elite boarding schools and summer camps. While in his second year of college, Jake had become estranged from his uncle, who had married again and Jake was disinherited. Was this all lies, then? If so, the man I loved did not exist. "Jake" was a carefully constructed fake.

"Multimillionaire?" I asked. "I'd rather have an honest man." Shoving back my chair, I started to rise.

Before I knew it, Jake had grabbed me by the hair, tugging hard to twist my face toward him while he hooked my legs from under me with his foot. He struck me four times—open-handed, contemptuous slaps on my left cheek and that side of my face soon went numb. I felt as if my scalp was being torn from my head as I swung helplessly. "You dummy," a harsh, rasping voice, the voice of a stranger, bellowed. "I've worked and planned for years! We'll live the way I want, or you'll regret it. That whining brat of yours could go bye-bye, you know." Almost to himself Jake added something that chilled my blood. "A child under six years old brings a fortune on today's kiddie market."

"Jake!" I cried in horror, my physical pain forgotten. "Your own child?"

To this day, I cannot believe Jake would've carried out this vicious threat to sell our daughter. Still, my love for Jake died in that hour. That he could think of such a monstrous thing was enough to show me I was indeed dealing with a stranger—a selfish and hardened criminal.

Suddenly remembering himself, Jake solicitously helped me to my feet. "Sorry if I lost my temper," he said. "I didn't mean to hurt you. Listen, please don't try to saddle me with the sticky emotions and obligations of parenthood. I hadn't planned on children, but you rushed into things. That particular problem of ours is all your fault. But why can't we live like civilized people? Amy, I've got too much invested in this deal, and in you, to lose out now. Didn't I take you from a slum and groom you into a society beauty? I've treated you like a queen and you know it."

Then he smiled boyishly. "Can you blame a man for wanting to give nice things to the woman he loves while they are both young enough to enjoy life? Please don't rock the boat. Now, why don't you go brew us a pot of coffee?"

All the charm was back—the charm that had persuaded me so often to act against my better judgment. But now my heart was like a heavy stone inside me, and I couldn't answer.

Silently, I made coffee and brought in the tray. Jake was writing in his notebook, a pile of papers from his briefcase pushed aside, and the newspaper open to the business page. Without looking up, he said cheerfully, "Five of my stocks are going up, three down. I'm getting the hang of it. Won't be long now until I can give up, well, certain activities that bother you. I'll have made my fortune."

Later I heard Jake showering. Then he dressed and went out. For a long while I sat in my room, in the dark, watching the street. My hopes and dreams were shattered. There was an empty aching inside me where all my love had been. My thoughts churned wildly: Should I ask for a separation? But what good would even a divorce do, since fathers have visiting and vacation privileges? Wendy can be snatched out of my life forever at any time, unless I do exactly what Jake wants—from now on.

Jake didn't return and I spent the night in Wendy's room, sitting in a chair beside her bed. Looking down at the face of my sleeping daughter in the dim glow of the night-light, I swore that she'd never again be sacrificed for Jake's interests, as she had been in the past.

In the morning I found a note Jake had left, as if nothing had happened between us. It read: "Don't forget the Sedgewick bash is tonight. If you don't have a presentable turquoise dress, get one today. That's the old man's favorite color. Chin up, dearest."

Leaving the note where it was, I made breakfast for Wendy. When I had dropped her off at kindergarten, I drove directly to Smithtown. My jaw was slightly swollen and a molar had been knocked loose. It was a tooth with a crown on it, and it had given me trouble in the past. My scalp hurt when I combed my hair, too, but in the mirror my appearance had seemed normal enough—no obvious bruises.

It was just ten o'clock when I walked into Dorrance's Drugstore. Karen wasn't in the store and Mac came hurrying toward me, his face alarmed.

"Is something wrong?" he asked.

Talking with Mac wasn't part of my plans, but I found myself saying brightly, "What have you got for a loose tooth? I ran into the bathroom door last night."

"Come in here," he said quickly, holding open the door to the pharmacy area. Under the bright fluorescent light, he tilted my face with a cool, professional hand. "Which tooth is it?" he asked.

"The one farthest back, with the crown." I felt idiotic as I opened my mouth wide.

"Keep your tongue away from it," he said shortly. With a cotton applicator, he painted a pink paste tasting of mint around the tooth. "This will numb the gum. The tooth should tighten in its socket in a day or so," he told me. "Just remember to chew on the other side, and if it acts up see your dentist."

"I will. I mustn't lose the tooth. Thanks, Mac," I said. Then our eyes met and I looked away quickly from his searching gaze. Suddenly aware of how close together we were standing, I moved back.

Mac's hand brushed my cheek gently, and he said, "Tell me the truth, Amy. Did he hit you?"

To my horror, I found my eyes brimming with tears at the sympathetic note in his voice. I nodded.

He said, "So that's the problem you wanted to consult Dr. Curtis about. No, things are worse than that—I can tell by your face. I knew he was wrong for you the first time he stepped inside this store. It's my fault for not warning you. What's his racket? Protection or drugs?"

I found myself blurting out the whole story—the farmhouse, the charge accounts, the flintlock, the big weekend parties, everything all garbled together. Somehow it didn't seem quite as bad as what Mac suspected, although the threat against Wendy, which I held back, made any kind of life with Jake unthinkable. Mac, however, wasn't inclined to urge me to return to my husband. But he spoke soothingly, and, just when I was getting my sniffles under control, Karen appeared in the doorway.

"What's going on?" Her sharp eyes lingered on my jaw, which felt huge.

"Her husband hit her," Mac said tersely. "Knocked a tooth loose."

"But that's not the whole story, is it?" Karen asked. "You wouldn't have that sick look, Amy, if it were. He's a psychopath of some kind, I'll bet. You remember, Mac, I always told you he had cold eyes."

Since what Karen suspected also seemed worse than the truth, I said, "He's a professional thief, and I found out. We had an argument about it last night. He warned me not to rock the boat, but I can't live with a criminal. Knowing all this," I paused uncertainly. "Karen, do you still want to hire me?"

Karen beamed. "Like a shot! Say, haven't you got a little girl? You two could board with Mrs. Torino, who could baby-sit while you're working. The money will solve her problem, too. She's got two grandchildren to raise. She's neat as a pin and a good cook. You could stand some hearty home cooking, I'll bet."

I smiled wanly, seeing some hope for my future. With a job, I could support my child and myself. Boarding in a private home would be better for my purposes—hiding out, that is—than an apartment or house where the phone and utilities would be in my name, and therefore traceable.

Things were that simple. At noon, I picked up Wendy at school and drove the sports car downtown. I left it parked, the keys inside, at the bus terminal. That was my good-bye to the "good life." When the police reported the abandoned car to Jake, surely he would think I had left the state. Then, holding Wendy's hand tightly, I led her onto a city bus for her first trip by public transportation. She was thrilled and all eyes. Because the bus was crowded she had to sit on my lap, which she enjoyed. She cuddled against me, but didn't try to speak. Her voice was quite soft, a near whisper that was sometimes inaudible, to the annoyance of her teachers and Jake. But from her bright eyes and excited smiles now, it was clear that she knew something important and different was happening in our lives.

By one o'clock we were sitting in Mrs. Torino's homey kitchen. I was eating an enormous plate of stuffed cabbage, while my daughter explored the same food with the cabbage wrappings removed and extra sauce added. The food tasted delicious, and I realized I hadn't eaten a real meal in days.

Our new landlady, who asked to be called Maria, was a middle-aged woman of Lithuanian descent. She explained that although she had married an Italian, she had never mastered that cuisine, and did I mind? "Not at all," I answered, savoring every mouthful. Wendy emptied her plate, too.

At first I was disappointed, though, that Mrs. Torino's grandchildren weren't old enough to be playmates for Wendy. The boy was two years old, the girl an infant. But Wendy was delighted, and couldn't get enough of peering into the crib and marveling about how tiny the baby was. "Look, Mommy, she's got my finger," Wendy said happily. "I think she likes me."

Hearing my daughter speak in a high, clear voice, not a whisper, warmed my heart. Our family doctor had repeatedly assured me that Wendy's throat and larynx were normal—that her only problem was extreme shyness—but I hadn't really believed him until that moment.

That afternoon I made the rounds of used-clothing stores nearby, replacing our wardrobes with serviceable clothing that cost very little. I selected subdued colors for myself. When I had washed my hair that evening and set it in a simpler style, I doubted that any of my friends from Rosedale would recognize me now. Happily, I phoned Karen. "When do I report for work?" I asked.

"Let's wait until that swelling of your cheek goes down. Rest up for a few days," she said. "The other girl may as well finish out this week. I've talked with her already and she tells me she'd rather work as a cocktail waitress anyway, so that's that. We'll see you next Monday."

"Sounds fine," I said, and hung up.

For the next two days I simply ate, slept, and played with the children. Wendy was now inseparable from the tiny tots. Seeing her so filled with enthusiasm, so pleased with her new life, did much to keep me from worrying about the dark cloud over our heads.

The cloud was still there, though. One afternoon Karen phoned, warning me to stay off the streets. Jake was searching the area for us.

From shop to shop he went, asking questions, and also stopping passersby. But nobody had seen a woman, a little girl, and a small sports car. Smithtown had closed ranks to protect one of its own from an outsider.

Before this, I hadn't given any thought to the effect that my desertion would have on Jake. What had he thought on returning home to find us gone, but all the furs, jewels, clothing, and expensive gifts he had bought for us left behind? Also, the credit cards and bankbooks were lying on top of my desk, clearly unwanted. If he was searching for me in Smithtown, then the police hadn't yet reported to him that my abandoned car had been found at the bus terminal. Had Jake filed a missing-persons report? Probably not; he would avoid the police wherever possible.

Fortunately, either Jake's failure to find us in Smithtown convinced him we weren't there, or the abandoned-car report finally came through, directing his search out of state, because he didn't return to Smithtown.

In the weeks that followed, I slipped easily into the life of my old neighborhood. At the store, I worked hard. Although technically I had two bosses, by tacit agreement I took my orders from Karen. Mac kept to his cubicle, rarely speaking to me except to say hello or good-bye.

Once, though, he paused beside me to smile encouragingly. "The roses are coming back to your cheeks, Amy," he said.

Fat was coming back to my hips, too, although, wisely, he didn't mention that. I gained fifteen pounds fast, another three more slowly, then leveled off, although I kept eating big meals. Wendy gained weight, too, and seemed to grow inches taller all at once. I had kept her from school, fearing that Jake would find us if I registered her. Since she was already ahead of her age group, I felt that the warm experiences in family life she was having now, especially helping to take care of Maria's grandchildren, were what she needed most emotionally. In fact, it was some time before I realized that not once since our flight from Rosedale had Wendy asked about her father, and I sensed just how unhappy she had been there.

Then one day I came home to find the house filled with a rare, lovely sound; my daughter was singing. And in a foreign language! Her "Auntie Maria" had taught her an old lullaby in her native Lithuanian, and Wendy was singing the baby to sleep. Her happiness was so obvious that I shed my last doubt that I had done the right thing in bringing my child to live in Smithtown.

Then, on a Saturday evening four months later, everything changed. Maria and I were watching the news on TV and I think I stopped breathing until the announcer stopped talking.

An attempted burglary in Rosedale at the Sedgewick mansion, which housed a rare coin collection, had left an aged caretaker with a fractured skull. He wasn't expected to live. A burglar alarm had gone off, and the caretaker had prevented the burglars from entering the house, but he had been struck with a gun butt by one of the two men as they fled. Police had pursued the fleeing vehicle—a dark van—and shots were exchanged. Traveling at high speeds on the expressway, the van had gone off the road at a curve, crashed, and burst into flames. One man escaped on foot. Judging by bloodstains left behind on the passenger side of the front seat, he had been wounded. The body of the driver, killed on impact, had been severely burned but the police had obtained partial fingerprints.

The room swam before my eyes. Maria looked at me in alarm.

"That was him?" she asked. "Your husband?"

"How could I know?" I choked. "We haven't been told the man's name."

"Always there's some clue," she said. "A woman knows when her man's in bad trouble."

Indeed, there was a clue for me. Sedgewick's. We were to attend a party at the Sedgewick mansion the night I ran away from Jake.

All that long night Maria and I sat huddled, first before the TV and then beside the radio in the kitchen, the sound turned low so as not to disturb the sleeping children. When I broke into hysterical sobbing once, Maria held me in her arms, rocking me and saying softly, "I know, I know. It's bad."

No new findings were given until morning, when it was reported that the caretaker was improving and seemed likely to live. The fingerprints of the dead man hadn't identified him; he had no prior criminal record, and hadn't been in the military service. So, with no new developments, the story was already being replaced in the news by more sensational crimes. It seemed likely that the dead man in the van would remain unidentified. And that was a thought I couldn't bear, somehow.

Since Karen was out of town that weekend, visiting a married daughter, I reluctantly called Mac. He sounded sleepy at first, but became wide-awake when he heard my voice.

Soon he interrupted my anguished flow of words to ask, "Why are you so certain the dead driver is your husband? Maybe he's the one out there who's wounded."

"No. Jake wouldn't ride in a car unless he was behind the steering wheel," I said. "And he always sneered at the kind of person who has to use a gun to get what he wants in this world. Jake preferred using brains and charm."

"I see. Well, Amy, if your husband had been a lone wolf as I first thought, I'd drive you to a police station. But with other people in the background protecting their interests—and they may have a few million dollars' worth of stuff in that kitchen safe alone—it wouldn't be wise for you to surface just now as a witness. Sit tight. I'll be over in about an hour, bringing a person you can talk to. See if Mrs. Torino will cook up a hearty breakfast to improve his state of mind after being wakened so early."

The mysterious person proved to be Sergeant Dale Strickland, now a detective uptown but once a rookie walking the beat in Smithtown.

"No reason why this can't be kept off the record," he said when I finished explaining why I thought Jake was involved. "We'll check it out, anyway. Chances are good the loot has been moved from the farm already, but we'll set up a stakeout there in case the wounded man or anyone else tries to use the place as a hideout."

222

"Will I have to identify the body?" I asked, dreading the possibility.

"No use. His own mother wouldn't know him," Sergeant Strickland said. "We'll check his prints against those in your husband's bedroom—ones on his shoes in the closet, for example. Give me his dentist's name, too. Dental work is often used to identify bodies. We'll let you know what we find out."

The body was identified as Jake's, as I had known from the first. The funeral was private, with just myself and a minister attending, since Jake's death wasn't mentioned in the news—not even when a shoot-out at the farm ended in the capture of three armed suspects, since that happened in another county. For the city police, the case was unofficially allowed to drop into oblivion.

Unofficially, too, Sergeant Strickland returned to hand me an envelope containing a check, the reward Mr. Porter had posted for the return of his heirloom flintlock.

The money came in handy because Jake had left no insurance. His financial affairs were chaotic, too. Nothing was completely paid for—even the stocks had been bought on margin. House, farm, cars, furniture—even the jewelry and clothes I had left behind—were all seized by creditors.

Throughout my ordeal, it was Mac who was always by my side. He arranged the funeral, bought me meals, and made sure I got some rest. Emotionally drained, I leaned on him, grateful for his kindness. Even in the months following Jake's death, Mac remained a constant comfort to me, and I soon found myself attracted to him, both as a friend and a man.

I'm still living in Smithtown—some two years later. Mac and I were married a year ago, and not a day has gone by since then that I don't thank God for bringing him into my life.

The End

WHY WOULD A 17-YEAR-OLD GIRL DO IT?

Afterward, I had no clear memories of the funeral at all. Only jumbled, hazy images of blurred faces and a horrible, oblong box that held my child. Thank God the ordeal was finally over. I was numb, devastated—and there was no way I could recover from the terrible wound in my soul. My firstborn—my older daughter—had committed suicide.

The doctor had given me pills to ease the shock. They did take the sharpest edge off my grief, but nothing could stop the incessant question that tortured me: Why?

Why would a seventeen-year-old girl take her own life? True, she had been deeply troubled for several years and had caused us untold worry, but we'd never dreamed she'd even consider killing herself. Only crazy people did that, and Michelle was just mixed up, not crazy.

Why had she done such a thing, just when we thought she was getting along so much better? In the weeks before she died, she had been actually cheerful, after years of moodiness and outright rebellion. I clearly remembered a conversation Howard and I had had just days before the tragedy.

The girls were both out on dates, and we were sitting in the living room waiting for the news to come on television. "Have you noticed the change in Michelle the last week or so?" I asked. Howard was scanning the paper and I was knitting.

"Yeah," he said, glancing up. "Looks like she's finally beginning to come out of this awful teenage phase she's been in. And about time, too, I'd say. Maybe we can have a little peace around this house for a change."

"It's beginning to look that way," I said. "She's finally showing some signs of becoming the kind of girl she ought to be. I always knew she had it in her. She's finally learning to control her feelings, too. She hasn't had one of her tantrums for almost a month now." I drew a deep sigh of relief. "Maybe the worst is finally over."

Howard folded his paper and grabbed the remote. "And, would you believe, it seems our constant harping about her greed and selfishness has finally paid off? I was talking to David Patterson the other day, and he just happened to mention how much Caroline was enjoying the records Michelle had given her. 'Don't tell me Michelle was able to part with any of her records long enough to loan them out?' I asked. 'No, she gave six of them to Caroline outright,' David said. 'Told her she wouldn't be needing them anymore.'"

"Well!" I exclaimed. "She's finally realized that stuff is junk! Talk about miracles!" Then I stopped knitting and gazed at Howard in amazement. "You know, I just realized I haven't had to yell at her to turn down her music all week—because she hasn't played any. Do you suppose she's developing a new interest?"

"I certainly hope so. Anyway, it's nice to see some improvement at last." And we both smiled, completely unaware of the true significance of Michelle's actions.

Later that week, there was bitter conflict between us again, and we decided our optimism had been premature. The argument was about a weekend trip to the city. We lived in a small town about forty miles from Milville, and Michelle wanted to go there with a group of her friends.

"Absolutely not," I answered when she asked for permission.

"Why?" she persisted, and I braced for battle.

"Are there boys going?" I asked bluntly.

"Sure," she said with scorn.

"There's your answer," I said. "You think I don't know what goes on nowadays? You know your father and I don't go along with all this permissiveness. You have no business getting mixed up in something like that, and you should know better than to ask."

"Dad?" Michelle asked, a quaver in her voice.

Howard looked up from his magazine. "The answer is no," he said abruptly.

"But—"

"There's no use coaxing," Howard said. "You ought to know by now that when your mother and I say no, we mean no."

"When are you ever going to stop treating me like a child?" There was a wild note in Michelle's voice, and my anger flared.

"When you stop acting like a child," I said, trying hard to keep my voice calm and my words reasonable. "A nice girl—a responsible young woman—would not want to take part in a wild orgy."

"Mother, it's not going to be like that. We don't plan—"

"What's planned and what actually happens can be two very different things." I couldn't keep the irritation out of my voice.

"Mom, I don't even have a steady boyfriend now. You know that. We aren't going as couples. There are just a bunch of us who want to see this rock concert and—"

"Why not go to the concert and then come home? You don't need to stay overnight."

"But we want to!"

"I'm afraid not," I said brightly.

"But you won't even listen to me!"

"Michelle, we're always willing to let you do anything that's

225

reasonable and respectable, but this is not. It's simply not wise for a bunch of young people to be running around on their own in the city on a weekend. It's just asking for trouble. You're not being very mature, or you'd realize that for yourself."

"There you go again, trying to force me into some mold you picked out for me." Michelle's voice was tinged with hysteria and her face crumpled. "You want me to be some perfect little lady you can keep under your thumb. Well, I won't be. I won't be!" She ran from the room, sobbing.

That was Wednesday, and I expected her to keep right on badgering us, but she didn't mention the matter again. In fact, she seemed once more to be on her best behavior—pleasant, if unusually quiet; docile instead of argumentative.

On Friday evening after dinner, she said, "I'm going for a walk," and left. Once I looked up from the sink and saw her strolling slowly across the yard, stopping to gaze at certain plants here and there. I was puzzled, but then I forgot about it.

She came back just before dark, made herself an enormous milkshake, and cut a huge slice of the German chocolate cake we'd had with supper. Then she sat down and began to eat slowly, as if savoring every mouthful. She'd just eaten a huge dinner not two hours earlier, and I was astonished. Inclined to be chunky, Michelle ordinarily dieted like a fanatic, but for the past few weeks she'd been eating ravenously.

"What happened to your diet?" I asked.

She merely shrugged, then rinsed her plate and left the kitchen.

An hour later, I went upstairs to look for a knitting instruction book I'd mislaid. Michelle's door was open, and she was cleaning her room. Usually, it required relentless nagging to get her to touch it, and even then she never gave it more than a lick and a promise. Now, however, her bed was made smoothly, the bottles on her dressing table were clustered in neat groups, and I could tell she'd rearranged her bookshelves. She was sitting on the floor at the door of her closet, sorting things. There was a pile of items she apparently planned to discard, and I could hardly believe my eyes. Michelle, an incorrigible pack rat, voluntarily throwing things out?

"Goodness, Michelle, what's going on here?" I asked. "Have you decided to turn over a new leaf?"

"I just got tired of this mess," she mumbled.

"Well, good for you," I said, and went back downstairs.

Twice Michelle made trips to the garage to discard things there. Later in the evening, she appeared in the living room, rosy from a bath, her hair neatly pulled back in a ponytail and wearing a spotless nightgown.

I looked up questioningly as she bent to kiss her father. It had been ages since she'd kissed us good night.

"All ready for bed?" I asked.

She leaned to kiss me and I marveled. Was this the same girl who screamed at us two days ago? "Good night, dear," I said. "Sweet dreams."

She turned at the archway and looked from her father to me and back again. "Good night, Mother and Daddy." She still stood, oddly uncertain. "Good-bye."

Then she whirled and was gone. Frowning, I returned to my knitting, feeling a moment's disquiet. Good-bye? Would she try to sneak out and go with her friends? But then I relaxed. I knew they had left before five o'clock.

The rest of the evening was uneventful. Denise came in from her date, Howard and I watched the news, then we all went to bed.

The next morning I was wakened by a terrifying scream from Michelle's room. It was Denise. "Mother! Daddy! Come quick!" Then she was screaming again.

In a daze, Howard and I fumbled to our feet and staggered down the hall to Michelle's room. Michelle lay on her stomach, one arm hanging over the side of the bed. Mystified, I looked from one daughter to the other.

"What's the matter?" I asked.

Denise was clasping her hands together, her whole body shaking. Stark terror shone from her eyes. "Mother, Michelle's dead!"

I shook my head in denial. "No, she's just asleep."

I leaned down to touch Michelle's arm, and it was icy cold. Then I saw an empty bottle of sleeping pills on the floor and I fainted.

With Michelle's death, something in me died, too. I simply collapsed and didn't care about anything. For weeks, I did nothing but grieve and try to find answers to the terrible question of why my daughter had destroyed herself. Then the answers began to come, and that was even worse.

Suddenly, every magazine I picked up contained an article on suicide. A surprising number of them were on teenage suicide, and as I read them, my entire being rebelled against what I was learning. I realized that Michelle had given us unmistakable warnings of her intentions. A devastating sense of futility gripped me.

Why hadn't I learned these facts earlier, before it was too late? Why was there a sudden rash of writing on suicide after my daughter was gone? Angrily, I went through back issues, and I found them there, too. I had to face the awful fact that the truth had been there all the time, but I hadn't been interested. The entire idea of suicide was so alien to my mind that I'd refused to even acknowledge it. Because of my complacence, my ignorance, my unforgivable blindness, Michelle was dead.

I was to blame—and so was Howard. We had driven Michelle to kill herself. But when I tried to tell him this, he protested.

"Howard, she as much as told us what she was going to do," I said. "Giving away her belongings, the sudden personality change, her abrupt switch from starvation dieting to stuffing herself—those were all definite signs of suicidal depression. And her uncharacteristic cheerfulness—that was the plainest clue of all. She was literally broadcasting her intentions, and we paid no attention."

"Barbara, we didn't know all that."

"But we should have known." I waved a magazine at him in agitation. "There was no excuse for us not knowing. It's all here—symptoms of serious depression, warning signals of potential suicide—in half the magazines we read each month. Yet, in our unforgivable ignorance, we gloated over her 'sudden improvement.' How could we have been so blind?" I was sobbing again, tortured by my crushing burden of guilt.

"Honey, you've got to get ahold of yourself," Howard told me. "Maybe we weren't very informed about the subject of suicide, but I doubt if it would have made any difference."

"What do you mean?" I screamed.

"I think Michelle would have done it no matter what. She's been in trouble for so long—shoplifting, drugs, boys—I'm afraid nothing would've stopped her."

"You sound like you're glad she's dead!"

"Oh, Barbara, no. Don't you think my grief is torturing me, too? But we can't spend the rest of our lives wallowing in guilt."

"But we're to blame!" I insisted, and my tone was so sharp, it was scarcely recognizable. "We handled everything wrong. Michelle's death is our fault, and there's no way we can deny it."

Howard shook his head. "No, Barbara. You're wrong. I'm not saying we were perfect parents, but I think we dealt with Michelle just as decently as anyone could have. If we're doing everything wrong, how do you explain Denise? She's our daughter, too. Who could possibly want a more stable, dependable child? If all Michelle's problems were our fault, then why isn't Denise the same kind of girl? No, Barbara, with Michelle, I don't think it would have mattered what we did."

"You just don't want to take any responsibility for what happened," I lashed out. "You want me to bear the whole burden of blame."

"Honey, that's not true! I guess I just don't see it the same way you do. But I do know one thing—Michelle's dead. She's gone, and nothing we can do will bring her back. Of course, we feel grief, but we have to pick up the pieces and go on. Please let the wound heal. Don't keep digging at it until it poisons all of us."

"You want me to forget Michelle!" I cried in shock.

"No, Barbara. I want you to remember Denise and me. You still have another daughter and a husband that you've completely forgotten about since Michelle died."

I recoiled as if he'd slapped me. "You're just plain selfish!" I hissed. "Not only are you unfeeling and uncaring and determined to evade any responsibility for what happened, but you're selfish, too. At a time like this, when I desperately need your comfort and support, you've got the gall to complain because you're not getting all the attention. I can't believe it."

Howard was looking at me oddly, as if trying to decide whether to say any more. "What about my needs?" he said finally "You say I'm selfish, but have you even once, in all this time, given a single though to my needs or Denise's? You think about that for a while, Barbara." He turned and left.

I cried for a long time, then stretched out on the sofa, hoping sleep would come to blot out my tormenting thoughts. The memories of Michelle were bad enough, but now there was also the shock of what Howard had said.

What was happening to him? He had always been marvelous—understanding, considerate, everything a woman could want in a husband. But now, just when I needed him the most, he was turning against me. Oh, what was I going to do? I tossed restlessly, wishing to slip into the quietness of sleep.

A long time later, I was awakened by sounds from the kitchen. Denise had just gotten home from swimming. I felt vaguely irritated with her for awakening me. I sat up and was rubbing my eyes absently when she came in carrying a tray.

"Hi, Mom," she said, smiling cheerfully. "Are you feeling any better?"

"No, not really," I told her.

"I brought you some tea. And I baked these cookies last night. They're pretty good, and I thought you might like some."

I glanced at the tray without interest. "No, I don't think so."

"Oh, come on, Mother," Denise insisted. "I'll bet you haven't eaten a thing since Daddy and I left this morning. Daddy bought this tea especially for you. It's an orange spice blend—just the kind you like."

"I don't want anything," I mumbled.

"But, Mom, you're getting so thin," Denise protested.

"Just leave me alone," I said sharply, and Denise shrugged helplessly and left the room.

Mercifully, I managed to go back to sleep again—a dreamless, empty, deep sleep. Then someone was shaking me.

"Wake up, Barbara," I heard Howard say. "Time for dinner."

I resisted weakly as he helped me up and guided me to the bathroom. "Wash and comb your hair for a change," he instructed.

Sick to death of his constant nagging, I didn't even answer. I made a couple swipes at my hair with a brush, then allowed myself to be guided to the table. The very thought of food nauseated me, but the only way I could get any peace was to eat a few bites. I almost choked, but I'd learned that if I refused to eat at all, there would be an awful uproar, and I couldn't take that. True, I was getting thinner, but I didn't care.

Throughout the meal, Denise and Howard kept up a meaningless conversation. I couldn't wait to get away from their incessant tales and the trivia that seemed to occupy them these days. I was just pushing my chair back from the table when Denise spoke to me.

"Mother," she said, "I need a couple of shirts and some new jeans. Will you go shopping with me tonight?"

I frowned. "Why? You've been shopping for your clothes for two years. You don't need me to go with you."

"Yes, but I want you to go. It's been a long time since we went shopping together. I thought it might be fun."

"Fun?" I snapped. "How can anything possibly be fun for me, after—" And I covered my face with my hands.

"But, Mother, you need to get out. You just sit here day after day and brood."

"I wish everybody would quit telling me what they think I need!" I exploded. "What I really need is some peace and quiet, and to be left alone."

"You know what you're doing, don't you?" Howard said coldly. "You're making an invalid of yourself. You aren't even sick, but if you keep moping around this way and refusing to eat, you soon will be."

"Well, I'll tell you one thing," I said in a rising voice. "If you both keep picking on me like this, I'm going to be a nervous wreck."

"Don't you ever intend to resume your family responsibilities?"

"I can't!" I cried. "I can't concentrate on anything. Whenever I try to do something, all I can think of is how hard we were on Michelle."

Howard's hands were clenched alongside his plate and his mouth was a thin line. "Barbara, this has got to stop."

He paused as if at a loss for words, then went on. "What are you accomplishing with all this terrible regret, this constant crying and whining? It's not going to change anything. If moping and mourning would bring Michelle back, I'd join you enthusiastically, but they won't.

"And here's something else for you to think about," he added. "Despite what you might think, Michelle's death has hit Denise and me mighty hard, too. But what would have happened if we had

230

followed your example? If I refused to go to my job and Denise hid in her room day after day, grieving? We'd all have gone down the drain by this time. We've forced ourselves to go on, and we've taken over your duties, but it can't go on forever. You've got to start making an effort."

Tears were running down my cheeks. "I never thought you could be so mean," I sobbed. "You just don't understand. Please go away and leave me alone."

But Howard only stared at me strangely. "That's something else you'd better think about, too," he said. "You keep asking us to leave you alone. Is that what you really want? If it isn't, you'd better quit saying it—otherwise, don't be surprised when it happens."

And with a stony look, Howard left.

I was hurt and angry, but a little scared, too. What did he mean by those last words? Well, it was obvious he didn't want to hear any more about Michelle, so I'd have to carry the burden alone. I made up my mind not to say another word about her. If that's what he wanted, okay.

So I withdrew into silence. I kept to myself the incriminations which plagued my mind, and I was very careful not to tell either Howard or Denise to leave me alone. Instead, I pointedly avoided them whenever possible.

Week followed week, and soon the summer was over. Denise started back to school, Howard began coming home from work later and later, and I retreated deeper into myself. At first, several of my friends came around, inviting me out for lunch, offering help of all kinds, but I didn't want to see them. What did any of them have in common with a mother who had goaded her child to suicide? So I rebuffed their overtures, and when they eventually stopped coming, I was frankly relieved.

One October day, Howard came home at noon with a touch of the flu, and so he was there when Denise arrived home from school. He was lying on the couch, and I was absently leafing through a catalog when she burst into the room, all smiles.

"Mother! Daddy! Guess what!" She flung her books down on a chair and actually skipped across the room. "I was chosen to be one of the sophomore homecoming attendants! Can you believe as it?"

By now Howard was sitting up. "Hey, that's great!" he exclaimed. "Congratulations! Come here and let me give you a big hug."

She danced over to him, then she was back in front of me, her face aglow. "What do you think, Mother?" she asked expectantly.

I just stared at her, appalled at her excitement. "What does this involve?" I asked.

A faint shadow crossed Denise's features. "Why, the queen and her court reign at the homecoming game and at the dance afterward. You know."

231

"Dance?" I exclaimed in horror. "What are you thinking of? We're still in mourning for Michelle. I won't have you cavorting around at some dance!"

"But, Mother!" Denise protested in dismay. "I was chosen. It's an honor, a really big honor!"

"I don't care," I answered. "You can thank them sincerely for the honor and gracefully decline. Out of respect for Michelle, that's the least you can do."

Denise's joy evaporated and now she was in tears. Her eyes had the baffled, hurt expression of a wounded animal's. "But, Mother, Michelle's dead. What—"

"She hasn't been dead six months, and already all you can think about is fun and good times. I'd think you'd want to show a little more respect for your dead sister and not have to be reminded of it all the time. Surely, at least six months of mourning isn't too much to expect."

"Barbara, this isn't the dark ages," Howard burst out. "Today when a person dies, his family grieves sincerely, but then as soon as possible, they try to take up their regular routine. That doesn't mean they love or miss their loved one any less, it only means they recognize that life must go on, and that it's necessary to return to normality with dignity and grace. It's an act of real consideration for the living, an effort to make acceptance of the terrible loss easier instead of harder."

"Preach, preach, preach!" I snapped. "Is that all you can do? I'm the only one around here who shows the least bit of interest in the memory of Michelle, and then I get criticized for it."

Howard's eyes narrowed. "Barbara, as long as you're going to be obsessed with Michelle's memory, let's at least be honest about it. Can you ever remember, even once, Michelle bringing honor into this house?" He shook his head emphatically. "No, you can't, because she caused us nothing but worry and disappointment. Oh, I'm not saying we should've loved her any the less for it—and we didn't—but when our other daughter brings us joy and recognition, we should rejoice with her. Respect for the dead should not cancel out appreciation for the living."

Denise was weeping softly, and I just glared at Howard. I knew there was truth in what he said, but I didn't want to hear it.

He went to Denise and put an arm about her shoulders. "Honey, I'm really thrilled about your good news," he told her, "and I'm sure that when your mother's had a chance to think about it, she'll be glad, too. There's nothing in the world wrong with your accepting and enjoying the honor you've won, dance and all."

I shook my head grimly. "I still say it's not appropriate," I insisted.

Denise looked up at me with confused, hurt eyes. "I might as well be dead, too," she said in a choked voice and ran from the room.

Howard turned to me fiercely. "If you cause problems in Denise's life with your insane notions, I'll never forgive you!"

Denise didn't come down to fix dinner, and at seven o'clock, Howard came and got me. "You get out there and fix us something to eat," he ordered. "There's no sense in your lounging around while Denise and I do everything."

So I reluctantly made grilled cheese sandwiches and opened a can of peaches, but the food repelled me, so Howard ate alone. He took a tray up to Denise, but soon he was back with the food untouched.

"She won't eat anything," he said. "She's all upset, and it's no wonder. I'm telling you right now, Barbara, I've had it. If you don't shape up soon, I'm finished."

His tone was angry, but in his eyes I could see evidence of uncertainty and despair, and for the first time since Michelle's death, felt a stirring of feeling for Howard and Denise. Perhaps I was overdoing my suffering. Maybe it was time to put the past behind and try to face the future with courage.

The next morning, without any prompting from Howard, I prepared breakfast for us all. I could tell he was impressed, but Denise was very subdued.

She hardly said two words, and for a girl who normally beamed with happiness, she seemed extraordinarily downhearted.

I probably had been too rough on her. Although it was very hard for me to accept, perhaps Howard was right. There was nothing to be gained from brooding over Michelle's death. In my heart, I knew the wound would never heal, but that was no reason why I should take it out on the rest of the family.

All day I pondered the dilemma of what Denise should do about being homecoming attendant. I was no more in favor than before, but I did see how important it could be to her. I grew more and more tense as the hours passed, and to my amazement, I had a sudden urge to do something.

After pacing restlessly from room to room for a long time, I decided to bake a pie while I tried to reach a decision. As I measured shortening and sifted flour, I realized with a start that this was the first time since Michelle's death that I had concerned myself with anything relating to Denise. I sighed deeply. Something else to feel guilty about. Would the time ever come again when I could feel good about something?

By four-thirty, the kitchen was fragrant with the aroma of freshly baked apple pie, and I had put on a clean shirt and pants and tried to do something with my hair. I was beginning to wonder why Denise hadn't come home, and I tried to remember if she'd said anything about a meeting or something after school. For the life of me, I couldn't remember that she had, but perhaps she'd mentioned something to her father.

He didn't get home until seven-thirty, and by then I was really worried about Denise. But the first thing Howard noticed was the pie.

"Hey, what's this?" he asked in surprise. "An apple pie? Great!"

I cut him a piece and poured coffee.

"Aren't you going to have some, too?" he asked.

So I cut another piece and sat down with him. "Did Denise tell you what she was doing after school today?" I asked.

"No, she didn't mention anything. Why?"

I frowned, feeling the beginnings of panic. "She hasn't come home yet."

Howard froze. "What? Are you sure?"

"Of course I'm sure."

"Have you called anybody?"

I looked down, ashamed. "I—I don't even know who Denise's friends are now."

Howard was on his feet, the pie forgotten. "I'll call Caroline Patterson."

I twisted my hands together nervously while Howard dialed and then waited for an answer.

"Hello, is Caroline there?" he asked. Then, a few seconds later, "Caroline, do you know what Denise was going to do today after school? She hasn't come home."

There was a short pause, then Howard's face blanched. "She wasn't at school at all today? Are you sure?"

Caroline spoke some more, then Howard said, "Did she say anything to you about any unusual plans she had? Well, could you give me the names and numbers of some of her other friends? Surely, somebody will know something."

Then he was writing on a pad, and I was fighting full-fledged panic.

Howard made call after call. Nobody knew anything. No one had seen Denise since school yesterday.

When Howard was finished, he looked at me bleakly. "Nothing," he said briefly.

"The police?" I asked, trembling, and I couldn't keep the tears back. "Do you think she's been kidnapped, or—" I couldn't bring myself to voice my worst fears.

"No, I don't think she's been kidnapped," Howard said. "I think she's run away."

"Run away!" I exclaimed in disbelief. "Denise? She would never run away."

"I think she took absolutely as much as she could of your senseless behavior, and then she just had to get out."

"But Denise's a good girl. She's always been helpful and dependable and—"

"And what did it ever get her?"

"What do you mean?" I asked.

"I mean, from the time Denise entered fifth grade, everything was Michelle, Michelle, Michelle. Michelle was the problem, so she got the attention."

"But how could it have been otherwise?" I protested. "When your child gets into the kind of scrapes Michelle did, you have to deal with the situation."

"To the exclusion of all else?"

"I still don't see what you're getting at," I said wearily.

Howard was dead serious. "Denise was good, sweet, a model child, so we ignored her. Just look back, think back, and you'll have to agree that I'm right. Well, every child needs attention and approval. But even after Michelle was dead, Denise still had to compete with her for any attention from us—especially from you. And she could never win. Even with Michelle gone, she couldn't win."

"But—but—" I faltered. "I didn't realize."

"Neither did I," Howard said, shaking his head despondently.

He began to pace, and his face was stiff and cold. "But at least I haven't been hounding her with Michelle like you have. You're so determined to wallow in guilt—so anxious to blame yourself. Well, now you've really got something to blame yourself for. You've driven Denise away, and for all I care, you can sit here for the rest of your life whimpering. At least you've got something to whimper about."

He began to walk away. "Where are you going?" I asked, terrified.

"I'm going to try and find my daughter."

"When will you be back?" My body was icy cold, and I thought my heart would surely stop.

"I don't know," Howard said bluntly. "Maybe never."

Without even a backward glance, he left, slamming the door behind him. I sat stunned, waves of misery washing over me. If I had been devastated before, I was totally bereft now. For hours I sat motionless, too numb to move, my mind in such a turmoil that I had no idea what to do next.

Shortly after midnight, I called the police and they informed me that Howard had already been there about Denise. An impersonal voice said that our daughter wasn't gone long enough to be listed as missing—that they would keep an eye out for her, but couldn't do too much yet.

I thought the early morning hours would never pass. I didn't sleep at all, and when daylight finally came, I felt battered and worn and hopeless. As the hours stretched ahead of me, I realized I had never in my life felt so alone.

Twice during the day I called the police, and they began to get irritated. I also called Denise's school, but they had no information. Beyond that, I could think of nothing to do, and as I sat or paced in my empty home I felt utterly helpless. If I had a car, I would have scoured the entire area, road by road, but Howard had taken the car, and I had no idea where he had gone.

The second night, I began to pray. I prayed that Denise was safe and would come home, that Howard would return, and that I would be able to fulfill my responsibilities wisely.

My whole body ached with weariness, and I felt terribly anxious. Finally, shortly after dark, I dropped off to sleep from total exhaustion. But just after midnight I awakened, more upset than ever. On impulse, I decided to call my sister, who lived in Rutherford, fifty miles away. Not even thinking about the time, I dialed her number and waited tensely while the phone rang. At last Danny, her husband, answered, his voice muffled and fuzzy with sleep.

"Danny, this is Barbara," I said. "May I please speak to Alice? It's an emergency."

"Do you know what time it is?" Danny demanded.

"I'm sorry, but I simply couldn't wait any longer," I told him. "Please, let me talk to Alice."

"Okay," he grumbled.

A few seconds later Alice was on the phone, and I poured out my whole miserable story. Alice said very little, and I soon got the idea that it wasn't news to her.

"Do you have any information about Denise?" I asked frantically.

"Why do you ask?"

"Why do I ask?" I screamed. "She's my daughter and she's missing! I'm frantic with worry. I'm going positively crazy! Please help me."

"You mean you want her back?"

"Want her back?" I was aghast. "Of course I want her back."

There was only silence on the other end of the line.

"Have you seen Denise?" I asked urgently. "Have you talked to her?"

"Yes, I've talked to her."

"Is she there?"

"No, she's not here with me, but I've seen her."

"And Howard?"

"I've talked to him, too."

"Oh, Alice, please, you've got to tell me what's going on. I've been

236

so foolish. I've been so crazy with grief over Michelle that I've driven the rest of my family away. Now I'm ready to change, if they'll just come back."

"I don't know if they will or not," Alice said, strangely distant.

"Alice, can you please come down here? I've got to talk to you." Now I was beginning to cry. "I need somebody."

"Barbara, it's the middle of the night."

"In the morning, then? First thing in the morning?"

"All right. I'll leave as soon as I get Danny off to work. You try to calm down now and get some sleep."

"Thank you, Alice. Thank you so much," I babbled.

Somehow I did manage to sleep for a few hours. When I woke, sunlight was streaming through the sheer curtains. I felt sick and suddenly realized I had eaten nothing since Howard had left. I ate breakfast and then felt somewhat better.

As the hours passed, I paced through my empty house, waiting for Alice's arrival. Finally, at eleven-fifteen, she came. I greeted her tensely.

"You say you saw Denise?" I asked eagerly when we were seated at the kitchen table. "What did she say? Why did she leave home?"

"She arrived in Rutherford by bus at about eleven in the morning and called me to come for her," Alice told me. "She'd been crying all the way from home. She's crushed—literally crushed—by the way you've been treating her. She talked and talked about how she's felt through the years when everything revolved around Michelle and her escapades.

"Your family was in a constant state of turmoil because of Michelle. Denise behaved herself, did well in school, helped around the house, got along with everybody, but she never got any credit for it. Then when Michelle died, all you could do was harp on how guilty you felt about the way you'd treated her. Denise knew very well that all the family's emotional resources had been spent on Michelle for as long as she could remember. Finally, it was more than she could take."

"I see it all now," I said brokenly. "Howard and I were completely unaware of what we were doing to Denise." I covered my face with my hands. "Am I always going to be doomed to realize the truth too late? What should I do, Alice?"

"Well, you understand what happened. At least that's a step in the right direction."

We talked for a long time, and Alice told me many things that Denise had shared with her. I was heartsick to learn of the unnecessary suffering I'd caused my child, and longed with all my heart for a chance to make it up to her.

It was long past noon when I realized that Alice might be hungry.

I fixed soup and sandwiches, and while we ate, I considered plans for bringing my family back together.

"Where is Denise?" I asked.

"I promised I'd keep that a secret," Alice replied.

"What about school?"

"It's all being taken care of."

"But the homecoming celebration—she was so thrilled about that. Won't she come back to—"

"You've completely ruined that for her."

"And what about Howard?" I asked with a heavy heart. "Do you think he'll come back to me?"

"Not right away," Alice answered.

I stared into space, trying to envision existence without Howard and Denise. The prospect was terrifying. Once again I turned to Alice in anguish. "Isn't there anything I can do to get them to come back? I've already changed inside, because I really see the truth for the first time. Does it all have to be for nothing? Have I driven them away for good?"

"I don't know, Barbara. You'll just have to give it some time." She looked around the cluttered room. "Get yourself together, do something to this place, get some kind of an outside interest, and there may be a chance."

"But Howard and Denise are gone," I wailed. "How will they know what I'm doing? Oh, please, Alice, convince them to give me another chance."

She nodded. "I'm certainly willing to be a go-between. I'll come down a couple of times a week to see how things are going, and, yes, I'll try to get them to give it another try. But I know it won't happen immediately."

"But you do think there's hope?"

"Sure, there's hope—if you're ready to do something about yourself."

"Oh, thank you, Alice. I really am grateful," I said, and the tears came again. "At least I know Denise's safe, and that's worth a lot."

Alice looked at her watch. "I must be going now," she said. "I'll call in a couple of days, and I'll tell Howard and Denise about our talk." She hugged me. "Keep your chin up. Everything will be all right."

I wasn't at all sure, but I smiled and waved good-bye.

Then the loneliness began in earnest. It required all the courage I could muster, but I began to eat properly and made myself take care of the house.

The very next time she was down, Alice commented on the improvement and told me to keep up the good work. The empty house was depressing me terribly, so I got a part-time job in a nearby hospital. That helped keep my mind off my problems at least some of the time.

Every time I saw Alice, I asked about Howard and Denise, but she never said much. Howard sent me money every week, and I knew he was back at his job here, but he never once contacted me. Although I considered calling him, somehow I knew he wouldn't return until Denise did.

Three months passed. Christmas was nearly unendurable, but somehow I made it through to the New Year and then to Denise's birthday. I had decided to make her a new outfit, and when I sent it with Alice, I included a long letter to Denise. I poured out my heart, trying to explain how sorry I was. I assured her that if she would only come home, I'd show her every day how much I appreciated her.

After Alice had taken the gift and letter, I was on pins and needles. Would Denise ignore my gift? Would she refuse to trust me again?

Then three days later, I got a letter from her. With a wildly beating heart, I tore open the envelope. Dear Mom, it read, Thanks for the outfit. It fits perfectly, and I really like it. Thanks even more for the letter. I guess I can see how easy it would be to get entirely wrapped up in Michelle's problems. It just finally got to me, though, especially after Michelle was dead. I am kind of homesick and I do miss you a lot. I would like to come home right now, but since I'm in school up here, I guess I'd better finish the term. Aunt Alice is having a belated birthday party for me next Saturday, and she said to ask you if you'd like to come. Dad will be there, and we both want to see you. Love, Denise

My heart sang as I read the letter over and over. I was filled with hope as I thought of the party. I knew it would be the first step on the pathway back to a normal life for my family, and I could hardly wait for Saturday to come.

The End

I HITCHED A RIDE
WITH A MADMAN!

The February day was cold and dry. It would probably snow before nightfall. If it hadn't been for little three-year-old Katie, the long hours would've been empty, except for bitter memories of that Sunday in December when all my happiness had been swept away. My husband hadn't left me, or fallen in love with another woman. He'd just been the careless, reckless cause of our boy's death—five-year-old Andrew, with his thick curls and happy eyes.

Terrible things shouldn't happen on beautiful mornings. It makes grief all the harder to bear. The sun was bright, the sky was blue, and it had felt spring-like outside despite the recent snowfall the morning Warren took Andrew outside for his first skiing lesson—a treat he'd been promising him for a long time. It was a rare weekend that Warren wasn't on the road. He was a pharmaceutical salesman.

"Let's go, Daddy!" Andrew had shouted.

"Just a minute!" Warren had laughed. "You'll get dunked in the snow soon enough!"

They'd waved as they started out and I'd called out, "Please be careful, Warren. Don't let Andrew take any unnecessary chances."

"Stop being a worrywart," he had said, grinning at me.

The ski area was just a short walk from the country back road on which we lived. I stood, looking around at the lawn and the trees covered with snow, thinking of Andrew and the snowman he planned to make when he returned from skiing. Warren and I loved children, and we were going to have as many as we could afford. This place was perfect—no neighbors crowding us, and schools near enough as our brood grew older. I drew a deep, satisfied sigh, glanced at Katie playing in the snow, and hurried into the kitchen to make gingerbread cookies.

I must stop nagging Warren about his skiing, I told myself. Someday, he'll get angry instead of teasing me. I do fuss too much, but he is reckless; he does take chances. He adores high slopes—the more dangerous, the better. But he's an excellent skier, and he wants Andrew to be one, too. So, talking to myself, I forgot my uneasiness as I spread the cookies to cool, prepared the vegetables, and saw that the chicken was browning in the oven.

Then cars were turning into the driveway—state police, an ambulance—Warren coming to me, his face drawn, haggard, his hands trembling on my shoulders. The ambulance doctor sat beside something covered with a blanket, something small, limp.

"Andrew!" I'd screamed, fighting against Warren's hands, beating at him with clenched fists.

"Sweetheart—" He'd tried to hold me closer.

I'd jerked back my head. "The last thing I asked you was to be careful! You just smiled! You've never listened to me! And now—now Andrew's dead!"

"Don't, Melinda, don't."

"You weren't careful! You enjoy taking risks!"

"Stop! Let me tell you—" His lips were trembling; his face seemed to crumble.

"So sure of yourself! You couldn't deny yourself your fun—not even for him!" His fingers were bruising my arms; the black-and-blue marks were to remain for days. "That isn't love!"

"I loved him!" There was a hot, fierce light in his eyes.

"He'd be alive if I'd been there! I was his mother!"

"And I his father! Be careful, Melinda." His lips were tight, set, his face a frozen mask. No muscle quivered now.

The doctor sat beside the still, limp form inside the ambulance. "I'm going to him—let me go to him!" I was struggling once more.

"One second. Listen, will you? You won't even give me a chance to tell you what happened or how it happened! How do you know I'm to blame? You talk about love—prove it! I was thinking of you—to get to you, help you, give you what little comfort I could. I hadn't a doubt but that we'd stand together, share our grief as we've shared our happiness. I've been through something, too!"

He let go of me and I staggered, and heard, at last, Katie's frightened crying. Warren bent, picking her up, holding her close, whispering gentle words till she smiled.

"You can't think of her, either, can you? Come on—stop making a scene before strangers. There are things to do."

He walked toward the house and I followed, stunned by grief and shock. Feeling that, more than the fact of Andrew's death, the words we'd said to each other had done their work. Later, I found the courage to face the cruelty of my wild reaction. Then I'd think: Warren should have understood, should've come to me and told me that he did. He hasn't even tried to explain what really happened. And sometimes, especially at night, my heart would cry: Go to him.

I never did, though. We went our dreary ways, talking very little, our meals strained and quickly eaten. He slept on a studio couch. I didn't know which was the harder—being alone or having him home. I dreaded his return from his present business trip this evening, or early the next morning. But mixed with that dread was an aching need.

As the wind grew and storm clouds gathered, I gave Katie an early bath, and in a short while, put her to bed. She was all right then; I swear she was.

About two hours later, the first flurries of snow came. Then the wind rose with sudden fury, bringing more snow. I ran to Katie's room to shut the windows. Above the noise of the storm, I caught another sound—choked, struggling breathing. The dim nightlight showed Katie's flushed, feverish face, tangled bedclothes, and half-open, unseeing eyes. I lifted her higher on the pillows; she didn't know me.

"No, no!" I whispered.

As I reached the telephone in the living room to call for an ambulance, the house lights dimmed. I dialed again and again, my fingers trembling. No answer. The overhead wires were going down, one after the other. I'd be in total darkness any second. Panic, numbing and dreadful, held me rigid.

Then I heard my voice crying out; I felt myself move. I realized I must get her to the hospital in Hillsdale, the nearest town. The small car we used for errands was outside. Before the lights had completely blacked out, I had Katie bundled up and ready to go. I put on a coat and, holding her carefully, I climbed into the car and swung it onto the country road, already deep in snow.

At the next turn, the two front wheels sank into the snow and the car stalled. I sat there, tears running over my cheeks. Where I found the strength I never knew, but I took Katie into my arms, and while every nerve in my body cried out for me to hurry, I slowly reached the highway.

I stood under one of the lights. A car passed in a swirl of spray, then another, their drivers indifferent to my frantic signals. Once more, headlights gleamed through the snow. Desperately, I sprang forward.

There was a scream of brakes, and then a man's voice shouted, "What the—get off the road!"

I ran to the door, pulled at it, and struggled in, gasping. I sank onto the seat. "Take me to Hillsdale—the hospital—my little girl—may be—dying!"

The driver stared at me, his face a white blur under the pulled-down brim of a soft hat. "I'm not going to Hillsdale." His voice was flat. "Find someone else." He reached across me to open the door.

"Who? Where? I can't wait. My own car stalled. Don't you understand?" I pleaded, close to despair. "She's unconscious!"

"I understand. It's you who don't understand. I tell you, I can't."

"What kind of a man are you that you'll let a child die?" I cried. In the light of a passing car, I saw his eyes, filled with pain and bitterness, with a suffering too deep for words. Like Warren's eyes on that Sunday in December when I turned on him.

Slowly, as if it hurt him, he bent forward and turned off the car radio. He straightened; the car moved, gathered speed. "All right. I'll show you what kind of a man I am!"

"God bless you," I whispered, weak with relief.

"You believe in God." It wasn't a question. "I did, once."

The black road was unwinding behind us, but not fast enough. I could feel the fear in the man beside me, and in the glare of another passing car, I saw the sad, deep lines etched in a face that was neither young nor old. I had to say something.

"You're kind. I'm sorry—don't think I'm not. You see, I lost my little boy in December. He was killed in an accident." Drawing a long breath, I went on, "My husband's away on a business trip. I had to have help. If I lost Katie, too, I—" My voice faltered and I closed my eyes.

Suppose when Warren returns, Katie is gone. Then he'll blame me as I blamed him—say I must have been careless—that if I'd been watching her, I would've seen something was wrong before the storm broke. Now, I need him as never before, I thought. I need him now, this minute. Slow, hot tears slid down my face. He needed you as never before then. Didn't you realize?

"Were you alone when the accident happened?"

"No." I'd already said more than I'd meant to say to this stranger.

"Be grateful for that. Grief shared is bearable. And he'll be back when?"

"Late tonight or early in the morning." I opened my eyes, wiped tears from my face, and bent over Katie. She struggled weakly and her eyes were closed.

The car stopped with a jerk. I lifted my head and saw the state trooper. His powerful flashlight turned on us was almost blinding. The man beside me neither moved nor spoke. But I rolled down the window and cried out, "Don't stop us! We must get to the hospital as soon as we can! My baby is ill!"

"Sorry, lady. We've got orders to stop all cars going north. There's an escaped—"

"He'd hardly have a sick child and her mother with him! This delay could be fatal, Officer!" The stranger's words were hurried, impatient, though he kept his face averted.

The light swept over us, and was turned off. "Have to obey orders," the trooper said. "Now, get moving, and good luck to you and your kid."

Once more, we were racing north, and I had the answer to much that had puzzled me—his first angry refusal to help me, the fear I'd felt in him, his pain-filled eyes—some of the things he'd said, I could now understand. But he'd taken a terrible chance to help me. He couldn't be all bad.

243

"Why didn't you give me up?" he asked. "You must have known."

"Yes. But I couldn't," I said simply.

"We're almost there."

I saw the lights of Hillsdale and I gathered Katie closer to me. "I don't know how to thank you. If I can ever do anything for you—"

"If you mean that, don't tell anyone how you got here. Don't say anything about me," he said softly.

"I won't. I promise."

The snow flew in my face as I pushed open the car door. "Good luck," I called to him as I slid to the ground.

"Good luck to your little girl," he called out, driving off into the night.

I pushed open the wide hospital doors and ran to the reception desk. A bell rang, and then there was an intern beside me, another nurse, a doctor who took Katie into his arms and bent over her. I caught his crisp orders.

"Take care of this lady."

Then he was gone. The hall was suddenly empty.

"Don't be frightened," the nurse said gently. "You'll hear from Dr. Dawson soon. I'm sure she'll be all right." She rang a bell and said, "If you can fill out these forms now, it'll make things easier. But first, you'd better get out of those wet clothes."

They were very kind through the agony of the next hour while I waited, starting at every footstep, every voice. An aide took my wet coat, and the nurse helped me to fill out the necessary forms. Then someone took me into the reception room, brought me hot, strong, sweet tea, and stood over me until I drank it. I put my head in my hands. The heat of the tea and the warmth of the room had stilled my shaking.

If she is dead, I thought, I would have heard by now. Such faint comfort!

"Mrs. Dixson," a voice said.

I sprang to my feet. It was the young doctor who had taken Katie from me.

"There's more than a fifty-fifty chance that your little girl will pull through. She's under an oxygen tent now, and her heart has responded to the injections. Has she ever had an attack like this before?"

"Never. What is it?"

"Croup, combined with a violent attack of asthma."

"She's never had asthma."

"It comes, at times, without warning. There must be some allergy. That can be tested when this attack is over. It's the heart that must be watched now, because of the strain on it, and that, as I told you, is as strong as it should be. Try not to worry." He stepped farther into the room. "There's one question I'd like to ask you, though."

244

"Yes?" I said, wondering what it might be. I was weak with relief, and yet, I had prayed for complete assurance that all danger was over. I waited, watching his face.

"We don't always know what causes asthma. Sometimes, it's brought on by nervous tension, distress that the subconscious feels and is fighting against blindly."

"But not in little children!" I cried.

"Oh, yes. It often begins then, and grows worse as they grow older, or, if the trouble is resolved, it often disappears as suddenly as it came."

"And you think Katie—I can't believe it. She's been such a happy child!"

"You said that there had never been the slightest trouble before. I may be wrong, but think back through the last weeks. Could there be anything that could have thrown her off balance, however slight it seemed to you?"

I reached for the arm of the couch behind me and sat down, fingers clasped tightly. I heard again her frightened crying as I'd screamed, struggling against Warren, my voice high and loud, blaming him for the death of Andrew. She'd never heard angry words or known anything but gentleness, kindness, protection, and laughter.

Warren had said, "You can't think of her, either." He'd picked her up, soothed and comforted her until she smiled, but the damage had been done. She'd been shy with me for a while. In my grief, I hadn't realized why. Now, though, I buried my face in my hands. How could I have been so cruelly selfish to her, to Warren?

"What is it, Mrs. Dixson?" Dr. Dawson asked.

My hands dropped to my lap and I told him the story. "Could that be the trouble?" I asked when I had finished.

"It might be."

"But—two months? Wouldn't it have shown at once?"

"Not always. Cases of shock are impossible to define. Sometimes, they show at once, sometimes years later."

"Then you think—"

"I couldn't say till I have more facts. Has anything else happened since then to startle and frighten her? I hate to ask you these painful questions, but it's necessary."

"I'll answer anything, do anything to help her," I said quietly.

"Does she miss her brother?"

"Yes, at first she did. I'd find her looking for him, calling his name. She was lonely. He'd played with her a lot; he'd made himself her protector. Once, she cut her hand, and he kept her laughing while I dressed the wound. Of course she's lonely!" I cried, my voice breaking.

He raised a hand. "I understand. Life, at times, demands great courage from us, as it has from you and your husband, and your little girl."

Where was my courage? I'd acted like a spoiled child, expecting only sunny days. My parents had loved me, and Warren had brought such richness into my life that I'd cracked under the first real blow. My thoughts should have been centered on making our home a haven in which Warren could find solace, where Katie could feel safe. I'd tried to keep her happy, not realizing how the strange, new silence between Warren and me had brought insecurity into the very heart of a baby not yet three.

"God forgive me," I whispered. I looked at Dr. Dawson. "I'm afraid I haven't been a good or wise mother."

"Don't blame yourself too much," Dr. Dawson said. "I've got to leave now. I'm the resident day physician; I'm late tonight. Dr. Stanton is the night physician. He'll be in touch with you. Do you know when your husband will arrive? You'll feel better with him here."

I stood up, not too steadily. "I don't know. Tonight or early morning. He may be coming through Hillsdale now over Route 22. He always does when he's been calling on doctors, at hospitals west of here. He'll go straight on home." My eyes widened. "There won't be any lights! The wires were breaking before I left. It'll be empty. He won't know what's happened! He'll be frantic. I never thought of leaving a message. He mustn't go there!"

"You've been through a lot. Don't panic now. I'll see if the troopers can make contact. He must be familiar to them."

I nodded.

"I'll ask them to have the radio stations put out a call. Give me the make of his car, and its license number."

I gave him the information and watched him as he walked quickly away. Now Warren would have another burden added to those already so heavy. I walked to the window, but the snow beating against it shut out my vision as I pressed my face to the cold glass.

Shortly, the doctor returned and told me, "All's in order, Mrs. Dixson. The troopers know him, and the radio stations were glad to cooperate. People are usually kind when there's trouble. Come and sit down. Turn on the radio so you can know what's going on."

I sat down, and it seemed as if time had stopped since I'd arrived at the hospital with Katie. I looked up as Dr. Dawson bent over the radio. "You haven't had much rest tonight, have you?" I asked.

He smiled a warm, friendly smile. "Don't bother about that. What doctor counts on that? And there's something else I'm interested in; maybe the news will tell me. Here, listen."

"Calling Warren Dixson. Please stop at Hillsdale Hospital before you go home. Mrs. Dixson is there with your little girl. Don't be alarmed. All immediate danger is over. An attack of asthma augmented by croup made it imperative to hospitalize her. She is under an oxygen tent and her heart is responding as it should. Mrs. Dixson has been wonderful." Then, another voice added, "Good luck! We're all pulling for you!"

I choked up a little. People are kind. I wasn't listening to what followed until a sudden movement from Dr. Dawson startled me into attention. The next words from the radio brought a faint warning.

"Earlier, during the height of the storm, a car was seen leaving the Hillsdale Hospital at a dangerous speed. A pedestrian recognized Alan Byrd, an escaped inmate from the state asylum. He was sure, he said, from the description of the car and the man given in an earlier broadcast. If it was, indeed, Byrd, he seems to have vanished into the night."

I was sure, too.

It all tied in—the stranger's first refusal, the fear I'd felt in him when he'd given in to my frantic pleading, our being stopped by a state trooper, his asking why I hadn't given him up, his request as I'd left the car—"Don't say anything about me, how you got here." I'd promised, but if he were. . . .

"Insane!" I exclaimed.

"He's no more insane than I am or you." Dr. Dawson's words were abrupt, angry. "There's many a free man or woman walking around who should be taken out of circulation, but not Alan Byrd."

"You know him?"

"I took my psychiatric training up there." He jerked his head to the south, where the state institution crested a hill. "I was there when he was committed. I got to know and respect him."

"But—but—" I stammered, "—if he wasn't insane, how—it couldn't have happened!"

"Oh, yes, it could, and it has, and it'll happen again. And through no fault of the doctors. There are evil people in this world who'll stop at nothing." He stopped. "I'm sorry. I shouldn't run on this way, but it rankles me to think of what she got away with."

"Who?"

He was walking up and down the small room, hands thrust deep in his pockets. "His wife, the woman he loved—the woman who drove him into the condition where he could be committed by her." He shrugged, walked to the window. "At least it's a good night for an escape. I hope he makes it. Anyway, I'd better be getting on. When your husband comes, get in touch with Dr. Stanton. Don't worry about Katie; she's doing splendidly."

"You can't leave me like this!" I exclaimed. I had to know more before I made up my mind about whether to keep silent, or tell him what Alan Byrd had done for me. It was difficult to think clearly with weariness creeping over me. "Please, tell me the rest!" I begged.

"Why?" He turned from the window and looked at me.

"I want to know," I said stubbornly. "I—I—have a reason. Please."

Again, he shrugged. "All right. Alan was a brilliant architect on his way up when he met her and married her. She was beautiful, knew how to stir men. He was easy game for her; he'd never had time for women. It's the old story." Dr. Dawson came over and stood in front of the small table, facing me. "He adored her. He bought a home and made it over to her. They had a joint bank account. He wanted children, but she refused at first. Then a big contractor asked him to design a new city college. She turned all sweet and willing then.

"He learned after work had begun that the whole business was rotten with graft and corruption. Alan threw in his hand and there was a big stink. She showed her claws then and told him she'd had an abortion since he couldn't think of her and their child. She let him think the contractor was her lover. That night, Alan disappeared. He was found two days later, wandering up in the hills, unable to speak, hands almost useless—in traumatic shock."

I shivered, my body cold, remembering the eyes I had looked into during my ride.

"He was in my care. I liked him from the first. I had to get him to talk, clear up his conscious and subconscious memories if he were to be saved. It took a long time, and only a brave man could do it. Finally, though, he could talk frankly without being struck dumb again. He suffered, and I pitied him, but he was cured."

This man's eyes had reminded me of Warren's. Was this what I had almost done? What I might have done—failed him through weakness and folly? I'd left him alone to carry the burden of his dead son. I pulled myself back to the present, to what Dr. Dawson had just told me.

"If he's cured, why isn't he free?"

"Because she'd left him to rot. When Alan was pronounced cured, she vanished, having sold the house in her name and having drawn out the last cent in their joint account. He had no place to go, no one to take him and be his legal guardian for the year, as required by law. His parents were dead; he had no near relatives. He was left a sane man in an insane asylum. And so he sent for me. I did all I could, but I couldn't take him. I was living at the hospital. He didn't crack up, although I was afraid he might. Now, please," Dr. Dawson asked, "will you tell me why you're so interested? There's more than ghoulish curiosity behind your questions."

I flamed into quick anger. "I should hope so. Because it was Alan

Byrd who brought Katie and me here. My car had broken down, and I'd struggled with Katie in my arms down to the highway. Two cars passed us; I sprang in front of the next one—it had to stop. The driver refused to come here, at first."

It was pouring from my lips—the frantic desperation of those minutes. Dr. Dawson couldn't miss it. "Then, because of Katie, he brought us here. He didn't want to. I felt the fear in him, and the terrible effort he made." I was talking so fast, I began to stammer. "He asked me not to—say anything about him. I promised." I drew a deep breath and went on more slowly, "But he was seen leaving here, wasn't he? He wouldn't have been if he hadn't helped me. Now I want to help him, if I can."

The doctor smiled a little. "What you've told me may help. You should be grateful; if there had been a much longer delay, it'd have been impossible for us to save your child."

A siren was wailing outside, coming nearer and nearer. I raised my head. Cars were stopping.

"I hope they've contacted your husband," Dr. Dawson said.

I sprang to my feet as he moved to the door. I caught his arm. "We could give him the home he needs, couldn't we?"

"If he's found, yes."

The entrance door swung open. There was Warren and a state trooper, but it was only Warren I really saw. Warren standing tall and straight, his strained face seeking an answer to one question, his lips saying one name.

"Katie?"

"She's out of danger; Mr. Dixson," Dr. Dawson said.

"He got your message, all right, Doctor. He was speeding, and I went after him. Then, seeing who he was, I escorted him down here quickly," the trooper explained.

I moved toward Warren, hands outstretched, knowing only that I had to be near him, touch him, hear his voice and try to get into words some of the whirling emotions inside of me. But all I whispered as I lifted my eyes to his face was, "Warren, you're here. Forgive me for everything. You needed me, and I failed you."

He took my hands, bent, and kissed me. He put an arm around my shoulders as I sagged against him.

"Your wife's about all in, Mr. Dixson," Dr. Dawson said. "She's been through a great deal, both physically and emotionally. You'll be proud of her when you hear the full story." He stepped over beside me. "Would you both like to see your little girl now? I think Dr. Stanton will allow it, if you are quiet and don't disturb her." He spoke to the nurse at the desk. "Find out please, if they may come. I advise you two to spend the night here. There's a small inn just outside the hospital grounds. You can get food there at any hour." He looked at me directly. "When did you eat last?"

"I—don't remember. I had some hot tea when I first got here. Before then, I guess . . . breakfast. I wasn't hungry at noon, and then the storm and Katie—"

"We'll make up for that. A hot, light meal and a good sleep and you'll be a new person."

Warren's arm tightened about me and I tried my best to stand straighter, but weariness dragged at me.

"An attendant will show you the way." I heard the doctor giving orders as a nurse appeared to take us to the children's wing. "Telephone Mrs. Michaels and tell her that Mr. and Mrs. Dixson will need a warm supper and a room for the night."

Everything was being arranged. I didn't have to think or plan. That was good. I was beyond thinking and planning. Warren was with me! That was like a sudden ending to dreadful pain.

Dr. Stanton met us and we stood by Katie's bed. She was sleeping quietly, a natural flush on cheeks that before had been such a ghastly white. Then we went back to the corridor and thanked Dr. Stanton.

"See you in the morning," he said. "She'll be up and playing in a day or two."

The snow fell on the roof and the windows of the inn as we ate. The warmth of the room made my eyelids droop with sleep. I felt secure because Warren was just across the small table from me. If one has been living in a cold, bleak world, a world haunted by pain and regrets, and fear of happiness ruined, one accepts the unexpected peace.

But I hadn't forgotten that there was still a lot to be said. I hadn't forgotten Andrew, or that I must rebuild what I'd almost destroyed. But Warren had no pretense in him. He wouldn't have kissed me—the first kiss in two months—or taken my hands, or put his strong arm around me to steady me, if he hadn't still loved me.

"Finished, sweetheart? Up we go."

"Get a good night's sleep." Mrs. Michaels smiled, calling after us. "It's a comfortable room."

"If it's as good as your supper was, we couldn't ask for more," Warren answered.

The lights were on, the beds turned down, a nightgown laid out for me, and Warren's bag brought up from his car.

"I've so much to tell you, Warren." I moved farther into the room. "Such a lot to explain."

"There's tomorrow and the next day and the next. From what I've been able to gather, you've been quite a heroine. But follow the doctor's orders now—get out of those snowy clothes and go to sleep. You're out on your feet."

I smiled, my lips unsteady. I knew him in this mood. Often, he'd half-babied, half-bullied me, and there'd never been a chance of changing him. I was out on my feet. Meekly and thankfully, I gathered up my nightgown and headed for the bathroom.

I dropped my wrinkled clothes on the bathroom floor, took a hurried shower, and then combed my hair. How clean and sweet the nightgown felt! I fumbled at the doorknob. Warren pulled the door open, picked me up as gently as he would a child, and carried me to the bed. Pulling the covers farther back, he put me down and pulled them over me. My head on the pillows, I looked up at him.

"Warren," I asked, "will you kiss me again? It's been so long."

"Too long."

His lips were gentle on mine, then hard, hurting. He lifted his head and moved away. The light went off. In the darkness, the only sounds were his quiet movements, the steady beat of snow falling against the windows.

Warren and I are sleeping in the same room once more, was my last thought.

I opened my eyes to a gray sky, but light was spreading across the clouds and the snow had stopped. I sat up, pushing away the mists of heavy sleep, suddenly remembering where I was, all that had happened.

Warren!

Was it true? Could it be true?

Yes, yes!

I threw aside the covers and was kneeling by his bed when he opened his eyes. His arms gathered me to him until I lay beside him, and then he drew me closer, closer to him.

Later, as the sunlight filled the east and swept up and over the earth, my head on his shoulder, his arm across me, we talked. Or rather, I talked, telling him of Katie's sudden illness, the ride with the stranger, and what Dr. Dawson had said might be the cause of that illness.

"Oh, God, how stupid and wrong I've been," I said. Then I told him all about Alan Byrd, the stranger who had saved Katie's life. "If he hadn't gotten me to the hospital when he did, she would have died."

Warren drew a sharp breath. "I heard the news reports about him. He can't be crazy. No crazy person would act like that," he said, raising himself on his elbow, looking down at me. "Isn't there anything we can do? Take him home for the necessary time, maybe?"

I nodded. "We owe him that for saving Katie's life. But first, he has to be found. He may be dead by now."

"Might be," Warren said, framing my face with his hands, kissing me. The next instant, he was up on his feet. "Let's get moving, sweetheart." He gathered up his clothes and disappeared into the bathroom. While he went down to see about breakfast, I dressed.

It was a crowded, busy day for us. A visit to Katie who knew us and was almost herself, and wanted to go home. A long talk with Dr. Dawson, who repeated more fully and concisely to Warren what he had explained to me about traumatic shocks.

"It may not be that," he added. "I believe it is, but bring her to the hospital next week and we'll test for an allergy. If it's shock, don't spoil her. Just be natural, keep her happy, but be firm. Why don't you give her a pet to play with—a puppy to grow up with her, or maybe even a kitten?"

"There'll be a puppy at home to greet her," Warren answered, smiling.

We asked about Alan Byrd, but there'd been no trace of him.

"Too bad," Warren said. "Anything we can do to find him, we'll do. We'd like to keep him for a year."

"I won't forget your offer. I want to find him, too. If ever a man deserves a break, it's Alan," Dr. Dawson answered.

As we drove home later that morning, a tow truck came along to move my stalled car from the middle of the soggy back road. Men were busy restoring phone wires, electrical wires. Trees were down and broken branches were everywhere.

"Do you mean, Melinda, that you walked from here to the highway in that storm carrying Katie?"

"I had to."

Some of our rooms had snow in them from the open windows I hadn't closed. Yes, it was a full day's work. But that night, after our afternoon visit with Katie and dinner in Hillsdale, Warren and I slept in our own room, in our own bed, with the new puppy we'd bought, content on his mat in the kitchen.

I thought of how Andrew would have loved him. "Why didn't we think of a dog before, while Andrew. . . ."

"Don't think about it. Andrew was happy, don't forget."

"We'll never forget him."

"No, we'll never forget him—he was such a happy child." After a long silence, Warren said, "I want you to know, Melinda, that I wasn't to blame. We were on the beginners' slope. It was hardly much of an incline, but some fool kid shot out of nowhere, lost control, and plowed Andrew into a tree. The other kid had only minor injuries." His voice broke. "God," he muttered, "if there's a hell, I found it then. But Andrew didn't suffer, Melinda. He didn't even know what hit him."

"And I made your hell worse, Warren."

He put his arm around me, his face to my shoulder. He didn't deny what I said; he couldn't. He'd said that terrible Sunday: I thought we'd share our grief as we've shared our joy.

Alan Byrd had said: Grief shared is bearable.

Tonight, we were sharing our grief.

But of Alan Byrd, who had unknowingly brought the first hint of this truth, there was no word. If he still lived, he was alone, beyond our eagerness to pay our debt.

The days passed, busy and full. Warren was away on his business trips, home and gone again. I took Katie to the hospital for her tests. There was no allergy; her complete cure was up to us. And if it's up to us, she'll be cured, I thought. She went her sunny way with two little boys from the nearest house who, finding she had a dog, came often to play. I'd hear their laughter, I'd see them romping, the four of them together.

Then one evening, the telephone rang. It was Dr. Dawson.

"I've had a short letter from Alan." His voice was excited. "He's in a small town up north, working as a dishwasher. He says he's all right, but that's no life for him. He has talent; he must get back to his career. You're still ready to take him?"

"You don't have to ask that, Dr. Dawson." Warren came and stood beside me. "We meant it, and we'll always mean it," I said.

"Then—is your husband home?"

"Yes."

"Let me talk to him, please. But, first, I want you to know that Alan wrote for two reasons. He wasn't asking for help. First, so I wouldn't worry about him as he knew I would, and, second, to find out if your little girl was alive. He kept wondering about her and you."

"Bring him here," I said, "and let him see for himself."

Dr. Dawson laughed. "Right, I'll bring him. I'm going up tonight and I'd like your husband, if he can, to come along with me."

"Warren," I said, and gave him the receiver.

"Yes, yes, of course. I'll drive you. I'll get going now and pick you up at the hospital," Warren said. He hung up and said to me, "At last, it's all working out. I think we'll get along together, but whether there's friction or not, we owe this to a brave and kind man." He gave me a hug, a quick kiss, and in less than five minutes, his car flashed through our entrance onto the country road.

It did work out all right. There was no delay over the legal end. Katie took an immediate liking to Alan Byrd, and he, from the first sight of her, adored her. She filled, I suppose, his empty heart, which had longed for a child and been denied a wife's love. Bozo the puppy adored him, too. Still, Alan was shy. It took some time to draw him into the family, make him one with us. When we did, though, we found a rare friend. Alan went back to his plans and designs before Christmastime. I know he'll do splendid things in the future.

253

Life can be wonderful. It can also be sad. But, from that strange mixture, we can make a fuller, better existence. I stood on the porch last evening watching the sun set, and suddenly, Andrew seemed close again. I haven't lost him forever. I must tell Warren this when he's home again; I hope he'll understand. I believe that he will.

The End

FLIRTING WITH DISASTER...
SCHOOLGIRL CRUSH!
She wrecked my marriage

My wife, Summer, and I didn't get along too well after our daughter, Chelsea, was born. We'd intended to stop with our son, Micah, but Summer's birth-control method wasn't effective. Micah was eight months old when Summer got pregnant again. There were seventeen months and three days between our children, and somewhere during that time, my wife disappeared into self-pity and depression. That, plus her neurotic concern over the children, left me out in the cold.

But I loved Summer. I felt somehow we'd work our way through this and come out with our original intimacy renewed.

Meanwhile, Summer agreed to my vasectomy. We'd reached our emotional limit. I hadn't really wanted kids, and she had wanted one. It was my responsibility to see that our marriage didn't collapse under a third pregnancy. I felt that much of her strained tenseness at my caresses was fear that she'd get pregnant again.

The vasectomy helped. Some. A month later, Summer agreed to family counseling. Fortunately, an evening session was available, because she wouldn't leave the kids with any sitter. She didn't trust me much, either. On her first night, she called home four times during her two-hour session.

The therapist, Dr. Clayton, insisted Summer was overprotective and housebound, which worsened her basic problems. He recommended she start working part-time.

I thought she'd have a nervous breakdown at that idea, but Dr. Clayton stuck to his guns. I backed him up. Finally, Summer went job hunting.

She screeched all the way out the door, "Jonah, what'll become of Micah and Chelsea—"

I tried to reassure her. "Mrs. Trenton upstairs will be happy for the money." Mrs. Trenton had raised a big family, and now she kept an orphaned granddaughter. It was tough trying to manage on their Social Security checks.

"Her kids were grown thirty years ago!" Summer wailed.

"Honey, we still diaper the same end," I said, edging her out the door. I'd taken a day's sick leave so Summer could job hunt. Dr. Clayton and I strongly agreed she needed to climb out of her narrow, child-absorbed rut and work her way back to the vibrant, enthusiastic woman I'd first met.

I took three days of sick leave before Summer found a job. She cried with frustration at getting it, though it was exactly what she'd sought. But she was furious at succeeding. She was to handle the library checkout stand from five until nine, evenings.

I was enthusiastic. I got home evenings around six-thirty from the shoe store where I was assistant manager. So we'd hire Mrs. Trenton for a couple of hours and I'd do the rest. As long as we had the kids, I didn't want to be an emotionally long-distance father. My handling of bedtime stories, baths, and that last dozen drinks of water would help the three of us grow a lot closer.

Before she had Chelsea, my wife had never let me change one diaper or feed a single bottle to Micah. She was even more smothering with our daughter. Her job would be the best possible thing for all of us.

But on the fourth day Summer worked, I came home to find not Mrs. Trenton, but her granddaughter, Linda, sitting.

"Grandma busy?" I asked, shaking out of my jacket and kicking off my shoes. "Bet she's making those fabulous spice cookies, or another terrific apple pie, isn't she?"

Linda ducked her head, glanced at me from the corner of her eye, and blushed. She was an odd, slight girl, looking more like a preteen than an intelligent high-school senior. She gulped. "No."

"No pie? No cookies? Cake, then."

Linda turned crimson. "No."

"I give up. Tell me."

"Grandma broke her ankle. She's upstairs in a cast."

"Hey, I'm sorry," I said. "How'll you manage? How can we help? How did Summer take it?"

Linda shook her head again. That seemed to be her standard social gesture.

"We're okay," she said. "Your wife phoned five times."

On cue, the telephone buzzed sharply. While I was assuring Summer that the house hadn't caught fire and our babies didn't have beans stuffed up their noses or safety pins stabbing them to death, Linda ducked out.

If Summer could have figured any plausible reason to quit, she would have. But no luck. Every evening I found Linda baby-sitting, with Micah playing peacefully, Chelsea drooling blissfully in her crib, and the phone about to ring hysterically.

With Summer working, I began handling some of the other chores she'd done, besides just baby-sitting. The first week I suggested my getting the groceries on Friday night.

She stared at me, aghast. "What'll you do with the children?"

"Honey, I'll take them. You do when you shop."

"But you aren't used to driving and watching them!"

"Honey, I'll have Linda along. She's got to buy their groceries. We'll both shop and she can manage the kids in the car."

"Well—call me when you reach the store."

"No!" I snarled. "Linda and I are capable of taking two youngsters shopping without dropping them on their heads in the parking lot."

"You're not funny!" Summer scolded.

I sighed. Once, her sense of humor had been nearly her most endearing trait. Now? I prayed she'd find herself again, because she was no pleasure to be near.

So on Friday night, with shopping list, children, and baby-sitter in tow, I headed off to the supermarket. I discovered that Linda knew more about shopping than I did. She could tell a ripe cantaloupe, which brands of coffee and fruit juice Summer used, and where the toilet paper was shelved.

Back in the car, I sighed with relief. "That wasn't too bad."

Linda ducked her head.

"I think we did splendidly," I observed.

"Grandma always took me. So I learned," she admitted.

"Well, I think we deserve a prize for not running over people with our carts or falling in the frozen fish and getting stuck forever."

There was a slight, smothered sound. A giggle?

"Don't you think we have a treat coming?" I asked.

She ducked her head again.

"Come on. I'll buy ice cream."

Once we arrived home, Linda took her groceries upstairs. I lay Chelsea down and parked Micah at the toy box before I unloaded supplies. On schedule, the phone rang.

"What took so long? Did you have an accident?" Summer's voice was shrill with panic.

I clenched my fists. Dr. Clayton had warned it would take months to overcome her postpartum slump, but the waiting was difficult. I tried to keep it light. "Have you ever shopped on a Friday night? It was a mob scene."

Summer snorted and hung up. I put away the groceries before the frozen peas thawed and did dishes, remembering something Dr. Clayton had suggested the last time I saw him.

"Mr. Preston, your wife didn't want this child. She can't yet face her resentment at getting pregnant again so soon. This buried anger makes her feel guilty. For everyone to automatically love children is an impossible fantasy. Let's face it, babies are a big responsibility. They're not always a pleasure. They're demanding during your own fun-loving years. In Summer's denial of her rage and guilt, she's overreacted with extreme protectiveness. Because she did not want Chelsea, she's terrified some disaster will happen. Of course, in conflict with these feelings is the love she does feel, despite her frustration. When Summer can accept this ambivalence, she'll improve. But it may not happen quickly."

"I had the same feelings, Doctor," I pointed out.

"Probably. But you appear basically quite open, while Summer had a rigid upbringing. Many legitimate feelings were not allowed—because they weren't 'nice.'"

I nodded. "I don't care whether I'm nice or not. I want to know where I am."

"That's your wife's problem. She's never come to terms with who or where she is as an individual. Your daughter's birth made this uncertainty more intense."

Our discussion helped me understand Summer's seeming irrationality, but it didn't always make handling it any easier. It was taking too long for my wife to come back. I don't mean physically. The body was there. I mean the intangible mental and emotional bonds that are so important to a good marriage. Now, except for the hours she worked, Summer was home, but her mind constantly hovered over the kids. If I'd set fire to my head, she'd have doused me absentmindedly and checked to see if Chelsea and Micah were alright. Whenever I said, "I love you," which I did, her response was, "Don't wake the children."

To keep from driving myself completely up the wall, I stopped trying to get the attention I craved from Summer. I drew back emotionally so she could work out her problems. I would wait for the time when she'd turn to me with her earlier warm hunger.

It was life in a vacuum. At least Linda was always there when I came home. I'd chat with her briefly before she left.

All that fall, our brief moments were the brightest part of my day, which wasn't saying much. Linda was abnormally shy. It seemed physically painful for her to choke out any response to whatever I said. That was a problem she'd have to overcome. It's a big, cold world for anyone who can't even hold a simple conversation.

But since Linda and I didn't have any emotional conflicts like Summer and I did, I decided that I could help Linda make progress with her problem.

I began making a point of telling her interesting things that happened to me, jokes I'd read, or bits of entertaining news.

The first few weeks she'd duck her head, turn fiery red, grab her books, and flee. But gradually her discomfort trickled away.

One night I came home to find fresh coffee perking. "It's so cold. I thought you'd like some before you start getting supper," she volunteered. Talk about progress!

"Only if you drink a cup with me," I said.

"Grandma doesn't like me drinking coffee." She turned crimson again.

"We won't tell. Anyone mature enough to baby-sit the efficient way you do is old enough for one cup of coffee before dinner." I felt good. I'd been home almost ten minutes, and Summer hadn't called in her usual panic.

We were halfway through our coffee when the phone did ring. "That's Summer," we both said simultaneously, and then we laughed. Linda's laugh was as musical as far-off silver bells. As I reassured Summer that the babies hadn't been kidnapped or smothered, Linda tiptoed out.

Maybe it sounds like I fell in love with her or something. No way. I loved Summer. I was never infatuated with Linda or made any advances to her. She was simply my do-gooder project while Summer fought her own private battles. My efforts to draw her out were a way to keep myself from being unbearably bored and lonely. Linda was a nice kid. But she never meant anything more than that to me. I didn't look at her as a woman.

As her shyness dropped away, she showed what a cute, beguiling youngster she was.

"How come you never go to the games or anything?" I asked one evening. "There are school dances, too, aren't there?"

"After my parents died, Grandma didn't think I should attend them right away. She's right. School activities are pretty childish."

"Oh, come on. You should start dating boys you meet in class. If you'd smile at them instead of ducking your head, they'd be goners. Have you tried?"

That blush again! Careful—or I'd embarrass her instead of building her confidence as I intended.

"Oh, Mr. Preston, the boys in class are just boys. They're like Saint Bernard puppies. They just . . . knock you over. I want someone who acts the way you do."

There went that inevitable phone, ending our conversation. "I forgot to leave a note about supper," Summer began. "Turn on the oven for half an hour and it's ready."

She was getting better. She was actually concerned about something besides our children. I was so happy about that that I ignored Linda's departure and gave no thought to what she'd said last, flattering though it was.

Later I decided I'd better point out the difference between boys her own age who might be interested in her romantically and a casual friendship with an older, married man. I chuckled at that. Twenty-five wasn't what I'd consider an older man, but to Linda, I must have fit that description.

However, the next three days Micah had a sniffle and Summer stayed home. When Linda came back, I'd forgotten what I'd intended to say. I continued my project of bolstering her self-confidence, though, while I gave Summer the emotional leeway she needed to come to terms with her feelings.

As the winter deepened, Summer grew better. She was getting really involved in her job, and she began thinking again about me, which delighted me to no end. She was still too protective as a mother, but she was making progress.

Her housework picked up, the meals got better, and our sex life regained that old zest, which for a time had seemed dead. Now, when I held her, she responded—the woman I loved, not just the available body.

Linda, too, blossomed. She did something to her hair—cut it, I guess, and combed it in a softly feminine way instead of just letting it flop. She continued sitting for us, because after Mrs. Trenton's ankle healed, arthritis settled in it.

I was glad to continue my experiment in making Linda lose her diffidence. Whatever I did—mostly just talking to her and listening for those few minutes every day—was working amazingly well.

At Christmas I got Summer a sexy nightgown and robe and a large bottle of her favorite perfume. As I shopped, I saw a makeup kit, one with experimental sizes of several different cosmetics.

"They're very popular with young girls," the clerk assured me. "They can decide which items are best for them."

It wasn't expensive, and it was something Linda could have fun with. I let the clerk pick the right color assortment, and I had presents for both my women.

That evening I wrapped their presents. With Summer's, I wrote, "I love you" on the gift card. I gave Linda's more thought, finally scribbling, "You can't gild the lily, but this might help others notice how pretty you are."

The first of the year Summer was offered work full-time, days.

"What do you think?" she asked me. "There's a good day care near the library that takes babies Chelsea's age."

I hid my smile. If this had happened a year ago, I'd have heard Summer's hysterical refusal blocks away.

"I'll help with more housework," I volunteered. "The day care will be more expensive than Linda, but we'll still be able to save a lot toward our house."

"That's what I thought, so I'm starting next week," Summer said.

"So why ask me?" I chuckled. "Your mind was made up."

"Just wanted to see if you'd agree," she said, sliding her arms around my waist in that old, exciting way.

"I only want you to be happy, baby," I whispered, nudging her toward the bedroom.

Her murmur of assent said she was. I'd gotten my wife back at last.

I told Linda the next night. She stared at me, frozen faced. Tears brimmed in her eyes.

"Hey, don't cry!" I protested. "You'll wash off all your new makeup. Linda, I'm sorry. You've done a beautiful job because you're a beautiful girl. But with Summer working days, we'll have to send the kids to a day care."

The way Linda stared at me, I felt like a heel. "Look"—I reached for my wallet—"if it means buying lunches and stuff, I'll give you some money for the rest of the school year. You can pay me back later."

"It's not the money," she whispered. Tears ran down her face. "I never spent a penny of your money."

"Why not? You earned it. Did your grandmother need—"

She shook her head. "Grandma said it was mine. I saved it, first for a new dress, but—you gave it to me. I couldn't bear to spend it."

Something felt sticky here. I wasn't positive what, but I was mighty uncomfortable.

"Look, Linda—" I wiped at my suddenly damp forehead.

"Don't you understand? Your wife doesn't love you, doesn't care that you're lonely. She isn't here when you come home."

"Hey, Linda—"

"If we were married, I'd never leave you alone."

"That's why she's switching," I blurted. "We want to be together more."

"She'll claim she's too tired. You'll see. Does she ever just talk to you, like I do?"

"Well—" How could I admit there'd been a long time, until recently, without any closeness? I couldn't discuss our personal problems with Linda.

"See? She doesn't love you like I do." I opened my mouth, but for once, I didn't have one single thing to say. I was too shocked.

"Let her go!" Linda begged. "I'm almost through high school. I could drop out even. I'll take care of you—and Micah and Chelsea."

"Linda—"

"I know you love me, too, but you're too honorable to tell me. You aren't happy. You wouldn't pay me this much attention if you were. Or buy me beautiful presents, like that makeup kit—or tell me the things you always do."

Boy, had Linda lost her shyness! Only the fact that I sat, frozen, kept her from chasing me around the apartment. Now her fingers brushed my cheeks, my ears, my neck.

"Go sit down," I begged. I loved Summer but Linda's teasing touch was getting to me.

Reluctantly, she obeyed.

"Look, Summer and I are happy," I began. "I'm not romantically interested in you. I never was."

"But the nice things you've said, the way you sit and talk to me."

I leveled. "You were very shy. I tried to bring you out of it. That's all."

"I don't believe you!" Even her voice held tears now. "We've meant too much to each other, shared too much."

"Linda, I'm older, married. I'm not the man for you. Start dating boys. You'll find the right one, but not me."

She stared at me, her eyes tragically hurt. I could hear Micah and Chelsea playing in their room. How I wished Summer was still preoccupied with them, so she'd call.

Almost on cue, the phone rang. "Jonah?" Mrs. Trenton asked. "Is Linda there? She's usually upstairs much earlier."

I hung up and turned to Linda. "Your grandmother needs you," I said curtly, sighing with relief as she left. That had been touchy. Thank heaven it was over. I couldn't understand why she felt I was personally interested in her—well, yes, I could—in a way. When I was seventeen, if anyone this much older had talked to me, asked my opinions, I might have misinterpreted, too. But now that Linda understood why I'd done it, there'd be no problem.

I couldn't have been more wrong!

Summer's first workday went fine. I got breakfast while she dressed herself and the kids, we made the beds together, and left simultaneously. She beat me home by five minutes and put the casserole she'd fixed the night before in the oven. We spent another few minutes kissing casually and finishing dinner preparations, and then played with the kids before we all ate. Later we both got them ready for bed, then spent another hour doing household chores and arranging tomorrow's dinner. After that, the evening was ours. We spent it curled on the sofa, listening to CDs like a couple of honeymooners.

We were in bed ourselves much earlier than usual. But we didn't go to sleep right away. There were more interesting things to do with a long evening and a loving partner.

Tuesday was hectic at work. We were taking inventory. I came home bushed and stepped out of my shoes at the door. Summer, still in her coat, was lighting the oven. "Just arrived myself," she said. Our warmly bundled angels stared up at me. "Let's see who I can undress fastest," I said, kneeling.

The doorbell rang.

Sighing, I answered it. Linda slipped inside. "Hello, Mr. Preston, Mrs. Preston," she said. "I came down to visit for a while."

"I'm sorry, Linda, but we're getting dinner," Summer said.

"That's all right. I won't bother you. I'll talk to Jonah."

"He helps me get dinner," Summer said.

"I'll help, too."

"I'm afraid this kitchen isn't big enough for three," she pointed out. "If you want to be helpful, why not get the kids out of their snowsuits?"

Linda sniffed. She didn't stay. After she left, I took the kids' winter clothes off and hung everything up.

Summer and I were cuddling on the couch later, when she said, "That girl has the worst crush I've ever seen."

"What girl?"

"Linda. She's gone on you. Not that I blame her. You're special."

"Come off it! I'm an older, married man."

"Maybe that's what appeals to her."

"But I never encouraged her," I whined.

"I know, sweetie. You're too nice to play with minors. I said she's got a thing for you."

I never felt less like laughing, but I managed a hearty, "Ho ho!" I hoped that indicated the idea was too ridiculous to even discuss.

If Summer actually believed Linda loved me, she might create unpleasantness—or slip back into her old emotional distress. So I had to deny it. Besides, it wasn't true. There'd simply been a misunderstanding on Linda's part. But without me to talk to daily, her loneliness would force her to turn to boys her own age. I prayed she'd do it before her unrealistic fantasies upset Summer.

Moments before my lunch break the next day, a clerk called me to the back phone.

"I've cut study hall," Linda announced. "I have to talk to you. Since she won't let us see each other, I had to phone."

"Linda, wait a—"

But she rattled on about how much she missed me and what she was doing.

"I got a B on my social studies paper," she said. "I worked hard so you'd be proud of me."

When she hung up, my lunch break was nearly over. Instead of a leisurely restaurant meal—which I needed during inventory—I settled for a burger and shake, which I wolfed down on my way back to work.

263

It wasn't a good afternoon. By quitting time I was exhausted enough to crawl under the car instead of into it. And, to make things even worse, thirty seconds after I got home Linda came along.

Summer made short work of her—she was out the door pretty fast. "She really does have a terrible crush!" Summer insisted.

"Look, this is the time that Linda was busy with our kids. She must miss them terribly. All she does is go to school and stay home with her grandmother," I said, trying to soothe her.

"She didn't say 'boo' to Micah and Chelsea," Summer pointed out logically.

I hate women's logic. There's never any good reply to it. I began praying that Linda would straighten herself out before Summer got mad.

But over that next week, nothing changed. Linda called me at work every lunchtime.

"I can't survive the day without hearing your voice," she moaned. "Life is completely empty without you."

I sighed, feeling hopeless. How had I gotten myself into this? All I'd done was try to give the kid a little confidence. Couldn't she understand that?

And every night, the moment I got home, she came downstairs. Summer discouraged it—very definitely discouraged it—but Linda continued to drop in.

"You must tell her she isn't welcome anymore," Summer said heatedly one night.

"I can't. It isn't polite. Besides, she'll think we're rejecting her."

"She isn't polite, either. And I'm fed up!" That was my old spunky Summer.

"Then you tell her to stay away," I hedged.

"Not me, lover. You got into this. Now you get out."

"Summer, believe me. I never did anything. I never touched her, never even thought about it."

"I believe you. But you must make it clear to her that if there wasn't anything between you before, there won't be now. I refuse to play the heavy-handed wife interfering with true love."

I gulped. Fortunately, Chelsea let out a screech and Summer hurried to see why. She was better, and I was glad to have the old Summer back. But Linda still had problems. I couldn't pull the rug out from under her until she straightened herself out. That would be vicious. I'd wait. Give her some time. Eventually, she'd realize she and I weren't going anywhere.

"Look, Linda," I explained tactfully the next day. "Summer gets mad when you visit. We're both busy after work. Please, cool it. I don't need any rumbles."

"I knew she'd make trouble!" Linda wept. "She doesn't understand.

If she did, she'd only want your happiness. I'll die if I can't see you, talk to you. I watch out the window every afternoon, just to see you come home."

"From now on, I'll wave. But please don't come downstairs. It creates problems."

"Then we'll have to talk like this. I can't go on otherwise."

How had I gotten into this mess? "All right," I promised.

I'd have done anything, at that point, to keep peace all around. And with time, Linda would come to her senses.

That night, casually, I suggested Summer and I start brown bagging it.

"We can save lots more toward our home," I volunteered.

She stared at me in disbelief.

"But you need a complete break and a hot meal at noon," she countered.

"That's true—but I could take stew or soup in a thermos. It would save a mint. And there's a corner of the stockroom to relax in."

"We've got the employees' lounge," she agreed. "The coffeepot's going all day."

So we bought an assortment of lunch fixings. That solved my noontime problem, until my boss got unhappy over my keeping the phone tied up. He wasn't sympathetic when I explained about having a neighbor with emotional problems who seemed able to trust only me.

Finally, I found a nearby phone on a street corner and gave Linda that number. I ate my lunch in the stockroom and then ran to the phone to talk to Linda. She did most of the talking. I listened and tried to make constructive suggestions. I was getting discouraged. This was wintertime and that phone booth was icy cold. But I remembered how long it took Summer to improve and I stuck with it.

I resigned myself to spending a good part of my lunch hour in the booth's scanty shelter while I tried to help Linda straighten her head out.

There were problems, though. I caught a fierce cold that dragged into February. Then I came back one sleety day to learn that Summer had called three times.

"I thought you spent your lunch hours in the stockroom," she said that night, puzzled. Micah had taken a bad tumble at day care. "The library had a very short staff today, and I wanted you to take him to the doctor on your break."

"I went for a walk," I lied.

"In this weather? With your cold? Are you crazy?"

Sometimes I almost wished Summer hadn't gotten quite so recovered. I could stand a little less forthrightness.

"I had to buy cough drops," I lied again.

"That took you an hour?"

"To be honest," I lied a third time, "I felt so dragged out I stopped in a bar for a hot toddy."

Summer stared at me with a complete lack of conviction.

"It helped. I started sweating, and I feel lots better now," I improvised.

She snorted and bent over her cookbook. I could practically hear her thoughts, though, and I didn't want to. So I vacuumed the living room.

I sure wished Linda would begin showing some of Summer's improvement. A year ago, Summer would have been hysterical for weeks over Micah's accident. Now, she simply took time off, rushed him to the doctor, reassured herself it was only a bad bump, and calmly returned to work. And tonight, outside of handing Micah a wrapped-up ice cube to hold against his bruise, she'd been unconcerned about it.

Dr. Clayton would agree. She'd recovered from her obsessive rejection and guilt feelings after Chelsea's birth.

Yes, sir, our family would make it! But Linda obviously needed longer.

The following noon was warmly sunny. I was glad, because that stormy day's session hadn't helped me one bit. Today was warm enough to leave the booth door open.

As Linda and I talked, I noticed a shadow fall across my legs. I ignored it. I'd been trying to make a point with Linda—she should attend the mixer dance, even alone. She should buy a pretty dress and meet someone her own age.

The harder I talked, the louder Linda cried. So I didn't try to figure out the shadow until I was about ready to hang up. Then, as I was trying to break off the conversation with Linda, I turned and saw what it was. It was the shadow of Summer leaning against the phone booth.

As I let out a gasp, she straightened, reached into the booth, pulled the phone from my suddenly nerveless fingers, listened, and then yelled, "You leave my husband alone, Linda! I've had it with this nonsense! If you don't butt out of our lives, you're going to regret it. I promise you that!"

She slammed the phone down, wheeled, jumped in her car, and pulled away.

Icy sweat trickled inside my shirt. Summer was all right. Her anger showed me that. But how had she found me? I'd worry about that later. Now I was concerned about Linda. What would this to her? I didn't have a phone number for her. She'd always called me. This would be a horrible shock for her.

I walked slowly back to work. Paul, the stock boy, asked, "Did your wife find you?"

So she'd been there. That explained it. She must have been suspicious enough of last night's lame excuses to come by and check up on me. Well, at least she cared.

"Yeah, she found me."

"That's good," Paul said. "She seemed pretty anxious to get hold

266

of you. I told her you were right across the street, talking to that crazy neighbor of yours." He was shaking his head and chuckling to himself.

I could have strangled him, I felt so frustrated. I had to work an hour overtime and I called home four times in that hour. No answer. Summer was probably too mad to talk.

When I got home, she wasn't there. The apartment was empty, there was no dinner started. Mad as she was, she'd probably stopped to buy the kids hamburgers. I'd better fend for myself.

I sloshed down some canned stew. Eight o'clock came, nine, then ten-thirty. No Summer. No kids. I didn't have the nerve to phone upstairs and ask if they'd heard from her. I did check closets and dressers. Everything belonging there still seemed to be there, so Summer hadn't moved out.

I waited.

At a quarter to eleven, her car pulled in. Gratefully I opened our front door. Summer stalked by me silently, Chelsea on one arm, a huge package in the other. Micah tagged sleepily behind.

"Summer, honey, let me explain——"

Micah wrapped his arms around my leg. Chelsea teetered unsteadily, peering up at us. "You worm!" Summer spat.

"Where were you? I worried myself sick."

"We went to dinner. We went shopping. We went to a movie. Here's your present." Summer shoved the parcel at me and went to lock herself in the bathroom.

It contained two fluffy new blankets. I got the message. I set up my bed on the sofa. Then I put the kids to bed. I changed Chelsea's diaper, tucked them in, and tried to talk to Summer through the locked door. She wouldn't even swear at me.

After a long while I settled down on the sofa. I never did hear Summer go to bed. The next morning was even more frigid than the night before. I was making toast when she stomped into the kitchen, picked up my empty bag, and pointedly threw it into the trash.

"Honey, if you'll just listen——"

"I don't want one word, you double-crossing weasel!"

A commotion began outside. We craned to look. An ambulance and a police car were stopping in front. Our argument temporarily forgotten, we ran to the door. The officer and attendants went upstairs.

"Mrs. Trenton broke her ankle again—or had a stroke!" Summer guessed.

But my sinking heart knew better. Call it what you want—I knew who'd come down, strapped onto that stretcher.

I was right. Linda's unconscious face moved by me, blurred through my sudden tears. The policeman helped Mrs. Trenton downstairs.

"She took every pill in the place!" Mrs. Trenton wailed. "Aspirin, cold tablets, my sleeping pills and pain medication—thank God, those were nearly gone."

The officer paused, and then asked curtly, "Jonah Preston? Wait here until I get back. The girl wrote you a note."

I gulped. Summer moved closer to me, the first time she'd willingly touched me since the noon before. "We'll both wait," she promised.

We phoned in to explain we'd be late. Summer put it as a family emergency and I couldn't say anything.

We waited endlessly. The kids played. Summer and I drank coffee. Sometimes she brushed my hand gently with her fingers.

"I'm still mad enough to kill you," she said. "At best, you're a stupid fool." I nodded. I agreed wholeheartedly. "But you're my husband. I love you. And I know you weren't playing around. You were just stupid."

"Thanks," I choked out. "So we're in this together. Right?"

"We'll see it through," she said.

"Who you trying to convince? Yourself or me?"

"Shut up, you fool," she said lovingly.

It wasn't pleasant when the cop came back. He let me read Linda's note—nine pages explaining her realization that, since she'd never have me, she must die. "Fortunately, she overloaded her stomach and vomited most of it," he said. "Now, tell me your side."

That wasn't easy. Maybe it was easier having Summer beside me, her icy hand tight in mine. Maybe it was harder.

"She was so withdrawn. I just tried to help her come out of herself," I ended.

Somehow that didn't sound good.

The cop snorted. "Mister, what you need is your head examined," he said, leaving.

Summer looked at me as if she'd never seen me before. Then, completely serious, she said, "You know something? He's right."

So I ended up phoning Dr. Clayton myself. He'd done a lot for Summer. I hoped he'd do half as much for me for my confusion and my guilt feelings and my regrets.

He worked me into an evening group, which I attended for months before I got my kinks ironed out. And I didn't like a lot of the things I discovered about myself.

First, I learned what I should've realized all along. Funny, I'd been smart enough to insist that my wife get professional help. Family, friends, and neighbors are not the ones to try straightening out anybody with a severe hang up. Sure, we should love them, but we shouldn't tinker, like I did with Linda. What I'd thought was a disinterested but friendly attempt to help her turned out to be destructive meddling with her emotions.

But the hardest thing to face was why I'd acted the way I did. It boiled down to one thing—my big ego! My childish desire to feel important. Though I hadn't realized it, I'd felt neglected when Summer became so overinvolved with the kids. And when she turned from them to Dr. Clayton and therapy, I grew even more jealous. Subconsciously, I'd wanted to show I was smart, too, and my behavior had pushed Linda to the brink of death. She didn't regain consciousness for nearly twenty-four hours after she took the pills, and she was hospitalized for three additional days.

Before Linda came home, Summer, the kids, and I moved. We talked it over and decided it would be best for all concerned.

So Summer and I combed the town for another apartment. We ended up paying almost as much for a one-bedroom dump, but it'll do for now. The kids got the bedroom. Summer and I sleep on a foldout couch.

I'm glad I have a loving, loyal wife who knows I didn't consciously intend to do wrong. I'm thankful her head was straight before I got loused up. If she'd still been depressed when this happened, our marriage would have collapsed, even though we do love each other and our kids need both of us.

But we're working it out, one day and one problem at a time. We both pray Linda will get straightened out, too.

The End

LOVE 'EM AND LEAVE
That was my motto—until I met her

Girls have always thought I was handsome—and most of them didn't hesitate to let me know it. I had more than my share of chicks who were always available for a date—and for parking. If I spent my time and money on a girl, she would have to pay for it. And she always did.

In those days, I bragged that no chick ever refused me. Some took more coaxing than others, but I didn't want my fun handed to me on a silver platter. I liked a little chasing; it added spice to the game. I always won out, anyway. The chicks were pushovers for a guy that knew his way around, like me.

It was all a game to me and the guys I ran around with. We stuck together. If one of us couldn't make out with a girl, it became a challenge to the others. It was just a matter of technique. I believed that any girl could be had if you just went after her in the right way. All you needed were clothes, looks, a good car, and a little money—and I had all that.

Some girls thought that if they held out long enough, they could get me to marry them. But I had ways of dealing with them. Take Karen Vox, for instance. She played hard-to-get like all the rest, but she played a little too hard. I finally got fed up on our fifth date. She had held out too long.

I remember that night well. I treated her to a movie and a snack, then headed for my favorite parking spot out by the lake. After we parked, she cuddled up, put her arms around my neck, and didn't try to stop my hands. I got things going, then I whispered in her ear, "Come on, baby, let's get in the back seat. It's a lot more comfortable back there."

She giggled, but wouldn't move. I didn't want to wait any longer. "Look, sweetie," I said, "you've teased me long enough. Now it's time to deliver. Let's get with it. Give now, or it's good-bye."

She sat up and tugged at her skirt. "If that's all you can think about, then just take me home!" she said haughtily.

I started the car. I wasn't going to plead with her. I had the feeling things were going to go my way in the end, anyway. "Okay," I said.

Karen tried to talk on the way home, but I gave her the cold shoulder. When I stopped in front of her house, she asked, "Will you call me tomorrow?"

I just said, "Maybe yes, maybe no," and waited for her to get out. I didn't even walk her to the door.

The next day when I got home from work, Mom said, "Jeb, some girl called and said to call her. She said her name was Karen."

"If she calls again, tell her I'm out," I said. I'd give her some more time to worry.

The next night she called at dinnertime, when she knew I'd be home. "Hello, Jeb," she said sweetly. "Why didn't you call?"

I played it cool. "I'm pretty busy. Who's this?"

"This is Karen, and you know it! I want to see you." Her voice got sweet again. "I'm sorry I made you mad."

"Oh, Karen," I said. "You want to see me? I'm tied up this week. Maybe next week."

"Please, Jeb! Don't be angry."

"Okay," I said. "I can see you Friday night at seven-thirty." That would teach her.

It was almost eight-thirty when I blew the horn in front of her house. She was out in a second, dressed extra pretty, smelling sweet. I could hardly wait for what I knew was coming. She smiled, as if she could read my thoughts.

"You know," she said, "after I got home the other night, I realized how much I like you. I was being silly about the back seat."

This time, I didn't even have to go to a movie. We stopped for hamburgers and headed for the lake. By the time I took her home, everything was satisfactory. My record was unbroken.

I dated Karen a few times, then dropped her. She called a few times, then I heard she moved. I felt a little sorry for her when she wrote me a letter saying that she loved me, but I didn't answer it. She meant nothing to me. Some men like to hunt deer or squirrels—I liked to hunt girls.

It was a dangerous sport, sure. But I was careful. A lot of the girls said they were pregnant, but I knew better. It's easy to avoid that, these days. They tried to get my sympathy, saying they loved me. I felt sorry for them, but what could I do? I wasn't about to get married, that was for sure.

My mom and my two older married brothers were always after me to find a nice girl and settle down. That was a laugh. A nice girl? There was no such thing. Some of them looked sweet and innocent, until I got them alone in my car. But then it was all over. They were all the same.

I was sitting pretty. My job at the brickyard paid good money, and the girls kept me busy. Marriage was the farthest thing from my mind in those days; it was the last thing I wanted.

Then I met Nelly. I saw her first at a dance given by the Chamber of Commerce. I went stag, and I was cruising around just looking, when I saw this strange girl talking to Colby Fossey. He back was to me, but she turned as I walked by. I almost fell over right there, she was so beautiful. Her hair was long and black, and she had big, soft-looking brown eyes. I had never seen anyone like her before.

I hung around until Colby had to introduce us. I could tell he wasn't too happy about it. Nelly smiled sweetly, shook my hand, and then took his arm again. She was friendly, but she seemed hard to get to know. She didn't flirt like most girls. I hoped Colby hadn't told her about me, my reputation, poison with a nice girl.

The music started up again, and Nelly and Colby danced. I watched, fascinated. She didn't dance with just her hips, she swayed like a willow in the breeze. Her dress showed her figure, but it didn't look as if the seams were about to burst.

It was the first time a girl had ever made me shy. It took me a long time to get up the courage to cut in. Colby looked mad, but Nelly was too polite to refuse. While we danced, I found out that she was from Charleston and the she was visiting her cousin here in Essex, Ginny Thurman. I didn't even ask her if I could take her home that night. Somehow, I knew she would leave with the same guy she had come to the dance with.

I went home alone. All the guys kidded me but I didn't pay any attention. I was thinking about Nelly. I had to get to know her. I just hoped Ginny Thurman hadn't told her anything about my reputation.

Saturday, I got up early, and drove by Ginny's, hoping that she and Nelly would come out of the house. I was about to give up when they came out and started walking downtown. I pulled up to the curb. "Hi, Ginny. Hello, Nelly," I said. "Can I give you girls a ride? Any place you go, I want to go."

"Sure," Ginny said. Nelly looked reluctant, but they got in the car. Ginny sat in the middle. "What are you doing out so early, Jeb?" she asked. "I thought you were a night owl."

"Oh, just passing by," I lied.

Ginny laughed and gave Nelly a knowing look, but she didn't say anything. I smiled at her across Ginny, and she smiled back timidly. I couldn't think of anything to say, either. But when I dropped the girls off, I did manage to ask: "Nelly, uh, would you mind if I called you sometime later this afternoon?"

"Not at all, Jeb," she answered. "Make it early, though. I have a date this evening."

I was worried. It looked like this was going to be tougher than I'd thought. When I called Nelly that afternoon, I came right out and asked her if I could take her to dinner Sunday night.

When she said, "Fine. I'd love to," I was as excited as a young kid who's just gotten his first date.

That night, Mom kidded me about not eating. "What is it, Jeb?" she asked. "I've never seen you like this."

My brother, Hal, laughed and said, "I believe some girl has him hooked. What about it, Jeb? Has lover-boy finally gotten bit?"

Mom laughed with him. "Jeb, have you fallen in love? I can't believe it!"

I left the table, even though I knew they were only kidding. But could it be true? Could I be in love with a girl I had only met twice? I knew I got weak all over when I thought about Nelly. No girl had ever done that to me before.

Sunday night, I drove downtown and bought the biggest box of candy I could find, putting it under the seat where the guys couldn't see it. If they found out I was taking candy to a girl, they would never let me forget it.

It was still early when I rang the doorbell. I waited nervously in the living room, talking to Ginny and her parents. They were friendly, but seemed suspicious. I was beginning to worry about the fast reputation I'd been so proud of. I wished that nobody had ever heard of me.

When Nelly came down, she looked more beautiful than ever. I gave her the candy and she said, "Thank you, Jeb. You're very sweet." That was all the thanks I needed.

We had a wonderful dinner. Nelly didn't drink, so I didn't have any cocktails either—we didn't need them. We talked and laughed about everything under the sun. I had never talked like that with a girl before.

I learned that Nelly had graduated from high school in Charleston two years before, and had stayed to work when her parents had gotten divorced and moved away. Now, she was spending her vacation with her aunt and uncle and Ginny. She was going to be in Essex two more weeks, and then go back home.

Although Nelly didn't say anything, I could tell she liked me, maybe almost as much as I liked her. That night, after we had kissed on the doorstep, we promised to see a lot of each other. We were together every night after that. We went dancing or to the movies, or just parked and had long talks out by the lake.

As much as I wanted to hold Nelly in my arms, I made myself be careful. I knew she had heard about my reputation, and I didn't want to frighten her. I wanted her to know that this was the real thing for me.

Everything went fine, until a few nights later. We saw a movie and had dinner afterward. Then we drove to the lake and parked. It was all right, I told myself. She was my girl, and I just wanted to be alone with her.

We just talked, until I put my arm across the back of the seat. Nelly leaned back, and I gently slipped my arm around her shoulders.

I was surprised when we kissed. I had kissed her before, but it had never been like this. I could tell by the way she responded that she was serious about me, too.

But something was wrong. I didn't want things this way. I kept telling myself that this was Nelly, that I loved her, but another part of me said, She's just like all the rest. She's not really a nice girl. They're all the same.

I knew it was wrong, but I had to know. As I took her in my arms and kissed her again, I was praying: Please, don't give in. Please, don't be like all the rest! Our lips met; my hand was on her knee. Please, don't let me, I prayed, as my hand moved slowly under her dress.

She slapped me—hard. I drew back. I hadn't expected this. My cheek stung, but my pride was hurt even worse. Nelly turned on me with flashing eyes. "So!" she said. "You thought I was just another conquest added to your list! Are you going to take me home, or do I have to walk?"

"Nelly, let me explain."

"I don't need any explanations," she said. "I've heard all about you. I thought, I hoped, that maybe you'd changed, but I was wrong. Take me home."

I drove slowly. I hoped that maybe she would relent before we got to the house, but she didn't. She sat silently in the car, ignoring me. I could have been a million miles away. At the door, I tried again. "Nelly, please—"

"Good night!" she said, slamming the door in my face.

When I drove off, I was mad, too. But that didn't last long. She'd done what I'd wanted her to do, only more. It was almost funny, except that I was too worried to laugh. I was afraid that I was going to lose her.

I called all the next day, and the next—but Ginny just said, "I'm sorry, Jeb. She says she doesn't want to see you anymore."

I knew it was useless, so I stopped calling. That night, I wrote a letter. I made it short and sweet, so she'd be sure to read it: "Dear Nelly: I'm sorry. Please, let me explain. I love you. Jeb."

I knew she wouldn't read it if she knew it was from me. One of my brothers work for the telephone company, so I put it in one of his envelopes so she would think it was a bill. I kissed the letter and dropped it into the box.

I waited three nights, but there was no answer. I had one last chance, even if Nelly didn't want to see me. I dressed up and bought a box of candy. This time, I didn't care what the other guys thought. I hadn't been seeing much of them anyway.

I smoothed my hair nervously as I rang the bell. As the door opened, I said, "Nelly, please." But it was only Ginny. "Please," I said. "Tell her I've got to see her."

Ginny looked sorry for me. "Okay," she said, and she ran up the stairs. I could hear her voice: "I know Jeb's a phony," she said. "At least he used to be. But I think this time he really means it."

Then she came back down. "I'm sorry. I tried."

I started down the steps, feeling sorry for myself. Then I remembered the candy. I gave it to Ginny. "For Nelly?" she asked.

"She'll only throw it away," I said. "Why don't you eat it? And thanks for trying."

I walked out to the car. I knew it was all over. Everything was ruined. Then I heard a familiar voice behind me.

"Jeb?"

I turned. Nelly was running toward me, the box of candy in her hand. "Jeb," she said breathlessly, "The candy, it's so sweet of you."

"You mean you're not giving it back?"

"I'll share it with you," she said. "Let's go for a drive."

We drove out to the lake and had a long talk. I said I was sorry and I asked her to forgive me.

"I do," she said. "I shouldn't have been so cruel, but you hurt my feelings so much. You just don't know how to treat a nice girl."

"I can learn," I said. "If you'll help me." Nelly did help me. We had a date that night, and things were wonderful. I told myself that I would never doubt Nelly again; I would never forget how to treat her.

My happiness was complete a few nights later when I asked Nelly to marry me, and she accepted. It was a little soon for marriage, maybe, but I loved her, and I could tell she loved me by the way she gave me her passionate kisses. I had to hold back that night, not Nelly. She trusted me completely—and I wasn't going to cheapen what we had by losing control.

Nelly was supposed to go back to Charleston in a week so we decided to get married as soon as we could. Then we would go back and get the rest of her things, and move to Essex.

We agreed to have a small ceremony—just a Justice of the Peace—because I knew that with my reputation, a big wedding would start a lot of talk. She would just invite her aunt and uncle and Ginny, and I would just have Mom and my brothers. When I told them about it they were very happy.

The next day we went to have our physical examinations for our marriage license. I dropped Nelly off at her aunt's doctor, and then drove across town to mine. It didn't take long. It was just a simple blood test. As soon as it was over, we went to the lake for a swim.

Nelly got her test results the next day, but I had to wait two days for mine. It seemed like forever. I wanted Nelly so much. Soon we would belong to one another completely. I could hardly wait and her kisses told me she felt the same way.

Finally, the doctor's office called. I went there on my lunch hour. I wanted to pick up the license as soon as possible.

The doctor looked very grave as he ushered me into his office. I couldn't figure out what was going on. Why all the formality? "Are the test results ready?" I asked excitedly. "Can I pick up the license now?"

The doctor sat down before answering. He looked at me and said, "Young man, you can't get married."

I couldn't believe my ears. "What do you mean? The date is set. Everything is ready."

"Young man, you have a venereal disease. You can't get married."

I couldn't even speak. It was as if he were telling me my life was over. I had found the most beautiful girl in the world, but I couldn't have her.

"Look," the doctor said, as if he could read my thoughts, "it's not the end of the world. Can't you postpone the wedding for a few weeks while you are being treated? It should take just about six weeks to clear this up."

I shook my head. Nelly would never agree to that. She would never agree to anything if she found out. I thanked the doctor and left. VD! I had been so smart. It had all been such an easy game, getting any girl I wanted. Well, one of them had gotten me—but good! It didn't even matter which one. I learned my lesson, but too late. My whole world had come tumbling down. What a fool I'd been!

I told my boss I was sick, which was true, and took the afternoon off. I drove out to the lake and parked. I had to think of something.

I couldn't tell Nelly the truth. I knew she would never understand, and I would lose her, for sure, this time. And I couldn't ask her to put the marriage off without telling her. She was too smart for that. She would know something was fishy, and she would find out.

I felt like killing myself. I thought of all the "good times" I'd had—the good times that I was now paying for by losing the girl I loved, and I wanted to drive the car into the lake and end it all.

And then I thought of something. I remembered there was no medical examination required in Maryland—only a two-day waiting period—and the line was only sixty miles away. We could get married, then I could tell her. She couldn't leave me then.

I had solved the problem. As I drove back to town, I felt like a jerk. I didn't like to have to lie to Nelly. But I told myself that whatever I was doing, I was doing out of love.

I didn't have too much trouble convincing Nelly that we should go to Maryland to get married. I told her there was some mix-up on the tests, and they wouldn't be ready for another week. And even after that, we would have to wait five days. In Maryland, we could get married right away. We could elope, I said. I didn't want Mom and my brothers around anyway. She was anxious to get married, too, so she agreed.

We left that night. We drove to Baltimore, got separate rooms in a hotel, and applied for the license. There was no difficulty at all. During the two-day waiting period we went to movies and museums and saw the sights.

I was miserable, but Nelly thought it was just because I was in a hurry to get married. "I feel the same way, darling," she said, kissing me passionately. "I can hardly wait until we belong to each other completely."

She made me feel like a criminal. I felt guilty even kissing her, but I couldn't avoid it. I just prayed she wouldn't get infected. But how could I tell her that our wedding night would be a sham? That we could have no sharing of newlywed love? All I would be able to give her on our wedding night would be a terrible secret. I dreaded it.

We were married in City Hall. Nelly cried and kissed me happily. The judge shook my hand. What would he think if he knew the truth? Could he believe that a man with a beautiful new bride was actually dreading his wedding night?

I kept putting it off. I told Nelly we needed a real honeymoon, so we checked out of the hotel and drove to Virginia, to a nice hotel on the beach. Nelly was so happy. She wanted to go to our room right away, but I talked her out of it. We spent the afternoon on the beach.

That night we went to a nightclub. If Nelly thought I was acting strange, she didn't say so. She must have thought I was just nervous. I insisted we stay and see the floor show twice.

Finally, it was twelve o'clock. I couldn't put it off any longer. We went to our room and locked the door. Nelly smiled and kissed me. "This is the happiest night of my life," she said. She said to wait, and went into the bathroom to get undressed.

I sat on the bed, trying to get up courage for what I had to do. I could hear Nelly humming as she changed. She sounded so happy, and now I was going to tell her the ugly truth and ruin everything.

Nelly came into the bedroom in her sheer, pink nightgown, her hair falling softly around her shoulders. I loved and wanted her more than ever before at that moment. She saw that I was still dressed, and she asked in surprise, "Jeb, aren't you coming to bed?"

"Nelly," I said mournfully, "there's something—"

She stopped me with a kiss. Then she got into bed and took my hand. "I'm a little nervous, too," she said. "It's our first night together, and—"

"No!" I said, standing up suddenly. She looked as if I'd slapped her. "I'm not nervous," I said. "I'm afraid it's something else. There's something I have to tell you."

277

She stared at me in horror. "What? What are you trying to say?" she asked in a small voice.

"Nelly—" I reached out for her hand, but she pulled away.

"Don't touch me!" she said. "Tell me. Tell me what's wrong."

"I—I can't sleep with you tonight," I blurted out. "Or any other night for a while." I looked down at the floor, and my voice grew weak. "Nelly, I have a venereal disease."

She just stared at me, then she fell back on the pillow. I went on in a rush of words and explained it all—about the test, and why we had come to Maryland to get married. "I know I tricked you," I said. "But, honey, I did it because I couldn't stand to lose you. I love you so much. It's only a matter of waiting it out for a few weeks. Please understand, Nelly, please."

"Understand?" she choked, sobbing. "You did this to me and you want me to understand?" She turned over and cried into the pillow. When I tried to touch her, she shivered and pulled away, as if I were something dirty.

I sat up for a long time that night, sitting on the side of the bed, watching Nelly cry. She looked so frail and weak as she lay sobbing her heart out. I wanted to comfort her, but I couldn't. It was hard to believe that I was the one who had hurt her so badly, the same one who loved her so much.

When Nelly finally fell asleep, I sat in the armchair beside the bed and stared out the window. I could never forgive myself for hurting the girl I loved so much. And I was afraid she would never forgive me, either.

I must've finally fallen asleep. When I woke up, it was daylight—and Nelly was gone. There was a note on the bed. "Jeb, I've had enough of your lies and your apologies. Don't think you've trapped me, because I'm having the marriage annulled. Nelly."

I wasn't really surprised. I ran downstairs and saw that the car was gone. It was too late. I had lost her forever. I paid the bill and went back to Essex. I didn't really want to go back, but I didn't know what else to do.

When I got back, I called Ginny. She said that Nelly had gone back to Charleston. She hadn't left an address, because she didn't want me to follow her.

I didn't tell Mom what had happened, of course. I just told her Nelly and I'd had a fight. She didn't ask me a lot of questions. I guess it was easy to see what bad shape I was in. She even tried to cheer me up, but it was useless. I was finally seeing myself, and it wasn't pretty.

I was a smart guy, all right—a real woman chaser—and look what it had gotten me. I knew it was useless to try and get in touch with Nelly. She had given up on me. All I could do was wait, and check the mail every morning for the notice that she was beginning annulment proceedings.

But by the end of the week, the notice still hadn't come. I called Ginny to see if she had heard anything. Nelly obviously hadn't told her what had happened, because she was very helpful and sympathetic toward me. She told me all she knew. She said Nelly had gotten back her old job, but she didn't know what it was. And she didn't know where she was living. But she did give me an address where I could write in care of someone else. Ginny said Nelly was using that address for her mail so that I wouldn't be able to find her.

It wasn't much, but at least it was something. I wrote to Nelly that night. I didn't ask her to understand anymore, or plead with her to come back. I just told her I loved her and needed her, how empty my life was without her. I also sent her a check. I said that as long as she was my wife, I was going to support her.

I got no answer. But when I checked a few days later, I found my check had been cashed. I felt some hope. Nelly was at least accepting money from me. And I knew how proud she was. That meant she still considered herself my wife.

I wrote to Nelly every night during those lonely months. I never saw anyone; I was through with the old crowd and their good times. I knew what that kind of thoughtless fun could lead to.

I told her that I still had the hope that she might come back some day. She never answered my letters, but they didn't come back to me. I didn't know if she read them or not. But she continued to cash my checks.

I also told Nelly that I was being treated for my disease. I'd gone to the doctor as soon as I'd come back to Essex. He's started a series of shots, which, he hoped would clear up the infection within six weeks. It was painful and expensive, ant it wasn't quite as easy as the doctor had hoped. It was more than two months before the doctor finally told me that I was cured. I guess he expected me to be overjoyed, but I wasn't. Without Nelly, it meant nothing at all.

I wrote Nelly that I'd been cured, but didn't expect an answer. I was surprised when an envelope came a few days later postmarked Charleston. I recognized Nelly's handwriting!

I tore it open excitedly. There was no letter inside: just a piece of paper with a telephone number on it.

I called the number four times that day but there was no answer. I figured Nelly must be at work, if it was her number. I couldn't wait any longer. I asked my boss for a few days off, packed a few things in the car and headed for Charleston. It might not mean anything, maybe Nelly just wanted the annulment. But I couldn't stop hoping.

I got into Charleston about nine that evening. I pulled into a diner and called the number again. It was busy. I felt I pang of jealousy. Who could Nelly be talking to? That was the one thing I had never thought of—she might have found someone else already. I ordered a cup of coffee, but I was too nervous to drink it. I called again. The phone rang three times, and then I heard her voice. "Hello?"

"Nelly!" I cried. "It's me, Jeb."

"Hello, Jeb." Her voice choked a little and then she asked, "How have you been?"

"Terrible," I said. "Where are you? Can I see you?"

"I'm not sure you'll want to."

"What do you mean? That's all I want in the world, Nelly. I love you!"

Her voice broke. "If you only knew."

"Just give me the address," I said. "Please."

She gave me the address, and then said, "Wait, Jeb, oh, forget it. Come on over."

I couldn't figure it out. Was something wrong? Had something happened to her? I rushed to the address she had given me.

It was an apartment in an old building on a run-down street. I looked on the mailbox and saw that Nelly was using my name: Nelly Crane. I hurried up the stairs, taking them two at a time, and knocked at the door.

Nelly opened the door. She looked tired, but as beautiful as ever. I tried to take her in my arms, but she stepped back. "Come in," she said.

I sat down on the old couch and she shut the door. "Nelly," I began, "you don't know what it means to me to see you again. I've missed you so much."

"Wait, Jeb," she said in a flat tone. "There's something you ought to know." She hesitated, as if she didn't know how to begin. Then she said, "Jeb, what you did was the worst thing you could have done. You made me pay for your mistakes, because you wouldn't admit them to me. Because of you, what should have been the happiest night of my life—my wedding night—was a nightmare! And still, you say you want me to forgive you."

She stopped and stared at me. I looked at her pleadingly. There was nothing I could say.

"You want me to forgive you," she went on. "And—and I do. I love you, too, Jeb."

I could hardly believe my ears. She had forgiven me! She still loved me. My agony was over. I got up and started toward her.

"Wait!" she cried. "Let me finish." I sat back down. "You say you love me, Jeb. You want me to forgive you because you make mistakes, and I do. But would you forgive me if I made the same mistakes?"

"But, Nelly," I said, "I know better. You're not that kind of girl."

She turned on me in anger, her eyes flashing. "I'm a woman, Jeb! I have needs, longings, desires, just like you! Do you love me, Jeb? Would you love me if I was pregnant with another man's child?"

I just stared at her, not knowing what to say. She looked at me coldly, and then turned away and stared out the window.

It couldn't be true, but one look at her face told me it was. I got up slowly. If I made one wrong move, I would collapse. I opened the door. "Nelly," I began. But there was nothing left to say. I shut the door behind me and ran out.

After I had driven a few blocks, I pulled over. I was too mixed-up to drive. All my dreams were gone. I turned on the radio, then turned it off. I just sat and stared down the street, at the rows of little houses, happy families.

I would never have that kind of happiness. I'd thought I'd found the right girl in Nelly, but I'd been wrong. She was just like all the others. I hated her for letting me down and turning my life into a nightmare, for turning my love into a lonely ache inside me. I saw what my life would be from now on, how empty and meaningless. I saw myself forgetting my troubles in the arms of some cheap girl with no face, falling into meaningless affairs as Nelly had done. . . .

As Nelly had done! The bitterness that I was feeling, the loneliness—it was the same that she had felt. Suddenly I realized something. I was afraid I was going to be sick. I recognized my hatred and contempt for what it was—hatred for myself! I saw for the first time what I had done to Nelly, my Nelly. I had hurt her so badly that I had driven her into the arms of another man. No, she wasn't a "nice girl"—but she had been. I had cheapened her, dirtied her. I had destroyed the person I loved.

And then I had deserted her! I had made a mess of her life and then walked out on her. "What kind of a bastard are you?" I asked myself. "You ruin a girl's life—you turn her into something she hates, and you hate, and then you walk out on her!"

But I didn't hate Nelly. I knew that now. She had hurt me, just as I had hurt her, but I still loved her. There was no need for me to forgive her. If I loved her—and I did—I would stick by her, no matter what.

Before I knew it, I was speeding toward Nelly's apartment. I ran up the stairs and burst in without knocking. She was lying on the couch, sobbing. I caught her in my arms. "Nelly," I said. "I'm sorry, truly sorry this time. I know now what you've gone through. I know how horrible it's been. But it's all over now. We'll make out somehow."

She looked at me through tear-filled eyes. "Do you mean?"

"I mean it's all right," I said. "I love you, you love me, and that's what counts. We're sticking together from now on."

"You—you forgive me?"

281

"It's you who should forgive me," I said. "It's my fault. I drove you to it."

"Oh, Jeb!" Nelly covered me with kisses. "I'm so glad you're back. I love you so. I was afraid I'd lost you forever. But I had to take the chance; I had to know for sure."

"Know what?" I asked, puzzled. "What do you mean?"

"I had to know if you really loved me. You see—" Nelly sat up. She smiled shyly, looking embarrassed. "There's something else I have to tell you, something bad."

"What?" I tried to keep my voice steady. What could be worse than what I already knew?

"I'm not pregnant. I lied to you. No other man has ever touched me."

"Nelly!" I stood up, shocked. "I can't believe it! You mean you put me through hell like that for nothing? Just to get even with me?"

"Not for nothing, Jeb. Don't be angry. I wasn't trying to get even. I just had to know if your love was real, if you had grown up enough to love me as much as I love you, in spite of all you've done. In spite of everything."

At first I felt like smacking her, then my anger slipped away as I looked at her and listened to her words. I felt foolish, but relieved—and happy for the first time in months. I took her into my arms. "Nelly!" I laughed. "What a crazy girl! But, you know, you were right. I had a lot of growing up to do. It hurt, but I did it all of a sudden tonight. I've learned a lot. That's the important thing. Now we know our love is strong enough to last. But tell me," I said, grinning, not that her answer would change the way I felt about her, nothing could do that. "Is it really true this time? You're really not pregnant?"

It was her turn to look shocked. "No, Jeb! Really! No man has ever touched me."

"Well, we'll have to do something about that," I said. "Right away." I locked the door and carried my Nelly into the bedroom. We were man and wife at last. It was our wedding night, even if it was a little late.

The End

THE GOVERNMENT
STOLE MY KIDS!

I was pacing the kitchen floor, wringing my hands nervously. Every so often my eyes were drawn to the letter on the table. Each time I could feel the tears begin to well up, but I fought them back. No point in getting the girls upset any sooner than necessary, I thought.

Suddenly I heard the garage door slam shut. "Good heavens!" I said out loud. Bill was home, and I hadn't even heard him drive up. He was whistling a happy tune.

Bill was a good man—one of the best, as far as I was concerned. He had a kind and generous heart, and a smile nearly as broad as his shoulders. He was a good worker, too. In the sixteen years he'd worked on his present job as a machinist, he hadn't missed more than four days.

A woman couldn't have a better or more loving husband than Bill. The way he'd been a father to the fifteen foster children we had cared for during our marriage was wonderful to see. We had four girls now, all sisters. We had had them for five years. And that's what the letter on the kitchen table was about.

Our noisy, laughing girls, excitedly running to meet Bill as they did each evening, caught my attention. As Bill walked in the front door, four pairs of outstretched arms reached toward his big frame. Even Georgette, our thirteen-year-old, always joined in the rush to greet Daddy.

"Well, now," Bill said. "How have our girls been today, Mama? Good or bad?" It was his usual homecoming routine, and the girls never tired of it.

"Good, Daddy!" they all squealed.

"Did you do your chores all week without being told?" he asked.

"Yes! Yes! We did!" four voices said at once.

"I dried the dishes all week," six-year-old Taylor said proudly.

Eight-year-old Madison and eleven-year-old Loretta said together, "We cleaned up the yard and took out the trash, Daddy."

Georgette, looking at Bill with her serious eyes, said calmly, "I always help Mama, Daddy."

"I know you do, honey," Bill replied as he gently patted her small face with his huge hand.

"Well, since you've all been so good, I guess you can have your Friday night treats," he told them.

Squeals of laughter followed Bill as he went to the door and reached out onto the porch where he always left their treats. He'd pretend he didn't have them, but the girls always knew better.

He opened a large brown bag and pulled out coloring books and crayons for Loretta and Madison—their favorite treats. Little Taylor was given a new outfit for her doll, and Georgette received her very favorite thing—a new book for her growing collection.

As I watched the happy scene before me, my eyes filled with tears. This will probably be the last time I see my girls like this, I thought hopelessly. As Bill came to me to give me my hello kiss, he noticed that I was upset.

"What's wrong, hon?" he asked, planting a kiss on my nose.

Bill's loving concern was all I needed to cause me to break into sobs. "Oh, Bill!" I moaned.

"Mama, Mama! What's wrong?" the girls asked, immediately running toward me. As their arms surrounded me, I cried even harder.

"Here now, honey. Nothing can be that bad," Bill consoled.

But as I continued to cry, he turned to the children and said gently, "Girls, how about playing with your treats for a while so that Mama and I can talk?"

With his arm around my shoulders, Bill led me to our bedroom and shut the door.

"Okay, sweetheart. What's this all about?" he asked as we sat together on the bed. I began to tell him about the letter, but I kept breaking into tears and was unable to speak.

"Darlene, take it easy. Let's see if I can get this straight. You got a letter from the Social Services Agency, and it said that they're going to take the girls away from us?"

"Yes, that's what it said," I answered.

"There's got to be some mistake," Bill remarked. "Where's the letter?"

"On the kitchen table."

When Bill returned, his face was white and he was looking at the letter in disbelief. "They can't! They can't!" he exclaimed. "Whoever heard of taking kids away from people because there's too much love! What the matter with that woman, anyway? Is she crazy?"

Bill was referring to Miss Green. She was the new social worker who was assigned to our case about a year ago, after Mrs. Finnegan had transferred up north to be with her husband.

"What are we going to do, Bill? What can we do?"

"I don't know, Darlene, but there must be something we can do. I've got to think about this. But we don't have much time—only a week. Why don't you go fix something to eat? The girls are probably hungry."

As I went toward the kitchen, Georgette came after me. Taking

284

my hand in hers, she looked at me with those oh-too-serious eyes. "What's wrong, Mama? Tell me. I'm big enough," she said.

Just then, Bill came into the kitchen. "Tell her, Darlene," he said to me. "In fact, I guess we'd better tell them all. They've got to know."

By that time, all the girls had come into the kitchen to find out what the trouble was. We seldom had serious trouble in our family, but when we did, everyone was told and shared in the solution, if possible.

Bill told the children what had happened. The two youngest began to cry, and little Taylor crawled onto my lap and clung to me.

Georgette reacted in anger. "We're not going!" she declared.

"But we're really not your legal parents, honey," I said.

"That doesn't matter. You're the only parents we've ever had." Turning to Bill, she pleaded, "Daddy, don't let them. Please don't let them."

Bill hugged her to him. "I'll try, honey, but I don't know if I can stop them."

I could feel myself about to break down in tears again, so I busied myself preparing supper. I had cooked chicken and dumplings earlier in the day. While I prepared the vegetable, Georgette made the salad. Usually, we teased her and called her our "little old salad maker" because she did such a good job, fancying them up and all. But tonight there wasn't any teasing or laughter in the kitchen.

Loretta and Madison set the table so quietly that I didn't even hear the dishes rattle. Taylor just sat huddled on a chair in the kitchen instead of collecting dandelions for the table "bouquet" as she usually did. Even Milo, the cat, lay quietly in a corner instead of swatting playfully at the girls as they passed by.

Even though I had made one of their favorite dishes, the girls barely touched the food.

"Eat your dinner, girls," Bill said, "and then you can have dessert."

"Please, Daddy," Georgette said, "we're not very hungry tonight."

Bill and I looked at each other, and then at our own plates. We knew how the girls felt. We weren't hungry, either.

"Darlene, I've been thinking about something," Bill remarked. "There's a guy at work, one of the union stewards, who's really sharp. He's been going to law school at night. He's a really nice guy, and we've been pretty friendly. He only lives a few blocks from here. I think I'll run over to his house and talk to him."

"What could he do?" I asked.

"I don't know, really. But maybe he knows something that we wouldn't know about the laws."

"Well, I guess it won't hurt to talk to him," I said.

Bill got up from the table right away. "I'll get over there right now. Be back as soon as I can," he said as he went out the door.

After the girls and I cleaned up the kitchen, I suggested we watch TV. I thought some singing and dancing might take their minds off our trouble—at least for a little while.

I turned on the TV and sat down on the sofa. Taylor came silently across the room and crawled into my lap. Madison and Loretta sat down on either side of me and snuggled close. Georgette sat on the floor and rested her head on my knee. Nothing was said as we all sat pretending to watch a musical variety show.

As I looked at Taylor, I remembered the day five years ago when Mrs. Finnegan had brought her and her sisters to our home. Taylor had been the youngest child I had ever received—not quite one year old. She, like her older sisters, was a tiny, skinny child, and her hair was sadly matted. It was appalling.

The children never seemed to get enough to eat, and the baby cried constantly. When I took them to the doctor for an examination, I found out why. They all had worms! They had head lice, too. What kind of mother did these children have? I had thought incredulously.

I only knew that the mother had voluntarily placed them in a foster home. Why, I didn't know. But it was apparent that the children had not had a pleasant existence. The few clothes they had brought with them weren't fit to wear. They had no toys. Not even the baby.

The State didn't pay enough to care for children in the way that I thought children should be cared for. But since Bill and I had never been blessed with children of our own, we didn't mind spending our money on our foster children. But to buy complete wardrobes for four little girls was a bit more than we could afford.

I told the girls that we would have to get some of their things second-hand at the thrift shop. I'll never forget their delight. It was the first time they smiled. The next day, all four children and I went to the thrift shop. We couldn't have had more fun if we had gone to the biggest and best store in town. I had told the two older girls, Georgette and Loretta, that they could choose a dress, two blouses, two pairs of pants, a coat, and a sweater for themselves. Their eyes lit up like they had just discovered Christmas. I chose for little Madison and the baby.

It was about a month after the children had come to live with us that I asked Georgette to put the baby to bed for me. She often took care of the others, and they listened to her. She had been upstairs a long time, and I went up to see if everything was all right. As I reached the top of the stairs, I heard her talking to the baby.

"You know, Taylor," she was saying, "I think everything might be all right now. These people seem real nice, and they treat us good. Maybe we'll really have a home and parents now."

As she continued to talk to her little sister, my eyes filled with tears, and I quietly turned and went downstairs. The poor little things,

I thought. There she is, an eight-year-old child, with the weight of the world on her shoulders.

At first, Georgette had been shy and aloof. But little by little, she came to trust and love both me and Bill. One time, when I was cooking, I asked Georgette if she would like to help. We spent many pleasant hours together and I finally learned the details of her past. It wasn't pretty! I also learned just how bright Georgette was. She caught on to cooking right away.

It was through her cooking that I received one of the most delicious gifts I have ever received.

It was my birthday. Bill had taken the children shopping so that they could buy me a present. But Georgette asked if she could buy some groceries so that she could make me something all by herself. She had never used the stove except when I supervised her, but after Bill explained the situation, I allowed her to use it by herself. As soon as she would get home from school she'd say, "Don't come in the kitchen. I'm going to cook."

"All right," I would laughingly answer. The present was to be a big secret until my birthday.

When the day arrived, we had the tastiest chicken cacciatore I—or any of us—ever tasted! Then Bill brought in a pretty cake he'd bought at the supermarket. It was all lit up with candles, and as he set it in front of me, everyone sang, "Happy Birthday." Each child gave me her present. Taylor, the baby, needed a little help from Bill, since she wanted to keep hers. I opened them up one by one, enjoying the look on each girl's face as I opened her present.

"Happy birthday, Mama!" they all cried with joy. Even the baby mimicked that one magic word: "Mama."

How happy could a woman be? The children were hugging and kissing me and Bill, yelling, "Mama and Daddy! Mama and Daddy!"

We had had other children who had called us Mom and Dad, and we had loved them. But these four little sisters were different. The other children had been with us because their parents had hit hard times, or because they had suddenly lost a parent. But these children had never really had parents. True, they had a mother, but she had never been a real mother. The girls had never been loved, or cared for, or protected. Bill and I couldn't love these children any more if we had been their natural parents. I guess we forgot that we weren't. They became ours, and we became theirs.

I selfishly dreaded the day that their mother would arrive for her first visit. Most of the parents of children we had cared for came about once a month to visit. Some came more often. As it turned out, I had quite a wait. The mother of our children didn't show up to visit them until they had been with us over nine months.

When the social worker, Mrs. Finnegan, called to say that the mother would visit the children that Sunday, I told myself not to be prejudiced. I had only heard the children's side of the story, and, after all, even Georgette was only a child. But I kept recalling the condition of the children when we had taken them in. As hard as I tried, I couldn't help but dislike the woman even before I met her. After I met her, my dislike multiplied.

The day she arrived she came into the house and immediately flopped on the sofa.

"Come to Mommy, Taylor," she said to the baby. But Taylor ran to me.

She urged again. "Come over here, honey. You look real cute." She reached toward Taylor, but the baby began to cry.

"She doesn't remember you," I offered. "After all, she was only a year old the last time she saw you."

She turned to the next youngest—Madison. "Come here, Madison. Come and give me a kiss." Madison stood absolutely still and said nothing.

"Well, if you don't want to kiss me, Loretta will—won't you, honey?" she said angrily. Loretta moved closer to Georgette, who was standing nearby.

"What's the matter with these kids, anyway?" the woman demanded. "These three are old enough to remember me."

Yes, I thought. They do remember.

The woman looked at her eldest child, Georgette. "There's no point in expecting you to be friendly, is there? You always were a strange one—just like your father. I couldn't get along with him, either. It's a blessing he died."

I gasped! To say such a thing to a child! When I looked at Georgette, I saw something in her eyes that I didn't want to see—hate! Hate for her natural mother.

I wanted to grab my girls and run—away from this woman who had given birth to them, but who didn't really care. But I couldn't, of course. She was their legal mother.

I tried to pull myself together and be polite for the sake of the girls. "Perhaps you'd like to take the girls to the zoo," I offered.

"Well, I don't have time, really," she said. "I have a date." As she headed toward the front door, she said, "Bye, kids"—obviously relieved that the visit was over.

I was still upset and angry when Bill returned home. "Can you believe the nerve of that woman?" I asked him. "I don't know if I can stand her visits too often."

"Calm down now, honey. She probably won't come that often."

As it turned out, I didn't have to worry about her visiting all the time. I didn't see our girls' mother again for a year. In the five years we had had the girls, their mother had only visited them four times, and then only briefly. We hadn't seen her for a year when the letter came from the agency.

Mrs. Finnegan, our former caseworker, had thought the girls were very lucky to have found a home with us. At first she had visited us every couple of weeks but after a while, she said that the girls were so happy with us that she didn't feel it necessary to check on us all the time.

Mrs. Finnegan visited us just before she left to go north, and she told us we would have a new caseworker. She assured us that the new woman would know all about the girls and us, and she was sure that everything would be just fine. She hadn't met Miss Green, though, and naturally, I began to worry.

Things got difficult after Miss Green was assigned to us. Immediately, she felt that the emotional stability of the children was threatened by our closeness to them. I really didn't understand that—and I didn't agree, either. We loved the girls, and they loved us. We were all happy. But Miss Green kept insisting that that was the problem. She said we weren't supposed to love each other that much— that we were only foster parents, not real parents. We knew we were foster parents—we had helped raise many children who belonged to other people.

Soon, Miss Green began to suggest that the girls would have to go back to their mother or to another foster home. I didn't see why. Their mother didn't want them, and they were happy and healthy with us. Why should they go anywhere else?

Miss Green came around all the time. She questioned the girls and upset them. She looked at their rooms. She even checked at their school. I couldn't understand why. I was frightened. There was no reason for her checking. The girls had good, nourishing food, the same as Bill and I ate. They had nice rooms, colorful and pretty, and filled with toys and games. They all did well in school, especially Georgette. She was so bright.

Then the letter came. The horrible thought brought me back to the present. I realized that it was dark in the room. The TV was still on. Taylor's weight seemed to be bearing down on me, and I realized that I hadn't changed my position since I had sat down. Taylor was fast asleep. Loretta and Madison had rested their heads on my arms and fallen asleep, too. Only Georgette was still awake, still sitting with her head on my knee.

"Come on, Georgette. Let's put the little ones to bed," I said. "It's been an awfully long day."

"Okay, Mama, but can I stay up with you and wait till Daddy comes back? I want to know what's happening."

I looked at her grave little face, so concerned about the situation. "All right, honey," I said. "You don't have school tomorrow, so you can keep me company."

She took Taylor from my lap and started upstairs while I roused the other two girls. They walked upstairs half asleep and didn't even wake up when I undressed them and got them into bed. They snuggled close to each other and slept like the innocent babies they were.

Please, God, don't let me lose these precious children, I prayed silently.

Although I had missed church occasionally, I believed with all my heart in God's goodness and mercy. I had never asked Him for anything that He hadn't granted, although He didn't always answer my pleas in the way I had asked—like when I had prayed for a child. I had had in mind a child of Bill's and mine—one I'd given birth to. But instead, God gave us many children to love and care for—especially our girls. I knew he wouldn't let the agency take them away, and yet, I was frightened.

Georgette and I had just sat down again when Bill returned home. We looked at each other anxiously and then at him as he came into the house.

"What happened?" I asked.

"Tony—that's the union steward—has a pretty good idea," Bill said.

"What? What?" I asked quickly.

"Now, just take it easy, honey," Bill cautioned. "It may not work, but it's worth a try."

He went on to tell us that Tony had called a few friends of his at law school. They told him that the best thing for us to do was to go to the Civil Liberties Union; they believed that we could fight the case on the basis that the girls had rights. I didn't know. I didn't see how little girls could fight a State agency even with both our help and that of the Civil Liberties Union. But Bill said that times were different now, and that children's rights were protected more than in the past. Like he said: "It's all we have, honey. At least it's a chance to keep our girls."

The next week went by like a nightmare. We talked with people from the Civil Liberties Union and so did the girls. The next thing I knew, we were all getting ready to take the girls to talk to a judge. He asked Bill and me many questions, and he also talked to the girls. I was in such a daze, I don't even know what I answered. But I guess the answers were all right, because the judge said that we could keep the girls temporarily until he had the situation investigated further.

A week later, we were just getting settled down from all the trouble when Miss Green came around. The girls wouldn't even talk to her, they were so frightened, and I didn't want to, either. . . .

"You know, Mrs. Burke," she said, "you are not going to be able to keep these children. They are only here temporarily until the judge decides what to do with them."

"That's not what the judge said," I answered defensively. "He said that he was going to investigate further."

"Yes, he did. But now there is a change in the circumstances. Their mother wants them back."

I couldn't believe my ears! Their mother didn't want them!

"What do you mean?" I nearly screamed at her. "She doesn't want these children, and you know it!"

Miss Green answered coldly, "I don't know any such thing, and neither do you. After all, she is their natural mother, and she has a legal right to take back her children."

"But how will she care for them? She isn't even working!" I exclaimed.

"I have arranged for her to receive welfare for herself and the children until she can be trained for a job. Then she can care for them on her own. The family will be together again."

My stomach turned over. I thought I was going to be sick right then and there. I fought back the nauseated feeling and tried to hold on to my senses. I heard myself saying, "You know she doesn't really want them. You know she doesn't care about them! She hasn't even visited them except for a few times in nearly five years. If she had wanted them, she would have tried to find some kind of work. She would have come to see them!

"And what about the few times she did come? She would only stay a few minutes, saying that she had a date. How can you believe that the children would be better off with her than with us? Putting people together under one roof doesn't make a family—love does!" Then I nearly broke down.

"She is their natural mother," Miss Green said unemotionally. "She gave them up voluntarily, and she can request their return. Of course, the judge will have to review the case first. But I'm sure he will feel that the children are better off with their own mother."

"They weren't better off with her before, and they won't be better off with her now!" I cried.

Miss Green turned toward the door. "We'll see," was her only parting comment.

As she left, Bill drove into the driveway. He barely got into the house before I collapsed in his arms, hysterically telling him what Miss Green had said.

Suddenly we heard Georgette's voice behind us. "I'm not going back with her, and neither are my sisters!"

The other girls were standing behind Georgette looking at us with tear-filled eyes and trembling lips. I thought my heart would break. My mind screamed: Why, Lord—why? Why do these little children have to go through this?

Georgette's voice cut through my thought. "We didn't get enough to eat when we lived with her. She had money from welfare, but she spent it on herself and her boyfriends. She left us alone all the time and didn't come home till late at night. And she brought men home—men we didn't know. She yelled at the baby and slapped me when Taylor cried. She told me to keep the others quiet. It was awful! We're not going back there, Mama and Daddy. We're staying here with you!"

We tried to explain to Georgette that we had to do whatever the judge decided, but she was too upset to understand. We finally just told her that her mother would soon change her mind. But Georgette's past experiences had left their mark, and she insisted things wouldn't change. In my heart, I knew she was right.

I pulled her close to me with one arm, and I hugged Loretta with the other. Bill's big arms encircled Madison and the baby. We just sat there in the darkening room, holding our girls close to us and looking at each other in misery.

About a month later, we received the notice to appear in court with the girls. The Civil Liberties Union sent a lawyer with us. He did everything he could for us. The judge even questioned the girls. Of course, they said that they wanted to stay with their "Mama and Daddy." Georgette and Loretta remained dry-eyed and brave, but little Madison and Taylor broke down in tears.

Miss Green was there, and I found out that she had given the judge her written recommendation in favor of the girls' mother. And their mother was there, too. I hardly recognized her—she looked so prim and proper. She had probably been advised by the agency to look neat.

The judge gave the girls back to their mother. When he announced his decision, I could hear Georgette yelling that she wouldn't go. I could hear the other three children crying. They were pulling on my arms. Then I fainted.

When I came to, I was lying on a bench in the courtroom. Bill had his arms around me. I looked at him, and there were tears running down his face. My husband was crying. As I looked around, I realized that except for Bill and me and the lawyer, there was no one else in the room. I looked at Bill, and he must have seen the question in my eyes, because he said quietly, "They had to go with their mother. We're to take their things over to them tomorrow."

I thought I was going to faint again. "You mean they're gone?" I whispered. Then I was sobbing, "They're gone! Oh, Bill—our girls!"

"Yes, sweetheart," he said. "They're gone."

I guess God takes care of us in His own way, because shock set in, and I was just numb. It was a sort of restfulness. My numbness probably saved me from a nervous breakdown.

The lawyer came the next day and said that it would probably be easier for us if he took the girls' things to them. He also said that he had begun an appeal of the decision.

I don't know how Bill put up with me for the next several weeks. I walked around like a robot. I don't even remember whether or not I cooked meals, but I suppose I did. I don't remember eating at all, and I had lost so much weight I hardly recognized myself when I finally "came to" and looked at myself in the mirror. When I really looked at Bill, I could see that he had been suffering, too. He was so thin! He looked older, and his broad smile had vanished.

I realized that we couldn't go on that way. We weren't helping either the girls or ourselves acting like that. The next day, I cleaned the house from top to bottom, except for the girls' rooms. I just couldn't force myself to go into those rooms yet.

When Bill came home, I was dressed in a clean, pretty dress and I had fixed my hair. I had a good, hot meal prepared, but I had skipped the salad—that had been Georgette's specialty. Bill looked pleased when he realized the difference in me and the house. After we finished our quiet dinner, devoid of little-girl chatter and laughter, I said to Bill, "Honey, maybe we could get permission to visit the girls."

For a second, Bill's face lit up, but then the look faded and he replied, "I don't know, Darlene. I just don't know if that would be best for the girls. Let's think about it a little bit."

It was a week later, about four in the morning, when I awoke and thought I heard a knock at the door. At first, I thought it was thunder—it had been storming all night. I listened for a minute, but all I could hear was the pounding rain hitting the roof and concrete walk. Then I heard it again. It was a knock!

"Bill, Bill! Someone's at the door! It's four in the morning!" I cried, panic-stricken.

Bill quickly grabbed his robe and was putting it on as we started toward the front door. When Bill opened the door, I couldn't believe the sight before me. Standing there were four soaking-wet little girls.

"Mama! Mama!" Loretta and Madison squealed as theft flung themselves at us. Georgette, who looked exhausted, quietly stepped inside and pushed Taylor toward Bill.

For an instant, Bill and I stood frozen. We couldn't believe our eyes! Bill spoke first. "Come, girls, let's get you out of those wet clothes."

We went upstairs, and I drew a hot bath. I put lots of bubble bath in it, the way I used to do. The girls were so cold and tired, they didn't even want to take turns bathing. They all got into the tub together.

"You'll all be lucky if you don't get pneumonia," I gently scolded as I smiled at them. I wanted to question them, but I held back. They need care right now, I thought, not questions.

After their bath, they dressed in my flannel nightgowns. Of course, the gowns were huge on them, but they giggled and pranced around the room, as tired as they were. The looked so silly and cute in those overflowing gowns as they held up the hems and pranced downstairs to show Bill. As we went toward the kitchen, the aroma of hot chocolate greeted us. Bill had gotten everything ready.

"Come on, gals," he called happily. As they entered the room and he saw them in the gowns, he broke into laughter. It was so good to see that big, broad smile of his again. He poured the hot chocolate for them, and dished out hot soup. The three little ones ate and chattered and laughed. But Georgette was silent as she lingered over her chocolate.

"Okay, girls, let's go to bed," Bill said.

As they followed him, Loretta called to Georgette, "C'mon, Georgette, let's go."

"I'll be up in a minute, Loretta. I want to talk to Mama and Daddy," she answered.

She sat silently until Bill returned to the kitchen. Then she told us the story. Her mother was using all the welfare money for herself—as Georgette had predicted. The mother completely neglected the girls, so Georgette was again taking full charge of them and the household duties. She didn't mind that, she told us, but she could never get any money to buy food.

The mother was rarely home and she only left the girls with bread and sandwich meat or peanut butter. Georgette said that there wasn't even enough of that. Their mother often brought a man in for the night, and the insecurity the girls felt, along with the lack of sleep and lack of food, was beginning to tell.

Taylor, who was six years old now, had begun to wet the bed, and Madison would wake up in the middle of the night crying. Although the girls shared two bedrooms, they had finally had to move together into one. It seems that one night when their mother and one of her boy friends came home, the drunken boyfriend had gone into the wrong room and flopped onto the bed—right on top of Madison and Taylor. They became hysterical and refused to sleep alone anymore.

Tonight had been too much for Georgette to bear. Her mother had come home late again, with a man friend. The noise had awakened Taylor, who had been restless anyway because she had a cold. Georgette tried to get her to go back to sleep, but she wanted a drink.

By that time, the noise in the apartment had quieted down, so Georgette went into the bathroom to get Taylor a glass of water.

When she was coming out of the bathroom, the man was standing in the hall between the bathroom and the girls' bedroom. As Georgette tried to pass by him, he reached for her. She ducked, and threw the glass of water at him, then ran into her room.

She made up her mind right then and there that she and her sisters were leaving. She awakened the girls and told them to dress. Then they all sat quietly in the dark waiting until their mother and her friend were asleep. Georgette then led the girls out of the apartment. Since they had no money, they had to walk. It was miles! Those little girls walked miles in the dark, rainy night in order to get away from their misery.

"Mama, Daddy—I don't know if you want us back with all this trouble, but I had to bring us home," Georgette explained.

"Want you! Oh, sweetheart, of course we want you!" I cried.

For the first time since Georgette had entered the house that night, she smiled.

"Come on, sweetheart," Bill said, holding out his arms. "You're still not too big to sit on Daddy's lap."

Georgette snuggled close to her daddy and in seconds, she was fast asleep. Bill lifted her gently in his big, strong arms. "Honey, let's put her to bed," he said to me.

When we got back downstairs, I asked him, "What are we going to do?"

"I wish I knew, hon. All I can think of right now is to call the lawyer in the morning and see what the possibilities are."

We had barely gone to bed when it was time to get up. Bill called in to work and took the day off. Then he called the lawyer. When the man heard what had happened, he came right over to our house.

After talking with the girls, he said, "It's hard to prove that a mother is unfit, but we're going to try!"

He decided to try to get a hearing that would give us temporary custody of the girls until he could get the appeal through that he had been working on. He believed that under the circumstances, he might be able to do that. But the courts are overloaded and slow. A few days later, Miss Green came again for the girls.

I couldn't help it; I got mad! "You must know what these children have gone through with their mother and her drunken friends! What kind of a person are you, anyway?"

She didn't say a word. She simply motioned to the girls to follow her. I couldn't believe that I was losing them again. They hugged me as tears wet my face—theirs and mine. Then they left. But Georgette whispered in my ear as she hugged me, "We'll be back, Mama."

The determination in her voice frightened me. What was she going to do? Taylor's cough worried me, too. She had been feverish during the night, and I had intended to take her to the doctor that day.

I called after them, "Miss Green! Tell their mother to take Taylor to the doctor!" But she ignored me.

That was on a Tuesday. Thursday night, the phone awakened me. I glanced at the clock. It was midnight.

"Hello?" I answered hazily.

"Mrs. Burke?" the voice asked. "Is this Mrs. Burke? Do you know a little girl named Taylor?"

My heart leaped to my throat. What was the matter?

Bill was awake and looked at me as I answered, "Yes, I know a little girl named Taylor. What's the matter? And who is this?"

"I'm a doctor at General Hospital. Taylor is here. She has pneumonia. She's been asking for you constantly. Her mother finally gave me permission to call you. Can you and your husband come over here?"

"We'll be there in half an hour," I said.

We left the house in record time and went to the hospital. When we reached Taylor's room, I had to grab Bill's arm for support. Looking at her under that oxygen tent—she looked so little!

She seemed to be asleep. The doctor filled us in on what had happened. Georgette had called an ambulance and taken her little sister to the hospital. Before she had a chance to call us, her mother had arrived at the hospital, angry and somewhat drunk. She had refused to allow Georgette to call us, and said that she would not allow us to see Taylor anyway. But Taylor had gotten steadily worse, and in her delirium, she kept calling for Mama and Daddy. Finally, the doctor had convinced Taylor's mother to let him call us.

Bill and I sat by Taylor's bed all night. We held her hand and kept telling her that we were there. Every so often she would cry out, "Mama! Daddy!" We would comfort her, and then she would rest again. I guess I fell asleep with my head on Taylor's hospital bed, because I suddenly heard her voice out of nowhere.

"Mama? Mama? Daddy? Where are you?"

"Oh, Taylor! Yes, baby, it's Mama and Daddy."

She was out of her delirium! Bill and I were so happy, we both started to laugh and cry at the same time. We didn't even hear the doctor come into the room.

He stopped short. He was surprised and grinning. "Well, young lady! You certainly are wide awake today!"

Taylor gave him a weak but big smile. "Can Mama and Daddy stay?" she asked.

"Sure," the doctor said. "But let's check your temperature and wash your face. You want to be beautiful for them don't you?" He was a nice, fatherly man. He motioned us outside, and a nurse entered to take care of Taylor.

When we went into the hall, he shut the door to Taylor's room and said, "Mr. and Mrs. Burke, maybe it's none of my business, but what's the story here? I'm very concerned about that little girl. Where do you fit into the picture?"

We related all the facts to him while he stood looking at us in astonishment. He shook his head. "This is unbelievable!" he exclaimed. "You mean that the girls want you, and you want them, and the court gave them back to a mother who doesn't care anything about them?"

"I'm afraid that's the way it is," Bill said.

"Give me your lawyer's name, address, and telephone number," the doctor said. "I'm going to have a talk with him. Maybe I can help you and the girls."

I suddenly felt that all was not hopeless. I actually felt better! I didn't know why, but I just believed that with a good lawyer who cared, and a good doctor who cared, we just had to have something good happen.

When we arrived home, Georgette was sitting on the front porch. There were several people with her, strangers to me and Bill. She ran to us and hugged us both, asking us about her sister. We assured her that Taylor was much better.

It turned out that the people there were the girls' teachers, and the principal from the new school they attended. It seems that they also represented many other teachers, and other people connected with the school.

Georgette had taken things into her own capable hands. She had written a brief story about her and her sisters' plight. Then she had added a request that people sign the petition she had attached to the story. The petition was to be presented to the judge at the time of the temporary hearing. Georgette had collected over three hundred names! Students, teachers, parents, and the principal had rallied to her cause. These people wanted to help us. Bill and I were overwhelmed.

I squealed in happiness and hugged Georgette. Everyone was so happy for all of us, and so kind. After we went inside and settled down, they asked us for our lawyer's name. We also told them about the doctor who wanted to help. By the time they left, I was so filled with hope that I could almost forget that Georgette had to return to her mother—temporarily, anyway.

I looked at my brave, little girl and reached for her hand.

"Don't worry, Mama," she said. "It won't be so bad going back there when I know it's only for a little while. Then we'll all be back together again. Forever!"

As I hugged Georgette to me, I prayed she was right. She had to be! Our fate—the girls', Bill's, and mine—would be decided by a judge—and God.

The End

MY SECOND MARRIAGE
WILL BE MY FIRST

Love for a boy wasn't something I'd experienced before, but I was sure that I was in love with Peter Russo the first day I'd met him. He entered school in midterm, and he joined our crowd in the Chocolate Shop for sodas that first afternoon.

It seemed natural for us to talk as we left together and, as we walked toward home, he told me all about himself. His parents were divorced and he was living in the old Morton house on the hill. He was eighteen to my fifteen, and he could use his dad's convertible any time he wanted to—and he was asking me to go out with him that night.

I could hardly take my eyes off of him as he talked. He was about six feet tall, with dark eyes and dark hair. I was proud to be seen with him. When I asked him if he was going out for our team, he said he never played because his dad didn't stay long enough in any town to make it worthwhile.

He talked so sadly about his dad and mother that my heart went out to him. In my mind, I could see him as a poor little unloved boy, wanting someone to share his hopes and plans. I could hardly bear to tear myself away from him, but Mom was expecting me home. "See you tonight at seven," he called after me, and I floated all the way home.

"Oh, Mom!" I cried, throwing my arms around her neck as I ran in. "I've got a date tonight!"

"Well, now, that's nice, Marina." She laughed. "I didn't know any of the fellows you knew rated so high."

"Oh, it's nobody I've dated before." I dismissed them with a wave of my hand. "It's a new boy in school. You'll love him, simply love him." I sighed.

"I'm sure I will," she answered dryly. I followed her into the kitchen and we chattered like two kids. Mom was like that. We were more like friends than mother and daughter. It was the same with Dad. I was their only child and they never criticized anything I did. We always had fun kidding each other, and I never gave a thought at that time as to how my actions might destroy all this.

That evening, when a car horn sounded out in front, I ran to the window and saw it was Peter in a cream-colored convertible. I grabbed my coat and started to run. "What's wrong with him?" Dad asked from his chair. "Can't he walk up to the door?"

"I guess he's in a hurry, Dad. He'll come up next time." I kissed him on top of his head and then kissed Mom, pretending not to see the displeasure in her eyes. "I'll be in early, Mom," I said over my shoulder.

Peter opened the car door for me. "Hi, baby. You're still as beautiful as I remembered." I was so excited I could hardly breathe. The way Peter looked at me I felt he surely must feel the same way that I did. He must love me! I couldn't stand it if he didn't.

We saw a movie that night, and I couldn't tell you a single thing about it. All I can remember is Peter holding my hand and looking over at me every few minutes. After the show we went out for sodas and hamburgers. To me, it was ambrosia and nectar. "How about a ride out around the lake the next time?" he asked on the way home.

I said, "Sure, but come to the door for me so you can meet my folks."

He hesitated a second. "Well, okay, I suppose I can."

"See you tomorrow then," I said, and I started to open the door.

"Wait, baby, aren't you going to say good night to your guy? Like this. . . ." He pulled me to him and kissed me hard. It wasn't the first time I'd been kissed by a boy, but it was the first time I'd been kissed like that. Rockets exploded inside me and I felt as if I were suffocating, then I was off in the sky somewhere floating. I almost fainted. I almost died. I loved him so.

Finally, I opened the door and ran up the walk. His lazy, smug laugh floated after me. "Tomorrow, baby." And he gunned the car away from the curb.

I patted my hair and hoped it didn't show—my happiness, I mean. I didn't want to have to explain anything just then. Not that I'd ever had to explain, you know, but I just wanted time to savor Peter's kiss by myself. I needn't have worried because Mom and Dad were both in bed. I sat in the window in the moonlight and thought about love. I'd never felt like this about anyone before, not about any of my other dates. There had been boys, fun, yes, but not like Peter. With him I could imagine a home, children, all the things girls dream of.

The next day passed in a daze. I lived only for seven o'clock. I was on pins and needles because Mom and Dad were so disapproving of Peter's behavior the night before. I made all sorts of excuses for him because I couldn't bear the thought of my parents finding any fault with Peter. I loved him so much.

When he arrived, I let him in myself. He was so handsome I just felt like dying; I was so proud of him. He brought candy for me, and flowers for Mom. How sophisticated of him! I was thrilled.

But I couldn't understand Mom and Dad. Generally, they were so friendly and polite to my friends, but tonight they acted cool. I was hurt. Peter was trying so hard to be nice. Wasn't he talking to Dad, smiling so sweetly at Mom that it made her heart turn over? Wasn't he treating them like all the man-about-town actors did in the movies? But Mom and Dad weren't in the least impressed. I just couldn't understand it. So to keep Peter from realizing how they felt, I suggested we leave right away. "Be back early," Dad said gruffly.

"All right, Dad," I answered in hurt dignity. After all, what was I, a baby?

With a perfectly charming smile at Mom, and a flip of his hand to Dad, Peter escorted me to the car. As we drove off, he said, "I knew it wouldn't do any good to meet them. They're just like everyone else. They don't like me at all."

"Oh, no! Don't say that. I can't bear it for you to feel hurt. Mom and Dad are just a little old-fashioned, and they don't always see things just like we do. They will like you. I know."

"I guess I don't even care if they do like me or not, just as long as you do." He gave me his crinkly smile again and my heart did flip-flops.

What in the world was the matter with me? I wanted to put my arms around him and tell him that no matter what anyone else thought, I loved him. No matter what Mom and Dad were sure to say, it wasn't puppy love. I loved Peter the way a girl loves the man she wants to marry. I guess that's what made what happened later so awful. But that night, I was happy.

We drove around the lake and then parked on the shore. The moon made a zigzag path of pure gold on the lake. Peter pulled me to him and kissed me, again and again. "I love you, baby," he whispered. "I guess it's crazy, but I sure do love you. I've never felt like this before about any girl. I can't understand it."

"Oh, Peter, it isn't crazy. It's wonderful, beautiful! I love you, too!" I kissed him back as recklessly as he kissed me.

"Do you love me enough to marry me after graduation?" he asked.

"Oh, of course I do. I'd marry you tonight if I could."

He laughed and smoothed my hair. "We'll have to wait awhile, baby. My old man's pretty tight with money. Right after graduation though, I'll go to work and make my own dough. Then we can really go to town." He hugged me again.

When I finally looked at the clock on the dash, it was one o'clock. I told Peter we'd have to fly before my folks had a fit.

"Just awhile longer, sweetie, another hour won't matter," he coaxed. "Your folks probably won't even be up."

Why couldn't I see then that there was something wrong with him? Anytime a boy tries to get his girl to disobey—well, there just has to be something wrong with him! But then, I was so in love with Peter I let him talk me into staying out until two-thirty.

He left me in front of the house with a final hard kiss. I tried to tiptoe up on the porch, but the door opened as I reached for the knob.

Dad stood aside as I came in. Mom was in the living room and both of them looked like thunderclouds. "Well, young lady," Dad thundered. "Do you realize what time it is? Where have you been? Don't you care that your mother and I have been frightened to death because you didn't come home? Or is a little consideration too much to ask for?" It wasn't like Dad to be sarcastic.

I glanced quickly at Mom, but I could tell there'd be no help from her. I turned back to Dad. "I know I'm late but—"

"I should say you're late!" he roared. "And if that smart Alec had a flat or something, why didn't you call us? And more important, why didn't he come to the door and explain? I don't believe I've ever seen a more boorish, inconsiderate, rude person in my life, and I thoroughly disapprove of your seeing any more of him! Do I make myself clear, Marina?"

I gasped. He was unfair. He wouldn't even give me a chance to explain before he started to blame Peter for everything. "Don't blame Peter," I said, as grown-up as I could. "We were so busy making plans. We're going to be married in June and—"

"Oh, no!" Mother sounded like a wounded animal. "Marina, you're only fifteen."

"I know, Mom, but I'll be sixteen before school is out. You were only seventeen when you and Dad were married."

"But that was different," Mother wailed. "Your father and I grew up together. We were next-door neighbors. You've just met this Peter. How in the world could you even know him, much less love him, in that length of time?"

"Oh, but I do! Mom, truly I do," I tried to tell her, but Dad broke in savagely.

"That's enough! You're not going to see this fellow anymore! And you're certainly not going to marry him."

My blood froze in my veins. My daddy, my own father, talking to me like that! I burst into tears and ran up the stairs, crying back over my shoulder, "I will see him!"

I saw Peter in school the next day and hurriedly whispered the news—my parents had forbidden me to see him. He looked at me quickly. "Do you agree with them, Marina? Do you want me to stay away, too?"

"Oh, Peter, no. I couldn't stand it."

"We'll get a soda after school at the Chocolate Shop and talk it over, baby. Don't you worry."

The rest of the day simply crawled. When at last we were seated in a booth together, Peter took both my hands in his. "Baby, listen. I've been thinking and I've got an idea. I have to go to Midland next Saturday to see a guy for my pop. You go with me. Tell your folks you're going to visit a girlfriend over the weekend. Then we'll get married in Midland. When school is out, we'll tell our folks we're married. See? My old man wouldn't say so much if we were already married."

I didn't want to do anything against my folks' wishes, but hadn't they proved how unreasonable they were? Why should I let them ruin my chance for happiness? "Oh, Peter, I'll do it." I cried. "A friend of mine moved to Midland last winter. Mom knows her. I'll say I'm staying with her."

"No, Marina," Peter protested quickly. "Don't let on that you're going to Midland. Pick someplace else."

"But why?" I asked, puzzled.

"Because we don't want them to have an inkling of which direction you're going." With Peter holding my hands I'd have agreed to anything. We arranged to meet at the library corner at eight-thirty Saturday morning.

I was walking on air. By this time the day after tomorrow, in forty-eight hours, I would be Mrs. Peter Russo, and my folks couldn't do a thing to stop me. Something deep down inside of me seemed to caution me, Careful, Marina, this isn't the way to handle things. But I told myself that the way my folks were acting wasn't the way to handle things, either.

At home, it was hard to act natural. Neither Mom nor Dad mentioned last night, and neither did I. Surprisingly, I didn't have any trouble getting permission to spend the weekend with Cara. I guessed they were sorry they had flared up at dinner yesterday and they were anxious to make up. Poor darlings, I felt bad deceiving them like that, but I didn't let it hurt too much.

I got to the library the next morning just as Peter pulled up in his convertible. I hopped in and he kissed me quickly before he pulled out in the stream of traffic. All the way to Midland, we laughed and sang like a couple of kids. We pulled up in front of the first Justice of the Peace sign we saw. The Justice was a sweet old man. He questioned me about looking so young, but before I could answer, Peter spoke up. "She's eighteen, can't you see the license? Hurry up, we don't have all day."

I was surprised that Peter could be so rude to an old man like that, but I put it down to the fact that, like me, he was anxious to hurry up and get married because he loved me so much. So the Justice read the service before his wife and their maid and we were man and wife. I was so proud when Peter slipped his ring on my finger and kissed me.

We drove straight to a motel and got a room. Peter carried me over the doorstep and kicked the door shut behind him. He held me tight. "Marina, baby, baby, this is what I've been waiting for." And he buried his face in my hair.

That day and night were perfect. Peter was everything I'd dreamed he would be, and I loved him, body and soul. And I felt, yes, I believed that he loved me the same way. I was so happy I could barely breathe. If only we could have had Mom and Dad's blessing, my happiness would have been complete.

On our way home Sunday night, Peter said, "Now listen, Marina, let me keep the license so your folks won't find it by accident. Let me keep the ring, too, because then the times we're able to be together I can place it back on your finger just like I did yesterday. It'll seem like getting married all over again."

"Oh, sweetheart." I cried. "I didn't know you were so romantic. I thought that was only for us girls," I teased him. At the library corner I caught the bus home. Dad and Mom didn't suspect a thing. I loathed myself for lying, but I kept telling myself it was all their fault for not giving Peter a chance. Sweet, wonderful Peter—my husband.

Peter and I managed to be together every weekend after that, though I had to lie like a fiend to manage it. But I was too happy to care. Then came the day I woke to find the room reeling and rocking. I fell back on the bed. I must be pregnant! The feelings I had are hard to define—fright, gladness, a little bit of fear. Now, Peter and I would have to let our families know we were married. Oh, I was so happy. I knew that even Peter's father wouldn't hold our secret marriage against us once he knew about the baby. But how would I tell Mom and Dad? I'd better tell Peter and let him be with me when I told them. Then they'd see that he really was trying to be a husband to me.

I got to school a little early. I wailed anxiously to Peter and at the last minute I saw him. "Peter!" I called.

"Morning, baby. How's my favorite girl today?"

"Great." I laughed, but in a whisper, I went on. "Come to the lockers. I've got to tell you something."

Peter gave me a sidelong glance. "Okay, baby, but hurry. I've got a class in a minute."

Down at the lockers I told him what I suspected. He turned red to the ears, then looked away. He wasn't taking this at all the way I thought he would. He cleared his throat and kicked a wadded up piece of paper with his foot. "Now, look, Marina, are you sure? I mean, is it for certain?"

"I haven't been to the doctor yet, but I'm sure enough for me. Just think, Peter, a baby of our own—a little son, or maybe a daughter." I was so excited.

"Keep your voice down! Do you want to tell the whole school?" He spoke sharply as he glanced furtively around.

"But, Peter, aren't you glad?" Tears were trembling on my lashes. "Just think, now we can tell the whole world we're married and we can move into a little place of our own." I was so pitifully anxious for him to want us to be together as I did, that I couldn't understand his attitude. I started to cry.

"Cut it out! Do you want to cause trouble?" He glanced around again. "Tell you what, I've got to go now or I'll miss class. I'll meet you tonight at the Chocolate Shop. Be there at seven. We'll talk things over and make plans then."

I got there at five before seven. I walked back to "our" booth and waited. Seven, seven-fifteen, seven-thirty. Oh, why didn't Peter come? Could he have had an accident? I finished two drinks, and then at seven forty-five I walked to the phone booth and looked for his number. I couldn't find it, so I called information. She told me the number had been disconnected that afternoon!

I came back to the booth. Eight o'clock—I was getting panicky. Why should they have had their phone cut off? Where was his father? Suddenly it struck me that I didn't really know anything about my husband, and less about my father-in-law. Peter had told me his father was in an office, something about imports, I thought. I went back to the phone booth and asked for information again. "Could you locate Mr. Russo's business office?" I asked her.

"Do you know his initials or first name?"

"No, but it has something to do with imports."

"We have two Russos listed. One is a service station and the other is a florist."

"Thank you, but those aren't the ones." I felt sick.

I walked out. It was eight-thirty and Peter wasn't coming. My feet dragged as I slowly made my way home. I knew deep down inside of me that he was gone. What would I do now? I had to find him somehow! I just had to, for our baby.

The next day I could hardly wait until I got to school. Peter would surely be there. But he wasn't. I couldn't understand it, but I didn't dare ask anyone, either. I cut classes after lunch and caught a bus to his house. The bus stopped at his corner and I waited until it was out of sight before I went up the curved walk. Then, even before I got a clear view of the house, I saw the sign "For Rent or Sale." The doors were locked tight. I walked clear around the house and tried them all. I couldn't believe it. But my heart told me the truth—he'd run out on me.

I walked every step of the way back home. I was ill, physically and mentally. Now I'd have to tell Mom and Dad, as badly as I hated to. I had no choice. That was the only way. Strange, now that I knew what the score was, I didn't feel like blaming Peter for all of it. I felt like blaming my own stupidity. I was as much to blame as he was.

Then suddenly, a thought struck me—my marriage license and the ring! Oh, dear God, why had I let him take them? How else could

I prove to Mom and Dad that I was really married? The county clerk, of course! I felt better. There was the proof I needed.

Peter, my heart cried, why did you do this to me? It must have been his father. That's it. Peter told me his father wouldn't like it, but I didn't think he'd go so far as to take Peter away from me. Why? I simply could not admit to myself that he was as bad as my dad said he was.

At home that night I couldn't get up my nerve to tell Dad and Mom. They were all dressed up and in such a good mood. It was the night of Dad's company dinner, and he'd never missed one yet in the twenty years he'd worked for the factory. No, I couldn't tell them tonight. I'd wait till morning.

Out of all my unhappiness, that's the only thing I'm really glad for—that my parents didn't know of my disgrace, for they were both killed in a car accident that night. A truck hit them broadside, and they were killed instantly.

The next few days were a nightmare. I had no other relatives, and I was an orphan now. Two weeks before my sixteenth birthday I was an orphan, a deserted wife, and a prospective mother. I didn't know what to do, or where to go, or whom to turn to.

The neighbors were very kind to me, and two of them begged me to make my home with them. But expecting a child as I was, I couldn't. Mr. Reed, Dad's employer, arranged to sell what furnishings we owned, and get rid of our house lease. He took care of all the details of Dad's insurance, too. There wasn't much—only one thousand dollars after all the funeral expenses. Poor Mr. Reed. He was so worried about me. He came to ask me if I had a place to go. "Of course," I lied. "I have an aunt up in Hillside. I'm going there."

Only one thing kept me from buying a ticket out of town. I'd made up my mind to get a copy of my marriage license. That morning, after Mr. Reed left, I went to the County Clerk's office in the courthouse downtown. I couldn't believe it when the clerk said, "I'm sorry, but there is no record of any license issued to you."

I was stunned! There had to be, there simply had to be. "But we were married by the Justice of the Peace in Midland only three months ago!"

"I don't know what this is all about," the clerk said crossly, "but I do know that this office did not issue a license to these parties. If you wish, I can call the Justice of the Peace in Midland, but I don't see what good that will do!"

"Would you please call anyway?" I asked in mounting terror. This wasn't turning out at all the way I'd thought it would.

"Didn't the Justice give you a certificate?" the clerk asked.

"No," I said quietly. "My husband has both the certificate and my ring. You see, we were keeping it a secret but now he's left me. I don't have a thing to prove my marriage." The tears were in my eyes again.

"My advice to you, Mrs. Russo, is to take this up with the police. Either the license was forged, or it was obtained from some other county. Either way, the police can help you. I can't."

"Then, I'm not even married?" I whispered.

"Well." The clerk shrugged. "There's something wrong someplace. You go to the police like I say."

I was numb all over as I walked out of the clerk's office. I wanted to be alone. The next day I left town without telling anyone so no one would be there to see me off.

I'd decided on a good-sized town of about ten thousand people, miles away from my old home, to settle in. Once there, I found a job in a factory where I would be able to sit most of the time, and I bought a cheap wedding ring for myself. I told my landlady and the girls in the factory that I was a widow.

I settled down to wait for my baby. The thousand dollars from Dad's insurance would just see me through the birth of my child. My time came at last, and early one cold, raining February day, my son, Neil, was born. Now I truly had something to live for and not just dreams, but my son, my beautiful Neil. He had dark eyes like Peter's, but his hair was blond and curly. He was an angel.

My landlady consented to keep my baby for me when I went back to work. That way, I could still take care of my own baby, at least part of the time. That's the way I lived for almost three years, then I was laid off at the factory. I collapsed on the bed that night. My world once more had tumbled around me. I sobbed. Without a job, how could I keep Neil? I had no savings.

The next day, I tried to find another job. I walked and walked and walked. It was a dull, small town and there were not ever many jobs. The fact that I had not graduated from high school and had limited experience didn't help. After a week, I saw no hope of getting a job and my money was almost gone. I spent fifty cents of my remaining money on a newspaper. Maybe I could find something in it that I could do. There were only a few ads—two for traveling salesladies, one for a stenographer, and three ads for housekeepers.

What about a housekeeping position? I didn't need a high school diploma there. Of course, I'd never done any housework besides keeping my own room clean at home, but it would be worth a try, especially if I were allowed to keep Neil with me. Two of the ads gave telephone numbers, one a newspaper box number. A woman demanded in a serious tone of voice if I was experienced. "No," I said. She was sorry, but I wouldn't do. The next call, a man answered the phone. Then when I mentioned my child he said I'd have to put him in a home. I hung up. I was going to keep Neil with me at all costs.

I sat down and answered the last ad, giving my age, name, and qualifications—or rather, lack of qualifications. I added the fact that I had a small son. Putting Neil's coat and hat on, I went out with him and mailed the letter.

Two days later I received my answer. Mr. Brian Lawrence said he'd be in to see me the next day. I was excited and I kept telling myself that I would have that job. I had to have it. I didn't dare think of what would happen if I couldn't find work where I could keep Neil with me. He was the whole core of my existence. I loved him so much it almost scared me.

Now, worried over what our future would be, I tried not to let Neil see how upset I was. Just for a change that night I told Neil he'd have to tell me a bedtime story. "Once there was a little boy, like me," Neil began. "The little boy had a bear, too, and he cried. Neil kissed the bear and he stopped."

I hugged him tight and when he was asleep I laid him in the bed and silently thanked God again for my baby. For an instant my thoughts turned to Peter. Where was he? Where had he gone? And why? Did he ever wonder about his child? Then I scolded myself for thinking of him. I should know better by now.

The next day when Mr. Lawrence came, I felt a surge of sympathy for him. He was clean, but his clothes were patched and not ironed. "You must be Mr. Lawrence. Come in and sit down, won't you?" I held the door open. "This is my little boy, Neil."

"Hello, young fellow." His huge hand completely swallowed Neil's little baby hand.

"Hello. You got bear?" Neil asked.

"Well, no, I don't think I have, but maybe someday I'll get one. Would that be all right?" he asked with a laugh.

"Yes. Get me bear," Neil said, and I knew he liked this kind man at once. So did I. Mr. Lawrence was medium height, about five-feet-ten or so, and stocky—a rugged, outdoor type of man. He had the kindest, saddest eyes I'd ever seen, deep-set in his square face.

"Mrs. Russo, I have two girls," he said now, "and a boy of five. Their mother is dead. I've had first one housekeeper, then another in the past three years. We live on a farm and they don't like it that far out of town."

"I've never lived on a farm," I said dubiously. "But I think I'd like it. And as for the children, I know it will be easy to love them. I have a child, too, as you see."

"I can't pay you much. And I think I'd better tell you, Mrs. Russo," he went on, "things are in a mess out there. We've been by ourselves for about a month now. We try to do the best we can, but that's not too good."

"That will be perfectly all right. I understand. I'll be frank with you, too. I've never tried this kind of work before. But I need a job where I can keep my son with me. I'll promise to do the best I can."

"Well, now, I think everything will work out just fine." He smiled. "How soon can you be ready to go?"

"I can have our things packed in an hour," I answered.

My landlady had tears in her eyes when I brought her the key. She told me to be sure and come back to her if my new job didn't work out. I promised I would.

The farm was about ten miles out of town and as we drove in the yard, a big, black dog dashed up, barking madly. He was followed by a ragamuffin little boy. "Hi, Daddy," he called, then stopped as he saw me, gazing at me in awe. The poor little fellow. My heart went out to him. His clothes were clean, but the knees were out of his jeans. His shirt was too small and he was barefoot. Freckles across his nose were the finishing touch.

"Dave, this is Mrs. Russo, our new housekeeper. Come say hello," his dad called to him. "And here is her little boy, Neil."

"I'm glad to know you, Dave," I told him with a smile.

"Where are the girls?" his father asked.

"Here we are, Daddy." Two shy, thin little girls came out of the house. Nicolette, aged eleven, and Rachel, nine. Here again my heart went out to these little motherless waifs. Their hair was stringy and dull. Both had gray eyes like their father's and again, those enchanting freckles.

"Can't you say hello to Mrs. Russo?" their father asked them.

"Hello, Mrs. Russo," they said together. "Hi, Neil."

"Hello," Neil answered. "You got a bear?"

"Bear?" The children laughed. "We don't have any."

"That's bear." Neil pointed to the big black dog.

"Don't tease him," Nicolette, the oldest, said. "He's playing make-believe." And she took Neil's hand, leading him off with the others.

I went indoors. It was a six-room house—kitchen, dining room, living room, and three bedrooms. The beds had been made, but messily. The floor had been swept, but under the beds there was dust. The windows were plain and the lower panes were liberally sprinkled with finger marks. Mr. Lawrence had certainly not exaggerated when he said things were in a mess. I most surely would have a job.

After a lunch of peanut butter sandwiches, which Nicolette served proudly, I went to work. The first thing I did was to shampoo the children's hair. Had I thought their hair was dull and drab? Nicolette had bright chestnut hair, with gold highlights through it. Rachel's was the color of honey and had a natural wave. Nicolette's dried straight, but I cut some bangs and trimmed it evenly. Both girls were so pathetically pleased over their appearance I almost cried.

Then we all got busy cleaning up. Even Neil tried to help. There was so much to do I could hardly decide where to start. We tackled the kitchen first. The two girls tried so hard to please, and my least little word of praise made their eyes sparkle with pleasure.

When Mr. Lawrence came in at six o'clock, the table was set for supper on an old cloth of mine. The dishes and silverware sparkled and there was a platter of fried potatoes, gravy, ham, fresh tomatoes, and onions. I had coffee for us, and milk for the children.

Mr. Lawrence took one look at the table, blinked, looked again, and a smile lit up his face. "I can see you are going to do a good job here," he said. "I haven't seen things look like this since Eva died."

"Look, Daddy! Don't we look pretty? Mrs. Russo washed our hair for us." Rachel was so excited. "And, Daddy, do you know what? Dave has white hair! Come here," Nicolette called, "and show Daddy your white hair."

Dave came running in from the yard with Neil in tow. His light blond hair was just as full of dust as before. "Oh no! Dave, how could you? Your pretty hair, what have you done to it?" Nicolette wailed.

"I just crawled under the porch to see if there were any eggs." He ruffled his hair and a puff of dust rose in a cloud above him.

"Hey, son, you cut that out. I'd be ashamed after Mrs. Russo did all that work on you." Mr. Lawrence laughed.

That day was the turning point in my new life. I slipped into the housework as if I'd done it all my life. After the washing and ironing was finished, I started in on the house itself. I washed the walls in the living room till they were bright and clean. Then I washed the woodwork and the windows. You'd never have known it was the same room. I scrubbed the wood floor until it shone, promising myself I'd make some rag rugs as soon as I could learn how.

After the living room was finished, I did one room at a time, until in a few weeks I had the whole house completed. We were all so proud of it, because we had all helped. You'd never have thought it could look so new and neat. Now, if I just had some curtains, I thought. Maybe I could do something about it the next time I went to town.

Neil and I had been there about six weeks when I discovered the feedbags out in the barn. How can a man be so dense, I wondered? There those poor youngsters were, running around practically in rags, and out here was a stack of printed bags that had been emptied and thrown over a board. Now I could make dresses for the girls, shirts for Dave, and curtains and slipcovers. Oh, I would learn how.

Funny, I, only a paid housekeeper, would want to go to all the extra work. But this house seemed almost like my own. My heart as well as my labor went into the making of it. Odd, wasn't it? Here I was, only nineteen years old, but I felt like I had found a home at last, and also a family.

309

The weeks since Neil and I had come had seen a change in Brian, too, as I called Mr. Lawrence. He lost his harried, defeated look. He held his shoulders back, his head higher, and even his eyes were brighter. He laughed a lot now, too.

Often I'd catch him looking at me in a way I didn't care to examine. But I was happier than I'd been at any time since I had lost my mother and father. I went around in clouds, singing, feeling quite at peace with the world. Sometimes, I couldn't help wondering just what Brian would say if he were to learn about Peter and my fraud marriage. He was so kind to Neil, and he never took Dave anywhere that he didn't take along Neil. Nor did he ever bring anything to his own children that he didn't bring a share of to Neil.

The summer passed, filled with work and happiness, and at times, I almost forgot my past. It was as if it had never been, except for Neil. Then, just before school started in the fall, I promised Nicolette a home perm for being such a sweet girl, and such a help to me. I took both girls into town to buy it, but how I wished we hadn't gone, for on the street I came face to face with Peter Russo.

I looked away hurriedly, hoping against hope that he wouldn't recognize me. I prayed silently for him not to. I almost dragged the two little girls into the drugstore and into the last booth. I ordered orange juice for them and coffee for me, which I could scarcely drink for the trembling of my hands.

I kept watching the door, afraid that he would walk in, but when he didn't my breath came a little easier. Maybe he hadn't recognized me. After all, it was almost four years since he had seen me. I had changed a lot, I knew. Maybe he'd just think I was an ordinary married woman with two little girls.

At last I had to leave. I tried to keep up a reasonable conversation with the girls so they wouldn't know anything was wrong, but I could tell by Nicolette's puzzled looks that she felt something was bothering me. Children are very quick that way. Please don't let him be there, I prayed on our way out the door.

"Hello, Marina." My hopes crumbled like a house of cards around me. I knew I couldn't pretend not to know him. He could tell by my eyes that I did. I decided to brazen it out. I started to push past him, but his hand closed around my wrist. "Hello, Marina." The hard, mean glint in his eyes belied his smile.

"Let me go—I haven't the slightest desire to speak to you, now, or at any time." I tried to keep the fright out of my voice.

"Oh, but we have lots of things to talk over. Who are these two kids?"

"I take care of them," I answered him.

"Where are you living?"

I didn't answer him because I didn't want him to know, but I hadn't figured on Rachel. She spoke up and told him where the farm was.

I was afraid of creating a scene. I didn't want anyone to know of my past, nor of my illegitimate son. He didn't let go of my arm. "How many other kids are there?" he asked. I told him one.

Rachel spoke up again. "Mrs. Russo, you forgot your own little boy, Neil. He makes four of us." She couldn't realize the harm she'd done!

Peter's eyes narrowed, and he looked at me with an evil smile. How could I ever have thought that smile charming—ever have loved him? "So you do have a child. When you told me about it I figured it was a trick to get me to live with you. How old is he?"

"He's three!" I said coldly. "Now will you please let me pass by?" He didn't move. "Will I have to call an officer?"

"I don't think you will. I'll come out to the farm though. I'd like to get acquainted with my own son."

"No, I won't let you see Neil. You walked out on us when we needed you. We're doing all right now and I won't have you upsetting my life!"

"I want you to come back to me, Marina." Peter was pleading with me now. "I'm out of money—I need a job and it would be easier to get one if I tell people I have a wife and child. Wouldn't you rather live in town, in an apartment? You're much prettier now, you know."

I lost my fear now and became an angry mother fighting for her young. "You're about as low down as a human can get!"

"Remember, you're still my wife." He smirked.

That did it. "You think I still believe that? I have proof that you forged our marriage license and if you try to find me, I'll have you arrested. That's a promise!" I was shaking all over.

Then I knew I had made an error in threatening Peter. There was such a look of hatred in his eyes, I was afraid of the revenge it promised. At that moment he spit out a foul word at me, and that's when Rachel hit him, or rather, kicked him. Then Nicolette joined in and doubled up her fists and began to hit him. By the time I could grab the girls and run for the truck, people were beginning to gather.

"Mrs. Russo, he called you a bad name. Daddy said we were not to let anyone call us names like that," Rachel said as I quickly pulled the truck out of the parking place and headed toward the farm.

"He was just a mean man, but I don't think he'll bother us anymore." I tried to sound convincing.

"Mama—I mean, Mrs. Russo, we forgot my perm." It was the first thing that Nicolette had said since the meeting with Peter.

"Oh, darling, I'm sorry. I'll get it the next time we're in town. Will you mind, dear?" I was genuinely sorry.

Brian was at the house when we got home, and I was glad the

children ran off to play because I wanted to tell him the story myself, in my own way. As soon as I could prepare our supper, I fed the children and sent them to bed. I knew now my only salvation would be to tell Brian the whole story and find out if he were willing to help me. It meant dredging up the past, which I had hoped to keep buried forever, and revealing what a fool I had been to run away with a boy I scarcely knew.

But I was thankful that Brian was different from other men and I trusted him.

Sitting across the kitchen table from him as we had coffee, I told him everything about the tragedies that had made my life so miserable in the four years before I came to the farm. I told him I was sure Peter was determined to have me back and I was full of fear for myself, as well as Neil.

Brian sat quietly listening. "That's an old trick, forging a marriage license. It means Neil doesn't have Peter's name legally, but it also means Peter hasn't any legal rights to him. I don't think he would dare to start anything."

"I hope you're right." I sighed.

"I'll take care of him if he shows up." And then he added tenderly, "If you'll let me, Marina." Then I knew I was in love. I stared at him with my heart in my eyes.

"Marina, do you know what we've gone and done?" he asked in a whisper. "We've fallen in love with each other, or at least, I've fallen in love with you."

"Oh, Brian, I didn't know! I never realized—yes, yes I do love you." I cried.

Suddenly we were in each other's arms and laughing. We kissed and I felt a peace I had never dreamed of steal over me. These kisses were infinitely sweeter and more tender than the wild kisses Peter and I had shared. "Honey, I love you so much. Will you marry me tomorrow?" he begged as he kissed me again.

"Well, not tomorrow, darling. Tomorrow is Sunday." I laughed.

"Monday, then. We can be engaged until Monday."

Brian had taken a burden of worry from me, but peace wasn't to be mine for long. We were playing hide-and-seek with the children the next afternoon and Neil hid too far away and I couldn't find him. I ran through the trees and out to the corner of the farmyard looking for him. I was just in time to grab Neil, because Peter was just getting out of a junky old car.

I gave Neil an awful shove. "Run quick, Neil, and tell Brian to call the police. Now run!" Then I screamed as loud as I could, "Brian! Help!" But Peter had reached me and he grabbed me in his arms and forced me into the car and started off. He was going so fast I couldn't get out. After a few moments I could see Brian's old pickup following way behind.

Then a police car came wailing toward us. I guess they could see that Peter just went faster and that he wasn't going to stop. As they cut in ahead of us, Peter swerved to avoid a collision and the car turned over on the shoulder of the road and smashed into a tree. I was thrown free of the car and was knocked out for a few minutes. When I came to, an ambulance was there and another police car and Brian was beside me.

All at once, I knew something terrible had happened and I struggled to my feet. They told me that Peter had crawled out of the wreckage and tried to run away and a policeman had shot him when he pulled out a weapon. I saw them lifting a stretcher into the ambulance. Brian wanted me to go to the hospital, too, so a doctor could check my condition, but I only wanted to get home and hold Neil in my arms and convince myself that he was really safe.

The next day we learned that Peter had died soon after reaching the hospital. I broke down and wept in Brian's arms, but now there was peace in my heart. I hoped that God had forgiven the sins I had committed when I was too young to know better. I knew that the years of hard work and loneliness I had gone through in order to keep my baby with me had now brought their reward.

The End

I HIRED A WOMAN
FOR DADDY!

She was different from what I expected—younger and prettier, with her blonde hair and gray-green eyes and a little tilt of her head just before she smiled.

"Hi, come on in," I said. I was fifteen and a sophomore at Bayview High. She appeared to be about my age as she stood there in the bright October sunlight. Only, how could she be my age with that baby she carried and the way she reminded of my mother who had died a year ago?

"I guess you came about the job of baby-sitting my little brother, Neil."

She nodded. "I'm Mary Gilroy," she said in a musical voice with a slightly foreign accent.

"I'm Amanda Wade. Mandy around here," I said when we were inside. I patted the sofa so she could put the sleeping baby down beside her.

The job interview I conducted wasn't really for real. If she didn't confess to a couple of axe murders, she was in, because how could I go to my classes at Bayview High School without somebody to watch Neil, my four-year-old problem brother? I told her about the hours and the pay. It was the same as Mrs. Jacobs got until she had to go to New York to look after her daughter's family while her daughter had her fourth child.

"There's just my brother, Neil, he's a really active little boy, and Daddy, and yours truly," I said. "Daddy wouldn't be in your way if you decide to take the job." I explained that my dad worked at two jobs, and though he was home a good part of the day, he would be sleeping while she was looking after Neil.

What I didn't explain was that Daddy worked at two jobs because he wanted me to attend a fancy college like the one Mom had gone to in New England, or that he was set on the idea because he'd never been able to provide for Mom the kind of life he felt she deserved, or that Daddy was living in his own isolated world since Mom had died.

Naturally, there were a lot of things like that I didn't explain—the main one being that what I wanted to do more than anything was to snap Daddy out of his own little world and make him the way he used to be, a great guy who laughed a lot and called me Princess. I was Daddy's favorite, and maybe Mom had leaned a little toward Neil, but we'd all been very close. But now, with Mom gone and Daddy on his crazy work kick, life was a real downer.

314

Daddy was my main problem. I figured if I could only get him back the way he was, then I could really try to help Neil. My brother was four now, and it was time he outgrew those two imaginary companions he had—Piggy and Wiggy. I worried about this, because the average kid outgrows the imagery companions bit by the time he's three. And here was Neil, four, and deeper in the Piggy-Wiggy routine than ever.

Sometimes I thought maybe I was a problem, too. It went back to the time Mom died unexpectedly of a heart condition nobody even knew she had. Daddy nearly went out of his mind with grief, and little Neil was like a lost soul. All the relatives turned to me. "You're the strong one, Mandy," they kept saying when all I wanted to do was go somewhere and cry my heart out. "You have to act as though everything was normal. Be strong, honey. Don't let your daddy and little Neil see you crying."

I was fourteen then. With all their demands of me and getting Dr. Sherborn to lecture me on the importance of setting an example, I never cried for Mom. Later, when I finally got a little privacy, I didn't cry, either. Something in me stayed partly frozen. It wasn't that I didn't feel things; I did. But I didn't trust my emotions anymore; they just didn't seem to be working.

Even as I was looking at Mary, I told myself: If I'm a problem, forget it! I just don't have the time to do anything about it.

"I need a job badly," I heard Mary say. Her direct honesty floored me and made me like her. "There's only little Mike and me." She explained that her husband, Mike Gilroy, Sr., was dead. He'd been a photographer with a big sport's magazine. They'd met three years before when he'd come to the tiny French-Canadian village where she and her family lived, and they'd been married after a few months. Her husband had died two months ago, shortly after Mike, Jr. was born, in a plane crash while on a bear-hunting assignment in Alaska, and she had lived on their small savings until her money was all gone.

"No use in my beating around the bush, Mary," I said, completely sold on her. "How does the job sound to you? Not that I want you to have to decide anything until you see Neil in action."

She smiled shyly. "The pay is fine," she said in that lilting voice. "But I'd work for less if you let us stay here. Little Mike and I . . . we need a home." Her idea surprised me. I hadn't figured on another two people actually living in our house, one of them a baby. I hesitated. "Mike is a quiet baby," Mary said. "He sleeps most of the time and almost never cries."

I couldn't see anything wrong with the idea, still, you never knew how such an arrangement would work. Then I remembered the out I had—Mrs. Jacobs.

"Suppose we try it till the regular sitter comes back and see what she plans to do," I said. I told Mary she could have the downstairs bedroom we'd been using for storage, then if Mike cried during the day he wouldn't wake Daddy. I explained that Daddy would have to give the final okay on the deal, but that he would go along with whatever I decided. A half hour later we had her and Mike settled in the bedroom after I hauled up some baby gear that had been Neil's from the cellar.

Gavin Valor burst in a split second behind his knock, the way he had been doing since he and I were six. He was a gangling sixteen-year-old and the nicest boy I knew—most of the time. "Wow!" Gavin yelled, spotting Mary. "Who's the new chick, Mandy?"

"She's not a chick," I said in what I hoped was a dignified tone. "Mrs. Gilroy, this character is Gavin Valor from next door." Mary acknowledged the introduction with a smile, then she tactfully excused herself and went into her room.

"She's hot," Gavin said. "Say, how about helping me out on that algebra assignment? I don't know what old Wilson's babbling about these days."

Mom had taught me good study habits, so school was no sweat with me. I drilled Gavin for a half hour before he began to grow disinterested. He was a sharp kid, really, but he had so many interests he didn't spend much time on studies.

"Say, Mandy!" he exclaimed suddenly. "You know what this Mary deal could mean if it works out? You won't have to hurry right home all the time. You can go out for cheerleading, the school play, the whole works. It could mean a whole new life for you." Good old Gavin. I felt a rush of affection for him. He was a kid who got as big a kick out of somebody else's good luck as he did his own.

I felt a rush of excitement at the possibilities. Mom had died just when I was starting my freshman year, so I'd never been to a school game, play, or club meeting because I always had to rush right home. But I shook my head. "Mary's kind of fragile. I wouldn't want to stick her with Neil that much. Although it would be nice if once in a while I could hang around and get to know the kids at school better."

I kept thinking about it after Gavin went home. It would be a blast all right. But I kept my fingers crossed because I knew I could never enjoy school or anything else until I got Daddy straightened out and made him and Neil happy again. What we needed to be was a real family again, the way we were before Mom died. Once we were in that groove, other problems would take care of themselves.

I heard Daddy's car pull up outside. The front door opened and my brother Neil rushed in, screaming, "My arm's broke, Mandy." He pathetically held his right arm against his chest, supporting it with his left arm. "Daddy says call the doctor right away." I bent over to examine the injury. His arm shot forward and his fingers pinched my nose painfully. Then he streaked off, giggling crazily.

Angrily, I started after him, but then stopped. Neil would hide in the house till he forgot why he was hiding. This would give me a chance to be alone with Daddy and fill him in on the baby-sitting situation, so I controlled my temper. When Daddy came through the door, he looked so worn and tired, I could have cried. He showed practically no interest when I filled him in on Mary and her baby. He just said, "Fine, fine. If you think she'll do, Mandy, I'm satisfied." He didn't even come inside the kitchen to meet her.

Up to now I had tried everything I knew to blast Daddy out of his shell. I'd even deliberately flunked everything one marking period last year, with no effect, then had to work like crazy to get my grades back up. And if low grades wouldn't get to Daddy, nothing would, because sending me to Mom's college was practically all he was living for.

"Oh, Daddy!" I cried impulsively. "Why don't you quit one of your jobs? I don't want to go to Mom's school. I can go to a state college and live at home and it won't cost much more than high school."

"Your mother wanted you to go to her college," Daddy said firmly, his eyes moist. "I failed her in everything else. I'm not failing her about what college you attend even if I have to work twenty hours a day." Daddy hadn't had as good an education as Mom had. That was why he was working two jobs, one from three in the afternoon till eleven at night, the other from midnight till eight in the morning.

"It's crazy," I argued. "When Mom went there it cost only two thousand dollars a year with that partial-scholarship she had. Now it's up around twenty thousand dollars a year and will probably be even more by the time I get out of high school. I can't let you ruin your health to put me through a college I don't even want to go to."

"It's settled," Daddy said. "Your mother wanted it."

"I need a father around," I said bluntly. "And so does Neil."

But Daddy didn't even hear me. "You want to help me with the basement project, Mandy?" he asked.

I started to say yes. I usually did, because it was the only way I could be with him. The basement project was an idea of Mom's, too. She wanted it fixed up for my sweet-sixteen birthday party, so Daddy was knocking himself out working on it during the weekends.

"I don't care about the birthday party, Daddy," I told him. "I want you to rest."

"I'll take it easy, Mandy," he answered. Sadly, I watched him go down the cellar stairs. If only I could find a way to bring him back to life again. What a wonderful day that would be for us all.

When I started Sunday dinner, Mary came in wanting to help. I

317

shooed her away, but finally allowed her to set the table. That baby of hers was an angel. Little Mike slept and slept. What really shook me was Neil. He followed Mary around as though she had him hypnotized. He even helped her with the table setting. The meal should have been dull, with Daddy being such a stick, paying no attention to Mary or any of us. Only Neil had such a good time talking with Mary, it was almost as though we were a family again. It was great to see Neil smiling and giggling. He really was an attractive boy with his darkish blond hair and wistful blue eyes.

Just as I was getting ready to clean up, Gavin Valor popped in, a book under his arm. "Bug off," I warned, "unless you want to do the dishes."

"Thanks, but no thanks. Did them at my house." He grinned. He gave me the book. "This is the play the school is putting on. I'm trying out for the part of the father. You're a natural for the older sister. Read it, will you?"

"Well, maybe," I half promised. Later, after finishing the dishes Mary insisted on helping me with, I opened the book Gavin had left. Before I knew it, I'd read a few lines of the play and was completely absorbed in it. It was about a poor family that stuck together through good times and bad, always working together and helping each other. I didn't put it down till I'd finished it.

Mary got excited about the play. "Go out for the part, Mandy," she urged. "With me in the house, why should you rush home from school?" After Neil went to bed, she helped me memorize the older sister's part. Later, she sat and studied from some kind of botany book. "I like to grow things," she explained. "Someday when Mike gets older, I want to work in a big nursery."

It was a lift, having Mary around. She was twenty-six, eleven years older than me and eleven years younger than Daddy. She was bright and quick, but in the way she got kicks from even the smallest pleasures, she was like a kid.

Several times that evening I asked Daddy to come up and join us watching TV after the studying was over, but he refused and kept working on that project for my sixteenth birthday next month. If only Daddy would get interested in people a little more, instead of knocking himself out for me, I thought.

Mary's presence changed my life completely, starting the next day. What a kick it was for me not to have to rush right home from school, to go over to Star Catcher, the high school hangout and have a soda and chat with the kids. Till Mom died, I'd always made friends easily and I knew most of the in-crowd at school to say hello to. But in the past year I'd felt out of everything because I couldn't hang around or participate in things.

Now suddenly, all that changed. Every day, right after school, a bunch of us would jam into Star's—cool girls like Mara Feldman, Judy Allen, who had been one of my best friends in grammar school, Pam Carnes, and Lynn Bishop, the prettiest girl in the sophomore class. The most popular boys like Sean Watson, Terry Wells, Frank Cassidy, Mark Arrio, and Chris Lester would join us briefly before going to football practice.

The biggest thing of all was the fact that Mr. Horace, the speech teacher and play director, gave me the older sister's part I tried out for at the end of the week. It wasn't for my looks or talent or anything like that. With my green eyes, dark hair, average features and figure, I knew I could get by, but I was not a raving beauty.

What got me the part was the fact that we were only going to have about five weeks of rehearsal. Mr. Horace had been ill, and with the late start, the fact that I had my part memorized gave me a big advantage. The only other girl trying out for the part was Josie Sinclair, a senior, who was the best actress in school. Josie had a horrible cold the first week and that cost her the part, because she didn't know her lines.

Mine wasn't the lead; the mother's part, played by Mara Feldman, was the lead. But as the oldest sister, I had to step in front of the curtain and set the mood for each scene before going back with the other cast members and playing my role.

"I told you that you were a natural," Gavin bragged. He had clinched the role of the father. "You nominating me for talent scout of the year?"

"I'm not that good, just lucky, Pop," I kidded him. "If I didn't have the part memorized and if Josie hadn't gotten sick—"

"Don't put yourself down, kid. Let others do that."

I didn't pay much attention to Gavin's thinly-veiled warning. I was too happy and confident then to see anything but the fact that I was making new friends every day, getting to know old friends better, and being a real part of the school, with kids phoning me all the time when I was home.

Bit by bit, Mary had taken over practically all the shopping, cooking, and cleaning chores from me. "I can't let you make a slave out of yourself, Mary, for the little we pay you," I protested.

"You're only a teen once," Mary said. "Besides, I'm living over all the fun of school days on that stage with you, Mandy."

Mary took Mike and Neil out every day the weather permitted and soon got to know all the neighbors. Best of all, Neil showed no signs of withdrawing into his little world of Piggy and Wiggy. Whenever he did, Mary showed an interest and took them for granted.

If only she can keep it up, I thought, the problem of Neil would be

319

solved. Sometimes I found Mary too good to be true. She was always helping somebody. Still, she found time somehow to keep the house neat, to teach Neil his ABC's and read him stories, and even to help me with my lessons, too. It was a thrill just to hear Mary's voice in the house singing or laughing or even just talking. It made us feel better—except Daddy. Nothing reached the sad, private world he lived in.

But slowly Mary had an effect, even on him. She kept Neil so quiet, Daddy slept better. She was a born cook and she coaxed him to eat. She went to a lot of trouble to see that he took hot food with him in a special insulated bag when he went to work.

Daddy put on badly-needed weight. He even looked a lot better, until you got to his dulled, expressionless face. I felt worse than ever about him, realizing he was slipping deeper and deeper into his dull, empty wasteland. "That poor man," Mary said one day. "I wish we could find a way to help him." Impulsively, I hugged her.

One evening about two weeks after Mary and Mike had been with us, I got a telegram from Mrs. Jacobs in New York. "Not bad news, I hope," Mary whispered.

I shook my head. "Mrs. Jacobs's daughter still needs her, so she's staying on in New York for a while longer." I remembered Mary's status as Neil's sitter was still temporary. I guess I had just taken it for granted that Mary would stay on with us, no matter what. Actually, Mrs. Jacobs was too old to handle Neil and had only agreed to be his sitter because she had thought the world of Mom. I knew she really wanted out of the job as soon as it was possible.

"So I'll stay on some more," Mary said.

"I'm glad, Mary," I said. "I was afraid you might let one of those ritzy families up on Palmer Street lure you away." I knew of at least three rich women who had been trying to get Mary to come work for them at more than we were paying her. She had become a neighborhood favorite.

"I'll stay as long as you want me."

"You got to stay, Mary. You got to stay all the time," Neil yelled excitedly before I could reply. His voice rose nervously. "I want you to. So do Piggy and Wiggy." Neil's words upset me. It was the first time I had heard him mention Piggy and Wiggy in more than a week.

She put her hand on his shoulder. "I'm not going away, Neil," she said softly.

I tried to concentrate on ways to help Daddy. I made an appointment with the school psychologist, but it was a bomb. I didn't ask the right questions and when he started asking me searching questions, I got tongue-tied.

Two more weeks went by, filled with excitement at school. Then it was the weekend again, with no football game scheduled. I slept late and it was after nine when I came downstairs. Half in a fog, I fixed breakfast. I was almost finished when I heard sounds in the cellar. I went downstairs. All of them were there. Mike was in the back of the basement asleep. The minute I saw Mary helping Daddy, I got a funny feeling. Helping Daddy had been something very private and very special between us.

Mary looked up with a smile and said, "Hi, Mandy," from where she was holding a panel for Daddy to saw. My glance swept past Neil, who was sweeping sawdust into a corner. I wanted Daddy to explain, to reassure me. That awful feeling grew.

"Morning, Princess," Daddy called with his charming smile of old I'd so long dreamed of seeing again. But all the time he was looking at her! It was terrible.

"Morning, everybody," I mumbled, like a stranger who had blundered in on an intimate family group.

Daddy proudly waved his hand at the paneled walls. "How do you like the job, Princess?" He looked almost boyish, as though he had never been in a depressed state. "The job has been going fast with Mary pitching in."

"It's great," I managed to say. That terrible feeling of loss, of being a stranger in my own house, went deeper at the tender way he spoke her name and the admiring look he gave her.

"Want to get in on the act?" Daddy asked me.

I said something about a test Monday and rushed back upstairs. Mary obviously had Daddy tied around her little finger and it must have been going on for days. I was shaken up. Daddy had come back from the point of oblivion, all right, but not to Neil and me, the way I wanted him to. He'd come back to Mary. It was so unfair when I'd been trying everything for a year to bring him back to us.

Now I began to resent Mary's sly, take-over pattern. Bit by bit, she had used Neil and then me to get to Daddy. She had gradually taken over this house and everyone in it, putting herself in a position where she was practically indispensable. I remembered that one time my instincts had told me she was too good to be true. If only I had awakened then. Now it was too late! She was practically in Mom's shoes, the mother of the house, the one everybody turned to. Well, I'm not turning to her, I told myself.

The rest of the weekend I pretended nothing had changed, while I tried to think of a way out of this scheming woman's trap. Saturday night I went to a double horror movie with Gavin and some other kids. I told Gavin what going on at home.

"You got rocks in your skull, Mandy, wanting to get rid of her." Gavin said. "Mary is okay."

"She has you fooled, too."

Except for the movie, the rest of the weekend was a drag—till around seven o'clock Sunday night when the phone rang. It was Mrs. Jacobs and she was back from New York. "Thought I'd let you know," she said, "in case you need me."

My heart beat wildly. What a heaven-sent chance to get Mary out of the house, to get her hooks out of Daddy before he fell for her completely! "We do need you," I said. After all, I'd never agreed to keep Mary on indefinitely, even though I'd wanted to at first. "Could you be here at the regular time tomorrow, Mrs. Jacobs?" She agreed, without enthusiasm. It was done. I'd had to do it to protect Daddy, I told myself.

I waited till Neil was asleep before breaking the news to Mary and Daddy that Mrs. Jacobs was back and ready to come to work the next day. I told Mary she could stay on, of course, till she decided which job she would accept from among the families up on Palmer Street who had been trying to recruit her.

Then she and Daddy talked privately. There goes the ball game, I thought. She'll twist him around her little finger. But to my surprise, Mary went to the phone and made a call. Less than an hour later, Daddy drove her and Mike to the home of a family named Templeton on Palmer Street.

Mary spread her charm on thick when she said good-bye to me and I acted friendly, too. I really didn't wish her any harm. I just didn't want her getting her hooks into Daddy. He was whistling when he returned from taking Mary to her new job. I was surprised and relieved. I'd been afraid he'd go back to his old ways. "It's for the best, I guess," he said, without explaining what he meant. "I hope Neil doesn't take it too badly, though."

Something in Daddy's manner convinced me he was going to keep on seeing Mary when he got the chance. Maybe he'd let her go so easily only because he was worried about what the neighbors thought of an attractive woman like Mary being in the house with him all day.

Neil sobbed his heart out when I told him Monday morning that Mary had gone away. When Mrs. Jacobs arrived, she agreed to sit the extra time with Neil while I was rehearsing, as long as she could stand him. I told her Neil had been behaving himself.

During the first period at school, I got word that Josie Sinclair was rejoining the cast as a special understudy for the top female parts.

"Horace likes her," Gavin told me. "She's played lead roles for three years. Between you and me and the clubhouse, I think she's after your part, since she can't get Mara's. So watch out, Mandy."

I was nervous when rehearsals started that Monday afternoon, worrying about Neil and Daddy and about Josie Sinclair, too.

Mr. Horace was a tall, gaunt man, who looked like President Lincoln. "You all have your parts down now. Starting today, we'll concentrate on actions and reactions," he told us. He explained how one actor had to emphasize the importance of what another actor said by listening and reacting to his words.

I understood, but I guess it just wasn't my day. Mr. Horace found fault with everything I did. "You're throwing your lines away, Amanda," he kept telling me. "And you're not reacting to the others. Instead, you're just waiting, thinking about your cue and your lines." I got steadily worse. When I tried to get emotion into my voice, I overdid it so horribly the whole cast giggled.

Things didn't improve for me all week long. As the other kids got better, I got nowhere. Finally, Mr. Horace asked Josie Sinclair to coach me. She was awfully good.

Friday the roof fell in. Mr. Horace made me stay after rehearsal. "You've worked very hard, Amanda," he said in a low voice, "but I'm afraid I can't take a chance on you in the part. You have to set the stage and mood for every scene. When you fail, everybody fails, and the play fails."

My heart sank like a stone. "You're taking the part away from me?"

"I hate to," he said gently. "Josie Sinclair is ready to step into it, but I don't want to take you out of it if I can help it. I'll give you a few more days. If you don't begin to feel the part, I'll have to use Josie. Eight hundred people are coming to this play and we owe them the best we can give them."

With Mary gone, everything changed at our house. I had the cooking, dishwashing, and cleaning chores again, and a dozen other jobs around the house. My savings were going fast, too, paying Mrs. Jacobs for the extra time she was staying each afternoon. Neil missed Mary. He was so quiet, Mrs. Jacobs called him a good boy, but his behavior worried me. When he spoke, it usually was to Piggy and Wiggy. And he wasn't eating nearly enough.

Remembering those wonderful meals Mary cooked, I couldn't blame him. And Daddy wasn't getting those hot meals she used to fix for him, either. I hated to admit it, but Mary took all the music and laughter out of our house when she left it. I didn't really admit it to myself, but I guess even I missed her, especially when I was doing my lessons late at night and she wasn't there to quiz me on them.

Why did she have to spoil everything by getting her hooks out for Daddy? We were almost a family again when she ruined it all. Now we were just three miserable people living in a house that had lost its sparkle again. Somehow, I was going to change all that and make us a family again, I told myself. But how? When you're fifteen it's rough trying to solve problems like that, especially when you don't really know any answers.

I exhausted myself the next week. I stayed up till all hours practicing my lines for the play. Yet when I was on the stage it was the same old story—no feeling in my words and gestures, no emotion in my face, or too much that didn't ring true. Then it was Friday again. I trembled as I went to rehearsal, knowing this probably would be my last day. Knees knocking, I gave the words everything I had but they came out flat and wooden. I felt like crawling into the woodwork when I got off the stage. It was the end, and I knew it.

I hung around, staying away from the other kids, knowing Josie would get the part now. I told myself Josie would be terrific. The kids would give a wonderful performance and eight hundred people would have a happy evening. Maybe Mr. Horace would put me on the makeup crew backstage. I'd still be a part of the play, helping it instead of hurting it.

Then Josie, who had not been around for the first-act rehearsal, was coming down the aisle and every eye in the place was on her, each filled with hope that Mr. Horace finally would give her the part. Nobody heard what was said. Josie seemed to be doing most of the talking. Mr. Horace seemed to be arguing with her, trying to make her change her mind. Josie shrugged. By that shrug she made everyone realize that whatever Mr. Horace asked was impossible. Then she waved at the kids, smiled a small, sad smile, and slowly walked out of the auditorium.

Talk buzzed onstage. A little later I got the word from Gavin. "How about that?" he said. "Josie's parents say she can't come to rehearsals anymore. She has to take the SATs and they're being held all day next Saturday, the day after we put on the play. And they want her to study for them every minute she can. So, you still have the part, daughter."

I nodded dully. "Yes, Pop," I told Gavin, "you're stuck with me."

"Oh, you'll be okay, Mandy," he said.

We went through the second act. Everybody was terrific, except, you know who. At the end Mr. Horace called us all together. "The play is not jelling," he said grimly. "Our only chance is work, work, and more work, especially on one or two of the key roles." I felt my cheeks flame as he looked right at me. "We have only next week. Starting Monday, we're going through the play twice each day. That means you'll be here from four o'clock each afternoon until about ten each night. Make arrangements with your parents. Bring something to eat. And maybe, if we work, we can avoid total disaster."

The kids let out a collective groan. Increased rehearsals were going to make their school grades suffer. It was all my fault and everybody knew it and was shooting daggers at me with their eyes. The way things were going, I was going to wind up the most hated kid in the history of Bayview High. And the late rehearsals posed another problem—getting a sitter for Neil.

Surprisingly, Mrs. Jacobs agreed to do it for that one week. "Neil is so quiet now, I don't mind," she said.

The last week flew by. I gave my part everything I had, but it was useless. Instead of getting better, I froze up and got even worse. We put the show on for the grammar school kids—a traditionally tough audience—Thursday, as a sort of final dress rehearsal. Those little brats nearly laughed us off the stage. You could have cut through the gloom with a knife when the disaster was over. Mr. Horace didn't bawl anybody out—not even me. He just announced another rehearsal for the next afternoon.

The final Friday rehearsal didn't help. Again, I ruined everything. What really hurt were those brief scenes when Mara and Gavin were onstage together as the mother and father. Then I could see how good the play might have been if I weren't around to louse it up. Finally, that last rehearsal ended. "Everybody," said Mr. Horace wearily, "be back here by seven-thirty this evening."

I rushed home. Mrs. Jacobs took off, promising to be back shortly after seven. I had a dozen last-minute things to do—fix supper, shower, press my costumes, wash the dishes. In spite of the rat race and the knowledge that I was going to make an idiot out of myself in front of eight hundred people, my heart went out to Neil when I saw him. He looked so pathetic and withdrawn, I could have cried. I started the meal. I couldn't help thinking how nice it would have been to have Mary around. She was a whirlwind of work and could cut everything down to size.

She hadn't come near us. Ever since she'd gone, I'd been feeling a little guilty about sending her away. But now I was sure I'd done the right thing. If she really had any feelings for Neil, she'd have come around to see him, wouldn't she? Or maybe, I told myself, trying to be fair to Mary, Daddy and she had agreed she should stay away to keep the gossips quiet.

I wondered whether she was going to use the ticket I'd given her for the play during those days when I liked her so much—or whether she might even go to the play with Daddy. It was confusing. Sometimes that nice feeling toward her would come back when I remembered her singing to Mike and Neil's happy laughter and those fabulous meals she fixed and how we all used to feel good when she was around. Then I would resent her for inching in on my family.

Somehow, I stayed on schedule showering, ironing the costumes, always with an eye on the clock, till I heard that blast upstairs. I ran up to my room. I nearly exploded with anger at what I saw—the drawers in my dressing table pulled out and all my stuff piled in a heap on the floor. The perfumes and other things I kept on top of the dresser were all scattered around the room. Neil!

Anger boiled up in me. But it died down when I found him, his eyes dazed, that pitiful look on his face, in his room. "Wash your hands, Neil," I said, feeling a tug of pity, "and go back downstairs."

I lost precious time straightening up my room. When I got back to the kitchen, the reaction hit me hard. This house and this family—what a mess it all was! Daddy hadn't been really close to me since the night Mary left. Neil was a worse problem than he'd ever been before. And I—the would-be strong character, the part-time mother—was a full-time teen in trouble, well on the road to making myself the most miserable, hated kid in school.

Head buried in my hands, I prayed for a storm, a hurricane—anything to postpone the play. I wished for a magic pill that would make it tomorrow with the play behind me, or better still, three years from now, with high school behind me.

Daddy came in, having taken off from his early job. "Am I in time, honey?" he asked.

"The food is ready when you are, Daddy."

He nodded. "I'll shower and dress. Give me fifteen minutes."

While Daddy was showering I heard the small voice coming from the room Mary and Mike had used. There was something strange in the tone, something so creepy the goosebumps started dancing up my back. Shivering, I went over and slid open the door.

Neil lay across Mary's bed, sobbing quietly, repeating the same words through the sobs, over and over again. His little body shook. "First Mommy went away," he said in a voice that tore at my heart. "And I never, never saw my mommy again. Mary come and Mike and I had fun. Piggy and Wiggy had fun. And Mandy and Daddy." I listened, scarcely breathing, as little Neil's voice vibrated through the room. "And Mary went away." Neil's voice filled with an awesome fear. The sobs came faster. "Will Daddy go away, too? And Mandy and my Piggy and Wiggy go away?"

My eyes were wet. Like a fool, I had sent Mary away without explanation and Neil thought she had died because that was what we told him when we lost Mom.

I leaned against the door for support, suddenly seeing how it was with Neil the day he woke up and found Mary gone.

Pain cut across my heart. I stopped, but the pain of guilt stayed with me. If I had thought of Neil as my little brother instead of one of my problems, I would have taken the time and trouble to ease Mary's departure for him. I even could have taken him to visit her.

Suddenly, I began seeing everything more clearly. I shouldn't have sent Mary away at all. Nothing had been right in this house since it happened—not for Daddy, for Neil, or even for me. While she had been with us, Daddy had become himself again. Neil had practically outgrown Piggy and Wiggy, and I had been happier, too.

That was what I had wanted for us ever since Mom died. Only, when it happened because of somebody else and not because of me, I had jealously and stupidly sent her away because I could not have their happiness on my terms. How selfish I'd been—like the older daughter I was playing in the school play, before she changed to a better person. How loving and good and devoted to us Mary had been—like the warmhearted, unselfish mother in the play.

Filled with pity for Neil helped me to understand myself better. When Mom died and my relatives bullied me into being strong for Daddy's sake and Neil's, I'd held back my tears, locking heartache in, afraid to weep, afraid to let myself feel anything. Now I realized it wasn't right to stifle feelings for a loved one. No wonder my emotions had been scrambled so I couldn't trust them in real life. Now I understood with my head, and my heart, too, why I'd been spoiling the school play. Distrusting my emotions since Mom died, how could I project them truthfully on stage?

I rushed to Neil, sweeping him up in my arms as a wild, fierce love for him shot through me. "Please, Neil," I pleaded softly, "don't worry about Daddy and me going away. We will never go away and leave you—never."

"Mary went away," Neil said haltingly. I saw the pain and grief grow in his eyes. "She was here and she went away with my friend, Mike, like Mommy."

Like Mommy. Neil's words scraped against my heart. Suddenly my mind was transported back in time. I saw Mom's sweet face as she lay in the coffin and my long pent-up sorrow burst forth. Scalding tears stung my cheeks. I don't know how long I cried my heart out, purging myself of that long, locked-up sorrow before I became conscious of Neil's calling to me over and over again, fright in his voice, "Don't cry, Mandy. Please, don't cry."

I nodded and wiped my eyes. "Mary didn't go away like Mommy, Neil. I swear it," I told him softly. "You can see her again, I promise. She lives only a few blocks from here."

He shook his head and began to cry again. "Mary went away. Mary went away and I'm never gonna see her again."

"Neil, please, just wait." I dashed to the telephone book and looked up the number of the Templetons. I had vowed I'd never call her, no matter what happened. I hesitated, with one last feeling of pride that did not want to admit that she was more important to this house than I was. Then I admitted it by dialing the number.

Mary answered. She seemed happily surprised to hear from me. Yes, she planned to go to the play. She was nearly ready. "Mary, please, could you come by the house first? Neil misses you so much and—" I broke down again. Sobs tore out of me. "We—we all miss you so much."

"Relax, take it easy, honey," Mary soothed in her cheery way. "I'll be right there." She arrived quickly. Daddy and Neil, seeming to sense something special even before she rang, came into the hall. When I opened the door, Neil flew into Mary's arms like a small missile. She caught him and whirled him around, her eyes sparkling. In seconds Mary's magic seemed to make our house a home again.

Daddy advanced shyly after she finally put Neil down. She held out her hand. He took it, his boyish smile growing. "It's so good to see you all," Mary said, shedding her special radiance. Only when her glance held on me was there a brief hesitation. "Mandy," she breathed, her eyes half laughing, half crying and full of love.

I didn't understand what was happening to me, the sudden warmth, the feeling of being part of life again, the rush of strength I felt, the sense of belonging in a special way to Neil and Daddy and Mary—and in another way, to Mom forever. Mary held out her arms. I was in them instantly, whispering to her how sorry I was that I had made her go away.

She clutched me tightly and patted my back. She released me and stood back, looking right into my eyes with her wonderful charm. "Well, I don't have to stay away, do I?" she said cheerfully. "Tonight we're all together for the play, the triumph. Isn't that so?"

"I want to go," Neil yelled excitedly. "I want to see you in the play, Mandy." I hesitated. "Can I go, Mandy?" Neil pleaded. "Can I? I'll be good."

I looked to Mary standing there, to Neil's eager, happy face, and then to Daddy's. Daddy was smiling, encouraging me to say yes. My glance darted back to Mary, so frail and yet so strong, so poor and yet so rich, because she had the gifts of love and strength and cheerfulness to give to us all.

In the minutes since she'd arrived, she somehow had made us a family again. And I understood with my heart at last, what my life and our school play was all about—the giving of love unselfishly, with no strings attached, because that is the only road to lasting happiness. And with this my last fear of the play died forever.

"Mandy?" Mary said.

"It's a wonderful play," I said in a voice vibrating with new confidence, "and I want everybody to see it. I wouldn't want you to miss the triumph."

And it was a triumph, because we all—Daddy, Neil, Mary, and I, the rest of the cast, and the eight hundred people in the audience— shared it. Only for Dad, Neil, Mary, and me, it was extra special because we knew an even bigger, more lasting happiness was coming when we all would be together again.

The End

I DROVE
MY LOVER INSANE!

Moving very carefully, I put down my suitcase and looked numbly around the room. It seemed strange to me because my parents had moved into this house just a few weeks before I'd left home to take a nursing job in another town.

It was a bungalow with two bedrooms, one occupied by Mom and Dad, and the other by my younger sister, Dana, who was sixteen and still in school. This, naturally, had raised problems when my elder sister, Michelle, came to stay, with her husband, Ray, and their baby. There was also my brother, Jack. So my father had transformed the huge loft into a vast room divided with curtains like a dormitory. At the moment, however, I had the loft all to myself. And at this moment of my life, I sure did need privacy! Meeting my family's questioning looks when I arrived had been a strain.

Now my mother called up through the hole in the floor of the loft. "Do you want anything to eat, Barbara?"

"No, thanks." I felt that food would stick in my throat.

"Would you like a cup of tea then?"

"No, thanks." Mom had forgotten that I didn't like tea. However, I thought I'd better not sound too miserable, or she would start to fuss even more. "I'll have a cup of coffee, though," I called down to her.

"All right, love. Do you want it up there, or are you coming down?"

"I'll come down," I answered wearily.

I wondered if I had done the right thing, after all, in coming home. If it was going to be like this all the time, with Mom fussing over me, then I had definitely made a mistake. The trouble was, that although I wanted more than anything else to be left alone, I had returned because I just couldn't bear the thought of living by myself in some lonely apartment, or with a lot of other too-curious girls in the nurses' home.

All these seething, conflicting emotions were making my head pound and my knees tremble, and I felt myself always on the verge of tears. Weak, helpless tears came so easily. I must stop it, I thought desperately. If anyone sees me like this, they'll know for sure that I'm on the brink of a breakdown. I was afraid that Mom suspected something was seriously wrong the way she lovingly held me when I came back. If she had any inkling that I was so near to nervous collapse, her love would become smothering in its intensity. This would be the last straw, and I really would go over the edge.

"Coffee's ready!" Mom shouted.

With an effort, I held back my tears and shakily climbed down the retractable ladder to the hallway. One part of me was glad and relieved that I was amid people who loved and wanted me, no matter what happened. But the other part of me was dreading the thought of the tomorrows that would follow.

In the big, sunny kitchen, Dad was reading a newspaper, and Dana was dreamily watching some birds through the window. Mom was bustling around getting out the coffee cups and looking very busy. The atmosphere seemed heavy with tact. "Here you are, love," fluttered Mom, placing a cup of coffee in front of me. "Help yourself to sugar. Would you like a cookie?"

I subdued the hysterical thought that they were being too polite— almost as if I were a stranger—and spooned sugar into my cup. "No, thanks," I muttered. It seemed to me as though I had said nothing but "no thanks" ever since I arrived.

"How about offering me a cookie then?" demanded Dana. I looked at my buxom teen-aged sister affectionately. With her candid blue eyes, and thick, honey-colored hair, she seemed refreshingly uncomplicated and natural, good to have around, especially now. "You're getting too fat!" Mom cried to Dana.

"Oh, I'll work it all off when school starts again," she replied unconcernedly, reaching for the cookie tin. "Anyway, Jogger says he likes big girls."

"Oh, he does, does he?" growled Dad, coming out from behind his newspaper. "Who in the world is Jogger? What a name!"

"It's just a nickname, and I've had a couple of dates with him, that's all."

Dad snorted, and turned to me. "Are you going to work at our local hospital?" he asked casually.

I hesitated. "No." Suddenly, I thought that this was as good a time as any to break it to them. "I'm giving up nursing. I'm going to take a commercial course and do secretarial work."

Mom and Dad looked at each other, while Dana cocked her head quizzically. Then they all began to talk at one time.

"Whatever for?"

"All that training!"

"What's wrong with nursing?"

"But, Barbara, you're twenty-five, and have no experience in computer work," cried Mom. "You can't expect to get a top-notch office job for several years."

"My mind is made up," I said as calmly as I could. "I've saved enough to take the course. I've decided to chuck nursing—I've had enough of it."

"But you're a very good nurse," Dad objected. "Why do you want to give it up?"

"I can't explain at the moment, but I've got to have a change, and this is as good a way as any."

"Okay, if that's how you feel," said Mom, sensing the despair in my voice. Suddenly I felt the familiar waves of misery washing over me again. I realized that my father and mother would find it hard to understand me—I had always been different from the others. Michelle used to be a social worker and was now happily married, the mother of a beautiful baby boy (how I envied her that baby!). My brother, Jack, was well on the road to success as a surveyor and was thoroughly enjoying life in his bachelor apartment. And Dana was happy and serene with her boyfriends and school life.

I was the odd girl out, a changeling. Michelle, Jack, and Dana were blue-eyed blondes. My hair and eyes were dark brown and my skin was olive. Because I looked so different from the others, when I was thirteen I conceived the notion that I was adopted. For years I kept this secret thought locked up inside me. I was almost nineteen when I tremulously dropped a hint to Mom that I was an adopted child. She was horrified. She dug into the attic trunk to pull out my birth certificate, then found some half-faded photographs of her younger brother who was killed in a car accident a year after I was born. She pointed out the strong resemblance I bore to my uncle.

She held me close to her as if I were a little baby, saying over and over again, "How could you think that way, my darling?"

I couldn't answer her, but I knew that something had happened when I was a child that made me feel insecure. I was always being hurt by the most innocent remarks others made.

But the greatest hurt, inflicted by Christopher, the man I had loved, had shriveled my spirit. I had always managed to hide my feelings, but he had left his mark on me. I was home only a day and I could tell that Mom and Dad—and even Dana—sensed there was something wrong with me. How could they help but notice? How long could I manage to choke back the tears? How could I keep my hands from trembling or my heart from pounding every time I thought of him? I knew that I couldn't keep penned within me the terrible hurt I felt. I would have to talk to somebody, or else become as insane as Christopher now was.

For more than a week I did nothing much except sit upstairs or loll around in the garden. Our large, beautiful garden was Dad's pride and joy. Most of his life had been spent underground as a miner, but now that he was retired he whiled away long, enjoyable hours in his garden, getting his fill of the sunshine and fresh air he craved. He was a quiet, thoughtful man, content with his family, his pipe, and his cabbages. I wandered around while Dad did his little chores, sensing that I didn't want to talk.

One day, while I was walking aimlessly amid the shrubbery, I heard a shout from the house. Mom was standing in the doorway, excitedly waving a letter. I hurried indoors, feeling wobbly.

"Here you are, dear." Mom smiled, almost quivering with curiosity. "It's a most peculiar letter. There's writing all over the envelope—hardly room for the address. Wonderful how the mailman managed—" She broke off. "What's the matter, Barbara?"

I must have gone pale. I was staring at the letter as though hypnotized.

"Barbara! What's the matter?"

"N-nothing, Mom," I managed.

I couldn't think of anything to say. I walked into the house, clutching the letter. I climbed the ladder to the loft and sat down lifelessly on the bed. It was several minutes before I could nerve myself to open it. It was from Christopher. But it wasn't the man I once knew and loved. This was a horrifying, frightening person. It wasn't a letter, but a list—a list compiled by a deranged mind—of the "good and bad" in me. My dazed eyes skimmed down the page and saw words like "marvelous," "beautiful," "vicious," "brilliant," "evil," and even "holy." I felt sick as I read this outpouring of an unbalanced mind, remembering how brilliant that mind had once been. I fell back on the bed, moaning, "Christopher, Christopher, it's my fault you're like this. Why did it have to happen this way?"

For a while I just lay there, reviewing the whole searing story of Christopher and me. Then gradually the sounds of clattering dishes broke into my thoughts, and I realized that lunch was nearly ready. I climbed down and went to fix my face in the bathroom, feeling glad that I had chosen to come home instead of remaining at the hospital.

To my relief, no questions were asked when I entered the kitchen. Instead, there was an air of excitement, and Mom was reading from letters in each hand. "From Michelle and Jack," she explained, beaming. "They're all coming here this weekend. Isn't that just great?

"Wonderful!" Dana cried. "Where's everyone going to sleep?"

"You'll have to go upstairs with Barbara," replied Mom. "Michelle and Ray can have your room, with little Trent in the crib, and Jack will have to make do with the couch in the living room. He won't mind. Let me see now—"

"When you've finished waving those letters about," interrupted Dad, "I would like to read them."

"Oh, sorry, dear. Here you are. They both say they're coming Friday night. The baby will need taking care of, and Jack won't bother to feed himself before he leaves, so I'd better have a hot meal ready. He'll probably bring all his dirty laundry, as usual, so—"

"Whoa! Hold on, Mom." Dana laughed. "Take it easy! There are two days to go yet. If you start like this now, you'll be worn out by Friday."

"I won't be if you'll do a little work around the house, instead of messing with your hair and mooning over the telephone," retorted Mom.

"Okay, okay," Dana answered snappily. "How about Barbara doing something to help, too? She's been here three weeks now, and it takes her all day just to make her bed. Why should I have to do all the chores?"

"Now, now," interposed Dad. "Let's have a little quiet."

I could see Mom was on the verge of saying something about me being ill, so I said hastily, "No, she's right. It's time I did my share. Tell you what, I'll do some baking this afternoon."

"Well," said Mom doubtfully, "you can help, dear, but you know how Jack and Ray love my apple pies, so let me handle the baking."

I felt the familiar shrinking feeling inside me at this rebuff, although Mom hadn't meant to be unkind. The fact was that I just couldn't bake very well. In the past, to cover up my hurt, I would probably have made a sharp rejoinder, but I forced a laugh and said, "All right, Mother."

Mom knew that she had hurt my feelings. "Tell you what," she said to me, "my legs ache terribly, so I think you'll do the baking, Barbara, while I sit down and supervise. It's time you learned to bake. Once you're married, you wouldn't want your husband running to his mother for a decent slice of pie."

"I'll never get married," I cried out.

"Why not?" asked Dana in surprise.

"Nobody'll have me," I joked, trying to keep the conversation light.

"Of course they will," said Mom. "You wait till you meet the right man." I felt my throat tighten as I thought of Christopher.

"Well, you'll never meet him in this town," Dana mused. "All the decent men over twenty-three are married. No bachelors here. Let's see now." She laughed, then said, "How about Jogger?"

"Oh, shut up!" I cried angrily and stormed upstairs.

I lay on the bed, listening to the clatter of dishes and the murmur of voices. After a while I realized I ought to go down and help with the baking and apologize for my outburst. I didn't really feel like baking pies, and wondered why I had offered my services when my heart wasn't in it.

That's me all over, I thought. All my life I'd done things I didn't want to do, and not things I had wanted to do. Why am I such a contrary creature?

My thoughts went back to my childhood. Michelle and I both played the piano well and won prizes, but it was Michelle who was always asked to perform for visitors and at parties. She was three years older, and for children, three years make a big difference. I always seemed to walk in the shadow of my older sister, whether it was at school or in other activities.

Our paths had diverged now. Michelle had gone where I ached to follow. I yearned with all my soul to be married to a man I could love, and who would love me, someone who knew and understood all my faults, yet loved me in spite of them. I yearned for the feel of a baby in my arms, my own baby.

But all these things would never be mine until I could rid myself of this terrible aversion to men. I would draw back in fear at the mere accidental touch of a man in the street or on the train. I knew enough psychology to realize that eventually, with love, patience, and understanding, my bruised spirit would probably recover, and I would be normal once again. But when will this be? I wondered despairingly. I am already twenty-five. Oh, Christopher, Christopher, what have we done to each other? There you are, sick in mind and broken in spirit, and here am I, on the brink of nervous collapse. Where will it all end? Forcibly shaking these thoughts from my mind, I gathered myself together and went downstairs.

I must have looked ashen when I entered the kitchen, for Mom glanced at me and put down the rolling pin. She wiped her flour-caked hands and came to me. "Barbara, are you having a baby?" she asked.

I looked at her, shocked. "Oh, no, Mom!"

"What is it then? Talk to me, Barbara. I know there's something wrong. Wouldn't it help to talk things over?" She put her arms around me and kissed me. I broke down, sobbing hysterically.

When I calmed down somewhat I said, "I only wish I were having a baby. It's what I want more than anything else."

"I don't understand, darling," said Mom. "But if you don't want to talk—"

"I've got to talk to someone!" I cried. "It's just that I don't know where to begin."

"What about that letter?" she asked gently. "Is that from—him?" I nodded. "Where is he?"

"In a mental hospital," I said in a hushed voice. "And it's my fault that he's in the hospital."

"Oh, no!"

"Yes!" I blurted out. "Maybe he wasn't well before I met him, but I was the cause of his breakdown."

"No! That can't be true!" exclaimed Mom protectively. "You're too lovely, too good, too decent. You were always shy as a little girl. You never had dates like Dana and Michelle. Why, you were afraid of boys!"

I smiled to myself. I sat down at the table and began sifting flour through my fingers. Mother's hand was caressing my hair lovingly. Words began to pour forth from me.

"I was madly in love all through my last years at high school with a boy who never even knew I existed. At college, I was badly let down by another boy. You didn't know about them, Mother, did you?"

"I wish I had," she said gently.

"It wouldn't have helped much if you had. They left me feeling shy and rejected, afraid I'd be hurt again, so I started behaving very coldly and distantly toward them. It got to the stage where I could be myself, and act naturally, only with men who were considerably older than I, and safely married. Bachelors frightened me. Last year, I met a doctor who had just come to the hospital. He was much older than I, and married, the father of three children. This was Christopher. Dr. Christopher Markum. I felt safe with him and laughed and chatted a lot. He was a brilliant surgeon, and I admired his work. His children were bright and lovely—oh, it was terrible." My voice shook as I thought of Christopher and his charming little family. "He fell love with you?" Mom prompted gently.

"Yes. And I with him. When it was too late, I realized what was happening, and tried to end it by acting cold and indifferent. I couldn't bear the thought of breaking up his family. I'd met his wife and kids, and they were wonderful. Besides, he had his career to consider."

"What happened, dear?"

"It was then that a sudden change came over him. He'd come to my apartment, force his way in, and we'd argue for hours and hours. Mom, he used to get down on his knees and shout and rave and wave his arms about. God, it was awful. He wanted me to run away with him, but how could I? I had become afraid of him, and the slightest breath of scandal would mean the ruin of his career. There were times I thought he was going to attack me. He started to write crazy, twisted poems to me and leave them about where I would be sure to find them. I was petrified in case other nurses should pick them up.

"He even sent his wife to try to persuade me to go away with him! It was a nightmare! I loved him, Mom, and it was horrifying to see what was happening to him. I nearly gave in to him, just to stop him, but when I thought that he was going insane, I became terrified. I changed apartments, but he trailed me. I told him that I didn't love him, that there was another man. I thought it would help, but he lost his nerve while operating and made mistakes in diagnosis. It was obvious to the hospital authorities that he was losing his mind. One day he ran wild through the corridors and had to be committed to a mental institution. He's still in there, terribly sick. Read this letter. It's from the man I once loved."

Mom read the letter in silence while I choked back the tears. She laid the letter on the table and put her hand on mine. "What happened to his family?" she asked.

"I don't know. I've ruined their lives just as I've ruined Christopher's."

"No, dear," she said. "It wasn't your fault. No normal man would've behaved like that. Think what your life would've been if you had given in to him. What did you know about him, his childhood, his youth? Maybe the seeds of insanity were planted long before you ever dreamed of meeting him. You mustn't blame yourself."

"It's my fault, Mother. I loved him."

"Love is beautiful when it's returned," she said. "Try to put this horrible affair out of your mind. Maybe you can go back to nursing later."

"I don't know, Mother. It's just that somehow I can't stand people. I thought I'd get a job in an office. Then I could be by myself most of the time."

"Perhaps, dear, when you feel a little better, you'll want to go back to nursing. Anyway, don't worry. I'm proud of the way you acted. Now, your dad will be in from the garden soon. He's gathering apples and blackberries for the pies and I haven't even made the pastry yet! Come on, we'd better get a move on. Dana will soon be in—she always gets hungry about this time."

Baking proceeded calmly, and soon the kitchen was filled with wonderful aromas. I felt a measure of peace stealing over me, and in the serenity of the big kitchen my nightmare began to recede a little. I was sure now that I had done the right thing by coming home. Home was not the irritant I had at first feared, but a haven for me and my bruised spirit.

That Friday evening I relaxed and watched my brother slouching in his favorite position in an armchair. He was holding court, his "women" grouped around him. We girls had a deep affection for Jack—he was easygoing, bright and witty, and loved teasing us. Mom kept popping in and out of the kitchen, beaming, and Dad sat contentedly sucking his pipe, happy at the prospect of having all his family together under one roof again.

Jack was baiting Dana. "Hey, Dana, what's all this about you having a boyfriend named Jogger head?"

"Do you mind!" she retorted. "His nickname happens to be Jogger, but his real name's Zeke Fulton."

Jack thought about it. "Isn't that the boy who was four or five grades below me in school? I remember him, because I always thought he looked like Huck Finn. Does he still wear a straw hat and go around barefoot in summer?"

"Of course not!" she cried indignantly. Then she realized he was only pulling her leg. "Anyway, you'll meet him tomorrow. We have a date."

"Good!" Jack grinned.

"Listen," Mom called, bursting into the room, "isn't that a car stopping in the drive?"

"Yes!" Dana shouted, bounding up. "Yippee! It's Michelle and Ray." She charged out of the room, the rest of us following eagerly.

"Hello, there!" Mom beamed, kissing them and gathering up the baby as she spoke. "My, but you're a big boy now."

Michelle smiled, looking proud and happy. "He's running everywhere and getting into all sorts of trouble. Got two new teeth as well."

"Please let me hold him," I begged. "Hi, there, Trent." I carried the baby into the house, looking at his little face with a pleasure too deep for words.

"You're lucky," I remarked to Michelle, who had followed me in. "Wish he were mine," I told her.

"Well, you know how to get one. Beats me why you've come back here to live. There isn't a marriageable male within miles. You'd do a lot better to get away from here, in a place of your own. Why did you leave the hospital? At least you see a bit of life in a big place like that, which is more than can be said for this town."

Although I knew Michelle didn't know anything of my story, and that her remarks were made in all innocence, they jarred on me. Mom, who had just come in, caught the tail end of Michelle's speech. "Look," she said hastily, "this poor little fellow is more than ready for sleep. Go and make his bed, Barbara, and we'll pop him into his crib. Michelle, do you and Ray want anything to eat?"

"Just a cup of coffee, Mom. We ate before we left home. Got any apple pie?"

"Sure, I have," Mom said with a chuckle. "I know what you come here for. Barbara made these."

"Heavens!" Michelle laughed, taking Trent from Mom. "What next? Is Barbara blossoming out as a cook? Mmm, they look quite good."

"They are good," I defended, trying to keep my tone light. "Don't you go knocking my pies."

Michelle laughed and took the baby to bed, while Mom and I busied ourselves in the kitchen. I felt very proud of my last remark. A few weeks ago, I would have bristled at Michelle's criticism. This time I had managed to react normally, returning a light remark. I was pleased with myself.

After the baby was in bed, we all sat around contentedly eating and drinking. Jack stretched out his long legs and Dad lit his pipe again. Everyone chatted easily, and soon we were up to date on each other's news.

"So you're chucking nursing, Barbara," Michelle remarked. "I can't understand you. Still, if that's what you want, I admire your courage. I wouldn't enjoy that secretarial college myself, I'm sure, not among all those teenagers."

"And what's wrong with teenagers?" Jack asked, with a sidelong glance at Dana. "They always have such gorgeous names, like Loggle, and Toggle, and Huck." He ducked as Dana heaved a cushion at him.

"Oh, she'd be all right," Mom said comfortably, returning back to the subject of me, "though I think you ought to smarten up a bit, Barbara, or you'll be thought an old fuddy duddy." She was right, too. Since I'd been at home, I'd become very careless and sloppy in my dress, not bothering with what I wore, and never putting on makeup. I just couldn't raise the slightest bit of interest in my appearance these days.

Disgruntled, I said, "You're always fussing about me, Mom. If people can't like me for what I am, instead of what I wear, then I say they're not worth knowing."

"That's not a very good philosophy for life," Jack commented.

"Right!" Michelle cried. "You must have a bit of window dressing to attract people in the first place, especially men. Ray, what attracted you to me when we first met? Was it my sweet nature, my brilliant brain, my dazzling beauty, or what?"

"Well," mused Ray, "I haven't come across any of those assets yet. Ouch!" Michelle pretended to hit him, and I laughed, glad to be part of this silly bit of family playfulness. "No," continued Ray, "seriously I think it was the way you dressed that first caught my attention. I'd always thought social workers were on the dowdy side, and dressed in sensible clothes. When they told me your occupation, I couldn't believe my eyes."

"There you are," said Michelle triumphantly, and I had to admit she'd made her point. Suddenly, she was smitten with an idea. "Dana," she enthused, "we'll start a campaign to marry off Barbara!"

"That's a good idea," exclaimed Jack and Dana together, drowning out my protests.

"We'll start in the morning by setting her hair," went on Michelle, warming up to the scheme. "Then we'll raid her wardrobe, and see what she has worth wearing. Then we'll make up her face."

"And then what?" I demanded. "I'll just sit at home and watch television afterward, I suppose."

"Not on your life," Jack asserted. "I'll hang around and watch the transformation and, if the result is worth it, the four of us will go out to dinner and dance. I'm sure Mom and Dad won't mind baby-sitting.

Wait a minute though! I've got a better idea. I'll call a girl I know, and Howard Davis, a surveyor who works with me. We'll have a party. Howard, by the way, is very eligible."

"Oh, no!" I said in dismay. I certainly didn't feel like going on a blind date. How could I, in my agitated state? But everyone thought it a brilliant idea and overrode my protests. I couldn't refuse to go without hurting their feelings.

"That sounds settled." Mom smiled, standing up and making for the door. "I'm going to bed, and I think you'd better hop off, too, Dana. It's nearly midnight."

We all elected to turn in then, and as we were going up the ladder I said to Dana, "Hope you don't mind, but I'm going to read. If you draw your curtains, the light shouldn't bother you."

"Oh, that won't worry me," she said, unconcerned. She went over to her bed and started to undress. "Aren't you tired?"

"Yes, but it takes me hours to fall asleep," I said.

"Why don't you take a pill?" Dana, my dear, sweet, extrovert sister had never had a sleepless night in her life.

"I'd rather not get into the habit," I replied.

"Oh, well," she said, yawning and climbing into bed. "It's your life. Good night."

"Good night," I echoed, and clambered into my own bed. I took a book from the shelf above the bed and lay back on the pillow. My life! It sure was! But what had I done so far with this life of mine?

I thought bitterly: I've messed up another life as well as my own. There was nothing I could do for Christopher, but I owed something to myself and to the people who loved me. Fervently, I resolved to change myself, to try to put the past out of my mind, and free myself from my depression. I would take the secretarial course, get an interesting job—not the quiet, hideaway type I'd envisioned when I left the hospital. I'd save up, buy a car, and get out and meet people. To hell with my sensitivities. Tomorrow I'd let Michelle and Dana do their stuff, then in the evening I'd put everything behind me and enjoy myself. What's done is done. I can't change the past, but I have to face the future.

I wondered whether or not I was fooling myself. I knew that it would not be easy, that only I, myself, could climb out of my private little pit. But when I turned out the light and curled up on my side, I felt more at peace with myself than I had for a long time.

Down below I heard a whimper from the baby, then quiet again. Probably Michelle and Ray had disturbed him while getting ready for bed. He's a lovely kid, I thought sleepily. Someday I mean to have one of my own. Someday. . . .

I sat stiffly at the table in the restaurant with the lights, music, and people swirling around me. By all accounts, I should have been one of the happiest girls in the room. In a dusky pink dress belonging to Michelle (nothing in my own dowdy wardrobe had been considered suitable) and with my hair and face looking their best. After my sisters' combined efforts, both my mirror and Howard's eyes had assured me that I was one of the prettiest girls in the restaurant. I was intensely aware of Howard beside me, looking like a big, blond Viking—he was Danish. That was the trouble. I was too aware of him.

Throughout dinner, I trembled every time he accidentally touched me and afterward, when the others got up to dance, I pleaded an excuse and remained at the table. I was doing my best to stick to my resolutions of the night before, and was making an effort to be upbeat and charming. But dance with a man I could not. Not yet, anyway. I had to have more time. I could see Howard was puzzled by my refusal to dance.

During one of the pauses between dances, I went to the powder room. Michelle followed me in and bluntly asked, "Do you like him?"

"Yes, of course. I think he's very good looking."

"Well, why don't you dance with him then? The poor man is probably thinking he's got bad breath or something. You're acting rather foolishly, you know." I didn't say anything, but went over to the mirror and began fiddling with my hairdo. What could I say? Without knowing my whole story, Michelle would never understand if I just said that I couldn't bear to have a man touch me.

As if reading my thoughts, she asked, "Can't you stand the guy touching you?" I looked at her in amazement, and she smiled. "Sorry, Barbara. I didn't mean to let on, but Mom told me the story you told her. She thought it best, since she knew we were dragging you off on a blind date. I hope you don't mind too much."

I shrugged. "Doesn't matter."

"I think you've had a raw deal, Barbara, and I'm sorry. But you can't go on this way all your life!"

"I know," I said. "One half of me yearns to love someone, to be married and have a beautiful baby like yours. But the other part of me is scared to death of sex, and of anything to do with it. That's why, when a man touches me, I feel like cringing."

Michelle sat on a stool and began fiddling with her evening bag. "Tell me, do you feel this way when any man touches you? Do you feel this way with Jack, or Dad, or Ray?"

"No, only with bachelors and people who I think might be interested in me."

"By 'interested,' do you mean romantically?" she asked.

"I suppose so." The answer was wrung out of me. All of a sudden, I could see what Michelle was leading up to. "Are you trying to tell me that my aversion to men is purely a sort of inverted sex urge? That when I flinch away from a man, I—I'm really all the time wanting him to hold me in his arms?"

"Well," she hesitated, "I wouldn't have put it as strongly as that, but you've got the general idea."

The powder room was invaded by a bunch of girls just then, so no more discussion was possible. In a daze I followed her back to our table, careful not to look at Howard. The band struck up a slow dance, and Michelle and Ray got up to dance. Howard rose to his feet, and asked Allie, Jack's date, to dance. Jack left to talk to an acquaintance at another table, and I was left alone.

I watched Howard circling the floor, his well-shaped head bent over Allie. I thought over the conversation with Michelle. More and more it seemed to me that she was right, and that my fear of men was an obsession that could destroy me. And if I didn't do something about it soon I might get worse and end up a bitter, frustrated old maid.

Jack came back at that moment, and I made up my mind. Quickly, before I could lose my resolution, I said to him, "Jack, I'm going to butt in on Howard and Allie. Will you come and rescue her so she's not stranded out there?"

"Why, sure," Jack answered in surprise. "But what's the idea? You wouldn't dance with him before."

"Never mind. I'll tell you later maybe. Come on, before the song's over."

He jumped up, and together we approached the whirling couple. Howard said nothing as I slid into his encircling arms, trembling. If I was shivering like a trapped bird, he made no comment. He just stood there a moment, then gently moved forward, and my feet miraculously followed his. The music stopped and, while people around us broke apart and clapped for more, Howard continued to hold me close. I looked up and saw his gray eyes looking into mine, and I felt his arms tighten around me. Although he didn't know my troubles, he seemed to sense them.

Gradually I stopped trembling and relaxed against his broad chest. The band gently slid into slow, dreamy music, and I moved off in the haven of Howard's arms.

The End

ENCHANTED BY
A KIND STRANGER
He stood by my side

It might have been a wonderful holiday season, but I felt sick at heart. I'd just seen the doctor and I couldn't accept what he'd told me. The phone rang. I groaned in pain while reaching for it.

"Hello, Tracy? This is Chris Lyman. You don't know me, but Alan Daughtry gave me your phone number."

"I see." I dated Alan occasionally, but he lived forty miles away and with the distance between us, nothing serious had developed.

"Tracy, Alan told me that you were great at skiing. He told me to get in touch with you because I've never skied in my life."

I burst into tears.

"Tracy? Are you all right?"

"No," I said miserably.

"I'm sorry." He paused. "I'd really like to meet you. I've always wanted to take up skiing. Alan told me you'd been to a lot of resorts."

"It's nice talking to you, Chris, but—"

"Tracy, please don't give me the brush off. I just want to learn to ski, that's all. I'm harmless. Ask Alan. I'm a technician for one of the engineering firms here. I have a really close friend who owns a cabin up on Blueberry Hill. Please, won't you let me talk to you?"

Tears streamed down my face. "It's just that," I choked, "it's just that I'll probably never ski again."

"Why not?"

How I'd loved skiing! "The doctor told me that just a couple of hours ago."

"Why can't you ski again? What's this about a doctor?"

I didn't want to explain anything to this stranger. I just wanted to stare at the ornaments, situated across the living room in a pile, minus their tree. For so long, when I'd closed my eyes, I'd envisioned this nice, healthy, bushy Christmas tree. Now I closed my eyes and thought of tree limbs smashing, falling. . . .

I wouldn't be able to chop down a tree now. I wouldn't even be able to haul one out of a tree lot. I could barely drive a car; I may never ski again—and this stranger kept asking me questions.

Impatiently, I blurted, "My back is out."

"Oh, gee, I'm sorry. It must be awfully bad, if the doctor says you might never ski again. How'd it happen?" Chris asked.

"I'm a recreational therapist. I work with the mentally disabled. Two months ago, a couple of really big guys started a fight. I fell

342

flat on my back on concrete stairs, trying to break them up."

I heard Chris's deep indrawn breath. "Wow! I guess the last thing you'd want to talk about now is skiing."

"That and everything else. This isn't a good time for me." The doctor was pessimistic. I'd been working my job for only a year.

I told Chris that the doctor said the X-rays indicated the beginning of arthritis in my back. "So I may never ski again. I may never even go back to work, except with limitations."

All the money I'd saved, just to get through college, and I'd been allowed only one year to work at my chosen profession. I had no other skills, and a stranger was still talking to me on the phone.

"I'm really sorry," Chris said again. "Is there anything I can do? Would you like me to bring over some food or something? It must be painful to even move, with—"

"It is," I answered him. "It's painful to drive, it's painful to talk, move, to do anything."

"Is your family helping you?"

"They're in Pearl River." He started talking again, and I tried to listen to him. I refused to accept what the doctor had told me. I would ski again and I would work again. I would not give up.

"Tracy, I'd really like to help you out. Do you need a ride to the doctor's office?"

I'd been independent for so long that my automatic response was no. Then I thought of how I could barely climb out of a chair right now. What would I do, alone and single now? To make matters worse, I'd transferred from another state hospital only six months back. Because I'd been paying off my move, I'd worked so much overtime that I'd hardly met a soul in my new hometown.

Chris kept on talking, but my mind kept drifting, while I gazed at the ornaments. "Yes, you could take me to the doctor's," I said finally.

"Anything. Wow, what an awful thing to have happen."

I closed my eyes and felt like I smelled pine. "I was warned that the program I worked on had a thirty-six percent injury rate, but it's always hard to believe it could happen to you."

I explained to Chris how we were on an outing to a museum, when two patients started the fistfight. My fall distracted them, and they stopped fighting. I didn't feel the searing pain until the next day. I closed my eyes, remembering my fall, and then I saw a skier sliding out of control down a mountainside.

"Is there anything you need to buy—presents or something, for Christmas?"

"Sure, a plane ticket to Pearl River, to see my parents, except I can't afford it," I joked. I glared at the Christmas ornaments. "If you really want to help, there is something. Would you help me chop down my Christmas tree? I've seen the tree farms up in the mountains. I planned on doing it myself, but—"

"Fantastic! I'd love to."

I almost felt like gloating. I'd have a Christmas tree, after all. Chris was going to help me. Of course, once he saw me, hunched over in a back brace, he'd probably never want to see me again, but at least I'd get my tree.

Once, at nineteen, I'd been too sick with pneumonia to buy a tree. I'd sat alone in my apartment then, staring at the boxes of ornaments. I vowed it would never happen again. I told Chris about my one year without a Christmas tree.

"How about Friday? I can come over right after work."

I smiled, thinking how much fun it would be. I closed my eyes and a tree farm came into view, but it wasn't dusk, it was morning! Strange. "Will you help set the tree up on the stand, too, and put the lights on?"

"I'll help you from start to finish," Chris promised. "I wouldn't leave you stranded."

He called me every night. I started looking forward to his calls; often, he was the only person I spoke to all day. We talked for hours. I'd hardly met anyone outside the hospital, because of all my hours of overtime, and Chris became my lifeline to the outside world. It scared me, how dependent I became on him in such a short time. I'd never depended on anyone like this before, but I'd never felt so helpless, either. I could barely cook or move around. Sometimes, I crawled, because I couldn't get up or get down.

I discovered I had a host of "fair-weather friends," friends who wanted to party, not people I could turn to if I had a serious problem. A lot of people called, but they said they'd be in touch with me later, after the holidays. That depressed me even more. I felt very much alone.

We had to cancel our first date because Chris had the flu, so we made plans for the following Friday. Meanwhile, I struggled to drive myself to the clinic for my physical therapy. If I didn't get there, my worker's compensation payments would be discontinued. I could barely twist my neck to see the road and I felt every bump my car hit.

Then I drove to my old job and dropped off the mounds of paperwork that proved I really had a problem. I felt like I was a road hazard; I was in so much pain I could hardly drive, but I'd be penniless if I didn't file the worker's comp. All my treasured independence dissolved to nothing during December. That hurt.

The rest of my time I spent in bed, in agony, my mind still working. Perhaps I thought a lot about trees because I was going to get a Christmas tree after all. But I kept having visions of skiers and trees, and excruciating back pain. A tree limb would snap and I'd feel it in my back, waking up with a jolt.

Finally, my back felt slightly better, and Chris recovered from his flu. Since his office was close to my apartment, but he lived miles away from his job, we made arrangements for him to come over to my apartment right after work.

That Friday, I tugged on my back brace that made me look far too fat, and grimaced in the mirror. My hair needed a good stylist, and after not having worn them, my contacts burned my eyes. I planned on meeting Chris down in the garage area, because the apartment complex was so large. We planned on leaving right after we met, so that we could make it to the tree lots before they closed for the evening.

I locked my door and walked slowly to the elevator. With each step, I felt excruciating pain, but worse than that, I wondered if my back would ever heal. And what would I do for a living, if I couldn't do what I'd been trained for? Much as I loved my parents, I didn't want to live with them again. How would I support myself? I never felt as depressed as I did right then. I had visions of Chris, a blond hunk who was brainy and gorgeous. He'd said he was balding slightly, but the other clues he'd given made him sound absolutely electrifying. I'd already discovered that he was great to talk to.

Painfully, I tried to smile—walking hurt so much. I spotted Chris in the parking garage, standing alongside my car I'd described. There were no sparks, nothing. Perhaps we could still be friends.

Warmly, he shook my hand. "You must be Tracy."

I nodded and tried to smile. "That's me. Nice to meet you in person, Chris." We studied each other for a moment. He was average, but nice somehow, like a worn quilt or something. He was balder than I imagined. For his late twenties, his hairline was receding dramatically. His hair was browner than blond, but he was in good shape physically and his eyes did make me catch my breath.

He had huge green eyes that dominated his face, a dark green, the green of Christmas. He continued to gaze at me, which was insane, considering how I looked and felt, but he acted like he really liked me, bad back and all! For weeks, my friends had been promising they'd stay in touch, but nobody wanted to deal with the shape I was in now, except this stranger with the dazzling green eyes.

"Ready to go? I thought we'd use my car. It's old and beat up, but it won't matter if it gets littered with pine needles." While he drove, Chris continued talking. "I used to have a good car." He explained how he was still trying to get back on his feet financially. "My ex-wife and her boyfriend took everything," he said finally.

"You're kidding! How'd it happen?"

"One day, I came home and they'd rented a truck and had moved

345

everything away. They even took my clothes, so it was hard going, for a while. We're divorced. I share a rented house with another guy, but he's always with his girlfriend."

I felt so sorry for him. "What about your family?"

"They live in the area, but my mother likes traveling during the holidays."

He hit a bump in the road and I groaned in pain.

"I'm so sorry, Tracy. It sure is getting dark fast. Did you check to see how late the Christmas tree farms stay open?"

"No, but you're right. They might not be open at night like the tree lots."

Chris grinned. "Well, we'll see."

We continued talking while Chris drove. I felt amazed at how comfortable I was becoming with him, back brace and all. Maybe he wasn't as gorgeous as some of the men I've dated, but there was something compelling about him; he seemed to care so much. He seemed real.

Up the hill toward the mountains, the scenery changed to majestic fir trees. "I love it up here," I said. "Sometimes, where I came from, I missed the seasons. It's nice to be reminded of winter—"

"There's no snow," Chris said.

"I know, but it still makes me think of winter."

Chris turned down a road that had several signs posted, advertising tree farms. He rounded a bend and I cried, "Stop! This is it! We have to get my tree here."

It was the farm of my dreams and it felt right, but it was dark and cold and all the lights were out.

"It's closed," Chris said. "Maybe we can find one that's open."

"No! It has to be this one." I knew it sounded crazy, but I had to buy a tree at this farm.

"All right. Do you want to come back tomorrow? They're sure to be open on Saturday."

"But you'd have to drive clear back here again on your day off and—"

"I have no other plans."

I agreed and Chris drove his old car down the mountain. He offered to take me out to dinner, and after I agreed, he asked, "Tracy, would you have seen me, if your back hadn't been out? You're so gorgeous, and Alan said you dated and partied a lot."

"I gained weight from this injury and I'm certainly not ready to party now."

"That's my point," he said quietly.

He was silent the rest of the way. I thought hard about what he'd said. I'd always been bored with "nice" guys. I loved dancing all night and I hung around with a crowd that liked constant motion and activity. But where were those friends now? "I don't know, Chris, but I am glad I met you."

"Are you really?"

"Yes." Would I have dismissed someone like Chris? In his own quiet way, he was very attractive, and very genuine.

By the time we reached the city, we were too late for some of the restaurants. Others had long waiting lines, many seemed too crowded, and I wanted a booth because of my back. After we'd gone to yet another restaurant with hard chairs, I finally said, "Look, I've got some chicken I could microwave. Why don't we go home and I'll fix dinner?"

Chris nodded. He stopped at a store on the way home. "I'll just be a minute." When he returned, he gave me a small bottle of wine and some roses.

"Wow. Thank you, Chris!" I sniffed the roses while he drove to my place. I suddenly felt self-conscious. "I get crabby with the pain. I guess I'm not a fun date."

"You're doing just fine." He swung the old car into the complex. "How am I doing?"

"Great! You're a lot of fun."

"You don't find me too quiet to be around? Alan told me you especially like to dance. I hate dancing."

I opened the car door. "Well, I won't be dancing for a while. Can you help me climb out?"

He raced to my side and literally lifted me out of the car. I gasped, "My back gets worse at night."

"How did you ever drive to therapy?"

"It wasn't easy. I worried the whole time. The traffic's so bad here and I couldn't turn my neck, so I had to rely on the mirrors."

"I'm sorry I had the flu. You shouldn't be driving, Tracy."

In my apartment, Chris helped me set the table for dinner and cook. And, after the table was set and everything was ready for dinner, he came up to me in my tiny kitchen.

"Tracy?"

"Yes?"

"Do you have time for a hug?"

It was only our first date, but somehow it felt right, he felt right, and he hugged me, gently massaging my back, never asking for anything more than that.

I closed my eyes, smelled pine, and opened my eyes to his green gaze. And that's when I realized how devilishly handsome Chris Lyman really was. . . .

We talked all through dinner. I felt more and more drawn to his soft, deep voice, and to the way his beautiful eyes looked so trusting.

Why would he want someone like me, anyway? None of my other friends wanted to have anything to do with me right now! Still, he was willing to help and I wanted, no, needed a Christmas tree. I also enjoyed having Chris near me, the caring way he held my hand until I could almost forget the pain. Maybe I wouldn't have to face my problems all alone anymore.

We talked way into the night about our childhoods—about everything. I told him what it was like to grow up in a tiny town in Pearl River. Chris had been raised by a divorced mother, who'd had a hard time making ends meet. "Anyway, I was on my own at a young age, working at a movie theater," he explained.

We didn't notice the time until it was three o'clock in the morning. "Goodness. You'll have to leave."

"What time do you want me over today?" Chris asked.

It seemed so ridiculous that I gestured toward the sofa. "Look, you can sleep here tonight, if you promise to be—"

He interrupted my offer with a kiss so sweet and gentle that I couldn't remember ever being treated with such reverence. "I really like you a lot, Tracy." He massaged my back, which ached in spite of the excitement I felt.

"I like you a lot, too. Look, you can stay here, but—"

"Do you want me to rub your back?"

"I'm too sore and it's too soon for—"

"I know. I understand." Gently, he took my hand in his and led me to my bedroom.

His touch was as gentle as he'd been all evening, more giving and more effective than the muscle relaxants the doctor had prescribed. I fell into a deep sleep.

By late morning, I woke with a start, finding Chris in the bed alongside me. I was dressed and so was he. Nothing had happened, had it? What power did he have anyway, with those hands of his? My back felt well, relaxed, and without pain.

At least it did until I removed his arm that had draped over me last night, and tried to get out of bed. The pain was still there, but I hurriedly threw on my brace and threw on another outfit that fit too snugly, with the big brace. I cooked breakfast and served it to Chris, who was still asleep.

He woke up with a start. "Wow! I'm sorry. I meant to use the sofa, but—"

"Sure you did," I teased. "Thank you for that back rub. You have no idea how much it helped."

Chris grinned. "That's some omelet you made. I'm glad you're a good cook." He explained that his mother was a notoriously bad cook. "All I've ever wanted out of life was a decent meal."

"Keep rubbing my back and you'll be fed," I promised, "as long as I can afford to feed you."

He grinned. "I eat a lot." Then he grew more serious. "It must be rough, being out of work."

I explained about my problems at work while we continued to eat. After breakfast, we went to the tree farm. Like my dream, it was brightly lit by the morning sunshine and I knew exactly what tree I wanted. Several people walked by it. One woman pointed to it. "They should chop that one down. Nobody would want that tree."

"That's a strange tree," Chris observed.

I touched the misshapen limb and just like my dream, it spoke to me that day. "That's the one I want."

"Are you sure?"

I nodded, touching its bough. I felt a strange tingling in my back. "Yes. It's the one I want."

For a short while afterwards, I felt a strange energy, so much so that I was able to play with Chris a bit in the mud and the rain, getting dirty and full of tree sap, but having a great time. "This is great! I can't thank you enough for helping me, Chris." I laughed while he tied the tree to the top of his car.

Spending time with him had been wonderful. I dreaded being alone, coping with my problem, but I knew he'd have to go home.

On the way back down the mountain, Chris asked, "When do you see your doctor?"

"Early tomorrow morning. Then I have more physical therapy. After that, I have to drop my papers off at work."

When he parked his car in my complex, he started to untie the tree. He touched the misshapen limb of the tree and the expression changed in his green eyes. "Look, I'm on flex time, which means as long as I work my eight hours, they don't care exactly when I come in. Do you want me to drive you to the doctor tomorrow?"

"It takes a couple of hours. You don't want to wait around the office."

"Could you wait? I could drive you home at lunch, after we drop off those papers. The industrial clinic is close to where we both work, right?"

"Well, yes, but," I gulped, "you weren't planning on spending another night here, were you?"

Chris grinned. "I could sleep on the sofa this time. I could go home now, get some clothes, and we'd still have time to decorate the tree tonight."

I stroked the tree, concentrating, but somehow, when I touched the tree all sensible thoughts left me. Why not have him help out? "All right! Sure."

After he returned with his work clothes, we had a marvelous tree-decorating party, complete with pizza that Chris "delivered" to my apartment. We joked and laughed and I finally gasped, "Chris, I can't believe I'm having so much fun with this rotten back!"

Late that night, my back started to throb. I shifted in bed, trying to find a comfortable position. Nothing helped. Finally, I walked, hunched over to the living room. I stared at the tree, situated in the corner. Chris was snoring softly on the sofa.

It felt to me like the tree talked to me again. I can't explain it. I walked over to the tree, touched the misshapen limb, and felt its healing energy travel down my spine. It had to be in my mind, because I'd been unable to have a tree that one year. But why did I have to have this tree?

Chris stirred on the sofa. "Tracy? Are you all right?"

I squeezed my eyes shut, still grasping the tree. "No. My back hurts."

"Want another back rub?"

I'd have nodded, but it hurt my neck. Instead, I kept touching the tree. Chris left the couch and joined me, taking my hand that touched the bough and leading me to the bedroom. Again, he gave me a fantastic massage until I drifted off to sleep.

The next morning, I saw the doctor. He said, "This will help you, because you can continue on full compensation while on limited duty. I suppose you may have a problem driving to work, but—"

"I would have to drive, huh?" My heart sank. "Can you just keep me on—"

"If you must stay home, you'll get disability. It's half of what you were earning, however."

"I can't possibly live on that and pay my rent!"

"Those are your options," the doctor said.

I held onto the papers approving my work status while I waited for Chris to drive me to my job, where I'd be dropping them off. I had lots of time to think. Much as I wanted to go back to work, I didn't know how I could drive back and forth to any job. Sitting up for eight hours would also be extremely painful, let alone driving home afterwards. I sighed, wondering how I could live on disability when my rent already took half my income.

When Chris picked me up, I clung to him, explaining what the doctor had said.

"Are you ready to go back to work?" He pulled up in front of the administration building.

"I don't have much choice, do I? I can't afford to stay home."

He offered to help me out of his car, but I refused, climbing out and walking quickly, considering my back pain, to the claims office. I

350

didn't want Chris to be late getting back from his lunch. The secretary immediately signed me up to work in the volunteer office, while my back recovered. I'd be doing clerical work. "Can you start tomorrow?"

"I'll try, but it's hard to drive."

"That may be a problem, but you have to work on limited duty in order to receive full pay. You're lucky you have office skills," the secretary told me coldly.

"I'll be there," I said, equally coldly, grimacing in pain when I stood up and walked back out to Chris's car.

"I have to get a bus schedule." I told Chris what had happened while he drove me home. He walked with me up to my apartment. It was strange, but I felt compelled to stand by the tree again.

Chris fiddled with one of the ornaments.

"Look, Tracy, I know we don't know each other that well, but I'd really like to help you. If you'll allow it, I'll stay with you this week and maybe the next, until your back is better. I'll drive you to work, it's on my way anyway, and it's certainly closer and more convenient for me than where I live."

"Are you sure? What about the house you share?"

"Oh, it'll be fine. I'll still pay rent there, and I'll only do this until you feel better, but—"

"I'd love it, Chris. And will you spend Christmas with me?"

He agreed and I became the happy recipient of his magical massages that later turned to radiant lovemaking. And by Christmas, when we opened our gifts under the tree, I'd managed to give Chris a little something and he'd managed to buy something for me. But nothing was as big or as generous as what he'd done while I'd been in so much pain.

Maybe I wouldn't have seen Chris's virtues if I'd been the same partying woman I'd been before my injury, but I like to think I'd have noticed just how special he was, even without my rotten back. Somehow, I'm convinced the tree also had something to do with it.

My most painful day happened when we decided to take the tree down. Somehow, I had some spiritual connection to it, some strange relationship. I touched the misshapen limb and pine needles fell to the floor. Chris had teased me about my attachment; it was the end of January and I'd insisted we keep the tree up.

"Tracy, we have to take it down."

"I know." Fondly, I touched the limb. The tree was so brittle the limb came off in my hand. I decided to save it. While Chris took down the tree, I put the limb in a plastic container. For a few months, I kept it in the closet and forgot about it.

Although my back improved, I still had to change careers. Chris's roommate moved in with his girlfriend and Chris moved in with me.

351

We never really separated after we first met, but it took us a while before we felt sure enough of each other to get married. The next November, I taught Chris how to ski, but I never skied as well after my back injury. I'm still limited at times with what I can do.

Right before Christmas, we skied again. I swished down the hill and slid on some ice. I skidded face first in front of a pine tree. The tree had a misshapen limb in exactly the same place as the tree we'd bought last year at the Christmas tree farm. A ski patrol guy skied by.

"You all right, lady?"

I stood up and brushed the snow off. Amazingly, I was all right. Entranced, I touched the tree.

"Bad accident there. Someone skied down the hill and hit that tree a year ago. He died."

"What from?"

"Spinal fracture," the man said.

Chris had walked up the hill and had joined me. He draped his arm around my shoulder. I shuddered and buried my head against his chest. Of course it wasn't the same tree, so why did I want to touch it? Why did I feel so drawn to it? Was I drawing strength from someone else's misfortune?

Chris and I skied down the mountain. Later at home, I pulled out the container with the misshapen tree limb. I wanted to remind myself of how we met and how we'd fallen in love. But when I opened the box the limb was gone. I asked Chris about it, but he said he hadn't touched it. Maybe we don't need it anymore.

But for a while, we were blessed by a special tree, a rare tree—rare as the love that Chris and I have. And our love grows with every Christmas we share.

The End

Made in United States
Orlando, FL
05 July 2023